MAKING A
COMEBACK

By the Author

Never Too Late

Making a Comeback

MAKING A COMEBACK

by
Julie Blair

2015

MAKING A COMEBACK
© 2015 By Julie Blair. All Rights Reserved.

ISBN 13: 978-1-62639-357-8

This Trade Paperback Original Is Published By
Bold Strokes Books, Inc.
P.O. Box 249
Valley Falls, NY 12185

First Edition: July 2015

CREDITS
EDITOR: SHELLEY THRASHER
PRODUCTION DESIGN: SUSAN RAMUNDO
COVER DESIGN BY GABRIELLE PENDERGRAST

Acknowledgments

Thank you to Radclyffe for giving me the opportunity to be part of her extraordinary publishing company, Bold Strokes Books. Thanks to senior editor Sandy Lowe for walking me through my first book proposal and helping me get this story headed in the right direction. Thanks to all the talented and dedicated staff who helped my story become a polished, published book with a beautiful cover.

Again, working with my editor, Dr. Shelley Thrasher, was a privilege and an education. Thanks for treating my work with care, thoroughness, sensitivity, and a keen editing eye.

Writing this story was a long and difficult journey. I couldn't have done it without the support and guidance of my writing coach, Deb Norton. Her story wisdom shows on every page.

Thanks to Carol McComb for checking my musical facts, answering endless questions, and providing invaluable insight into the life of a professional musician.

Beta readers Ginny, Greta, and Suzy graciously read many drafts.

I'm grateful for friends and family who provide support, encouragement, and common sense when I need it—Dena and Susan, Ginny and Greta, Suzy, Patricia, Jac, and Summer.

I've always loved jazz, and writing this book gave me an excuse to immerse myself in it. A nod to Liz Story, Bill Evans, Duke Ellington, Miles Davis, Dave Brubeck, and Benny Goodman, to name a few of the jazz greats whose albums provided my writing soundtrack.

Thanks to all the readers of lesbian fiction. Your support of the genre keeps it alive.

Dedication

A writer could not have better friends than Ginny Hagopian and Greta Muller. For all your support, this one's for you.

CHAPTER ONE

Why did everything have to be harder alone? Liz blew out an exasperated breath as the car in front of her backed into the parking space she wanted. It was the third time that had happened.

She circled another block, creeping along in the line of cars slowed by stop signs at every corner. Tourists, unfazed by the rain, strolled along under umbrellas. Strolling seemed to be their only speed. She couldn't blame them. She'd been coming to Carmel her whole life, but the English-village-style architecture and unique shops and galleries that helped make the small seaside town a year-round tourist destination still captivated her.

Was someone pulling out in the next block? She couldn't see for sure around the pickup in front of her. Tears stung her eyes. Two days of feeling like her old self, and now parking was making her reach for the Kleenex that had become part of her attire in the last six months. Usually one of them drove while the other scouted for a space. A perfect collaboration. At this rate she'd be late getting back to San Jose, but then, when wasn't she late?

"You were even late for our wedding."

Teri's voice had always been too loud, but she was a drummer and never did anything quietly.

Liz smiled, as if Teri were sitting beside her, teasing her, making her feel loved in spite of her faults. "Not without reason," Liz said aloud, as if it were a real conversation. As long as she remembered Teri's voice, it felt real.

"Must have been a good reason."
"Just a last-minute tryst with the sexiest woman I'd ever met."
"I couldn't wait hours to have you," Teri would say, adding the smug grin that showed her dimples and made Liz's insides go soft.
"But I was on time."
"You didn't have to fix your hair and makeup."
"True. I only had to wash my hands."

Teri would tap a finger against her lips, a reminder that she'd refused to wash away Liz's taste.

The memory still brought a flush to her cheeks. After sneaking Liz away from the guests gathering at her parents' home and up to her bedroom, Teri had made love to her with an urgency that left her breathless and relaxed on the most important day of their lives.

Her heart skipped several beats, lost without Teri's steadying rhythm. Dabbing the tears away, she breathed a sigh of relief as she backed in between two sedans, right in front of Galerie Plein Aire. Perfect.

She pulled up her jacket hood as she stepped out of the Yukon and strode around the rear to avoid seeing the dented bumper she still hadn't gotten repaired. If she'd known she would end up driving it, she wouldn't have agreed to buy something so big. Perfect for their band's tour back East last summer, but now, like everything else, it was more than she could handle.

Sidestepping tourists, she hurried up the alley flanked by shops and took the steps up to the gallery at the end in two bounding strides. She regretted the exuberance when her calves complained. In her search for new routines, she'd thought a jog on the beach the last two mornings was a good idea.

"You're here for the Morris," the redhead at the desk said. "The framing worked beautifully. We can unwrap it if you want to check it."

"No. I'm sure it looks great."

"Do you want help carrying it out?"

"I can manage. I don't want you to get rained on."

The painting barely fit between her arms, and she pinched the top and bottom to keep from dropping it. She could do this. She backed out of the gallery, watching the painting's corners so they didn't knock against the doorframe.

As she reached the bottom step she misjudged the height of the railing, and a corner of the painting hit it with a crack. Trying to correct, she backed up and collided with something that grunted. She watched helplessly as a woman fell into a brick planter full of flowers.

Liz set the painting against a storefront and turned to help the woman up, almost tripping over a dog that stood patiently amid the commotion. "I'm so sorry. I had this painting…well, you can see. Are you all right?"

"Max?" The woman knelt, and the dog pushed its head against her hand. She ran her hands over his sides and down his legs. "Is he hurt?"

"He seems fine." The dog's harness and the woman's panicked tone finally registered. "Oh, my gosh, you're blind."

"Keen observation," the woman said, cupping the dog's chin and stroking his head.

"Are you all right, Jac?" The gallery employee rushed down the steps.

"I'm fine, but is Max?" Jac ran her hands down his legs again.

"He's not bleeding anywhere and he's wagging his tail," the employee said.

Jac gave the dog a biscuit from her pocket and kissed his head. Standing, she pushed the hood back from her face.

Liz was horrified to see blood oozing from a cut above Jac's right eye. "Um, you're bleeding."

"Where?" Jac ran her hand over her forehead, smearing the blood.

"Here." Liz pulled a Kleenex from her pocket, wrapped it around her finger, and dabbed at the blood.

Jac jerked back from the touch. "I can manage." She held the Kleenex to her forehead and handed an envelope to the employee. "Peg said to call if you have questions." She took Max's harness and started down the alley.

"He's a beautiful dog. Golden retriever?"

Jac stopped but didn't turn around. Her shoulders rose and fell once, as if she was taking a deep breath. "Yellow Labrador retriever."

"I'm sorry for bumping into you." She wasn't sure Jac heard as her long strides carried her away. Max guided her effortlessly around people, ignoring a yippy little white dog wearing a plaid sweater. What a great partnership.

"Let's get the painting back in the gallery and check it," the employee said, taking one side.

In the back room Liz watched anxiously as the woman cut the paper away. "Oh, no," she said, rubbing the chipped corner. Tears filled her eyes. She'd suggested to her siblings that the painting was the perfect birthday gift for her dad. He did so much for all of them, and she wanted him to feel extra special. Sometimes no matter how hard you tried, things went wrong.

"Let me call the framer and ask him to do an emergency repair," the employee said, giving Liz's arm a reassuring squeeze.

Liz knew why she was an easy target for tears today. The birthday party she didn't want to go to Sunday, afraid it would be like the last family gathering, when she'd broken down in the middle of opening Christmas gifts. She wanted to show people she was doing better, and the thought exhausted her.

"He'll fix it," the employee said. "Come back in forty minutes."

"Thanks." Liz checked her watch. The brown leather band was frayed so badly she worried it might come apart, but she couldn't face not having it the way it was when Teri gave it to her for their fifth anniversary. Surely it would last a little longer.

She left the gallery and headed to Sixth, turning left at the Corner Bistro toward another gallery she liked. The rain had let up and she unbuttoned her jacket. It was warm for mid-March. Passing the Bistro's patio she saw Jac sitting at a table off to the side under an awning that matched the Italian Villa orange of the walls. Her back was to the street, as if she was oblivious to the world. Her dog lay at her feet, head on his paws.

Eating alone made Liz feel lonely. Why not keep Jac company? She smiled as she approached the table and then felt foolish. Jac couldn't see her. Max looked up at her and his tail swiped the patio. "Excuse me. I'm the woman from the gallery. I wanted to make sure you're all right."

"Quite." Jac sat with perfect posture, hands on a white napkin draped across her lap. She was well-dressed in navy wool slacks and navy raincoat unzipped to show a fisherman-knit turtleneck sweater. Her mother had loved those sweaters.

"You know the signs of a concussion, don't you?"

"Shall I count backward from ten?" Jac lifted an eyebrow and tilted her head, pinning Liz with eyes that were pale blue, like the sky right after the fog burns off, and crystal clear. Shouldn't they be cloudy? Didn't blind people wear sunglasses?

"You can't take things for granted." She must sound ridiculous. Of course this wasn't a serious medical situation, but Liz's pulse jumped anyway. They'd been sure they would beat Teri's leukemia, as they had the first time. "Um, it's still bleeding."

Jac took balled up Kleenex from her pocket and dabbed the cut.

"I'm Liz Randall. Here's my business card in case you need stitches."

"Are you a doctor?" Jac took the card and tucked it in her pocket.

"No, but—"

"Who exactly are you?"

"A musician." Was that still true, with the band on indefinite hiatus and their plans for a fall tour in ruins?

"What kind?"

"I played the piano in a jazz quartet," she said, surprised at the question. "And I teach music at San Jose State." At least she still had that.

Jac laughed, and the sound trickled through Liz like the perfect pitch on a wind chime. The knots that bound her heart loosened a bit. It took her a second to realize what Jac was laughing at. Duke Ellington was streaming through the speakers mounted on the walls.

"'Black and Tan Fantasy,'" they said in unison.

Jac's eyebrow rose again. "Newport Jazz Festival, 1956." She tapped long, elegant fingers to the rhythm.

"Saved his career." Ellington had been on the verge of disbanding his orchestra before that performance. Liz wondered if a serendipitous moment would revive her career.

"The concert is in your honor," a waiter said, coming through the door from the restaurant. He set a glass of white wine in front of

Jac and a bowl of water in front of Max. "Tony said if you can name the album, your lunch is free. I'll be right back with another glass of wine for your guest."

"What's your quartet's name?"

"Up Beat." Liz pulled out a chair, morosely thinking she should change the name to Down Beat. They'd been so high the day the doctor said Teri's leukemia was in remission that they'd decided on the hopeful name. "Do you mind if I join you?"

"You apparently have." Jac lifted the wineglass to her nose, inhaled for several seconds, and took a sip like someone used to tasting wine. "Your album two years ago was very good. A little immature, but with potential."

"Thank you. I think." She stroked Max's back and he wagged his tail. "Does he like the beach?" She pictured walking the Carmel beach, throwing a ball for her own dog instead of watching all the dogs having fun with their owners. Max stared at her, ears lifted.

"Careful. He knows the word and he'll expect to go."

"Have you seen us perform?" Liz cringed at her poor choice of words.

"No. Are you here for a show?"

"I came over to spend a few days at our vacation home. It was my grandparents'. Are you a local?"

"Yes."

The waiter returned with a glass of wine for Liz. He set a basket of bread on the table, along with a small plate, onto which he poured olive oil and balsamic vinegar. "How's the wine?"

"Tell Tony to put this one on the menu. Should work with his swordfish and lighter pasta dishes and would be superb with his tomato bisque."

"Shall I bring you a bowl of bisque while he prepares your lunch?"

"Perfect," Jac said.

"Shall I bring the same for your friend?"

"Please."

Liz studied her companion as she listened to this exchange, grateful not to have to make a decision. Jac's face was beautiful in a classical way. Thick, wavy, blond hair rested on her shoulders. She looked to be older than her own thirty-two years, but it was hard to tell—she had a timeless quality.

Notes danced across Liz's mind, and she almost jumped in her chair. She hadn't heard even the hint of a new song since before Teri's death. Normally she'd hurry to write it down before she lost it, but today she let the notes drift away. "Are you a musician?"

"Just a music lover. If you did a follow-up album, I missed it."

"No." Her shoulders dropped. They'd recorded four nights in New York on their tour last summer, excited to release their first live album. She still hadn't chosen the songs to put on the CD. "Ellington's one of my idols," she said, pulling her attention back to the music.

"'Diminuendo in Blue,'" they said in unison again when a new song started.

Liz smiled at the raised eyebrow that seemed to be a common gesture with Jac. "The famous Paul Gonsalves solo," she said, letting the exuberant sax pull her away from fretting about the album she really needed to get done. She took a sip of the wine. "Who couldn't be happy listening to that?" She tapped her feet and moved to the addictive swing rhythm she loved. Teri would be drumming her fingers on the edge of the table and swiveling her shoulders to the beat. The memory landed softly, with no hint of dragging her under.

"What did you buy?" Jac dipped a piece of French bread in the olive oil, her movements as sure as if she could see.

"Buy?"

"At the gallery. You said you were carrying a painting."

"A present for my father," she said, around a bite of bread. "It's his sixtieth birthday Sunday. He loves the ocean but doesn't get over here often, so we thought we'd take the ocean to him. It's by a terrific artist named Peggy Morris."

The waiter set bowls in front of them and grated cheese over the soup. "It's a new Asiago. Tony wants your opinion."

"Perfect," Jac said, after tasting the soup with the same attention with which she'd tasted the wine.

"This artist does wonderful seascapes," Liz said when the waiter had gone. She rarely had an appetite, but this soup was delicious.

"Which one did you buy?"

"Umm, it's called *A Clearing Storm*. I confess I wanted it for myself." Something about it had tugged at her emotions—the loss and loneliness, the struggle of being on her own for the first time in her life. The painting captured that and also a sense of hope and peace she yearned for. "Rough, angry sea—"

"Waves crashing against the rocks, sun coming out through bulky gray clouds, two gulls flying high up in the sky. I was with her the day she painted it."

"The artist? That's amazing."

"Would you like her to sign a card for your dad?"

"Huh?" Liz scraped her bowl with a chunk of bread. Had she just wolfed down the whole thing?

"She's my sister."

"You're kidding." What an unexpected and pleasant encounter. Sometimes good things did come from disasters.

The waiter traded a plate of pasta for Liz's bowl. "This smells delicious." Gorgonzola cream sauce.

"Card?"

"My dad would love it." She watched Jac use her fork to push fusilli pasta onto an oversized spoon, bring it to her face, inhale like she had with the wine, and finally slide it past her lips. She'd never seen anyone eat with such measured grace, each bite like an event unto itself, each movement perfectly orchestrated. Her family loved food but devoured it like they were eating in a cafeteria.

"I'll call her and you can pick it up."

"Lunch is good?" A man about her father's age wearing chef whites approached the table.

"Excellent as always," Jac said. "Was the wine a Verdejo?"

"Haven't fooled you yet but I keep trying."

"Tony, this is Liz. Tony's the owner and creator of fine cuisine."

"So, am I buying you lunch?" he asked Jac.

"You stumped me on the album," Jac said.

Tony clapped his hands, winking at Liz. "Bravo! I'll send dessert and coffee out in a bit."

"Do they always just bring you food?" The staff was treating Jac like royalty. Carmel was known for celebrities, but she'd never heard of anyone famous and blind who lived here.

"Because I can't read the menu?"

"Oh, gosh, that's not what I meant."

"I abdicate the decision. Tony's an excellent chef and has never disappointed me."

Liz wished she could abdicate her responsibilities. Sammy, the band's sax player, and Regan, his twin sister and their bass player, would be at the party on Sunday. They'd be disappointed that she still wasn't making progress on the album. It wasn't just her career at stake. She'd have to decide soon if she should replace Teri and keep the band together or let them move on. Her chest tightened and that shadowy emptiness spread through her body, making her feel heavy. Everything was so much harder on her own. The conversation drifted back to music. Jac was certainly knowledgeable about jazz.

She flipped her hood up against the rain that had started in earnest and checked her watch as they walked through the patio gate of the Bistro. Right on time to pick up the painting.

"Peg will have it ready for you," Jac said, putting a cell phone back in her pocket. She gave the address and started to give directions.

"I know where it is. We're a few blocks away on Carmelo, near Tenth. Practically neighbors."

"Was your grandmother Mildred Randall?"

"How would you know that?"

"Your last name is Randall, you mentioned the house was your grandparents', and it's on Carmelo. Fifth house from the corner of Tenth, if I remember correctly. Peg took piano lessons from her. I was sorry to hear she passed away."

Five years ago and Liz still missed her terribly. Everything she knew about the piano she owed to her grandma. "Can I give you a ride to wherever you're going?"

"I'll walk."

"It was a pleasure meeting you." Jac was already several strides down the street. "I hope I run into you again." She cringed, hoping Jac hadn't heard.

Jac pivoted toward her. "Perhaps it's best you don't."

Was she teasing or serious? Liz still hadn't decided by the time she walked into the gallery. The time with Jac had been refreshing, like they'd been in their own world, away from everyday problems.

"You'll be pleased," the employee said, leading her to the back room. "The framer put wood tabs on all the corners to cover the repair work."

She ran her fingers along the frame. If only someone could repair her life so flawlessly. Notes darted through her mind again, and this time she hummed them. They faded after a few bars.

"I'll wrap it for you," the woman said, picking up bubble wrap.

Her phone rang. "Hi, Kev. I'm on my way."

"Don't bother." Her brother sounded stressed. "I have to work." He managed her dad's restaurant and the bar for the jazz club her dad had opened last year.

"Oh, no." She knew how much Kevin had been looking forward to the getaway with his wife, Karen.

"Three o'clock on Sunday. Don't be late." He ended the call.

She called her sister. "I'm not babysitting the boys tonight. I'll be home in a couple hours."

"Oh. Um—"

"I don't care if you didn't clean up." Letting Hannah move in with her had seemed like the perfect solution for both of them, but the reality of clothes and shoes tossed anywhere and Hannah's night-owl habits was getting harder to live with.

"I'm sort of having someone over for a cooking lesson."

She clenched her jaw. Another groupie from the catering company Hannah now worked for after losing her head chef position at a luxury resort.

"Since you weren't going to be home I invited her to spend the night."

They'd had this discussion. No sleepovers.

"I'll clean the condo and do your laundry," Hannah said in her cajoling voice.

"I'll stay here tonight." It wasn't fair to be mad at Hannah. She'd been through a lot, too. And she had to admit she'd felt better the last two days here in Carmel. Another day was an appealing prospect.

"You're the best, Lizzie."

This time she let the employee help her load the painting into the Yukon. She made her way down Ocean Avenue, toward the beach, in the slow crawl of cars typical on the main street through downtown Carmel. As she waited her turn at a four-way stop, Jac and Max crossed the street, her strides long and confident, his tail waving as he guided her around people. Driving through the intersection she realized something.

The conversation with Jac had seemed different because Jac didn't treat her like the grieving widow or the pianist without a band. She didn't see worry or, worse, pity on Jac's face. Just two people talking about music. When was the last time music wasn't about analyzing or critiquing or worrying? She looked in the rearview mirror, but they were out of sight. She hoped she would run into Jac again. She should have asked her where she lived.

A few minutes later she turned left onto Carmelo Street, drove past her grandma's slate-blue cottage with the driftwood picket fence her grandfather had built, and stopped in front of the property at the end of the street. She'd walked past this property more times than she could count, envying the unobstructed ocean view from atop the bluff. A wrought-iron fence was barely visible behind exuberant plantings of lavender and blue flowered shrubs she didn't know the name of. A one-story house sat well back from the road. Monterey pines dotted the property. The Pacific created a grayish-blue backdrop in the distance under the cloudy sky. She drove between the Carmel ledgestone gateposts that framed the entrance to the driveway, tires crunching on the gravel.

Ten minutes later she headed to her grandma's house with the card for her dad, an invitation to dinner next time she was here, and the information that Jac lived on the property. She'd see Jac again. The thought made her smile.

CHAPTER TWO

Jac unbuckled Max's harness as soon as the surface changed from hard street to gravel. Home. Half-an-hour late, thanks to Liz joining her for lunch. If she had to endure conversation, at least it had been a topic that interested her. Twenty-four seconds to cross the graveled parking area. The crunch of her soft-soled walking shoes stopped when the surface changed to flagstones at the walkway that skirted the main house where Peg and her family lived. Twelve seconds and she was on the large patio behind the house. A few minutes to check in with Peg and let Max be a dog, and then the hour nap that concluded her afternoons.

Max made his goofy grunting sounds, which he did when he rolled on his back on the lawn adjacent to the patio. The harness was custom-made not to chafe or bind, but it seemed to be his way of switching from on-duty to off-duty. Show tunes came from Peg's art studio at the far side of the patio, and Jac headed in that direction. Painting must be going well today.

"Guess how my day was, honey?" she asked in the Ozzie-and-Harriet parody they did with each other. She rubbed the soft leaves of the lavender plant by the door and sniffed her fingers.

"You have a cut over your eye that I'm supposed to keep careful watch over, and you met Mildred Randall's granddaughter."

"Did you recognize her?" She tried to create an image of Liz based on her grandmother. Her voice was a pleasant alto that sounded kind. It occasionally slowed and became a flattened monotone—one of the marks of sadness. She knew the reason for the sadness.

"No. I can see the family resemblance in her face. Hazel eyes like her grandmother. Wavy, chestnut hair below her shoulders. Younger than us." Paintbrushes clinked against a jar, and Peg's footsteps tapped across the cement floor toward her.

"It's fine."

Peg pushed her hood back, lifted hair from her forehead, and pressed around the cut. "Does it hurt?"

"Only when you touch it. I'll clean it and put Neosporin on it." She swatted Peg's hands away and backed up. "Blind isn't the same as incompetent."

"Thank you for reminding me. Liz couldn't stop talking about your musical knowledge and how similar your tastes are to hers."

"We're not going to be friends."

"Wouldn't you like someone at your level to talk music with?"

She wasn't going to encourage this discussion. It was a chance meeting that would not be repeated.

"I invited her to dinner the next time she's over here." Peg's voice was irritatingly enthusiastic.

"I'm late for my nap. What's for dinner?"

"Minestrone."

"Perfect." She held up the bag. "A new Asiago from Tony."

"He spoils you."

"He makes money off me."

"It's okay for people to like you, honey."

The comment didn't justify a retort. People had always liked her for what she could give them. Period. She headed for her cottage at the back of the property. Five minutes and she'd be on her bed with Max.

"Malcolm called again." Peg sounded reluctant to deliver the news.

"Damn it!" She stopped, anger tightening her muscles. How many times did she have to say no?

"You should listen to the message."

"Delete it."

"He's not going away this time. He wants to—"

"I know what he wants." Capitalize on the ten-year anniversary. Damn him.

"You should talk to him and try to work out a compro—"

"Never!" She left her hood off as she strode to her cottage. What was cold rain pelting her head compared to the icy resentment in her veins? On top of being knocked down and a too-perky lunch companion, she had to be reminded of one of the biggest mistakes she'd ever made in marrying that man. Too much for one day.

Max was waiting for her by the front door. "You're my perfect partner." Gentle, smart, loving, and totally incapable of anything but loyalty. He gave a final shake before they stepped into the quiet and order she craved. She'd always been solitary. Being blind had exaggerated that trait, and she didn't care in the least. As long as she had music, she had everything she needed.

Shoes and socks were discarded into the closet by the front door along with her jacket. After towel-drying Max, she walked barefoot to the kitchen, the heated slate floor warm and textured beneath her feet. She gave Max a generous handful of the oatmeal-peanut butter biscuits Peg baked for him. "Spoiled." He nudged her hand for more and she indulged him.

Taking a stiff brush from a drawer, she walked around the small dining table and opened the French doors. She stepped onto the wet flagstones of the small patio backed by a walled garden and the six Monterey Pines she'd helped her parents plant as a child. When it became obvious that staying here was the best option, she'd asked that the cottage be built on this spot so she'd have a visual image to associate with it. Those seedlings were now forty-foot-tall trees that provided additional privacy and some protection from the wind off the ocean. The property had the proverbial million-dollar view, but for her, the sight of the Pacific Ocean just beyond the cliff was a distant memory.

"You're such a goof." She brushed Max from head to tail, and he wiggled his rear end in appreciation. "That bastard. He's not undoing our life, buddy, but he has ruined our nap." Daily three-hour walks and the naps that followed were part of the routine that kept her back pain manageable.

Still bristling with irritation, she walked across the living room to the cabinets that contained the core of her life—a state-of-the-art sound system and her CD collection. Alphabetized by genre and artist and labeled in Braille, it was almost evenly split between classical and jazz, with a dash of Broadway musicals, blues, and opera. Thumbing through the jazz albums she found what she wanted—Dave Brubeck's *Time Out*, revolutionary for its unusual time signatures when it was released in fifty-nine. She envied Liz for having met him and, moreover, having played with him. Her credentials were impressive— the Brubeck Institute at University of the Pacific, a mere three hours away in Stockton, was an enviable school for jazz. Pianist in the institute's highly regarded quintet should have been a sure trajectory to fame, but fame in the music business was often a twisted path. She knew what Liz's path had been. Unfortunate for one so talented.

She hadn't listened to Brubeck in a long time, but the conversation with Liz about her favorite composers and jazz pianists had piqued her interest. All right, she grudgingly admitted, it had been one of the most interesting conversations she'd had in a long time.

She settled into the leather recliner positioned as close to the center of the space as Peg would allow for aesthetic purposes. As much as Peg had always been visually oriented, sound had been Jac's world. The loss of her hearing would have been a tragedy she couldn't have adapted to. Using the remote, she adjusted the various parameters on the equalizer until she was satisfied. In the never-ending darkness, music was light and shadow and color. Movement. Life. It was also laced with memories. Today those memories stayed pleasant enough, safely away from awakening darker emotions just as easily provoked.

If Liz loved Brubeck and Ellington, why were both of her bands unabashedly blues/rock style jazz? Her first group, The LT Quartet, had garnered two well-deserved Grammy nominations. Up Beat, her more recent quartet, was the same style with a sax player who wasn't a bad imitation of Coltrane, Liz's piano chord progressions solidly pinned to the twelve-bar blues, and a drummer who pounded with a rock beat. A drummer who'd died last year. Liz's partner. The twisted path of fate.

Jac pushed the recliner back and opened herself to the music. Max settled in his donut bed next to her chair with a contented huff. She scratched her fingernails through his damp fur. No, Peg was wrong. She was not going to be friends with Liz Randall. She didn't do friends.

CHAPTER THREE

L iz drifted slowly up from sleep. She hadn't slept through the night in longer than she could remember. Arousal licked at the edge of her awareness. The slow wake-up kind where she'd nuzzle Teri's neck and fondle her breast, the introduction to lovemaking. She snuggled back against Teri and then sat up so fast she banged her knee on the coffee table. The back of the couch, not Teri. Her grandparents' living room, not the master bedroom in their condo. She pulled the collar of the T-shirt over her nose. One of Teri's she hadn't slept in yet. Yes, there was the faintest trace of her slightly masculine cologne. Longing surged through dormant channels. She cupped her breast and let go with a groan. Slid her hand inside the waistband of her sweats—No. Not if it wasn't with Teri. She shoved off the couch and tugged on one of Teri's old UOP sweatshirts.

Opening the French doors beside the stone fireplace, she walked out to the brick patio. Blue sky and a chill in the air greeted her. Why was her body doing this to her? Another way grief didn't play fair—months of numbness and then it made you ache for the touch you'd never have again. Dropping onto a rickety chair at the wooden table her grandpa had built, she turned the gold band on her finger that meant they'd belonged to each other. Still belonged to each other. A jay squawked at her from the branch of the overgrown Japanese maple in the corner of the small backyard.

"Yes, I know there used to be feeders and a birdbath." The once-beautiful garden had been reduced to just a few brave roses that survived the long absences between family visits. Grandma had poured herself into the garden after Grandpa died. Dad had opened the jazz club after her mom's death. What was her widowhood project going to be? The dark thought sent her to the kitchen for coffee.

She measured water for the Cuisinart and then poured half of it out. She was still making coffee for two. Opening the cabinet, she remembered she'd used the last of the coffee yesterday. She'd wait until she was home. Darn it. She couldn't go home this morning. No way was she walking in on Hannah and Ms. One Night Stand.

She went to the baby-grand piano in the corner of the living room. The ebony-finished Steinway was her grandma's pride and joy, an extravagant wedding present from Grandpa. She'd left it to Liz but the condo was too small for it. She and Teri had hoped to buy their own home next year if the band took off. She lifted the keyboard lid and started "Spring Time," the first piece she'd composed for the quartet she and Teri started while still at UOP. The first time she'd played it since Teri's death. Her fingers slowed and then stopped under the weight of all the memories.

Shutting the keyboard lid, she stared out the floor-to-ceiling corner windows to the garden. Glass shelves across the windows held her grandma's cherished cranberry-glass collection. As a child she'd been entranced by the ruby color that glowed when the sun came through the windows, sometimes dotting the piano with red light. So many hours she'd spent at this piano under her grandma's tutelage. This house held so many happy memories of her childhood. Coming over for a few days had been a good idea. For ten years she'd arranged her teaching schedule at San Jose State and her private lessons so she was free Thursdays through Sundays. Plenty of time for composing and performing. Now the weekends loomed long and lonely. Maybe she'd start spending them over here.

Twenty minutes later, dressed in yesterday's jeans and her last clean T-shirt, she closed the front door. She'd go to town for coffee and do some shopping. A new outfit for her dad's party tomorrow might help her look forward to it. As she walked through the neighborhood of unique homes, most of them mere cottages that contributed to Carmel's charm, her mind kept wandering back to Teri. She searched for a happy memory to lift her spirits, smiling when her thoughts landed on the first time she saw Teri.

Sitting in the music-theory class on her first day at UOP, Liz had looked up to see a tall woman swiping a chunk of dark hair off her forehead as she stood in the doorway. She'd smiled that dimpled smile and taken the seat next to Liz, chatting in the easy way she had. Within weeks they were inseparable friends. And then one night everything had changed. After a dorm party she'd insisted Teri stay the night in her room rather than drive home. Her skin tingled from the memory, and her heart beat with anticipation. Did you ever forget your first time?

They'd tumbled onto her twin bed, Teri in Liz's T-shirt, too small for her. When she'd teased Teri about the difference in their cup size, Teri had pinned her and rubbed her breasts over Liz's chest, saying maybe some of hers would rub off on Liz. The joking had stopped when their nipples hardened. She'd tried to squirm away, embarrassed by her arousal. In an instant Teri's eyes had switched from confusion to desire, roaming her face before she'd leaned down to kiss her. The kiss that had changed everything.

They'd learned what to do slowly, tenderly, shyly at first. In the aftermath of her first orgasm with another person, floating in the warm enclosure of Teri's arms, something inside told her this was where she belonged. She'd blurted out, "I love you." A moment of panic had followed, but when Teri said the words back to her she'd thought her heart would fly out of her chest. They'd spent the rest of the night learning each other's bodies in that way that only happens once. Her first and only love. Like her grandma. Like her dad. Like Kevin. She'd found her one love at a young age. And lost her fourteen years later.

She waited for tears, but they didn't come. Another odd quirk of the grief that was quicksand one minute and completely gone the next. Notes trickled across her mind as she walked past the Tuck Box, her grandma's favorite breakfast place. She'd love a scone with their trademark orange marmalade, but she hated feeling conspicuous eating in restaurants alone. Maybe someday she'd have Jac's ease. The melody persisted and she hummed it. It sounded like more of the one from yesterday.

She bought coffee and wandered the downtown streets, popping in and out of galleries, soothed by Carmel's casual beauty and relaxed atmosphere. Every patch of ground and planter box was filled with plants and colorful flowers her grandma would have known the names of. Bowls of water sat outside doorways for the dogs that were welcome to accompany their owners into shops and restaurants. It was impossible not to fall into the ambience where everyone was friendly and in no hurry.

In Carmel Plaza she went into her favorite clothing store. Half an hour later she left carrying a bag containing her clothes, while she wore jeans a size smaller, a cheerful orange print blouse, and a yellow cashmere sweater too soft to resist tied around her shoulders. Realizing she was hungry again, she detoured back down Mission Street to Nielsen's Deli. It was too beautiful a day to leave yet, and she could manage a sandwich by herself in Devendorf Park.

❖

Jac leaned back against the park bench, stretched her legs out, and rolled up her sleeves. Her back was loose from the walk, and the sun was too warm and welcome after days of rain to pass up a few minutes' relaxation before heading home. Conversations faded in and out as people passed on the sidewalk behind her. The man with the Aussie who chased Frisbees was clapping and encouraging his dog from the far side of the park. "Leave it," she said to Max when his body tensed against her leg. "We'll play fetch at home."

"Okay if I share your bench? It's Liz from yesterday."

She stifled a groan as she scooted over. "I thought you were going home."

"Changed my mind. How's your forehead?" Liz set bags on the ground and something on the bench between them.

"Fine." She turned her head away from Liz in case she had any ideas about inspecting it. It hurt, and she hoped it didn't leave a scar.

"I'm so sorry I knocked you over. Does Max chase Frisbees like that dog? Oh, darn. I did it again. There's—"

"I know what chasing a Frisbee looks like." Blind wasn't the same as ignorant. Or stupid. Or deaf. Or uneducated. Or any of a dozen other assumptions people made about her. Last Sunday on the beach some idiot had asked if she knew what color her dog was.

"I don't mean to say dumb things." Liz's voice was kind and mercifully absent any trace of pity. "Isn't this sun glorious?"

"Quite." Jac weighed the pleasure of sitting in the sun against the annoyance of company.

"Would you like to share my lunch?" Liz opened the bag on the bench.

"No, thanks."

"Turkey and avocado from Nielsen's."

"I had lunch."

"Bistro?"

"Yes." Why was talking so important to most people? She started to get up. She'd enjoy the sun on Peg's patio. Alone.

"I wanted to go there, but I hate eating alone."

Jac sat back and crossed her arms. Apparently she was now the solution to that problem. Ten minutes, then she was leaving no matter what. At least Liz had a pleasant voice—medium rhythm, not squeaky or too loud.

"I spent last night listening to Grandma's old Brubeck and Ellington records. I also listened to our CD and you're right. It does have an immature quality." Paper crunched as Liz unwrapped her sandwich.

"I didn't say you weren't good." A moment of fondness for Liz infiltrated her. Many musicians would have discounted her opinion. "There's great musicianship. You hadn't gelled as a group yet, and the album seemed a bit premature."

"We were in a hurry to get it out." Liz's voice flattened.

That made sense. They would have been eager to regain the momentum their first band had. "Congratulations on your tour."

"How did you know?" Liz opened a tab, presumably on a soda can.

"I follow jazz." Impressive reviews. Too bad Liz had lost out again on the brink of major success. She couldn't help feeling sympathy for Liz's circumstances. Making a comeback would be a long, hard road. "Newport Jazz Festival. Boston. New York. Not easy places to perform."

"You're telling me. It's great because the audiences are savvy but—"

"Hard because you're always having to prove yourself."

"Yes. We recorded some shows last summer for a live album," Liz said as she chewed.

"That's a risky move."

"Why?"

"You don't have a big-enough repertoire of studio recordings." She pinched the edge of the bench. She'd never been able to keep her opinions to herself.

"And?"

"Most listeners prefer the polish of studio recordings." Jac didn't filter the sarcasm out of her voice. So many were over-manufactured, even faked with pitch correction. "When they think they know you and can 'air guitar,'" she punctuated with finger quotes, "then you shake them up with a live album where you give your songs a fresh twist, and they're hooked again."

"I wanted to do another studio album," Liz said under her breath, her tone flat again.

"Where did you record?" Just an innocent question.

"Hotel Kitano in New York."

"Outstanding club. How many nights?" Okay, she was a little curious.

"Four. Two sets a night."

"That's a lot." And would mean a lot of songs to edit down for the album. Not an easy task.

"That's what I said." That telltale flatness in Liz's voice again.

"Good acoustics?" Just curiosity.

"Excellent."

"Good engineer and plenty of mics?"

"Highly recommended and yes, twelve tracks." Her voice was strained, as if talking about it hurt.

"You did it right." Jac felt bad for bringing up a touchy subject.

"If only I could pick the songs," Liz said, chewing again.

"You haven't started engineering it?" Usually live albums were released quickly. Was that because of Teri's death? She clamped her mouth shut. Not her business.

"I should let you listen to them."

It would be interesting, but she didn't intend to encourage a friendship with Liz. When it seemed that Liz had finished eating she said, "I need to be going." She took Max's harness in her left hand and stood. "Enjoy your afternoon."

"I'll come with you." The sound of paper being crumpled as Liz apparently gathered up the remains of her lunch.

Jac clenched her jaw. Of course Liz would. When they reached the sidewalk she told Max, "Right."

"How did you know you were at the sidewalk?" Liz was a step behind her.

"Grass changed to pavement."

"Should I walk next to you or Max?" At least Liz had the courtesy to ask.

"Me."

"Because?"

"It gives him room to maneuver." At the corner, Max stopped. "Forward," she said after a moment and stepped into the street.

"How did you know it was safe to cross?"

"There are stop signs on all the corners, and car engines sound different idling." And Max would stop her if it wasn't, but she wasn't going to explain intelligent disobedience or encourage a discussion on the mechanics of how she dealt with her blindness. When they'd crossed the street, she turned right again.

"How does he know when to turn?"

"He doesn't." Fighting the urge to lengthen her already long stride, Jac kept her focus on the sounds and smells around her, and on shifts in shade and sun and wind against her skin that oriented her. Forty-five minutes and she'd be blissfully alone, napping.

"So you have to know where you're going."

"He's not a GPS." She moved away from Liz and whatever she was carrying that kept bumping her arm.

"Sorry. Dumb question."

More people were on the downtown streets today, but Max guided her with only an occasional slowing in their pace. A dog sometimes barked nearby, but he never wavered. Yes, he was the perfect partner, totally in sync with her. Liz was quiet for a block and she felt bad for her curtness. Grief wasn't easy to deal with. "Tell me more about your favorite composers." No, they were not going to be friends, but Liz was more interesting than most people.

She stopped half an hour later at the corner of Liz's block. "Your exit, I believe."

"I'll come with you. I want to say hi to Peggy."

Of course. They'd be great friends. As they walked, Liz talked about the jazz composition class she taught, and Jac resisted the urge to join the conversation. If Liz discovered how much she knew about music, it would only encourage a friendship. Finally her shoes crunched on the gravel driveway and she let Max loose. Ten minutes. Nap.

"Liz," Peg said from the direction of her studio when they were on the patio. "What a nice surprise."

Max grunted from the direction of the lawn. What a goof.

"Oh, my gosh, that's my album."

"I realized after you left yesterday that we saw you at Kuumbwa last year. Join us for dinner tonight? Roger's grilling."

"I was going home today, but I don't have to," Liz said. "What time?"

"Why don't you stay?" Peg suggested. "I need a break from this canvas that's frustrating me. We can chat while I do some gardening, if you won't be bored."

"Grandma loved to garden. I feel bad so little of it's left."

"Are you planning to restore it?"

"I don't know anything about gardening. Maybe you can teach me."

Max nosed Jac's leg, his signal he wanted to play fetch. She took the tennis ball from his mouth and threw it toward the lawn. Wiggling her fingers at Peg, she headed for her cottage. When Max didn't bring the ball back, she called his name.

"He's up here," Liz said and then laughed. "He wants me to throw his ball."

Traitor. "Treats," Jac called when she got to her door. He was there in seconds. Cookies for Max, then brushing and examining him. Peg kept an eye on him, but no one knew him as intimately as she did. If there was a lump or tender spot she wanted to know immediately. Losing Max wasn't her only fear, but it was her worst.

After changing into chenille sweats, she settled on her back on the king-sized bed, a pillow under her knees. Max did his three circles and snugged against her side, his head resting on her hip. She worked her fingers through his fur. "She's not our friend, buddy." Liz and Peg would get along just fine, and she'd be off the hook.

Chapter Four

Liz brushed her hands together to get the dirt off. She ran her fingers up the stalk of one of the lavender plants she'd planted and held them to her face. She loved the smell. "That was fun." And rewarding. A section of bare ground along the flagstone patio was now filled with plants. She liked Peggy's garden. A series of large beds hugged the patio and continued along the walkway to Jac's. Crammed with fragrant and colorful plants, it managed to feel intimate.

"It's my sanity," Peggy said, as they carried trowels and empty plant containers to the side of the house. "I'm forced to give up artistic control. The plants have a mind of their own and never fail to remind me that any creative endeavor is a collaboration."

"Like composing. I think I know where a song's headed, and then it goes in a completely different direction." Teri had always laughed at her for arguing with the piano.

"A lot like life." Peggy set the trowels next to a flat of seedlings on a potting bench.

"Yeah," Liz said, fighting the tug toward sadness. They soaped their hands at the sink next to the bench. "Grandma used to start seeds every spring. Is it hard?"

"Easy as open the packet, sprinkle them on soil, cover with more soil, and water."

"I could do that." She ran her palm over the tops of the tiny plants. They bent over but sprang right back up. Something new. Something easy.

They walked back to the house and through French doors into a large space that was a dining room and kitchen separated by a bar top. A mahogany-finished baby-grand piano sat in the corner behind a long dining table. "This kitchen belongs in a magazine," Liz said, admiring the cheery yellow counters and walls with accents of white and blue. Large windows afforded a view past the garden to the ocean.

"Do you cook?"

"My dad would disown us if we didn't. He owns a restaurant. My sister's a professional chef, and my brother manages Dad's restaurant."

"I want to show you something." Peggy set a plate of chips and what looked like homemade guacamole on the bar top and went to the piano. She held up yellowed sheet music. "It has your grandmother's notes on fingering in the margins."

Debussy's *Petite Suite* for four hands. The spidery handwriting she remembered well. "When I first learned this piece I had to sit on a pillow to reach the keys."

"Wow. Child prodigy if you were playing it that young."

She'd been called that before but never gave it any thought. She'd always known she was meant for the piano, like when you met someone you knew you'd be best friends with.

"Shall we?" Peggy set the music on the rack and opened it to the third movement. "This is my favorite."

"Treble or bass?"

"Your choice." Peggy sat on the bench.

She sat to Peggy's right, taking her usual treble part. Closing her eyes, she let her fingers move over the keys from memory. All that was missing was the scent of lavender she always associated with her grandma.

When they finished, Peggy put her hands to her cheeks. "I just had the most vivid memory of sitting at your grandmother's piano playing this with her. I remember the cranberry glass she had in those corner windows. I loved how the sunlight would reflect through them onto the piano. She must have been so proud of you."

Liz hoped so. Her grandma rarely missed one of her shows, right up to the week before the heart attack that took her in an instant. But a quick hug and "you played that section exactly the way I would have" were as effusive as she got.

"Sorry I'm late, honey." A man with sandy-blond hair walked toward them from the living room, taking off his suit jacket.

"This is Liz," Peggy said. "I invited her to join us for dinner. I know how you like to show off your grilling expertise."

"I'm Roger." He extended his hand, a smile on his boyish face. "I hear you knocked Jac off her feet yesterday."

Liz looked at her lap when he kissed Peggy. She wanted those moments of casual intimacy back.

"Shall we rouse Jac and get this party going?" He dipped a chip in the guacamole.

"I'll get her." Liz wished Jac had kept them company while they planted. It would have been fun to continue their discussion of composers. For a layperson Jac had an amazing grasp of music.

"Tell her she better get up here before I drink all the old cabs," Roger said. "Are the kids eating with us?"

"Jack's skateboarding and Susanne is sulking in her room. Her best friend is on a date," Peggy explained.

Liz took her sweater from the back of the patio chair and put it on as she walked to Jac's cottage, a couple hundred feet down the wide walkway that headed toward the ocean. Colorful plantings spilled onto the flagstones, and the ocean shimmered, reflecting the low-lying sun. The cottage was a miniature version of Peggy's house—the bottom half of the walls ivory-colored Carmel ledgestone, the top half cedar shingles stained gray green.

She knocked on the oak door, amused at the heavy knocker that hung from the mouth of a gargoyle. Several minutes later, as she was about to leave, the door opened. She swallowed hard. Instead of creased pants and pressed shirt, Jac was wearing a light-blue sweat suit, the top unzipped enough to reveal significant cleavage. She looked softer, younger, less intimidating. She tucked hair behind her ear with a slow, graceful movement.

"I'm working, Peg. I'll be up later."

"It's Liz." Jac's eyebrow went up and Liz smiled at the predictability of it. "Roger said you should come before he drinks the old cabs."

"He wouldn't dare." Jac closed the door and then opened it again. Max trotted out with a tennis ball in his mouth. "He thinks you'll play fetch with him." The door closed and Max dropped the ball at her feet.

She tossed the ball for him as she walked back to the patio. He was definitely friendlier than Jac. She joined Peggy at the teak patio table with chairs for eight. A sweep of orange from the setting sun streaked the darkening blue-and-white curls of the Pacific. A hummingbird chased another across the garden. "I feel like I've stepped into one of your paintings." The quiet and beauty wrapped around her, and worries seemed far away. "Do you ever get tired of the view?"

"I didn't appreciate it as a child. Now wild horses couldn't get me away."

"I haven't been here in almost a year. I forgot how beautiful and relaxing Carmel is."

Peggy got up and turned on patio lights and a propane heater near the table. "The scenery would be enough, and the long history of emphasis on the arts would be enough, but the two together make Carmel special in a way that's hard to describe."

Liz nodded. That was exactly it. It was hard to describe, but easy to feel. She'd felt better the last few days than she had in a long time. "Grandma said she couldn't imagine living anywhere else. She'd scold us if we didn't call it Carmel-By-The-Sea. She had a scrapbook of articles about Carmel. Some of them date back to when her parents settled here in the early nineteen hundreds. Both were teachers and artists who wanted to live in an artists' community."

"That's some family history." Peggy tucked hair behind her ear in a gesture reminiscent of Jac. The same blond, shoulder-length waves of hair. The same blue eyes. Both tall and slender. Very different personalities.

"Where are they?"

Liz startled and looked over her shoulder. She hadn't heard Jac approach. She'd changed into heavy gray slacks and the fisherman-knit turtleneck sweater she'd worn yesterday that accentuated her long neck.

"Kitchen," Roger said, carrying platters to the party-sized barbecue, one piled high with raw steaks and another with sliced vegetables. He'd changed into jeans and a pink Polo shirt. "If you get it right, the next wine-tasting trip's on me."

"You two are incorrigible," Peggy said.

Jac returned with a bottle of wine, corkscrew, and three glasses.

"So you're on their team," Peggy said.

"Their team?" Liz asked as Jac sliced the foil off and screwed in the corkscrew.

"Wine drinkers. It's practically a religion with them."

"And with my brother. I try to tell him it's just fancy grape juice."

"Nectar of the gods," Jac said, pouring a half glass. "Or goddesses."

Liz was surprised when Jac offered her the glass, stopping when it was a few inches from her. *How does she do that?* She eyed the diamond ring on Jac's left ring finger, the only jewelry she'd seen her wear. Tasteful. Expensive. She had the odd sensation she was in the presence of someone unlike anyone she'd met before. She sipped the wine as Jac faced her, head tilted as if evaluating her.

"Do you like it?"

"That's the best wine I've ever tasted."

"What do you taste?"

She hated when Kevin asked her that, like a pop quiz she usually failed, but Jac's voice was inviting and her posture casual with her hip against the table. She sipped again. "Oak? And fruit?"

"What kind?" Again Jac's voice wasn't at all intimidating, more like an encouraging teacher.

"Um, blackberry?"

Jac nodded and twirled her fingers to indicate Liz should continue.

"Something kind of smoky." She sipped again. "Herbs? And something chocolaty?"

"Good." Jac poured another glass. Holding the stem between thumb and two fingers, she brought the glass to her lips and rested her nose just over the rim, inhaling deeply. She swirled the wine and inhaled again. A smile curled the corners of her mouth before spreading up her cheeks. "Too easy." She held the glass up in Roger's direction. "Joseph Phelps. Backus Vineyard Cab. 1999." Jac enunciated each word with reverence, as someone might recite a favorite passage from Scripture.

"Show-off." Peggy went to the house and returned with a glass of beer.

Roger looked up from laying the vegetables on the grill. He shook his head, but he was smiling.

Liz read the label on the bottle. Exactly right. "How—"

"Practice. Like doing scales." Jac put the glass against her lower lip and tilted it so the wine slid obediently into her mouth. She held it for a moment before swallowing, that same slow smile making her face even more beautiful.

Mesmerized by the casual sensuality of the gesture, Liz let out a long breath.

"Sometimes a hundred-dollar bottle of wine really is better than a ten-dollar bottle."

Liz almost choked on the sip she'd just taken. "I thought you said yesterday wine was as simple as drinking what you like. Something about a ten-dollar bottle being as good as a fifty?" She regretted the flip comment when Jac tilted her head and stared at her with that raised eyebrow.

"That doesn't mean you can't like a hundred-dollar bottle of wine better than a ten-dollar bottle."

"This isn't a hundred-dollar bottle of wine." Surely Jac was teasing her.

"No."

Thank God. She took another sip.

"More."

This time she did choke.

"Careful. Swallow." Their fingers touched as Jac held Liz's glass to refill it. "You realize, of course, that we just freed a fifteen-year-old prisoner," Jac said, sitting in the chair closest to the heater. Max lay by her side, the tennis ball between his paws.

"Huh?" Why did she always feel three steps behind in conversations with Jac?

"The wine. 1999. Great year. Now free to be our guest for the night."

Liz's heart tumbled and she took quick breaths. That was the year she and Teri had met. It had been a great year. She wanted more wine, lots more suddenly, and took a long swallow. She didn't intend to let grief shred this moment.

"You missed our recital," Peggy said to Jac. "Which reminds me. I'll be right back." She went to the house, and a minute later Liz's CD started. "When's your next show?" Peggy asked when she returned. "Roger and I love live music."

"We're on a break at the moment."

"Jac said you had a successful tour last year. You'll have to let us know when you're performing again."

Liz stared at the base of the wineglass as she turned it slowly. Resentment felt like a hard block in her stomach. This was her life now. And it followed her everywhere. A widow. Explaining. Sympathy she was tired of. Conversations that died because people didn't know what to say. She kept turning the glass as she said, "My wife died last September." The first day of fall. A beautiful day, not too hot. The kind of day they should have been on a picnic, not—She clenched her jaw against the threat of tears. "She was our drummer."

"I'm so sorry. Jac didn't say anything." Peggy scowled in Jac's direction as she laid her hand on Liz's forearm. "Were you together long?"

Liz liked that Peggy asked what she wanted and didn't bat an eye at her being a lesbian. Jac's expression was unreadable. "Fourteen years."

"I can't imagine how hard it's been for you."

Silence ensued until Jac asked, "Are you keeping the band together?" She rubbed the backs of her fingers up and down Max's side.

"Good question." Liz took a long sip of wine. "I haven't even managed to get the live CD out."

"Jac can help you with it." Peggy looked pointedly at Jac, whose jaw tightened.

Liz wasn't sure what to say. She didn't want to be rude, but laypeople had no idea how hard it was to produce a CD. "Um, maybe you can give your opinion of which songs you like?" She did seem to have a sharp ear and a good grasp of jazz. If she didn't like Jac's opinion she'd just ignore it. What harm could it do?

Jac said nothing as she tapped her fingers against the arm of her chair in time with the rhythm, a subtler version of what Teri had always done.

"If you like live jazz you should come over to my dad's club," Liz said.

"Jazz club?" Peggy asked. "Jac didn't say anything about that either." Her tone carried indulgent annoyance.

"Jazz On The Side."

"Your father owns that? We've seen some shows there."

"You're not burning the steaks, are you?" Jac asked.

"No, your majesty." Roger set a juicy looking steak on the plate in front of Jac. "Rare for you." He returned with steaks for the rest of them and a platter of roasted vegetables and baked potatoes.

Each time Roger topped off their glasses with the last of a bottle, he disappeared into the house and returned with another. He let Jac taste each one and she identified all of them. From the conversation, Liz gathered that they'd studied wine for years, taken tasting courses, and that Roger had an extensive wine collection Jac had helped him acquire. Yes, Jac was unlike anyone she'd ever met. Sophisticated was the right word for her, and definitely interesting, if reserved.

"Are you sure I can't help you with the dishes?" Liz asked when they'd finally run out of food and wine. She hadn't eaten this much in months. Yes, Carmel was good for her.

"Don't be silly. Jac, why don't you walk Liz home? I don't think Roger or I should drive."

"I'll be fine."

"Nonsense," Peggy said. "What if you trip and pass out, and a neighbor finds you asleep on their lawn in the morning?"

"Wait here." Jac strode off toward her cottage, Max at her side.

Standing, Liz realized she was tipsy. She didn't care. It was the best evening she'd had in a long time. She clutched the back of the chair as she pulled her sandals on, almost losing her balance. Okay, more than tipsy. She still didn't care. "I'm going to move over here this summer," she hollered toward the house. "Will you help me with Grandma's garden?" Pretty flowers. Bird feeders. New patio furniture. Walks on the beach. It would be a glorious and relaxing summer.

"I'd love to." Peggy handed her a plate wrapped in foil. "Cake for breakfast."

"You're a bad influence." She hugged Peggy for longer than she should, but it felt good. When she let go, Jac was there with Max in harness.

Liz stumbled as she stepped from the squishy gravel of the driveway to the street. Holding onto Jac's shoulder, she took off each sandal and shook out offending pebbles, then tugged them back on. She hooked her arm through Jac's as they walked the unlit street, another of Carmel's quirks—no streetlights. "Why aren't you drunk?"

"Practice."

"I love all the connections between our families." Liz hiccupped, then giggled, and hiccupped again. It was glorious to feel happy even if it was alcohol induced. "I wish we'd met as kids. I like talking to you. When you talk. Would you listen to the recordings?"

"You don't need my help."

"I love Carmel." Liz looked for the moon, but all she saw were stars in the pitch-black sky. She could hear the faint sound of the ocean a few blocks away. She let go of Jac's arm and spun around in a circle, bumping Jac's shoulder.

"Careful." Jac steadied her. Such strong fingers.

"I had a dorm mate in college who was blind. Great sax player…" A cat darted across the street and then another one chasing it. The first one leapt over a picket fence, but the second one didn't and fell back before scrambling over it. Liz laughed, swinging her arms. God, she felt good. "Where was I? Oh, yeah. I tried to use his cane once with my eyes closed and nearly knocked myself out walking into a branch. He was blind from birth. When did you lose your sight?"

"If there was some reason for you to know, I would tell you. Drunken curiosity doesn't constitute a reason to know."

The unexpected harshness of Jac's reply penetrated her awareness. "I'm sorry. I didn't mean to pry." She struggled to keep up with Jac's lengthening strides. "I'd like us to be friends is all. I'd like—" The toe of her sandal caught, and the next thing she knew she was sprawled face-first on the street. Her left wrist hurt like hell. "Shit."

"What happened? Liz? Where are you?"

"Here." Liz cradled her arm as she struggled to her knees. The pain made her stomach clench, and she swallowed to keep from throwing up. Max nosed her cheek.

"Are you hurt?" Jac gripped her shoulder.

"My wrist." She flopped to her butt and rested her forehead against bent knees as she rubbed her wrist. A sharp pain shot up her arm and nausea hit her again.

"Damn it, I should have brought a flashlight for you. Can you get up?"

"I don't know." Tears sprang to her eyes from the pain.

"Take my hand." Jac pulled her up and gripped her waist. "Are you hurt anywhere else?"

"I don't think so." She pressed her palm to her forehead to stop the spinning.

"Give me your hand."

"It's fine. I'll put some ice on it." Was this what a sprain felt like?

"You're a musician, damn it. Give me your hand."

Jac's touch was gentle but thorough. "I'm calling Peg and we're taking you to the hospital. It's broken."

"How can—"

"I feel a ridge in the bone that shouldn't be there."

"I don't want to." Bile rose again. No hospitals. Bad things happen there, her drunken brain said.

"You don't have a choice."

"I can't." Her voice rose, and she clung to Jac's shoulder as her surroundings spun. She covered her mouth, but the sob broke through. "I can't." When Jac's arm came around her waist, she turned into her and buried her face against her sweater. It was soft and smelled faintly of perfume, a delicate floral scent. "I can't."

"Let's get you home."

Tears streamed down her face and her wrist hurt. Bad. It couldn't be broken. It just couldn't.

She was holding ice cubes in a towel against her wrist when Peggy and Roger came through the front door. Fear thrummed through her racing pulse, but she didn't argue about the hospital. She couldn't move her hand. "I'm sorry I ruined the evening." Her voice cracked, and she pressed another Kleenex against the flood of tears.

"Shh," Peggy said, wrapping her in a hug. "I should have had Susanne drive you home. Come on, she's waiting in the car. Do you want to call your family and have them meet us?"

"No." The last thing she wanted was her family to have to come to her rescue again.

❖

Jac stepped out of Roger's SUV and rubbed her lower back. She hated hospitals, and Liz's anxiety had added to the stress. Two hours in the hard ER chair was torture on her back. It throbbed and the muscles were tight bands under her fingers. Hot tub. Stretching. Bed. Maybe a muscle relaxer. She removed Max's harness and headed across the gravel. He must be as tired as she.

"I'll walk down with you," Peg said when they reached the patio.

"Don't." She knew what was coming.

"Why didn't you tell me about Teri?"

"It wasn't my place."

"Just because you ferociously guard every detail of your life doesn't mean everyone does. I feel bad it came out like that. She seemed to drink more afterward."

Jac said nothing because there was nothing to say.

"And you knew about her band."

"Yes." She didn't tell Peg it was the second time Liz had lost her chance at fame because of Teri. Losing everything—the dark side of love.

"You didn't see how defeated she looked when she talked about it."

As if she needed to see what was clear in Liz's voice—sadness, loss, fear.

"Can't you help her?"

"A review of a two-year-old album won't do her any good."

"Don't play dumb with me. Can you at least help her with her CD? It might give her the encouragement she needs to keep going."

"Why do you care?"

"Why don't you?"

She opened her front door. This conversation needed to end. "I don't get involved with—"

"Anyone. I know." Peg walked away and then her footsteps stopped. "Don't you miss it?" Peg's voice held nostalgia she didn't want to hear.

Memories followed Jac to the hot tub, which did little to relax her back, and then to bed, where she dozed in a half sleep, fighting the tug back to a past she didn't want to think about. Emotions surged and curled over each other like ocean currents—regret, guilt, and loss in an inseparable swirl. Max lay stretched out along her side, his undemanding presence comforting. No, she couldn't afford to miss what was irrevocably gone.

She finally got up and took a muscle relaxer. Getting involved was a bad idea. But…the chance to help a talented musician create an album that might be great. Maybe it wouldn't hurt to listen to the recorded material. If it was good…She tugged the down comforter up to her chin and clenched it. No. She did not get involved. Her life worked just fine, and opening it up for any reason wasn't smart. It would only lead to disaster. It always did.

CHAPTER FIVE

Liz woke with a dull ache behind her eyes and a fuzzy taste in her mouth—revenge of the old cabs. And a cast on her left forearm. She pulled it from under the covers. Peggy had drawn colorful flowers on it, but Liz found nothing cheerful about this. Lucky, the doctor said. No displacement. It should heal on its own. Then she'd told him she played piano professionally. His expression changed and he'd suggested she see a specialist. She was too scared to ask him questions.

She rubbed her finger where her wedding ring should be. It hadn't been off since the day Teri put it on. She tried to bend her puffy fingers. Would she ever play again? She groaned and rolled over, burying her face in the pillow. How could she explain this to her dad? To Regan and Sammy? Maybe it was a blessing in disguise. She'd take a break for a while. Regan and Sammy should find another band. She'd tell them today at her dad's birthday party. It would be better for everyone.

Making coffee with one hand was a new adventure, but her fuzzy head demanded it. Cup in hand, she headed for the shower, a necessity just slightly behind coffee.

She stopped halfway down the hall and looked at the cast. Darn. What had the doctor said? Wrap it in a plastic bag when she showered. She trudged back to the kitchen and tugged a Ziploc bag from a drawer. Not big enough. She pulled a trash bag from under the sink, slid it over the cast, and twisted the excess around it. All the rubber bands in the drawer were too small to fit over the cast. In frustration she took the bag off. A bath would have to do.

As she waited for the tub to fill she wriggled out of her T-shirt. Hers, not Teri's. She sat down hard on the edge of the tub, tears bubbling up along with the urge to laugh. How had what she slept in become so important?

She lowered herself into the bath feeling numb and lost. Six months next Saturday—she knew without having to count, as if a calendar had been inserted into her brain labeled BEFORE TERI and AFTER TERI. When had counting the days gone to counting the weeks? And now she was up to months.

She had to sit with her back lodged next to the faucet so she could rest her left arm on the edge. She closed her eyes, knees bent in the short tub. The last time she'd taken a bath, it had been with Teri resting back against her, the week before she died.

She replayed the moment they knew they wouldn't win the battle with the leukemia this time. For reasons the doctors couldn't explain, Teri's body wasn't responding to the drugs. It had been late at night, and the hospital had moved into its night sounds. Crawling into the bed, she'd cradled Teri, stroking through her hair, desperate to give comfort.

"Water?" Teri croaked.

Liz held the straw to Teri's mouth as she sipped and then spread lip balm over Teri's lips.

"Promise me something." Teri's voice was thick and slow.

"Anything." She kissed Teri's head, damp with sweat from the fever.

"Promise you'll go on with your life." And then in barely a whisper she said, "I'm not going to make it this time."

Tears sprang to her eyes and she hugged Teri tight as if she could stop time by the sheer force of her will and her love.

Teri stroked her forearm. "I fell in love with you in the space of a heartbeat. Loved you every moment since. If I can't have a long life, I've had a happy one. Because of you, baby."

Liz could barely swallow around the lump in her throat as she gave Teri more water.

"Remember the happy times. Let yourself make new happy memories."

No. She wouldn't have any happy times without Teri.

"Promise you'll keep playing."

She wouldn't promise that. Not that. Music without Teri? Teri *was* the music. Unable to hold back sobs, she'd buried her face in Teri's hair, run her fingers through it, kissed Teri desperately on her forehead, on her cheek, and then on her mouth, silencing words she couldn't bear to hear.

The next day she'd taken Teri home and called hospice. They'd had a few good weeks, laughing together, talking, and even making love. Friends and family had rallied around them, but all the love in the world hadn't stopped the inevitable. She'd died in Liz's arms in the quiet of the early fall morning.

"I can't do it. Not without you." Holding her arm up, she slid down until her head was underwater, squeezing her eyes shut, seeking comfort in the warm water. Had her grandma cried in this tub for her lost love? Grandpa had died in his sixties, and she'd lived almost twenty years without him. She had no idea how to live without Teri. She got out of the tub. She'd never make it through her dad's birthday party if she didn't pull herself together. The doorbell rang as she tugged on a robe.

"You forgot this last night." Peggy had a foil-wrapped plate in her hand. "How's the wrist?"

"Broken," she said humorlessly.

"I feel awful about it."

"Not your fault. Let me get dressed. There's coffee." Of course she'd made enough for two again.

"One-handed isn't fun," Liz said, joining Peggy at the ancient table on the patio, forcing her arm through a sweatshirt sleeve. She swallowed a pain pill with a sip of coffee and chased it with a big bite of cake.

"We definitely need to do something with this garden," Peggy said.

She liked the way Peggy said "we." She tried to ignore the throbbing in her wrist as Peggy talked about her kids—Jack, a freshman in high school and obsessed with skateboarding. Susanne, a junior and aspiring actress.

When cake and coffee were gone, Peggy carried dishes to the kitchen. "Shall I wash these for you?"

"No. If I'm going to be one-armed for a while, I might as well start practicing."

Peggy went to stand behind the piano, looking out the corner windows to the garden. "I can't believe I'm back in this house." She turned one of the cranberry-glass bowls on the shelf. "I'd like us to be friends."

"Me, too. I'd like to be friends with Jac, but I think I annoy her."

"*I* annoy her. Don't take it seriously. You two have a lot in common. You really should ask her to help you with the CD."

"I might not do it at all. I decided this morning not to keep the band together."

"I'm sorry to hear that." Peggy looked like she wanted to say more. Finally she shook her head.

She walked Peggy to the door and then went back to the piano and played the right-hand part to the first song she'd written for Teri. It was sweet and full of their new love. Jac would say it was immature. She liked Jac's decisive opinions.

Notes ran through her head and she plunked them one-handed. Another bit of the melody she'd heard Friday. Some songs came all at once. She suspected this one would take its time.

CHAPTER SIX

L iz tried to dampen her irritation with Hannah as she drove the two miles from her condo to her dad's house through the downtown San Jose neighborhood that was a mix of pre-World War II homes and small businesses. She'd stopped at home to grab a blazer that would fit over the cast. Messy didn't even begin to describe the state of the condo.

She pulled to the curb in front of her dad's house on the tree-lined street. The two-story house with the wide front porch had recently been repainted white with black trim, the only colors it had ever been. She was careful not to park under the canopy of the mulberry tree. Her mom hated the messy street tree whose berries stained sidewalks and cars purple in the spring.

She let the CD finish, devouring the memories of the last night of their East Coast tour. A hot Sunday in July. The stunning boutique hotel on Park Avenue they'd stayed in that featured one of the top jazz clubs in New York. The accommodating staff that made them feel pampered.

Four of the most amazing nights she'd ever experienced as a musician—playing out of their minds, high on adrenaline and hopes for their future.

One of the best weeks of her life—sleeping late, making love, exploring the city new to her. They'd gone to three shows at the Village Vanguard jazz club, promising each other they'd perform there someday. She'd always have those memories. Private memories she wouldn't have to share with the world on an album.

The pill she'd taken at home was kicking in, and the pain that throbbed in time with her pulse was manageable. No one used the front door, so she walked to the backyard along the walkway that ran between the house and detached garage that had been soundproofed and converted into a music room before she was born. She tugged on the sleeve of the loose-fitting out-of-style blazer she'd pulled from the back of her closet. By the time she reached the back door that opened into the kitchen, she'd kicked herself into a good mood. Her dad's birthday deserved her best showing. The smell of tomatoes and garlic greeted her when she stepped into the kitchen.

Her brother, Kevin, looked up from opening a bottle of wine and tapped his watch. Four years older, he'd added pounds to his linebacker build and more gray to the thick chestnut hair they'd all been blessed with, but he was still handsome. "Please tell me you remembered the painting."

"In the car." She held up her keys. "You'll have to get it."

His eyes widened when he saw the cast. "What did you do?"

"Tripped at Grandma's." She wasn't going to tell them she'd gotten drunk and face-planted in the street. She tossed the keys to Kevin, who took a long swallow of wine and went out the way she'd come in.

Rebecca looked up from stirring a pan of meat sauce at the six-burner stove. She wore an apron over jeans and a sweater in shades that complemented her red hair. "Oh, sweetie, does it hurt?" She was the longtime chef at her dad's restaurant and practically part of the family.

Liz nodded and softened into Rebecca's hug. She gave the best hugs. "Where's Dad?"

"In the music room with the boys."

Liz needed to tell her dad she'd decided not to keep the band together before Regan and Sammy arrived. He knew what it was like to lose one's wife. He'd be disappointed, but he'd understand.

Oscar, a huge orange tabby cat, scooted into the music room when she opened the door. The once-scrawny stray, adopted by her dad years ago, considered the space his personal apartment. He jumped onto his usual spot on the back of the couch as if he were the audience.

Her dad was sitting on his stool, front and center between the baby-grand piano in one corner and Teri's drum kit across from it. Foot hooked on the rung, he was strumming his Gibson Super 400 guitar. He broke into a huge grin when he saw her. Robbie, Kevin's oldest son, was sitting on a shorter stool, mimicking her dad's posture. He was playing his new Gibson guitar and not doing a bad job of it. His younger brother, Kevin, Jr., was standing behind the drums, slapping the snares. Teri had always set him on her lap and let him play with her. Liz kept her arm behind her back until they finished.

"Sunshine," her dad said. "Join us."

She held out her arm and slid the blazer sleeve up to reveal more of the cast.

His smile disappeared and his eyebrows pulled together as he stared at the cast. "What happened?" He set the guitar in the rack along the wall with the other dozen guitars in his collection.

"Tripped. Colles' fracture."

"Collies," her nephews said in unison as they rushed toward her. "Like the dog?" the older one asked.

"Not quite," she said as they stroked the cast as if petting it.

"Can I draw on it?" her younger nephew asked.

"Go find your dad, boys." He walked them to the door.

She sat on the old plaid couch with the squishy springs, cradling the cast in her lap. She flexed her fingers. In some scary way she felt compelled to make sure they kept working. The knuckles were more swollen than this morning, but the doctor said she'd have a lot of swelling at first.

"This isn't good." He sat next to her, staring at the cast. "We need to get you to a specialist right away. I'll make some calls first thing in the morning. This is your career." He walked back to his stool, hands in his pockets.

"I know."

He looked like he was thinking and then said, "Seven months until the first date on your fall tour."

She forced herself to meet his gaze. "It would be best to let Regan and Sammy move on. Next year, after everything calms down, I can form a new group."

His jaw tightened and he ran a hand through his thinning hair, gray at the temples. "You don't have that kind of time. This band. This year. It's your last shot to make it big."

She wanted to argue. She didn't. He was right. The music industry was fickle and she'd already had two opportunities. It should be simple—hire a new drummer and keep going. Nothing was simple without Teri. "It's not fair to keep them hanging."

"I love them like they were my own kids, but they owe you. They'll wait."

Again she wanted to argue, but again he was right. She and Teri had discovered the twins in a coffeehouse, playing the heck out of an old blues standard. Their raw talent was breathtaking. Impressed by what they'd heard, they offered the twins the opportunity to become part of their new quartet. It seemed symbolic—their own lives were starting from scratch after Teri's battle with leukemia. Why not do the same with a band? It had worked and they'd been so close to achieving their dream. Again. "Maybe I shouldn't start another band. Cassie has always said I could join—"

"Absolutely not." He crossed his arms. "You're going to make it big with your own band. That's what we've worked for."

"I can't do it alone."

He sat next to her again and put his arm across her shoulder. His Old Spice was familiar and comforting, as was the soft knit of the long-sleeved Polo shirts he often wore. "You're not alone. I won't let you lose your dream."

"It hurts too much without her."

"It gets easier. You'll be glad you stuck with it. We'll focus on the album. Without shows, it's imperative we give your fans something to keep their interest."

"I'm still picking the songs."

"Closing night was your best show. We can use it for the album."

"I want to pick the best versions out of all the sets." The album had to be perfect.

"We need momentum, sunshine."

His favorite word. How did you get momentum from a dead stop?

"It's been long enough. You can't let adversity get you down."

"I'll get them picked this week. I promise." Eighty-one songs to choose from. The enormity of it made her dizzy.

"That album has to carry us until your fall tour."

"I know, Dad."

"We'll get through this." He squeezed her shoulder and headed toward the door. "I'm going to pop over and check on the restaurant. We'll talk about this later." The restaurant he'd owned for over thirty years was across the street and the jazz club next door to it.

Liz looked around the room where she'd spent so much of her life. Dark paneling. Fluorescent lights overhead. Brown carpeting worn unevenly from where people stood or sat as they played. Shelves stacked with sheet music. Stools of varying heights and some folding chairs. Coat rack by the door. Not fancy, but oh…the music that had been created here. Surrounded by all the instruments, all the history, all the dreams born here, she felt very lost. She stroked Oscar for the three seconds he'd allow, the tip of his tail twitching.

Getting up, she went to Teri's drum kit and sat on the wooden stool. She toed her feet to the rung. "I broke my wrist." She tapped her fingers on the floor tom, then across the hanging toms to the snare drum. How could she face someone else sitting here? Not Teri's expressive brown eyes that anchored her. Not Teri's dimpled grin that never faded when she was behind her beloved drums. "I can't do it, sweetie. I can't keep my promise. I'm sorry." She fled the room that didn't feel safe anymore. She'd have to convince her dad that letting Regan and Sammy move on was best. When she had her emotions under control, she returned to the kitchen, as much the hub of family gatherings as the music room.

"Taste this." Her sister, Hannah, came toward her from the far end of the large kitchen, holding a spoon of chocolate frosting. "You broke your arm?"

"Wrist."

"Oh, Lizzie, that's terrible. Is it going to be all right?"

"I hope so." She licked the frosting off and glanced from the spoon to the conspiratorial grin on Hannah's face. "Looks like chocolate but tastes like—"

"Chocolate-raspberry ganache. Ta dah." Hannah bowed, her perfectly highlighted wavy chestnut hair flowing over her shoulders.

"Don't let Kevin find out," Rebecca said, putting two pans of lasagna in the oven.

"Find out what?" Kevin walked in from the direction of the living room. By the sound of it, his boys were playing video games.

"Nothing," Hannah said.

Kevin dipped a spoon in the bowl of frosting. "What the—" He worked his mouth as if it were full of peanut butter. Banging the spoon down on the counter he said, "Dad likes chocolate cake with chocolate frosting."

"And he'll get chocolate cake with chocolate frosting. Just dressed up a little." Hannah's hands were on her hips, and frosting dripped from the spoon she held.

"Can't you stick to anything?"

"It's cake, Kevin. Lighten up and live dangerously."

"Look what living dangerously got you."

"It. Wasn't. My. Fault."

"Your boss finds you in bed with his wife, and it wasn't your fault?"

"You're jealous because I have more fun than you."

"And welcome to it."

Hannah's face tightened. She tossed the spoon into the bowl and stalked out of the kitchen.

"She's trying to contribute," Liz said.

"She's ignoring tradition. Like always." Kevin rubbed the back of his neck and took a healthy gulp of wine.

"Where's Karen?" She hadn't seen her sister-in-law.

"Home. Sick."

"Oh, no."

"Yeah, whatever," he said, his mouth a hard line. It was a shame they'd missed their weekend getaway.

Benny Goodman blared from speakers in the living room, and seconds later Hannah bounced into the kitchen. "Dance with me, Kev." She grabbed his waist and whisked him through the kitchen and into the dining room, around the table, her yellow dress twirling out around her as she sashayed to the swing beat. Music had always been her family's salve and bond, and not even Kevin could stay mad in the midst of all that jazz.

A timer went off, and Hannah dashed into the kitchen. Opening the convection-oven door, she stuck a toothpick into the cake. "Perfect," she said, reaching for a hot mitt.

"Dare I ask what you did to the cake?"

"Nothing Dad won't like."

An hour later Rebecca carried pans of lasagna to the table, Hannah close behind with the salad and garlic bread. It was her dad's favorite meal. The back screen door banged and Sammy walked in from the kitchen, his wavy black hair hanging over the turned-up collar of his trench coat. He looked rough but played tenor sax like an angel, and his puppy-dog eyes were a hit with the band's younger female fans. "Happy Birthday, Pops." He shrugged out of his coat and hung it on the back of his chair.

Regan, his twin sister, appeared in the archway between the kitchen and the dining room, dressed head to toe in black, the only color she wore. "Hey." One hand was in its usual position half in her jeans pocket, and the other held a present. Her dark good looks and broody manner made her a heartthrob, especially with the fans savvy enough to know her preference for women. She was grinning. In the four years she'd known Regan, Liz had rarely seen more than a half smile.

"Saved you the best seat," her dad said, pulling out the chair to his left.

Regan set the present on the sideboard with the others. She stood next to Liz and held out a folded piece of letter-sized paper. "Read it."

Keeping her left forearm under the edge of the tablecloth, Liz took it with her right hand and snapped it open. An email printout. She frowned, read the "from" line, and peered up at Regan, who was rocking back and forth, still grinning. Liz read the first sentence. Her heart stopped and then started up, pounding like that of a horse about to jump a fence. By the time she finished the three paragraphs, her hand was shaking. The table was quiet, everyone staring at her.

"What is it?" Her dad asked.

She handed him the paper and stared at her plate, unable to speak, as confusion and anger collided in her stomach. Regan shouldn't have done this without asking her.

Her dad's smile grew as he read. "Congratulations!" He stood and waved the paper. "Up Beat is invited to perform at the Monterey

Jazz Festival!" There were confused looks and then clapping as everyone asked, "how" and "why didn't you tell us?"

"I sent it," Regan said. "Teri put it together."

Liz shot her eyes to Regan as the shock tumbled through her. Teri had done this? How? When? Why hadn't she said anything? Why hadn't they discussed it? *Promise you'll keep playing.* No, no, no. This couldn't be.

"Well, I'll be damned," her dad said. He squeezed Liz's shoulder and held up his glass. "Here's to the future of Up Beat!"

"What about your wrist?" Hannah asked. The table went silent.

"Nice timing," Kevin said, sarcastically.

Regan tilted her head, her fork halfway to her mouth.

"Collies," Liz's youngest nephew said. "I drawed on it."

She pulled her arm from under the table, and the excitement on Regan's face shut off so fast it was as if someone had flipped a switch.

"Damn," Sammy said. He set his fork down and chewed his bottom lip. "Damn."

"Excuse me." Liz bolted out the back door. Monterey Jazz Festival? They'd appeared there with their first quartet and had planned to submit for this year, but...Teri had managed that in the weeks—She walked faster around the house to the street, hugging the cast to her stomach, feeling sick. This was too much for her to handle on her own.

Regan fell into step beside her, head down, hands shoved all the way in her pockets. "Does it hurt?"

She resisted the urge to send Regan back. "Not too bad," she lied. Regan had faced plenty of tragedy in her life, and none of this was her fault. She caught a glimpse of the deep-brown eyes capped by shaggy bangs. Vulnerable wasn't an attribute she normally attached to her emotionally distant bass player.

"She wanted you to be happy, to have everything you worked for."

"Happy? She thought I could be happy again?" Liz laughed, the sound brittle, aware she was close to losing control.

"I couldn't tell her no. It's what we worked for. It was part of—"

"The plan." A CD release party in January. Follow-up tour on the West Coast for the live album. End the summer at the Monterey Jazz

Festival if they were accepted. Fall tour. Take a break over Christmas to compose new material. Back on the road in the spring. A new studio album next summer. She wanted to sit down on the curb just thinking about it all. And without Teri? "No. I can't do it."

"She said to give you this." Regan pulled a small envelope from her back pocket.

A tremor went through Liz's heart and washed down her arms. Out of the corner of her eye she saw LIZ in the center of the lavender envelope in Teri's all-capitals printing. She shook her head, fighting the throbbing pain in her wrist, the crushing pain in her chest, and the horrible emptiness of being alone. This wasn't fair. It was half a block before she took it. She shoved it in her blazer pocket. She couldn't read it now.

"I loved her, too. I miss her. I miss you. I've barely seen you since—"

"I've been busy." It was a lame excuse. It was hard to be around Regan and Sammy, the four of them now the three of them.

"The band. It's my life." What Regan wasn't saying screamed through the silence. Don't let my dream go. Don't send me back to the nowhere I came from. "You're the family Sammy and I never had." Regan turned away as she brushed the back of her hand across her eyes.

Liz had never seen Regan even close to tears. What she wanted no longer mattered. That paper on the dining table changed everything. Dreams. Everyone's dreams hinged on the Monterey Jazz Festival and the album. She put her hand on Regan's shoulder. "We'll do it. We'll make her proud." She infused the words with confidence she didn't feel.

She smiled at all the expectant faces when they returned to the table. She downed another pain pill and managed to eat, forcing herself to join in the conversation. Today was about her dad. Hannah sulked and Kevin gloated when her dad said the cake was interesting.

"Open this first," Liz said when they'd gathered in the living room. She pointed to the painting and slid in between Hannah and Kevin on the couch. Hannah put her arm around her shoulder.

Her dad pulled the wrapping off the painting. "It's beautiful."

"I met the woman who painted it." She gave him the card from Peggy. "She lives a few blocks from Grandma's and took lessons from her."

"Good job," Kevin whispered.

Something she'd done right. And alone. And she'd met Jac because of it. Should she let Jac listen to the recordings? No. She didn't have time to waste with a layperson. Regan and Sammy didn't have the skills to help her, and she was afraid she'd cave in to her dad's need to get it done quickly if she let him help. She was on her own. *Why did you do this, sweetie?* She knew the answer. Love.

"This is from me and Regan, Pops." Sammy handed him a present. Regan worked in a used-record store, and Liz knew she'd been looking for rare jazz records to give him for his birthday.

"Mine next," Hannah said, handing her dad a present wrapped in paper Liz recognized as some she'd bought last year.

"Well, I'll be," her father said as he read the front of the CD. "I heard this was coming out. Unreleased Wes Montgomery. How'd you get it?"

"It's who you know," Hannah said, beaming a smile.

"Nice," Liz said to Hannah. She wanted to be irritated with her for keeping it to herself, but that was Hannah. Even as a kid she'd always had an extra present for their parents at birthdays and Christmas that she was careful to say was just from her.

"Let's get over to the club," her dad said. "Customers to take care of." He was already putting on a sport coat and helping Rebecca into her raincoat.

They walked across the street to the jazz club her dad had opened last year, a longtime dream that had helped him get over his wife's death. She wanted to go home, but two of her friends' bands were performing as a birthday tribute to her dad. Parties exhausted her as much as they'd exhilarated Teri. So many ways they were different, but they'd blended those differences into something magical.

She settled at the far end of the bar that took up most of one side of the long, narrow space. The club was packed, and her dad made his way through the closely spaced tables, shaking hands and accepting birthday wishes. She took another pain pill with half a glass of wine after her dad announced they'd been accepted to the festival.

She endured the congratulations and questions about her wrist, trying to act excited instead of worried. It was after midnight when her friend Cassie's band finished their set and she was able to leave, so exhausted she could barely drive to her condo.

Too tired to care about the laundry basket blocking the door from the garage into the kitchen, or Hannah's shoes littering the hall, she went to her bedroom and collapsed on the bed. The envelope crunched in her pocket. Sitting up, she took it out and scooted up against the headboard. Her heart skipped beats as she traced her finger across her name. What was it about someone's handwriting that made it feel like they were still here?

Opening it, she pulled out a card. A cartoonish pianist hunched over a piano, notes flying from the inside of the piano. It was a joke between them—Teri finding cards with piano themes. Tears rolled down the well-worn paths on her cheeks.

Hi, baby. I just finished putting the packet together. If you're reading this, then you were accepted. I know you didn't expect it, but I hope you're smiling right now. Come on, please? I love it when you're trying to be serious and I can get you to smile.

She let the corners of her mouth pull up, but smiles weren't supposed to feel sad.

I watch you trying to hold it all together—taking care of me and enduring the intrusion of our family and friends. I know it's exhausting. You're so gifted and I can't bear the thought that you'll give up. We're so close and, for the second time, I've let you down. I want to give you a reason to keep playing. I want to help you get everything we worked for.

She went to the bathroom for Kleenex. To have Teri's words in her neat handwriting made her seem close enough to touch, but she wasn't.

"Spring Time" is playing from our first album. Do you remember where we were when you wrote it?

"I'll never forget it," Liz whispered. Spring of their freshman year. The hour drive to Daffodil Hill. The picnic afterward in the secluded meadow Teri took her to. Making love. All the promise of that day, all their hopes and dreams, were in that song.

I'm tapping the bed, always backing you up, baby. I'll be clapping for you at Monterey. All my love, Teri.

She put the card back in the envelope. Of course Teri would do this. She was the driving force—marketing, promoting, setting gigs, managing the million things so Liz could do one—compose. She had to make Teri's final wish come true. "I'll make you proud, sweetie."

She put on Teri's T-shirt, washed too many times to have her scent. She took another pain pill and tried to sleep, but her mind wouldn't stop cycling through everything she needed to get done. Midterms this week. A recital for her private students on Thursday. No time to work on the CD. Spring break next week. Could she get the songs chosen? Maybe start mixing them? She'd have to contact her sound engineer about his availability. The million things Teri did were now her responsibility. She finally wore herself out and sleep captured her.

She woke snuggled up against—

"Don't get up yet."

Her heart flailed wildly at the injustice of it. Not Teri's voice. Of course not.

She needed a pain pill but instead closed her eyes and pulled Hannah's arm tighter around her. Hannah had slept with her every night for weeks after Teri's death. She'd forgotten how good it felt to be held. Her mind picked up where it had left off, listing all the things she needed to do this week.

CHAPTER SEVEN

Liz checked her watch again. It looked wrong on her right wrist. So did the ring she'd had to force over the knuckle on her right ring finger. No way was she not wearing it. Their appointment was an hour ago. "Dad, the recital's in an hour."

"You have no idea what I had to do to get us in to see him." He crossed his arms.

She covered her mouth as she yawned. A nap would have been heaven. She'd been barraged during her office hours with students needing help, which meant she couldn't get midterms graded at school, which meant she'd been up late every night grading them. She'd lost track of how many phone calls she'd returned from parents nervous about the recital. And always the worry about her wrist. And the CD. And finding a drummer. The million things.

"Mr. Randall?" A young woman with cats on her scrub top held a door open across the reception area.

They followed her down a white-walled hallway. This wasn't a hospital and they were just here for information. She knew logically that a broken wrist and leukemia were different, but her churning stomach didn't. Specialists couldn't always make things better.

"Sit." Dr. Russell, tall, with salt-and-pepper hair, stood from behind a large desk and gestured to two chairs. No smile. No handshake. A bookcase behind him was filled with books. Diplomas and certificates hung on the wall. Proof he was an expert.

She sat in the chair, cast resting on her lap, flexing her puffy fingers. Did he know anything about being a musician?

"I reviewed your medical records." Dr. Russell typed and then angled the computer monitor toward them. "X-ray is useless beyond confirming the fracture. It can't predict healing. Your break is close to the joint, which increases the risk it won't heal properly. Surgery is your best option. It's predictable."

Predictable. The word clattered around in her head. He was wrong. Nothing was predictable. She studied the X-ray, vaguely listening to the conversation between the doctor and her dad: open reduction internal fixation, volar plate; yes, there's always the risk of infection but it's slight; yes, compressive neuropathy is a rare complication. Her father knew the right questions to ask. That thin line of black across the end of the white bone. Such a tiny flaw. Surely the ends of the bone would knit together. She tried to imagine screws sticking out of it. Her stomach rolled and she pulled the cast against it. Treatment options. Risks. Odds. Her mother's battle with a benign brain tumor. Teri's with leukemia. Both lost in spite of the experts' odds.

"How soon can you do the surgery?" her dad asked.

Dizziness made her close her eyes. Weren't they just here for information?

"I had a cancellation for Monday."

No. Carmel. Ten days to pick the songs, walk on the beach, and spend time with Peggy and Jac.

"Nothing sooner? She's playing at the Monterey Jazz Festival in September."

"What instrument?"

"Piano."

Dr. Russell's face tightened into an expression similar to the ER doctor's. "Monday's the best I can do. She'll need to come in tomorrow for pre-op workup."

"Good enough." Her dad shook the doctor's hand.

Back in the reception area she signed the forms where he told her to sign. Then they were in the parking lot. It was dotted with trees covered in pink blossoms. Flowers filled big containers by the entrance—pink, orange, and yellow. Happy colors. She wanted to know their names.

"I'll pick you up in the morning for the appointment," he said when they reached the freeway.

"I don't want surgery."

"I know you're scared, sunshine, but I'll be right there with you. The benefit of the surgery outweighs—"

"Do you still remember Mom's voice?"

He was quiet and then said, "Not as clearly as I want to." His voice was back to his dad voice. The one she needed.

Neither did she. Nor her grandma's. She couldn't bear the thought of not hearing Teri's voice in her head. She turned up the volume on the CD and directed the heater vent to blast her with hot air. She was shivering. Duke Ellington filled the car, but even music she loved didn't chase away the dread filling her. Hills along the freeway were green and full of promise, and she clung to that feeling. She'd composed "Spring Time" on a day like this. It had to go on the album, but they'd played it every night. Which was the best version? Her shoulders collapsed with the enormity of picking the best out of eighty-one. Rubbing the cast, she willed the bones to heal.

She checked her watch. She'd barely make it to the recital before her students. "Can we stop at McDonalds?"

"Rebecca can fix you—"

"I want a cheeseburger and fries and a chocolate shake."

"You bet. I've been thinking about the CD. How many songs have you chosen?"

"About half." She didn't tell him that half changed weekly.

"I should have gotten involved sooner. Now there's no time to waste. We'll spend the weekend selecting the rest of—"

"I'm going to Carmel." She'd felt better there, and she really needed to feel better before the surgery. "To work on it. I can't concentrate with Hannah around."

"It has to get done, sunshine." He looked over at her, all business again.

"It will." She needed to prove to herself she could do this. She couldn't disappoint Teri.

"It's your future."

"I know." "Black and Tan Fantasy" started, and she thought of listening to it in the rain with Jac. Maybe it wouldn't hurt to let her listen to the recordings.

"You okay with money? We can't scrimp on it."

"I'm—" Her head dropped. There'd be a deductible for the surgery. Teri's medical expenses had drained their savings. And she'd been paying Regan and Sammy a little bit.

"I'll finance it for you. When you make it big you can pay me back." He patted her thigh. "I take care of you and Kevin. When Hannah gets with the program, I'll help her, too."

Program. Was there a program? She closed her eyes and leaned her head back, but that didn't stop her mind from racing. Take care of her wrist. Get the CD done. Find a drummer. Get the band rehearsing again. Get the website updated. And their Facebook page. A million things. "I'm trying, sweetie, I'm trying," she whispered.

CHAPTER EIGHT

Professional ethics wouldn't let Jac skip even one song on an album she reviewed, although this one tempted her. She'd earned her reputation and people relied on her expertise. Finally the obnoxious music stopped and quiet reigned. Free jazz was one thing. Noise masquerading as free jazz was another.

"Nothing good in this batch, buddy." She loved discovering a worthy group or artist and giving their career a boost with a great review on her blog. She reached down. Max was right where he should be, in his bed beside her recliner. She scratched along his side. He stretched out and made his happy-moan sound.

"Why did it take me so long?" Peg had tried to convince her to get a guide dog for years. She rubbed his ears with the backs of her fingers. The softness went right to her heart. It wasn't the independence that made a difference to her. Going out in the world mattered little. It was his presence. After getting over the shock of realizing how lonely she'd been, she'd given in to his innocent but insistent seduction of her with his playfulness, devilishness at times lest she think he was perfect, and above all, his loyalty. He wasn't capable of hurting or betraying her, and for that she'd give him anything.

She went to the cabinet that housed her CDs and searched through Brahms. Like cleansing her palate after mediocre wine, she needed to cleanse the noise of the last album. She pulled out his second symphony, then stopped. Leafing through the CDs a shelf above, she found the one she wanted. Up Beat's last CD. Curiosity. Just curiosity.

She settled back in her recliner and for the next fifty minutes focused on Liz's music, as if she were searching around someone's home to find out who they were.

"Hmmph. I didn't listen closely enough." When she'd reviewed it she'd taken it whole, and her opinion that they had potential but were immature as a band was still true. But Liz...her playing sent pulses of pure joy through her. Emotionally powerful. Technically brilliant. Innovative and unique chords and progressions. But on too many of her solos it felt like Liz held back. Fit in. Easy to miss unless you really listened. Liz deserved every bit of praise she'd received, but Jac couldn't shake the feeling she could be even better.

Max stood and nosed her fingers. "I know." His sense of time was as accurate as hers. The perfect partnership. He went to the front door and she went for shoes.

She heard music coming from Peg's studio as they walked to the patio. Not show tunes. Jac pinched off a stem of lavender by the studio door and held it to her nose. French lavender. Velvety, narrow, serrated leaves and her favorite scent of the different lavender varieties Peg planted. "How's it going?"

"Why do I agree to these shows?"

"Because gallery owners wait long enough that you forget how much you hate them."

"I don't hate them."

"How many seascapes does she want?"

"Not funny. And I'll have you know I'm painting the garden."

"Careful. You have a reputation to uphold, an audience to please..." Something landed on her chest, pointy like a paintbrush. "Don't throw things at the blind woman." She tried not to smile, but she loved giving Peg a hard time. Every artist had to grapple with the balance between creative self-exploration and providing their audience with what they expected. It wasn't an easy line to walk.

"Aren't you late for your route?" Peg's nickname for her daily walks because she walked the same route everyday. Past Carmel Roasting Company, where the owner selected and ground coffee for her once a week. Past Pilgrim's Way bookstore for audiobooks the owner ordered for her. Past the Bistro for lunch. Past Diggidy Dog pet boutique so Max could get his treat from the clerks Jac trusted to supply her with the best supplies for him.

"Right on schedule." Everything orderly and familiar, just the way she liked it. "What time's Liz arriving?"

"Around one. You joining us for lunch?"

"No."

"I'm making pizzas."

"Trying to bribe me?"

"Yes."

"What wine are you serving?"

"Whatever you pick. Can you swing by the gallery? Marissa has a check for me."

Jac whistled. "Good month for you. Have I said how much I respect your talent?"

"You're in a good mood today."

"Sun is shining, birds are singing…" Her back felt great. She had the number-one blog in jazz. Max was healthy. What else was there? "Let's go, buddy." She carried the leather harness until they reached the street, then buckled it around him. "Want to trade half your walk for a beach romp tonight?" He barked. "Yeah, that's what I thought."

❖

"Hello," Liz called out, crossing the patio to where Peggy was kneeling, planting small plants along the front of a garden bed. "Pansies?"

"See, you know something about gardening." Peggy stood and brushed dirt off her gloves. In a pink T-shirt and purple drawstring pants, she looked as colorful as her garden. "How was the appointment?"

"Surgery Monday." Her stomach did the somersault it did every time she thought about it.

"Oh, Liz, I'm so sorry."

Liz followed Peggy around to the side of the house, where she put her garden tools in the shed. "My dad did a lot of research. It's the best option." Her stomach clenched again. She rubbed her palm over the seedlings on the potting bench. They'd grown a lot in a week.

"How was the birthday party?" Peggy asked as they walked toward the house.

"Dad loved the painting and the card. I got a surprise, too. We've been invited to play the Monterey Jazz Festival."

Peggy's eyebrows rose. "Congratulations. I thought you were going to dissolve the band. You didn't think you'd get accepted?"

"I didn't do the submission. Teri did. I'm excited. It's the break we wanted."

"That is some surprise. Your wrist will be healed?"

"I hope." Liz settled onto a bar stool in the kitchen and wiggled her fingers. The knuckles finally looked like knuckles. "Surgery will make healing more predictable. I can start rehab sooner."

"I imagine you're nervous about surgery," Peggy said when the pizzas were in the oven and they were sitting on the patio. "We'll have to distract you this weekend. I'm going out to Carmel Valley tomorrow to my favorite nurseries. Why don't you come?"

"I need to get the songs picked for the CD." She tried to be enthusiastic, but the enormity of the task settled like a heavy weight across her shoulders. Maybe her dad was right about using the last night.

"Ask Jac to help. You won't regret it."

She looked across the garden to the undulating Pacific, gray trying to be blue today. She loved how variable it was from day to day, a reminder that nothing stayed the same. "I don't want to offend her." If that many songs were too much for her, how would a layperson ever sort through them? "She seems to know a fair amount about music but—"

"That would be an understatement."

Liz jerked her head in the direction of Jac's voice. By her tone, she seemed more amused than offended.

Jac stood by the table holding Max's harness. Max ran to the lawn and rolled around on his back, legs pumping in the air. "You're wondering if I'm qualified." Jac set the harness on a chair and sat next to Liz. "You can always decline my suggestions." Max bounded toward them with a tennis ball in his mouth. He poked Jac's leg. She took the ball from Max and handed it to Liz.

True. Max bounced around her chair, his ears lifted and tail wagging madly. Liz threw the ball. Max streaked after it and snagged it on the first bounce. He pranced regally back to her and dropped it in her lap before dancing around her chair again.

Jac smiled as if at a private joke. "Do you know the blog *Jazz Notes*?"

"Who doesn't? Reviewed our last album and said—" Liz's arm froze as she was about to throw the tennis ball. She stared at Jac. No.

Jac tipped her head. "At your service."

"Shit." She flung the ball.

"It's been called that."

"No one knows who writes that blog." She shook her head. She was sitting next to one of the most well-regarded critics in jazz.

"And I intend for it to stay that way." Jac's expression looked dangerously serious.

Peggy was shaking her head indulgently. "I need to check the pizzas."

"Why didn't you tell me?" Max dropped the ball in her lap and she dutifully threw it for him. Yeah, it would be fun to have a dog.

"See comment above."

Liz laughed. "How about I give you the recordings and you pick?" The thought was both disturbing and such a relief that she inhaled a huge breath, as though she hadn't really breathed since Regan put the letter in her hand. She gulped when Jac didn't seem amused.

"I can offer critical evaluation, but an album has a heart and soul, and only you can find that." Max returned with the tennis ball. Jac gave him a hand signal, and he lay down by her chair but kept the tennis ball between his feet.

"There is no heart to this album." Liz studied a drop of water sliding down the outside of her iced-tea glass, her mood dropping with its descent.

"That's ridiculous. It's a tribute to Teri."

She stared at Jac. Yes! That was exactly it. If only she could get her dad to understand that. With him, it was about generating momentum for the band. She needed it to be personal. She needed it to be perfect. Maybe she could work on it with Jac.

"But the tribute comes from your feelings about Teri and the music you made together. It's not about her. It's about you."

Peggy was still in the kitchen, and time seemed to slow in Jac's quiet presence. Liz didn't want it to be about her, but Teri wasn't here to help. Teri's voice was in her head, but it had nothing to offer about the CD or how to accomplish what she'd set in motion. "I'd be grateful for any help you can give." She rubbed the cast. So much had changed since Teri's death.

"When do you want it done?"

"This weekend. Before I have surgery."

"Surgery?" Jac's eyebrow went up.

"Monday."

"Without giving it a chance to heal on its own?"

"It's too risky. We were accepted to Monterey and I can't take the chance."

Jac's other eyebrow shot up. "You applied to—"

"Teri did."

"Without your knowledge?"

Liz stiffened as something dark and hard clamped down on her heart. "It was her gift. A way to help the band keep going."

"And to put you in an awkward position." Jac's voice was sharp, and Max looked up at her. She petted him and he put his head back on his paws.

"We had dreams." Liz's voice was louder than she intended, and that hard place started to burn. "It took a lot of guts to do what she did when she was…" The unspoken word hung in the air like a dark cloud over the warm, gentle spring day. Six months tomorrow. Of course Teri had been secretly hoping for a last-minute miracle, as she had. Tears filled her eyes and she pulled Kleenex from her jeans pocket. Would grief ever stop ambushing her?

"I know." Jac's voice was soft, as if she saw her tears. "But it's your place to decide if, when, and how you continue."

"The band was never mine alone."

"It is now." It wasn't said unkindly, but it had a bite to it. Jac shoved her chair back and went to the house. Peggy intercepted her and said something to her.

"Are you all right?" Peggy set two pizzas on the table, both still bubbling from the oven.

"She doesn't pull punches." Liz's mouth watered in spite of her conflicting emotions.

"Her bark's worse than her bite."

"I can't argue with her credentials."

Jac returned with a glass of red wine. "I assume you played a core program each night and added different selections to mix it up?"

"Yes."

"Do you have them on a computer?"

"Just the original master."

"Put it on CDs with the same songs back-to-back. I don't care which night was which. Bring them by when you're done. Be here at nine tomorrow." Jac slid a slice of pizza onto her plate, and just like that it was settled.

Liz felt like saluting. She felt like hugging Jac. She didn't know what to say.

"Did you tell Liz about your show at Gallerie Plein Aire, Peg?" Jac cut a bite of pizza. Of course she wouldn't eat with her fingers.

"Your own show?" Liz shoved a big bite into her mouth. She loved eating with her fingers.

"Next month."

"God, this is good." Liz wiped tomato sauce from her chin. "Do you show in other galleries?"

"I used to, but as much as I love sharing my art, it got to be too much pressure. It was starting to feel formulaic—the gallery owners wanted me to keep painting more of what was selling. For a while I bought into that because I wanted to give buyers what they want."

"It's the same for me," Liz said. "I love shows, but I get tired of having to do the tunes we're best known for. Some of them I wrote fifteen years ago."

"Bands are successful if they create a sound that people respond to," Jac said. "But that becomes a trap. The greats like your Ellington, Miles Davis, Brubeck—they never sat still. Their music was constantly evolving, reflecting their new interests and creative development. Blocking that process leads to stilted artists, or musicians." She bobbed her fork at Liz. "And boring music. Your band will be different without Teri and your style might change. You have to trust that if you lose some listeners, you'll find new ones."

"It's easy to get caught in expectations, isn't it?" Peggy asked. "I'd rather do fewer paintings, enjoy each one more, and be able to explore different subject matter and styles. I've been working with pastels this last year and exploring new ways to look at color and form."

Liz listened, adding a comment occasionally, as Jac and Peggy talked about the creative process like it was something they discussed often. She missed these kinds of conversations with Teri. So many gaps left by her death.

"Nap time," Jac said when Peggy took the plates to the kitchen. She stood, her head tilted as if in thought. "Ten years. I've been blind ten years." Without another word, she ambled off toward her cottage, Max trotting by her side.

Liz stared, her hand over her chest, until Jac disappeared behind the door with the gargoyle knocker. Would she ever not be caught off guard by Jac? She fought the urge to follow her, to see her home. She heard notes in her head—a new part to the melody from last weekend. Humming, she gathered the rest of the dishes and went to the kitchen.

Peggy handed her a plate of cookies. "Come by for coffee in the morning before your audience."

Again Liz heard both fondness and humor in the statement. She wished she and Hannah were as close as Peggy and Jac seemed to be. At her car, she stopped and went back. "Do you know where I can buy blank CDs?"

"I might have some in my office." Peggy was back in no time with a handful. "I'm grateful you're going to let Jac help you."

She was the one who should be grateful. She headed home, her steps light and her mind spinning in a good way. She imagined telling her dad she was getting help from—Darn. Jac was insistent she not tell anyone, but that was a big thing to keep from her dad. He read her blog religiously. She'd ask Jac about telling him.

Doubts surfaced as she loaded the music onto the CDs. What if they disagreed? *Jazz Notes*. Those were serious creds, but maybe she'd be too calculating and intellectual about it. Or think they were still immature. What would it be like to work on an album with someone other than Teri? A new bout of anxiety set her nerves jangling. What if she broke down?

"I'm trying, sweetie, but it's so hard without you. I met the woman who writes *Jazz Notes*. She's going to help me pick the songs." She could almost hear Teri's long whistle at the news.

The computer signaled the last CD was done. Almost twelve hours of music. How could Jac be ready to discuss songs tomorrow? Maybe this wasn't a good idea.

Jac knew she'd overslept the instant she woke. An hour nap refreshed her. Anything beyond that made her foggy and irritable. She twisted under the light blanket, nudging Max with her knee until he heaved himself up and resettled marginally farther off her legs. She rubbed her fingers along his back. There were worse things than a Labrador who was a bed hog.

How she had longed for Maria to sleep with any part of her body touching hers. "Too hot, darling," she'd say in her Italian-tinged voice, one leg flung out from under the covers in yet another luxury hotel. After Maria dropped off to sleep she'd inch as close as she dared and rest her fingers on Maria's thigh. She'd stay awake, aroused by their lovemaking, never satisfied as easily as Maria, wanting more, always wanting more.

Then Maria would turn away from her and the contact would be broken. That distance should have told her what to expect. How things would end. Anger erupted, shooting daggers through her heart. How could she have been so stupid?

Peg's three rapid knocks on the front door pulled her from unwanted memories. Max hurried off the bed. He knew Peg would give him treats.

"Here are the CDs from Liz. I put Braille numbers on them. Liz listed the songs on each CD and I transcribed them to Braille," Peg said, setting something on the dining table. "I'm proud of you for helping her."

"A moment of arrogance I'm sure I'll regret."

"Why did you change your mind?"

In part she hadn't wanted to be seen as a layperson, but it was more than that. "Her first quartet was a winner. Couple of Grammy nominations. They were headed to the top."

"And?"

"Teri got leukemia."

"Oh, how awful for her."

"She has talent, Peg. Real talent. She seems determined to go on without Teri. If she doesn't make it now, she may never. It's a fickle and unforgiving industry."

"Oh, honey."

"This isn't about me. I'll help her over this hump. It won't be hard to put together the songs for the CD. I just have to get her to use her emotions in the right way. Get her past the nostalgia and into what's there in the music."

"No one can do that like you can."

The reverence in Peg's tone made her chest tighten. She closed off that line of thought.

"You know I'll do anything I can to help." Peg was silent too long. "Malcolm left another message this afternoon."

That bastard. "What now?"

"He said he doesn't want this to become a legal issue."

Jac barked a laugh, but there was no humor in it. "Legal issue? That's not what this is about. Money. It's always money with him. The answer is no. Today. Tomorrow. Next year."

"We should hire an attorney."

Fatigue washed over her. "I want to be left alone."

"Maybe it's time to—"

"No."

"Is this really the life you want? You didn't do anything wrong. There's no reason for you to live—"

"Don't—"

"In exile."

She turned her back to Peg and stepped to the French doors. Palming the glass she absorbed the coolness. There was a garden she couldn't see and an ocean beyond that. She folded her arms and buried clenched fists in her armpits. If she didn't argue, Peg would leave.

"I want you to be happy." Peg's voice sounded like she was holding back tears.

She was as happy as she deserved to be.

Peg squeezed her shoulders and kissed her cheek. "Dinner at the usual time?"

She nodded once. The front door closed and the silence was unbearable. She took the top CD from its sleeve and put it in the changer. She settled in her recliner and Max settled in his bed. Everything as it should be. The first song allayed her fears that they hadn't advanced beyond their immaturity. By the end of the first CD her body was tingling and her mind was consumed by the beautiful music. Lively. Sophisticated. Exceptional arrangements. And Liz's playing took her breath away.

But she heard problems. Problems that were the wall between a decent album and a chart-topping album. It was going to be an interesting weekend, and an exhausting one.

CHAPTER NINE

Jac opened her front door. Liz was right on time. "Come in."
Liz's scent as she walked past—citrusy perfume and, today, a
hint of lavender. Subtle. Pleasant. "Did you sleep well?"

"Okay." Liz's voice said otherwise. "Hey, Max." Her footsteps
were barely audible on the tile and then disappeared. She was on the
area rug that covered most of the living room, a concession for better
acoustics. "Your home's lovely."

"Peg has good taste." Jac walked to the kitchen for coffee.

"That's some CD collection," Liz said from the direction of the
cabinets on the far wall. "I've had to go to mp3 for lack of space."

"I prefer the sound quality of a CD. How's your wrist?"

"I forgot my pain pill last night, and it's not bad this morning.
The swelling's gone in the fingers, and the cast isn't as tight. They use
screws and a plate to fix the bones together. Sci-fi, huh?"

"Quite." She tried to keep judgment out of her voice. It wasn't
her place to talk Liz out of surgery, and perhaps it was the best option.
"I want you to be comfortable here, but please don't move anything."
The space was so familiar that she never thought about it. She needed
all her concentration for the music and for Liz. She'd stayed up until
early in the morning to listen to all twelve hours. She knew what
needed to be done. Now it was time to find out if Liz was up to it.

"Sure. Where can I plug in my computer?" Liz set something on
the dining table.

"There is fine, but you don't need it yet. Come, sit." She went to
her recliner and motioned Liz to the couch.

She sat on the edge, hoping she was doing the right thing. Max didn't come to his bed. He must be with Liz. Good. "I know what today is." Six months since Teri's death. "Are you sure you want to do this?"

"It has to get done." Resolve in Liz's clipped words; sadness in the flat tone. "We need to build momentum for Monterey."

"Monterey is a showcase. You don't have to generate an audience."

"Dad says we need to get the album out before our fans forget about us, especially since I can't do shows for a while."

Dad again. "What's your slot at Monterey?"

"Opening the festival Friday night on the arena stage."

"Impressive." Yes, everything was riding on that show and the album. She took a deep breath. "Tell me about Teri." Liz was silent so long Jac thought she wouldn't answer.

"I'd rather not talk about her."

"I'm not asking to cause you pain. She's here in this room with us. She's in the music. She's who you want to be working with on the CD. I don't know her. I need to if I'm going to help you." Jac laced her fingers together and waited.

"Were you married?"

Not a question she'd expected. Was it worth it to help Liz? "Ten years. He was in the music business. It ended around the time I became blind."

"I'm sorry."

"Do you like Miles Davis?" Jac would need something to fill the silences and give structure to her emotions as she listened to Liz talk about loss and grief.

"Yes."

"Preference?"

"Something from his early years."

"No *Bitches Brew*?"

"Not this early in the morning." Good. A touch of humor.

Jac put in *Kind of Blue,* one of her favorite albums, and resumed her place on the recliner, sitting back but not reclining. And waited. Max was still by Liz and she missed him, but Liz needed him more.

"What do you want to know?"

"Start at the beginning." Another long silence.

"I met Teri at…" The cadence slowed and softened over her wife's name, much as Jac's voice had once spoken the syllables of her lover's name. It strengthened and sparkled with happiness when she talked about their years at UOP. Jac's days at college had been some of her happiest, too. Resentment coiled up from its nest in the pit of her stomach. Young. Idealistic. Arrogant. She'd thought she could have it all.

"We formed our first band…" Liz's voice rose and fell as she talked of juggling jobs and shows as their reputation grew.

Jac heard the sacrifice and struggle buried inside the excitement over their success. Anger flared like a match as memories paraded past her. She snuffed the anger out. This wasn't about her.

Liz's voice tightened around the phrase "diagnosed with leukemia," became strained as she talked about that battle. It lifted on the word "remission," became strong again when she talked about finding Regan and Sammy and forming a new quartet. It soared when she talked about the tour and then was barely audible after "it came back." And through it all was "us" and "we" and "our." And that was the problem.

Jac waited through Liz blowing her nose, through going to the kitchen for a glass of water. Max returned to his bed, and Jac buried her trembling fingers in the soft fur on his chest. When Liz returned she said, "Thank you. Shall we begin?"

"Yes." Her voice sounded weak, but clear. It was enough.

"Let's eliminate a quarter of the material." She needed to ease Liz into letting go.

"What if we did a double album?" Her voice was tentative, grasping.

"Your choice. Let's work on cutting duplications of the core songs you played every night."

By lunchtime they'd cut one version of each of the fifteen core songs. Fifteen out of eighty-one. They had a long way to go. They joined Peg for lunch. She would have preferred to eat while they worked, but Liz needed the distraction.

❖

"Looks like rain," Liz said, throwing tennis balls for Max as they strolled back to the cottage after lunch with Peg.

"I can smell it."

"I'm sorry you're giving up your walk. Should we take Max down to the beach?" They were in front of the door, and the gargoyle looked like a warning. More cutting. Liz knew it was the right way to begin, but it chipped away at her heart.

"Maybe later." Jac held the door for her.

Liz stepped into the cocooning quiet and simplicity and order. She put her shoes and socks in the closet by the door. She wanted to be barefoot like Jac and was surprised the floor was warm. Peg had done a masterful job in the space that was living room, dining room, and kitchen—sage-green walls, sand-colored leather couch and recliner, bleached-wood furniture. Beach-like. Casual yet elegant, like Jac. The dominant features were the Carmel ledgestone fireplace in the center of the far wall and the cabinet that took up the wall to the left—CDs floor to ceiling and a stereo system behind a glass door in the center. The sound was as good as she'd ever heard, even in a sound studio, and the acoustics were amazing.

"Let's go through the songs you performed only once and rank them."

"Yes. Good." No cutting. She sat on the couch, a notepad on the coffee table. How did Jac keep it straight in her head? This morning she'd pointed out differences in specific passages from memory. Jac's ear was as good as hers and, although she hated to admit it, better than Teri's. It was different than working with Teri but, so far, not uncomfortable.

"It's a great song," Jac said three hours later. It was the last of the twenty-one songs they'd played only once. "Genius how you arranged the melody to bounce back and forth between piano and sax."

"Thanks." Liz yawned and got up to stretch, walking to one of the windows that flanked the fireplace. She looked out to the small garden, obviously Peg's work. A hot tub was off to the left, and a chair sat next to a small table to the right side of the flagstone patio. Life for one. Jac seemed happy with it. Would she adapt in time?

"What's your first choice?"

"'Soaring Hawk.' It's one of Teri's favorites." She couldn't hear it without remembering the day that inspired it—a spur-of-the-moment picnic at one of their favorite open spaces, the meadow alive with poppies, Teri nuzzling her neck, the hawk appearing and soaring in circles, she humming the melody as the moment became song.

"Second?"

"'Rush Hour.' We were stuck in traffic up in the city, and to keep me calm Teri had me come up with melodies that mimicked the sounds. By the time we arrived at our destination we had a new song."

"Did Teri compose?"

"Not directly, but all our compositions were—" She knew where Jac was headed.

"Stay with the music."

"You mean ditch her favorites." Liz clenched her jaw, irritated at Jac's calm expression. Jac's insides weren't churning. Her chest didn't hurt.

"You can put anything you want on the album. It's your album."

That phrase again. Your album. She hated it.

"For the sake of argument, which are the ten best of the songs we just listened to?"

Liz stared at the door. She could be home in minutes. And then where would she be? Alone with an overwhelming task she hadn't been able to accomplish in six months, or with her dad who just wanted it done. She crossed her arms and listed them.

"I agree."

Good. That was good. Liz uncrossed her arms and went to the kitchen for more coffee. She liked Jac's vanilla French roast but still added sugar and cream liberally. So far they'd agreed on everything. Musically, they were a good match. Maybe this would work out.

"Let's cut the rest."

Liz sucked in a breath and her heart clattered. Cutting. Resentment bubbled up from that tender place in her stomach. She went back to the window. Few patches of blue remained amid the dark clouds gathering over the ocean visible beyond the Monterey pines, their heavy branches barely moving in the wind. She didn't hear Jac approach until she was beside her. Like sunshine on a cold day, her presence was soothing.

"Stay with the music and trust your instincts." After a minute Jac said, "Let's take Max out before it rains." She walked toward the hallway that led to the bathroom and two rooms with closed doors—bedrooms, Liz assumed.

She wanted to go home and take a pain pill and crawl into bed. She was exhausted and her wrist hurt again. Instead she put on her sweatshirt and tennis shoes and waited. She'd asked for Jac's help and she'd see it through.

She walked behind Jac on the narrow path that started at the back of the property and took them down the cliff to the beach in a series of switchbacks. Jac navigated it as if she could see. When they reached the bottom, Max dropped his tennis ball on the sand and barked at her. She threw it into the stiff wind that whipped her hair. It made conversation difficult, but she wasn't in the mood to talk. They walked all the way down to the end of the long beach, taking turns throwing the ball for Max. She was careful to walk out of range of the ice-cold water, but Jac seemed unfazed when it washed over her ankles.

When they got back to the cottage, there was a tray on the dining table. Cheeses, apple slices, French bread, and bowls of bean soup. Jac opened a bottle of white wine. She didn't go through her tasting ritual but set two glasses on the table. "I'm in the mood for a fire." With sure and graceful movements she set kindling, lit a square of fire starter, and stacked more kindling around it. In minutes flames appeared.

Liz sipped the wine. It tasted expensive. "You'll have to give me fire-starting lessons." She'd stopped after several dismal attempts that created nothing but smoke. Teri had always started the fire on the rare occasions they spent time in Carmel.

"Practice." Jac joined her at the table. "Turn lights on when you need to. The switch for the sconces is by the door."

No clocks. No art on the walls. Lights never on. Jac's world was so different from hers in some ways, but music was obviously the center of Jac's life. "Did you ever play an instrument?" Jac analyzed music with as much a musician's ear as a critic's.

"I dabbled. Do you mind if we work while we eat?" Jac was already headed for the CD changer. "Of your core songs, which five are your favorites? We're not cutting the others."

Liz listed their favorites. Easy. She and Teri had been so in sync in every way.

When Jac returned to the table, "Spring Time" from their opening night was playing. Liz's first choice. How did Jac find specific versions out of eight CDs?

They listened through dinner, through Jac adding more wood to the fire, through Peggy coming to retrieve the tray and bring slices of that delicious chocolate cake. Eight versions of each song.

She yawned and checked her watch. She could barely see it in the dim light from the sconces. Midnight? Jac seemed as fresh as she had this morning. "Maybe we should call it a night."

"Listen. What's your first impression?"

"Tired."

"Yes!"

She'd meant herself, not the music. She started to say as much, but Jac's hand was sweeping the air to the rhythm. And Liz saw it. Jac's hand slowed, wavered, then righted itself. No. She kept her gaze on Jac's hand as a sick feeling gathered in her stomach. It happened again. And then again. The beat wasn't steady. Tears filled her eyes and she pulled Kleenex from her pocket. She wanted to run. She wanted to scream. She looked away from Jac's hand, out to the dark garden and the moonless sky, but music filled the room with evidence of Teri's illness.

"I'm sorry."

"You knew all along." Liz's stomach hurt like she'd been punched. Why hadn't she noticed? Why hadn't Teri said anything? Sure, she'd been sleeping later, taking naps, but they'd all been exhausted after weeks of touring. She took the remote from Jac's hand. Where was the damn off button? The silence felt accusing and her chest tightened. She should have taken better care of Teri. What if they'd come home early…started treatment…"It's still a great song," she whispered. Maybe she could excuse not hearing the unsteady beat during the shows, but months of listening to the recordings?

"It is. The beat's fine—"

"Teri! Teri." God, were they all like that?

"Teri's fine in plenty of songs. You'll have enough material for a great album."

"But not a double album."

"I don't think so."

"How many people will notice? If I didn't..." She twisted the ring on her right hand.

"How could you?"

She cradled the cast as Jac's point hit home. She wasn't listening to music. She was listening to memories. Gravity was too much all of a sudden and she wanted to give in, to slide to the floor.

"Let's quit for tonight."

Liz packed her computer, put on her shoes and sweatshirt, and opened the door.

"Eight tomorrow?"

She closed the door and stepped into the drizzle.

Jac was in the hot tub, still consumed by the music, peripherally aware of rain spattering onto the water, when Peg paid the expected visit. Her back was stiffer than she wanted it to be, but no muscle spasms. One more day and she'd be back to her routine.

"Are you all right?"

"How's Liz?"

"Ragged. What happened?"

"The truth. If she wants it to be the best, she has to hear what's there. She has to separate the music from her feelings for Teri." The recordings were Liz's past, the album she created from them her future. She'd have to make a choice.

"Oh, honey, are you sure you're up to this?"

She climbed out and wrapped her robe around her, trying to keep in the warmth. The flagstones were cold on her feet. Rain landed on her head as she hurried into her bedroom. "I have to be." Liz would never be able to pick the material by herself, and if she'd had anyone qualified to help they would have already. The future of a gifted musician was at stake. That concern overrode personal discomfort.

An hour later she lay on her bed still wide-awake, keyed up, unable to let go of the music. Her body tensed against the rip current of emotions that threatened to suck her fully back to the past. Emotions and music. Such a tricky, delicate marriage. Emotion the musician put into the music made it powerful and alive. Emotion separate from music, outside those acceptable channels of expression…dangerous.

The German-accented voice of the man who'd been her teacher for twenty years filled her head. She clenched the covers. Who was she to advise Liz? She hadn't navigated that terrain well. Max whimpered, his legs pumping. Dreaming. She laid her hand on his shoulder and he quieted. Could she help Liz and keep her distance from emotions she wanted no part of?

CHAPTER TEN

I don't think I can do it." Liz paced barefoot, from warm tile to coarse rug, window to kitchen, in Jac's cottage. She wanted blue sky, not gloomy monochrome white depositing a steady rain.

"You already have."

Why did Jac get the recliner? She added more sugar to her coffee and filled Jac's cup. "We've narrowed it down to twenty-five songs. Let's cut five and do a double album."

"All right." Jac took the cup from her and set it on the side table without sipping.

Liz wanted to scream. She wanted to throw something. Jac's methodical calm infuriated her. *Listen. Stay with the music. Hear what's there.* "I can't afford it." She looked out at the plants drooping in the rain. Twice the cost to mix and master. Higher purchase price. Double albums didn't sell as well. She wanted to laugh. She'd asked for Jac's help, and boy had she gotten it—her unwavering attention to detail, her ruthless ear, her insight. Two of the most exhausting days she'd endured as a musician. Two days of the most exhilarating musical discussions she'd had since…She shook her head to clear it and checked her watch. By four this afternoon it had to be done. Long drive home. Surgery tomorrow morning.

"Don't think. First choice."

She named it, surprised when Jac agreed.

"Congratulations. One song. Don't think. Least favorite."

She named it.

"Excellent."

"Just like that?" She looked over her shoulder at Jac, still ensconced in her recliner. Two days of endless analyzing and they were down to grab bag?

"You have impeccable instincts. Trust yourself."

She bristled at what wasn't said. Eliminate Teri. "It's a tribute to Teri."

"Yes," Jac said too quickly. "It's a tribute to fourteen years of making music together. Not four nights."

She stared out the window. Those four nights in New York were the crowning glory of those fourteen years. God, she was sick of thinking in calendars. Fourteen years with Teri. Four nights of shows. Six months plus a day since Teri's death. "How do we make this final cut?"

"We listen."

She whirled around, angry words on her lips. Jac was petting Max, curled up in his bed. Their home. She was an invader. She'd asked for this. She tried to imagine doing this with her dad. A sinking feeling tugged on her stomach. He knew music, but he wasn't in Jac's league. She was barely in Jac's league. She squeezed the coffee cup. Her fingers worked. Tomorrow screws and plates would replace the cast. Music overshadowed the sound of the rain hitting the roof and patio. Opening night. Teri grabbing her before they walked onstage and kissing her. One of their core songs. The audience loved it.

"What do you hear?"

"Sammy on top. Regan underneath. Teri pushing them." The song ran its eight minutes. A different song replaced it. Closing night. An old song she'd recently revived. She'd put it in the set list on a lark because it was a great song for jamming. They'd had the audience on its feet, clapping along. A glorious end to the tour.

"Which one do you prefer?" Jac asked when it finished.

"The first." Liz stared out at the garden as she listened through the fifteen minutes of two more pieces. The rain had picked up, making flower stems bounce to its rhythm.

"Which one?" Jac asked.

"The first." She listened through two more pieces Jac selected, seemingly at random.

"Which one?"

"The first. Is this about cutting?" Liz turned and studied Jac.

"It's about what you're not hearing."

"Teri's rhythm is fine."

"Why did you pick those three?"

"On 'Sleeping Late' Regan has that great solo. She was hot that night. On 'Combustion' Sammy shows off his great upper register. On 'Late Night'—"

"Where are you?" Jac walked toward her, head tilted, her voice gentle.

"I don't understand."

"Those three songs you didn't pick are the only ones where we hear what Liz Randall is really capable of."

"What's your point?"

"You're holding back on all but a few solos. Why is that?"

"Soloing isn't the point." She crossed her arms. She didn't like where this was headed.

"It's not not the point either. You have fabulous technique. You have rhythm and style that have swing and stride and blues all wrapped up in a sound I've never heard. You have star-quality talent, and you show it off only once in a while?"

"It doesn't matter to me."

"What?"

"Standing out."

"Why not?"

"A band is collaborative. A group. I'm not a soloist. It's about our collective sound."

"You're one of the best jazz pianists playing right now. Show off that talent. Build a band around that talent. Like your Ellington and Brubeck. What you have is a watered-down version of what you could be."

"It's who we are. It's our sound." *It's who I am.*

"That sound is dead."

The sob welled up from that raw place deep in Liz's center, the place Teri had been ripped from. Jac laid her hand on her shoulder. She wanted so badly to turn into the touch. No. She wouldn't give in. She'd preserve their sound. She rushed to the door. The hell with Jac and her infuriating calm and arrogant assumptions. She hurried up to the house, the rain cold pinpricks on her skin. She'd say good-bye to Peggy and go home. Next week she'd make the last cut herself.

When she got to the patio, her thoughts were interrupted by conversation and laughter coming through the closed French doors. Peggy's Sunday brunch that was open to anyone who wanted to come. Two couples sat with Peggy and Roger, the table covered with plates of food. Peggy waved and came to the door.

"I was about to bring brunch down for you. Why don't you pick what you want?"

"I need to leave." She would put together an album of Teri's favorites. It was that simple.

"What happened?" Peggy cupped her elbow and led her to her studio.

"We don't agree on what the album should be."

"Jac said it was going well. She loves your music."

"Everything's different working with her." She missed Teri's laughter, the dimpled smile, the comfort of her eyes. The safety of her opinions.

"But is it bad different?"

Liz didn't like Peggy's tone, like she was talking to one of her kids. She wanted to snap back, but she couldn't. She shook her head. No, it wasn't bad different, just hard different.

"You have no idea what this is costing her." Peggy's expression was sad, like a sadness that had been there a long time.

Costing Jac? Serene? In her recliner? Unfazed?

"She never has guests in her home. People send requests to the blog all the time asking for help with albums." Peggy fixed her with a look somewhere between pleading and accusing. "You're the first one she's invited in, the first one she's agreed to help."

Liz shivered in her wet T-shirt. She'd made assumptions about a woman she barely knew. A woman who'd been nothing but kind to her.

"She's as invested in this album as you are."

Her chest tightened. None of this was Jac's fault. Her insights were pointedly accurate, and that was the problem. She didn't want them to be. She wanted Teri's beat to be strong and sure. She didn't want to be the star. She shivered harder.

"Don't walk out on her."

Abandoned. Liz knew how that felt. The studio smelled of paint. Peggy's creativity hung in the air, as potent as her emotionally powerful paintings stacked against the walls.

Peggy pointed to a canvas on an easel. "I thought this was going to be a simple little seascape, but it had other ideas. I wrestled with it all week, tried to make it what I saw in my head. This morning I just started painting and let it evolve through the brushes."

"It's beautiful." She held Peggy's gaze, absorbing the point and the kindness.

"Let's take brunch down to Jac. You know how cranky she gets if her meals are late."

Liz nodded, but her steps felt heavy as they walked to the kitchen. Did she have enough courage to do what needed to be done?

❖

Jac's arm fell uselessly to her side and her heart sank as the door closed behind Liz. Her scent lingered and she greedily inhaled the comforting smell. She had no agenda for the album other than helping it be the great album she knew it could be. Helping Liz reach her potential. It was a terrible dilemma for Liz. She admired her loyalty to Teri, but for the album to be its best Liz had to let go of the past that defined her. It was a lot to ask.

"Did I push too hard?" she asked Max. She returned to the recliner, warm from her body, and stroked him. This was her life. A good life she'd worked hard to build. She pressed play on the remote. A knock on the door. Peg with brunch. She'd lost her appetite.

"Is Liz all right?" she asked, opening the door to a bluster of cold air.

"No."

Liz. She'd come back for her computer.

"Can we talk?" Resolve in her voice.

"Of course." Liz's courage pulled at her heart.

"Brunch," Peg said, following Liz.

Jac turned the volume down and set the table, listening to Peg describe what she'd brought. She was hungry again.

"I'm sorry," Jac said when Peg was gone and they were seated at the table. "I'm not doing this very well." Her heart stopped for an instant when Liz covered her hand. She didn't like being touched, but Liz's touch felt strong and gentle, two qualities she felt sure Liz possessed. She liked the connection.

"You're doing a great job. I've never met anyone with your feel for music." Liz withdrew her hand. "Will you help me finish it? I won't leave again."

"Of course I will." She filled her plate with pancakes and bacon and quiche for good measure.

"I've never been on my own musically. I think band, group, solos written around my musicians, but not me."

"Ellington was a genius at highlighting his soloists, but he didn't shy away from taking center stage. You're not quite at his level." Jac smiled and hoped Liz would, too. "But you're close."

"I'm not, but thank you for saying so."

"You can build the future you want, but you have to take center stage."

"I don't know if I can."

"When you hear new music, are you always sure you can make it a workable composition?" Liz was silent. It was a big leap in her relationship with her music. "Don't you trust your instincts?"

"The band's dynamics will change."

"The personnel might change, too."

"Maybe I'm not up to it." Fatigue and worry in her voice.

"And maybe you are." They ate in silence for a while, surrounded by the sounds of rain and beautiful music.

"So we have five chosen." Liz took their plates to the kitchen.

"You should put 'Drum Roll' on it. Teri's solo is solid and riveting."

"Agreed. Let's listen to the best versions of the core program and pick four."

One by one they listened to the songs and talked about them, and Jac felt like herself again in a way she hadn't in a long time. Memories poked at her, accompanied by jabs of emotion, but she didn't have time to think about the past. There was only the music and Liz. At three o'clock they made the last choice. She put the recliner upright and leaned forward, tears stinging her eyes. She always experienced that moment of letdown when a project was finished.

Liz put her hand on her shoulder. Squeezed. Let go. "I felt bad about bumping into you. I don't any more. I'd like to give you credit on the album as co-producer."

"Absolutely not. It's yours. Yours and Teri's. I'm honored to have helped." An awkward silence descended. "It's beautiful. So very beautiful. Can I have a CD of those songs?"

"I'll go ask Peggy for a blank and burn it for you before I leave." Liz walked to the door but didn't open it. "Do you think I should have surgery?"

She thought before answering. Dishonesty seemed wrong. "If it were me I'd wait and see if it heals. Surgery isn't foolproof."

"Even with Monterey?"

"Worst case, if you have to cancel out of the festival, you'll perform there again someday. Trust your instincts and think long-term."

"Thank you for your honesty." The door opened and then closed softly.

"Shall we brave it, buddy?" Max's tail whacked the side of the recliner. The rain had stopped, and a walk would clear her head and chase away the memories threatening to escape the corners where they sat with sharp teeth. Other albums, but she'd never forget this one. Tomorrow life would be back to normal.

The door opened and Peg said, "Nobody goes anywhere until we've heard it. Roger has champagne waiting."

Jac smiled and knelt by Max. "I'll make it up to you tomorrow." She wrapped her arms around him and rubbed her cheek on the side of his head. This was one celebration she'd be glad to attend.

CHAPTER ELEVEN

I did my best, Dad." How many times had Liz said that this morning? Teri would know how hard it was to choose the songs, and she'd approve. One of the million things was done. A few minutes and they'd be at the surgery center. She was nauseous even though she hadn't eaten since last night. The celebration toast that turned into dinner. The memory of the fun evening made her smile in spite of the growing dread that was making her heart pound.

"Your core songs are less than half the album. You have to give your audience what they expect." How many times had he said that this morning?

"I picked the best material." It would be so much easier if she could tell him the woman behind *Jazz Notes* helped her, but Jac had staunchly refused. She flexed her fingers. No pain. No swelling. Were the ends of that bone knitting together? She slanted the heater vent toward her and stared out at the heavy gray sky.

"And only one that has Teri soloing. She's showy. It's a big part of your popularity."

"I explained that." What would happen when they gave her the anesthetic? Would it be like going to sleep?

"Maybe I should listen to the recordings."

"I like it." Peggy and Roger loved it. Hannah loved it. She hoped Teri would love it. She tapped on her leg to "Spring Time," giving her trembling fingers something to do. Plate and screws. A shudder rolled up her back. "Are you sure surgery's the right thing?"

"It's the best option." He looked at her and his eyes softened. "I'll be right there the whole time. I scheduled an appointment Thursday with the physical therapist Dr. Russell recommended. When are you mixing?"

"I need to call Mark." Liz yawned. She'd barely slept last night even with Hannah cuddled up to her, rubbing her back whenever she woke up.

"Shoot for Friday."

"He's probably booked out several weeks." Her mouth was dry, but they'd told her not to drink after midnight.

"Give me his number. I'll call while I'm waiting. If he can't get us in sooner I'll find another sound engineer."

"Mark's done all our albums." Why were they talking about this today?

He pulled into a parking space. The building looked solid, like a sure thing. The best option. How had her life come down to best options? He put his arm over her shoulder as they walked toward the door, and she tried to absorb his certainty.

Inside, she sat and he brought her papers to sign. She smelled coffee and it made her want to be in Carmel, sipping coffee, nibbling a warm chocolate croissant. Her phone rang and she took it from her purse. An 8-3-1 area code, but she didn't recognize the number. She answered it.

"I was thinking about you," Jac said.

The tightness in her chest loosened a bit. "A friend," she said to her dad and hurried outside.

"I listened to the CD again this morning. If you have any doubts about it, drop them. It's beautiful."

Liz closed her eyes and absorbed the comfort of Jac's certainty. Just what she needed.

"I have some ideas for the order to put them in if you want to talk about it."

"Yes. If we can get studio time, Dad wants to start mixing this week."

After a long silence Jac said, "Busy week for you."

"Have you ever had surgery?"

"Yes."

"I don't want to do it." Her stomach hurt and the dread made her feel cold, the kind of cold where you'd never be warm again. "Everything's happening too fast."

"Trust your instincts, Liz, and think long-term."

"They're ready for you," her dad said, holding the door open.

"I have to go."

"Let me know the outcome."

"Thanks for calling." She clutched the phone to her chest. Trust her instincts. Was dread a normal reaction to surgery? Was she unreasonably scared because of what happened with Teri and her mom?

Her dad hugged her. "I'll be right here, sunshine."

She gave him her purse and followed the nurse through the door and down a hallway to a cubicle.

"Leave your clothes in the closet. Everything off, gown open in back." The woman smiled as she held the curtain aside for her.

Liz's hands shook as she traded her clothes for the flimsy blue gown. Her lungs sucked air in and out in shallow bursts as the dread became unbearable. I don't want to do this…I don't want to do this… Her whirling thoughts suddenly halted. Her eyes darted around the cubicle, but her focus was on the melody running through her head. The Carmel melody that she'd been getting bits and pieces of since the day she met Jac. Lots of it. She pulled in deep breaths and the dread backed off. How many times had a song come to her when she was trying to work out the answer to something? She trusted music. She trusted her instincts. She looked at her hand as she moved her fingers. It would heal. Dressed, she threw the curtain aside and hurried down the hallway.

"I'm not doing it."

Her dad looked up from his crossword puzzle, and his face went from surprise to tight-lipped disapproval.

She bolted out the door into the rain and blustery wind and headed toward the car.

"You're not thinking clearly," he said, catching up and stepping in front of her. He put his hands on her shoulders. "I know you're scared, but this is the best option."

"I want to give it a chance to heal on its own." Long-term. If it didn't, then she'd have the surgery. She didn't want an arm with a plate and screws in it. She held it against her stomach. It would heal.

"Everything we've worked for is at stake." His hair flew about in the wind, and his brows were pulled so tight they almost touched.

"I know." She was betting her career and her future on a healing process she didn't understand. Music she understood. It couldn't be seen on an X-ray, but it was all she knew and she trusted it.

"This is our last shot, sunshine." He sounded almost desperate. "I want you to have your dream."

"I know." The melody returned, cheerful and insistent, and she let it be the good omen she needed. His expression changed from confusion to disappointment tinged with annoyance. He'd looked at Hannah many times with that expression. It hurt.

His jaw worked the whole drive home, and several times he shook his head. She kept her attention on the CD. Yes, she liked it.

"This is a mistake," he said as he pulled into his driveway. He kept the engine running. "Surgery's the best option."

"Doctors aren't always right." Finally he turned off the engine. "I'm going back to Carmel." A chance to rest up before the crazy last half of the semester, before the weeks of mixing the CD. Walks on the beach, working out the order of the CD with Jac, maybe helping Peggy in her garden.

"What about mixing?" He was frowning again.

Couldn't they catch their breath for a minute and celebrate that the songs were picked before rushing to the next thing? "I'll call Mark."

"Tell him if he can't—"

"I'll take care of it, Dad." If she hurried she could get to Carmel in time to walk with Jac.

"I've been researching band websites. I have some ideas on how to make ours really eye-catching. It's our most important publicity tool."

"I barely know how to manage this one."

"I'll do it."

"You shouldn't have to."

"We're in this together, sunshine."

Liz hugged him and went to her car. He was standing with his arms crossed as she pulled away. She hit the callback icon as she headed toward her condo to pack. Ten days in Carmel. Exactly what she needed. "I'm not doing surgery," she said when Jac answered.

"Good decision."

Her chest loosened and she clung to Jac's approval. "I'm coming back to Carmel. Can I walk with you?"

"Don't be late."

She punched the accelerator, but her confidence faded before she reached the corner. If her instincts were wrong, it wasn't just her dreams that would be lost. Her dad's. Regan's. Sammy's. Teri's. She flexed her fingers. It had to heal.

CHAPTER TWELVE

L iz turned off the Yukon. The sound of the garage door ratcheting shut replaced the CD, a demo one of her San Jose State senior students had made. Vicky's quartet had potential, but Liz would have to address their problems. Tactfully. Constructive critiquing was a delicate dance of honest feedback that encouraged more of what was working while suggesting ways to improve what could be better. She'd been lucky to have her grandma and dad as mentors—she'd never questioned their opinions. Until now.

Her dad had insisted on helping with the song mixing. It was the most important stage in the process and was always grueling, but this was a nightmare. Resting her head back against the headrest she closed her eyes, trying to muster the energy to walk the ten feet to her door.

Please don't let Hannah have someone over. Slinging her satchel over her shoulder she trudged to the door. Singing came from inside. Hannah showing off for whatever woman she was giving cooking lessons to tonight. She shoved through the door into the kitchen. "Can you tone it down?" Her anger deflated when she saw Hannah—alone, dancing around the tiny kitchen, pumping a spoon in the air and singing.

Hannah stopped in mid-twirl when she saw Liz. Holding the spoon like a mic, she continued her rendition of "I Will Survive."

"Is disco making a comeback?" Liz flopped the satchel onto the small table tucked into the corner of the dining area, too tired to fuss about the shopping bags piled on the two chairs.

"No, but I am." Hannah stirred something on the stove. It smelled delicious.

"You found a job?" Taking off her coat, she hung it on a peg by the door, next to Teri's.

"Not yet, but I will. Survive," Hannah boomed out. She had a beautiful voice.

"I remember watching you rehearse that song with Dad." She set the bags on the floor and sank onto the chair.

"Yeah, my talent-show standby." She did an over-exaggerated bow with a super-fake smile. "I'm better off as a chef than a singer. I'm really good at it and I've lived in some cool places. You got Dad's dream life and I got Mom's."

"She wanted to be a chef?" Wiggling a finger inside the cast, she tried to reach the itch that had been tormenting her all day. Was the bone knitting together? Twenty-six days since she broke it. Another three weeks until the cast was removed. A new calendar count.

"No, silly. Don't you remember all the travel magazines she subscribed to? She had a whole list of places she wanted to see. I've been to a lot of them."

"She did? How come I don't remember?"

"You weren't around the house a lot. When you weren't at Grandma's or practicing, you were doing shows."

"I liked playing piano more than anything else."

"Good thing. You were their last hope."

"Of what?" She yawned and laid her head on her forearm. She wanted to sleep till noon tomorrow, but they had a nine o'clock appointment at the recording studio.

"Here, taste." Hannah delivered a spoonful. "New curry I'm developing for when the blacklist gets lifted."

"Yummy." There were definite perks to Hannah living here. "Blacklist?"

"He trashed my reputation."

"Sleeping with your boss's wife was kind of risky, don't you think?"

"Just because he owns a bunch of hotels, his version isn't necessarily the truth." Hannah shoved a drawer closed. Silverware rattled.

"What do you mean?"

"It doesn't matter," Hannah said, her voice edgy. "I'm not giving up. I will survive," she sang in a loud vibrato. "How's the CD coming?" Hannah piled rice into a perfect mound on the plate and ladled curry over it, topping it with sprigs of something.

"Terrible. Three days in the studio and we only have one song mixed. Teri and I worked with Mark on all our CDs. It's never gone this badly. At this rate we'll be at Monterey before it's done."

"Let me guess. Dad's not helping." Hannah brought the plates to the table and went back for beers, pouring them into frosted glasses.

"He knows my music, but mixing requires a certain kind of listening. You have to be able to separate out each of our twelve tracks and hear what it needs to make it the best, while keeping in mind how it's going to fit into the song as a whole."

"Like a meal. You have to know each ingredient but also how the flavors work together." Hannah grinned as she moved shopping bags off the other chair.

"Exactly."

"He can't do that."

"He understands reverb, compression, EQ, etcetera, from a technical perspective, but he doesn't have the experience of knowing how to apply them. We have to keep repeating a track over and over for him, and then what he likes isn't what I like. I don't want to offend him so I try to compromise. I'm getting so confused I'm starting to doubt my own perceptions. Mark's so frustrated I'm afraid he's going to tell me to take it to another sound studio."

"Is Dad paying for the CD?"

"No." Now that she didn't have the deductible for the surgery, she'd decided to pay for it herself. "I can't afford extra sessions."

"Tell him you want to do it yourself."

"I can't. He's trying to help. This curry's amazing."

"I know." Hannah grinned, her bravado back. "You know, Lizzie, you're not a teenager anymore. He's still treating you like you are. It's your album."

"Maybe he's right that they're not the best songs, not our sound."

"It's a great album." Hannah's expression was fierce. "So what if it's not your same sound? Life changes. Don't let him make you doubt yourself because you didn't let him help pick the songs."

"What does that have to do with it?" She chewed one of the sprigs. Lemongrass.

"Oh, Lizzie." Hannah shook her head, an indulgent look on her face. "He likes being in charge."

"He likes helping us."

"On his terms."

"How would you know? You haven't been around for the last fifteen years."

"I had a different idea about my future than he did."

The comment hung between them. Was that what he meant about Hannah getting with the program? "Don't tell Dad, but I had help choosing the songs. A woman I met in Carmel. She's the sister of the artist who painted his painting."

"Can she help with the mixing?"

"I don't know." Liz stirred the curry around on her plate. If the mix wasn't handled right, all their work selecting the songs wouldn't make it a great album. She had no idea whether Jac had mixing experience, but if she did…Hope bubbled up. Even if she didn't have mixing experience, Liz could imagine what a help Jac's keen ear could be.

"Did you like working with her?"

"I barely know her, but she's brilliant, and musically we think alike."

"You don't have to know a lot about someone to click with them. Do it. Ask her to help. I dare you." Nobody beat Hannah in the cocky-grin department.

"How do I tell Dad I don't want his help? I hate that face he makes when he's disappointed."

Hannah imitated it.

"You're bad. I wouldn't have a career without him."

"And he wouldn't have one without you."

"What—"

"Never mind." Hannah patted her arm. "Have you talked to Kevin lately?"

"About?"

"Karen."

Was she that tired or was Hannah not making sense? "She's over the flu. I saw her at the restaurant last night."

"She didn't have the flu."

"At Dad's birthday? Sure she did."

"That's what Kevin told everyone. She refused to go. I heard them arguing."

"Why would she—"

"The trip they didn't go on because Kevin had to work at the last minute? It was their anniversary."

"Oh, shit." Anniversaries weren't something they celebrated as a family, but Liz had forgotten to get them a card. "He works too much." She covered her mouth as she yawned. Bed. Soon. Hannah gave her a funny look again. "What?"

"It's about priorities." They ate in silence for a while and then Hannah asked, "Are you going to Carmel tomorrow?"

"I wasn't."

"Oh." She scooted rice kernels around on her plate.

"Cooking lesson with benefits?"

"Yeah." Hannah grinned.

"Don't you want to find someone to settle down with?"

"Not my style." Hannah made an icky face. "I didn't get that Randall 'find true love young and mate for life' gene."

"You've just never fallen in love. When you do—"

"Love doesn't always come neatly wrapped up in happy-ever-after-forever."

"I wouldn't trade what I had with Teri, even though it wasn't the forever I wanted it to be."

"I know." Hannah squeezed her hand. "Speaking of settling down, what do you think about Dad and Rebecca?"

"What about them?"

"Don't you see the way she looks at him?"

"She's like family."

"My point. They make a cute couple."

"Mom's only been gone two years." Her dad and Rebecca? No.

"That's a long time not to have someone to cuddle up to."

"Long if you have the relationship attention span of a mosquito." Liz looked at the pictures of her and Teri on the bar top between the kitchen and living room. Fourteen years of memories she cherished.

"Don't be upset with me, Lizzie." Hannah's voice and expression turned serious. "I left everything behind. Keeping myself distracted helps me not think about what I lost."

Maybe she'd been too hard on Hannah. "If you promise to clean up the condo, I'll go."

"You're the best sister ever." Hannah threw her arms around her and kissed her cheek. "We need to take you shopping." She tugged the shoulder of Liz's blouse.

"Not hard when I'm the only sister." She ignored the fashion scolding. Teri had given the blouse to her. So what if it was a few years old?

"Details, details." Hannah brushed her hand through the air. "Mango-lime mousse for dessert."

Liz's phone rang as they were clearing the table. Reluctantly she answered.

"I was thinking about 'Spring Time,'" her dad said. "We should bring up the bass and drums, give it more punch." His voice punctuated the word. "It's your most popular song. It needs to be showy."

Liz propped her elbows on the counter, trying to hang on to her shredded patience. Showy. His second favorite word next to momentum. It's "Spring Time," she wanted to say. A delicate melody invoking new growth and the optimism of the season, not a march. "Can we talk about this tomorrow?"

"Sure, sunshine." He sounded disappointed. "This mixing is exciting stuff."

Hannah was shaking her head when she ended the call. "Chicken," she said as she laid mint leaves on the desserts.

Hannah didn't understand. Her dad was a big part of the band's success, and she didn't have it in her to disappoint him. She tried to imagine "Spring Time" with more punch. She grimaced. How could she let him be part of the mixing process but get the finished album she wanted?

Liz collapsed into bed an hour later, resting the cast on Teri's pillow. She flexed her fingers. They were puffy again, and she'd had to take pain pills this week after a week of not needing them. What if she'd made the wrong decision about surgery? What if it never healed? What if those New York shows were the last time she played? She hugged the pillow and tried to corral the terrifying thoughts. Trust your instincts. Think long-term. God, she hoped Jac was right.

"For you," Hannah said, entering without knocking as usual and holding out Liz's cell phone. "Sexy voice."

"Hello?"

"I've been assigned to call you," Jac said. "Susanne just got word she's filling in for the lead in her school play tomorrow night. Peg's trying to rally a full house for her. Can you come?"

"I'd love to. What time?"

"Peg said to come for dinner."

"Um, I'm mixing tomorrow. I can't get down that early."

"Play's at eight. Meet us there. How's mixing?"

"Slow going." She didn't want to think about what Jac would say if the mixing ruined the album.

"You've never done a live album before. It's different than a studio recording."

If only it were that simple.

"You have good reverb on the master. Bleed will be a bigger challenge than a studio recording. Your biggest problem will be getting definition from each instrument and balance among the tracks without over-refining it. What you lose in perfection you gain in energy, spontaneity, and that magic of a live performance you want listeners to experience."

"You have mixing experience." Jac's expert ear…working with someone she didn't have to explain everything to.

"Some."

"Will you help me?" She had no idea how she'd handle her dad, but it had to be perfect, and she wouldn't get that with him. "I could use a fresh set of ears on it."

"I thought you liked your sound engineer."

"I do, but he mostly does studio albums. And it's Dad's first time mixing."

There was a long inhale, a pause, and then a longer exhale. Jac's eyebrow was surely reaching for her hairline, but thankfully, she didn't point out the obvious.

"I won't come to San Jose."

"I'll bring it to you. Thank you. See you tomorrow."

She ended the call and picked up the picture on the nightstand. She and Teri in Provincetown, a few days' vacation in between shows last summer. They were wearing matching sweatshirts and grinning for the selfie. "I want it to be perfect."

She'd have to figure out a way to work on it with Jac and let her dad help. She flopped back on the bed and held the picture to her chest. "I'm trying, sweetie. I'm trying."

CHAPTER THIRTEEN

Liz bolted from the car the second her dad pulled into his driveway. She sprinted to the music room. "It looks good," the doctor had said as he put up the X-rays on the view box. "We won't know how much soft-tissue damage…" She'd tuned him out as she put her ring and watch back where they belonged and moved her hand in circles. It was stiff, but the black line between the bones was now a thickened white line he called a callus. Healed.

She slid onto the piano bench, flipped the keyboard lid up, and froze, hands poised above the keys. She looked over the piano to the drums and her heart stumbled. She desperately wanted Teri's reassuring smile and steadying beat.

Her dad appeared in the doorway, his brows pulled together. He seemed worried a lot lately. Oscar scooted in and dashed for his perch on the couch.

Liz closed her eyes and played a chord. The sound crawled inside her, and before it faded she played another and then another, greedily soaking up every note. Six-and-a-half weeks deprived of the piano had felt like a lifetime. Within the first few bars of "Spring Time" relief shifted to fear. Her fingers were slow and she didn't have her octave-plus reach. She flubbed notes and chord changes. She stopped and began again. The muscles in her forearm ached and sharp pains shot from her wrist into her palm. She dropped her hands to her lap.

"Best not to overdo." He smiled, but the hard look in his eyes betrayed what he wasn't saying—surgery was the best option.

"Physical therapy at ten tomorrow. I'll pick you up. Call the twins." He closed the door.

She rubbed her left forearm. It was visibly skinnier than the right. "What if I'm not ready for Monterey?" The words ricocheted around the room and landed heavily in her lap. She pulled her phone from her purse.

Jac answered on the first ring. "How is it?"

"It hurts and my fingers don't work right. What if I messed everything up?"

"I think the cast needs to be off for more than an hour," Jac teased her. "How did it feel?"

"It hurt and—"

"I meant how did it feel to play?"

"Like a part of me that was stolen away is back." Tears slid down her cheeks and she pulled Kleenex out of her pocket. Silence wrapped around her as if she were in the quiet calm of Jac's home.

"I talked to Alvin. He'll do the mastering for you." He'd been the head sound engineer at one of the top recording studios in New York with an impressive number of great jazz albums to his credit. Now retired and living in Carmel Valley, he worked only with select clients.

"Thank you. I know it's because of you." Liz couldn't imagine doing any of this without Jac. The CD was going to be the tribute Teri deserved.

"What did Mark think of the mix for 'Spring Time'?"

"Pure genius. He said it made him feel relaxed and peaceful, like he was lying in a meadow on a warm spring day." Exactly where she'd been when the song first took form. Jac had the uncanny ability to refine and sharpen the emotional impact of songs, making them powerful sensory experiences.

"I've been working on 'Soaring Hawk.' I finished one mix. You might not like it. I brought the sax solo out so it sounds distant."

"Like a hawk soaring." Another of Jac's talents—finessing solos in just the right way so they became centerpieces. Jac's ear was as astute with mixing as it had been when they were selecting songs. She'd made it clear she didn't want to talk about how she'd come by her mixing experience. Liz was too grateful for the help to risk offending her by pushing the issue. For all the connection they shared musically, Jac was a mystery in so many ways. "I wish I could come down this weekend."

"You need a break. I'll see you next weekend." Jac ended the call.

Babysitting her nephews wasn't going to be much of a break. Liz sat on Teri's stool and patted the snare drum. Working with Jac was different than working with Teri but just as satisfying. Her thoughts were snapped back to reality by her phone ringing. Regan. "It healed."

"Good. That's good. You played?"

"Um, gosh, that would have been a smart thing to do." She paused and then rescued Regan. "Of course I did. It'll be fine." She didn't need Regan worrying any more than she already did. "We'll be ready for Monterey."

"That's good. Your hand, I mean. You'll be there tonight?"

"Yes." Vicky, one of the most talented students she'd ever taught, was performing with her band at her dad's club tonight. She'd suggested Vicky expand from a quartet to a quintet by adding a bass. She'd recommended Regan and it seemed to be a good fit. "You sounded great yesterday at the rehearsal."

"It's good to be part of a band again." Regan ended the call. She never said good-bye.

Liz's stomach signaled its unhappiness that she'd missed lunch again, but it had been a small sacrifice for last-minute consulting with Vicky about the show. Mentoring young musicians was one of the best parts of teaching.

She walked across the street to the club. She needed to make sure the mics were set up correctly. She went in the back door, put her purse in the green room, and headed down the hallway toward the stage. She heard Kevin talking to someone.

"It was her decision." Kevin sounded as tired as he'd been looking lately. It was good he and Karen were getting away this weekend.

"It was a bad decision." Her dad's voice was dense with criticism.

"It healed."

"We don't know that yet, and now we're a month behind with rehab."

"She's always been a hard worker."

"Not lately. I don't understand this disappearing to Carmel the minute her classes are done on Wednesday and staying through the weekend. We need the CD done. We were making good progress with mixing, and then out of the blue she says she wants to finish it on her own."

"Liz knows what she's doing."

"Liz isn't thinking clearly right now. This is too important, Kevin. Her career. The club."

"Revenue's picking up. We'll be all right."

"We need Liz back on stage. She fills the club, and it gets us exposure we need. I took a big risk doing this for her."

Liz backed down the hallway as their conversation shifted to employee problems. He'd opened the club for her? That didn't make sense. The club was his dream.

Karen came through the back door. "How is it?"

"Hurts." She made a series of fists. Yep. Pain.

"I'm proud of how you've handled all this." Karen was soft-spoken like Liz's mom had been and just as rock solid. "Have you seen Kevin?"

"He was just talking to Dad."

"I swear, if anything interferes with our weekend away…" Karen's face turned stony.

Liz wasn't sure what to say as they continued down the hallway. Neither Kevin nor Karen seemed happy lately. She went to the stage and Karen headed toward Kevin, who was over by the bar. Liz repositioned a mic over the piano to pick up more treble, while her thoughts bounced between her hand and what her dad had said.

"I've blocked out Friday, June thirteenth, for the CD-release party." Her dad stood at the edge of the stage, his arms crossed.

"That's too soon!" She sat down on the piano bench and stared at him.

"We need to get people listening to the band again."

"I don't even know if I can play yet. How are we going to rehearse for it?"

"You don't need much rehearsal other than to get a drummer up to speed. Did you call Bobby? He's showy like Teri was. He'll be a good match."

"I asked Cassie to play Monterey with us." Jac had suggested it, pointing out it might be easier if the new drummer was someone Liz knew and trusted. In so many ways Jac's advice was astute and thoughtful.

"She's not Teri's style."

"We need to push the release back. We're not done mixing."

"You need to spend less time in Carmel and more time—"

"I'm working on it in Carmel with Jac. I know how important—"

"Who's Jack?"

Oh, God, had she said her name? She scrubbed her face as fatigue washed over her.

"Liz?"

"I'm working with someone on the mix."

"I see." His jaw muscles worked.

"No, you don't." She moved to sit on the edge of the stage, legs dangling down. She could trust him and it would eliminate part of the stress. "I'm working on it with the woman who writes *Jazz Notes*."

"The blog?" He looked puzzled.

"She's the sister of the artist who did your painting."

He frowned. "I'll grant she's a decent critic, but what does she know about—" He snapped his eyes to hers. "She helped you pick the songs." He shook his head. "It's not your sound."

"I needed someone impartial. We chose the best songs, Dad. You can't tell anyone about this."

"She doesn't want to be associated with your album?"

"She's blind and a very private person."

"I don't know." He looked at her like this was another of the bad decisions she was making.

Liz shoved up to a stand, grimacing as she inadvertently put weight on her left hand. "I do." It would be the best CD she could give Teri. That's all that mattered. She went back to checking the mics.

Liz slid onto a stool at the end of the bar in her dad's club, the dark end farthest from the stage. It was a good crowd for Thursday and an unknown band. Half an hour and Vicky's set would be over and she could go home. Liz pulled her phone from her pocket and added a comment in the notes app, happy to have the use of both hands. She would have a long critique session with Vicky and didn't want to forget anything. Regan was sensational. She'd obviously been practicing.

Her thoughts drifted away from the music. Her dad wouldn't budge on the date for the CD-release party. Six weeks. She was scheduled for PT three times a week for now. She'd researched the rehab process. "Unpredictable" appeared often in articles and on-line forums. She did circles with her wrist and made fists. It hurt. She was a hard worker. She'd have to do an hour or more of exercises daily on top of PT. But that word, unpredictable, kept jabbing her. What if hard work wasn't enough? Everything depended on her playing again.

"How's the wrist?" Hannah joined her, an arm around a young brunette.

"Good."

"Liar." Hannah whispered something to the brunette, who went to the other end of the bar.

"Hurts to play."

"You knew it'd take time."

"I guess I was hoping for a miracle." Cast off. Sit down and play like it had never happened.

"You deserve one." Hannah slid onto the stool next to her. "In the meantime I'll share my good news with you." Her smile was infectious. "You're looking at the head chef for East of Eden, the new hip Asian fusion restaurant in San Francisco. Opens in October. They want me to come on board right away to help with the layout and developing menus." Hannah's voice had an edge of snobbery that Liz disliked.

"Congratulations. Does that mean you'll be moving out?"

Hannah's smile faded. "Is it that bad living with me?"

"Only sometimes." She smiled and squeezed Hannah's arm. "Don't forget we have the boys all weekend." Hannah's expression went blank. She'd forgotten in spite of the note Liz left on her bathroom mirror. "So Kevin and Karen can get away? You're in charge of getting tickets to the new Muppets movie."

"No problem. Um, I sort of had a date tomorrow night. Maybe—"

"No." Liz wasn't going to sit in a theater with Hannah and the brunette.

"Yeah, bad idea. Okay. You, me, kids, and popcorn."

Vicky stepped to the mic. "This next song is dedicated to Professor Randall, my teacher at San Jose State and my mentor."

Liz recognized it as an arrangement of one of her tunes. This was what music should be—a living thing that passed from musician to musician. Teri lived as long as these moments existed. She fingered her wedding ring. Her grandma had never stopped wearing hers, and her dad still wore his. She had the band and teaching. That was her life now.

CHAPTER FOURTEEN

L iz drove between the stone gateposts and onto the gravel driveway. Parking behind Roger's SUV, she turned the key so the engine was off but the CD still played. Bill Evans's *Sunday at the Village Vanguard* kept the silence at bay. Jac and she hadn't talked on the twenty-minute drive from Alvin's mastering studio.

Dropping her hands to her lap and leaning her head back, Liz closed her eyes. Exhausted physically and mentally, yes, but more because she wanted a moment in Jac's reality. Sightless, the music seemed more visceral, more poignant, more intimate, or maybe it was just her teeming emotions grabbing for somewhere to anchor. For reasons they hadn't talked about, Evans had become their go-to music the last month in the few hours—during meals or late at night when their ears had lost their sensitivity—when they weren't working on the CD. Palate cleanser, Jac called it, and it worked—complex but ordered, restorative.

Her album was mastered. Done. She was relieved, but a new sadness was attached to it, a vacancy that scared her. It was like being in a room abruptly vacated, the occupant's belongings left behind but no trace of the person. Those four precious nights were the last music she would make with Teri. She didn't know how to say good-bye to Teri's music any more than she'd known how to say good-bye to her. That last conversation they'd had before the disease and the drugs separated them had been—

Jac let out a long breath, and it snapped Liz back to the present. There would be no CD, no tribute to Teri, without the woman sitting beside her. She leaned over the center console and hugged Jac. The gearshift poked into her ribs and she didn't care. Jac tensed and then relaxed, but didn't hug back. Liz sat back in her seat, embarrassed. Jac wasn't the hugging type.

"We went to three shows at the Vanguard." Liz closed her eyes again. "It gave me chills." Photographs on the walls spanning eighty years of jazz history. Knowing Evans and so many jazz greats had played there. Like meeting relatives she didn't know she had. "That was our dream gig. We were so sure we were back on track. So sure we'd perform there one day."

"You will." Jac sounded hoarse. She seemed tired. Not that it showed in her always perfect posture, or her endless patience, or her attention to detail, which was why they'd gone back for a fourth day of mastering. She seemed tired like someone who's reached so deep they've given away parts of themselves not easily replenished. She'd spent more hours on the album than Liz had. Her generosity was breathtaking.

The last song on Evans's CD started and Liz turned up the volume. "This album was recorded fifty-three years before our last show in New York, almost to the day. And not ten minutes away by cab." While dancing his fingers over the piano keys at the Vanguard on that Sunday in July, Evans hadn't known his band would be demolished by tragedy not long after the show. Jac knew jazz history as well as she did, but Liz kept going, as if feeding Teri's death into the long list of jazz musicians who'd died too young and her name into the long list of survivors forced to regroup after tragedy. "His bass player died ten days later in a car accident. That trio was his best group." Maybe her best group had come and gone, too.

"Until today this was my favorite live jazz album."

"I love his casual, singing melodies, balanced by those wonderful blocky chords. I feel like I'm looking at an impressionist's painting when I hear him." Liz opened her eyes. "The sunset is incredible. Oh, gosh, that was thoughtless."

"Describe it to me."

"Shades of orange and pink and—"

"What do you hear in it?" An inviting request, like when Jac asked her what she tasted in a glass of wine.

Liz hummed a melody as she stared at the colors evolving in the sky, translating what she saw and felt into notes. Change. Fading.

Longing. Letting go. Liz brushed away tears. She'd used up her Kleenex at the studio.

"Yes. You have to let go to make room for the next moment," Jac said, interpreting Liz's melody perfectly. "You created beautiful music with Teri, and now it goes out into the world, and you begin a new cycle."

"I'm afraid." That awful emptiness felt like a huge dark hole swallowing her. On the edge of it sat doubt that she could make music without Teri and fear that her wrist might not recover. Her future, Regan and Sammy's futures, depended on what felt like whims she had little control over.

"You have heart and courage and talent. You'll find your future. It's been an honor and a privilege to work on your album." Jac stepped out of the SUV. After arching her back and stretching her arms above her head, she headed toward Peg's house. Max, who'd stayed home because Alvin was allergic to dogs, ran to meet her, and she dropped to her knees and wrapped her arms around him.

Liz's phone rang. Her dad's ring. She let it go to voice mail. She wished she hadn't told him about Jac. Since she wouldn't let him hear the mixes, he wanted to know everything Jac said and then argued with it. She couldn't please him lately. She still hadn't mustered the courage to tell Jac she'd told him. Peggy walked from the house and opened Liz's car door. "You can't leave until we have a toast."

Liz should head home. There'd be heavy traffic and she had classes in the morning. But she wasn't ready to leave yet. She'd spent so much time here working with Jac, meals with them, grilling lessons from Roger, helping Peggy with her garden. She'd miss all of it. They walked to the patio where Roger was opening a bottle of champagne at the table. He offered the glass to Jac.

Liz stopped, watching the tasting ritual. Jac said something to Roger, probably naming the vintage. He smiled and shook his head. "How does she do that?"

"Immense talent." Peggy stood with arms crossed, head tilted, looking at her sister with that sad smile she often had when she talked about Jac. "It's hard, isn't it? When you put so much energy and focus into something and then it ends. Now that my show's over I feel lost."

Gone. Teri. Her music. The life they had. The love they had. She felt numb as they continued to the table and took the flutes of champagne Roger handed them.

Jac lifted her glass. "To—"

"To Teri," Liz said, a little too loudly.

"To Teri," Jac echoed. They all touched glasses and sipped in silence as the colorful sunset faded to twilight gray.

"I finished the painting for the album cover," Peggy said. "It's drying." They walked to the studio and Peggy turned on lights.

She'd been deeply moved when Peggy offered to do the painting. "It's beautiful," Liz said, standing in front of the canvas—an energetic, impressionistic rendering of the four of them onstage in New York. The past. If only Peggy could paint her future. "Teri would love it."

"It's yours to keep." Peggy hugged her for a long time. "I looked over the pictures you gave me of your grandmother's garden and made a plant list. Some of what she grew isn't available anymore and some I can't identify. She had a keen eye for structure and used color sparingly. We can create that same style. When do you want to start?"

"Thursday." Liz liked the idea of having a new project to fill the void left by the CD. It would also give her an excuse to continue to spend time in Carmel. "Maybe it'll be good for my wrist."

"How's PT?"

"She says the range of motion is coming back nicely. We add resistance exercises next week. Too early to tell if I'll be a hundred percent." Four weeks to the CD-release party. She couldn't play a song all the way through yet because of pain.

Jac appeared in the studio doorway. "I need to take Max down to the beach, and then I have a blog to write. I regret I can't review your album publicly. It's going to be the best jazz album of the year." She came to Liz and hugged her. Briefly, but a hug. Then she ambled toward her home, Max matching her stride, tail waving regally.

Liz's chest tightened and panic made her want to run after Jac. Without the album connecting them, they wouldn't have a reason to spend so much time together. "Can I come with you?" Jac stopped but didn't turn around. Liz took that as an invitation and trotted to catch up. Friends. She really wanted them to be friends.

Jac turned on her computer and opened a document. She wrote reviews of the three albums she'd listened to this week, making sure she wasn't overly harsh because they weren't of Liz's caliber. Drumming her fingers on the desk, she formed what she wanted to say in the blog. A band had a sound, but so did each individual in it. Where was the line between the collaborative sound and the soloist's voice?

Opening a new document, she wrote about how jazz invited the individual to step forward and claim her voice within the group. Noting some of the best soloists from bands stretching back to the start of jazz, she made the case that an individual could make a band, as with Liz, although she didn't name her.

She filed it as a draft she'd edit in the morning before posting and went to the living room. She poured wine, gave Max treats, sat, and then got up and paced. She felt lost without the focus of working on the album. Music she woke up to and went to bed with. Dreamed about. She knew every note, every drumbeat, every nuanced phrase in Liz's playing. And now that she knew Liz intimately, how would she let go?

She needed something to listen to, but what? Not jazz. Beethoven? No, her emotions needed something else. Billie Holiday. Putting several albums in the CD changer, she settled in her recliner. She stroked Max in his bed beside her and reached for the glass of wine next to the remote on the table. Everything was the way it should be, the way it had been before Liz. But everything was different.

Three raps on the door and it opened. Peg. "I brought chocolate cake, and Roger sent the bottle he bet you for naming the champagne. You're quite the show-off."

"Wasn't I always?" The energy from the walk on the beach was wearing off, replaced by a bone-deep fatigue that made her feel heavy.

"Are you happy with the CD?"

"Immensely."

"You know Liz wants to be your friend."

"Our collaboration is done. She doesn't need me any more."

"Liz isn't like that." Peg set a plate on the side table and gave Max something he crunched.

"They're all like that."

"Is cynicism another of your talents?"

"What do you want me to say, Peg? I like her? All right, I like her."

"She's coming over Thursday. We're going to start on her garden. I invited her to dinner."

Jac held up her hands in surrender. "You'll have to give me lessons in friendship."

"I thought you'd never ask."

"I admit I want to see if she reaches her potential." Jac took a bite of cake and chased it with wine.

"You think she won't?"

"It could go either way."

"You don't think her wrist will heal?"

"I'm not sure her heart will. If it doesn't, she won't be able to move on and find the sound that's truly hers. She'll be a cover band, playing Teri's music, maybe new songs in the same style, but it won't be what she's capable of."

"How do you know?"

"I know how she thinks and feels about music, who her favorite musicians and composers are. That blues/rock slant is the band's signature sound, but I don't think it's hers."

"What is?"

"That I don't know, but I want to be around when she finds it."

Peg kissed her cheek. "You should be proud of yourself."

"Thanks for the new bouquet. A couple of Mr. Lincolns, a couple of Double Delights, and one off the yellow rosebush near your studio that Mom planted and you don't know the name of."

"Show-off." The door opened and then Peg spoke again. "Doesn't working with Liz make you—"

"No." She couldn't afford to miss it. She turned up the volume as the voice that was made to sing the blues provided the perfect company to her mood. Anger roiled inside her. Guilt and regret joined it, and she was helpless as the storm of emotions battered her. She contained the pain, anchored it to the music. If only she'd kept her emotions under control ten years ago.

CHAPTER FIFTEEN

"We should have done the beach instead," Jac grumbled when her shoes squished on the gravel driveway. She was twenty minutes slower than her usual pace because of having to wind through the extra-thick coating of tourists on the downtown streets. Max paused, accustomed to being let out of his harness. "Not yet, buddy. We need to get through the minefield." Party paraphernalia—catering trucks in the driveway, tables and chairs all over the patio, people scurrying about as they set up. Memorial Day. The first of the summer-holiday parties started by her parents the year the house was completed. Peg had continued the tradition. Required socializing. No nap. Could this day get any worse?

An hour later she was sitting in her usual chair at Peg's patio table, the sun warm on her shoulders. Max lay at her feet. She rubbed her fingers along his back to soothe herself as she endured an ever-changing array of people joining her and asking the same "catch-up" questions they asked every year. As if her life ever changed. Bursts of laughter erupted sporadically from the growing group of guests, and kids' shrieks came from the bouncy-house Peg always rented for the parties. All the noise made her grate her teeth. "My parents are scuba diving in Australia," she said for what felt like the hundredth time.

"I remember when they were building the house. Must have been…"

"Sixty-seven." It was sad to hear the forgetfulness in Wayne's voice. He'd been a fixture in her childhood, the trumpet player in her dad's jazz band.

"We'd come over on weekends, play music, and have a bonfire on the beach. Those were the days." He patted her shoulder and pushed his chair back. "I'm sorry about the way things turned out for you," he said, before walking off.

Someone pulled back the chair next to her and she stiffened. Couldn't she have a few minutes to herself?

"I wasn't sure you actually had arms." Liz tugged the edge of her sleeveless blouse. "Pretty color."

Apparently gold still looked good on her. Irritation melted. Liz's company was the one thing that would make this day tolerable. "Tell me what you're wearing."

"Boring khaki shorts…"

Jac filtered out surrounding conversations as she formed a picture in her mind. Orange short-sleeved blouse…the dangerous sandals from the night she tripped…Earrings? A necklace? Certainly the ring and watch she always wore. "Why aren't you at your dad's barbecue party?"

"It took me half an hour to go five miles, and to be honest, I didn't want to. Over here people don't know about Teri so I don't have to worry about what they're thinking—am I doing okay, is the band going to make it? And we always play music at any party. I don't want the disappointed looks when I tell them I can't."

"Are you sure going ahead with the CD-release party is smart?" Jac tried not to sound judgmental. Liz already had enough stress over it.

"It won't be my best performance, but I need to do it. I wish you'd come."

"I can't." Every time Liz asked, she felt bad for saying no. She'd love to be there for her big night. "Try this." She held out her glass. "Talbott Chardonnay. One of the best of the local wineries."

"You're not going to tell me how much it cost and ruin it for me, are you?"

One day soon Liz wouldn't think hundred-dollar bottles of wine were expensive. Yes, her wrist was an unresolved problem, but if success didn't happen this year, it would happen soon. Jac would make sure of it.

Nancy, the owner of Pilgrim's Way bookstore and a longtime acquaintance, joined them. Jac half listened to their conversation about books as she snacked on cheese and crackers. The warm offshore breeze would keep the fog at bay, and the evening would be perfect for dancing. What would it be like to dance with Liz? Her heart skipped a beat and then another as she imagined Liz in her arms. Dare she ask her? An innocent dance with a friend? No. She crossed her arms and shut down that line of thought.

That's how things had begun with Maria. *Don't be so provincial, darling. Just an innocent dance with a friend. Women dance with each other here. When in Rome...* By the end of the dance Jac had been swept away by feelings she'd never felt before. A burning desire to touch and be touched. By the end of the night she knew what had been missing in her marriage. No, those kinds of feelings only led to disaster. She would not make that mistake again.

"What's that?" Jac asked after Nancy left. Liz was humming.

"That blasted melody is teasing me again. It's your fault. I heard it first the day we met."

"Met?" Jac fingered her forehead where the cut had been.

"Don't make me feel bad about that. You know you're glad." Liz rubbed her hand up and down Jac's forearm.

Just a friend, she warned her heart when it skipped another beat.

"Give me your napkin," Liz said. She rummaged in what sounded like her purse, then went back to humming. "Darn." Hummed some more. "I need paper. I'm hearing more of the song. Lots more. I don't want to lose it."

"I'll get the paper. Don't break the mood." Taking Max's harness, Jac went to Peg's office. She found the copier and grabbed paper from the tray. On her way back through the dining room, a hand on her arm stopped her.

"How are you?"

Of course Gwen would be here. She came every year, and every year it was awkward. "Good. I can't talk right now."

"Later?"

"All right." Jac hurried back to the table and set the paper down, saying nothing lest she break Liz's concentration. Scooting closer, she put her arm across Liz's chair, hoping the implied intimacy would deflect anyone from joining them. If she leaned toward her she could catch a whiff of Liz's perfume. Citrusy and sweet. Nice. Liz's humming continued, broken by silences when it sounded like she was writing. It was thrilling to be with her as she created new music.

Finally, Liz sat back against the chair, her shoulders against Jac's arm. "I think it's a suite." Liz's voice was sparkling.

"Describe it."

"The first part has…" Liz explained the technical elements, then hummed several different melodies as she tapped the edge of the table in a rapid beat.

"Reminds me of the day we met. Lunch at the Bistro. The rain hitting the awning over our table." She imitated Liz's tapping. "The melodies sound like variations on Ellington."

"Yes! The second part is more leisurely." Liz hummed. "It's how I feel when I'm walking downtown and meandering through art galleries. Then there's a new part I haven't heard before."

"Ocean. Walking the beach," Jac said after Liz hummed it.

"Yes!"

"Sketches of your life in Carmel."

Liz laughed and tilted her head back, and her hair tickled Jac's arm. "I guess it's fitting that you name it. How about 'Carmel Sketches'?"

"I'm honored."

"It isn't my usual style." Liz sounded apologetic.

"Let it be what it wants to be."

A cell phone rang and Liz answered it. "I'm sorry…I didn't decide until this morning…I'm not avoiding you…Yes, we're going to start rehearsing…Next week." Silence and then, "Arrrgh. Regan. I love her dearly, but she's driving me crazy."

"Worried? Doesn't handle change well? Give her time. Let her work it out through her guitar."

"How do you always know the right thing to say?"

"I've been bragging about you to everyone," Peg said, presumably to Liz. "A lot of people have heard of your band and want to meet you."

"Is there somewhere I can put these?" Liz gathered the papers and knocked them on the table, as if to line them up.

"I'll put them in my office," Peg said.

Jac caught snippets of Liz's voice as Peg took her around. Good. She needs to be reminded of who she is. An hour later Liz was back.

"Okay, that was surreal. Peggy introduced me to the head of the Carmel Bach Festival, who's heard us perform, an artist whose work I love almost as much as Peggy's, an author who's one of my favorite mystery writers, and Clint Eastwood."

"He drops by most years."

"Easy for you to say. He's a big fan of the Monterey Jazz Festival, and he knew Grandma from when she helped on his campaign for mayor. Dad's not going to believe it."

"Now you're officially part of the who's who of Carmel." People continued to join them, but her previous irritation melted away in light of Liz's presence.

"Dinner, ladies," Roger said some time later, setting plates on the table. "And one old cab for you, your majesty." Peggy and Roger joined them, and it felt like the many nights the four of them had dinner together. Friendship and nothing more, she reminded herself each time Liz's voice or an accidental touch made her heart leap in a way it shouldn't.

"The band's about to start," Liz said when they'd finished second pieces of chocolate cake. "They're moving tables to the perimeter of the patio to make a dance area. I love to dance. Teri hated to dance. Can you believe a drummer with two left feet? Do you like to dance?"

"Yes." The only part of these parties she liked was dancing with Roger.

"God, I love swing," Liz said after the band started with a Glenn Miller song. "Peggy and Roger are dancing." After a few minutes she said, "They're good."

Jac folded her arms and stretched out her legs. Her back would be sore tomorrow from too much sitting in a hard chair, but she could listen to this music all night.

"No sitting," Roger said several tunes later, taking her hand and pulling her up.

"Or you," Peg said to Liz.

"Don't have to twist my arm," Liz said as they walked to the dance area.

"I need a break," Roger said when the song ended.

"Me, too," Peg said. "You and Liz stay out here, though."

"I'm game," Liz said.

Jac was about to decline when Liz took her hand. Palm to palm. A shiver went through her, and her body overruled common sense. Ten years ago was the last time she'd danced with a woman. Not a happy night. Taking the lead position she preferred, she blocked out everything but Liz and the music. She loved West Coast Swing, and Liz followed as if they'd been dancing together for years—left side pass, an underarm pass, more side passes, then a whip. Yes, Liz danced beautifully. There was the occasional touch of their legs or arms and always Liz's hand in hers. Every point of contact was like a fire on her skin.

"You're a great dancer," Liz said when the song ended. "Shall we try another?"

Jac hesitated when the band started a slow ballad. Liz stepped into her arms, and all the feelings she'd been trying to contain exploded in a rush of fluttering in her chest. Liz's hand on her shoulder, her cheek close enough that she felt the rapid exhalations of warm breath, their thighs and breasts touching. When Liz hummed the melody the delicate vibration of it drifted through Jac's body, warming places that had been chilled for years. This connection couldn't last, but she drank up the guilty pleasure of it.

"I'll get us water," Liz said when they returned to the table.

Jac's heart was pounding and she squeezed the arms of the chair, fighting to rein in her feelings. Liz was just a one-night dance partner.

"We never danced together." Gwen's deep voice.

Damn it. Not now.

"Looks like you got over not wanting a relationship." She sat in Liz's chair.

"She's a friend."

"I know your body. She's more than a friend. I hoped we'd have another chance."

"I'm grateful for everything you did for me." She wouldn't be able to dance if not for Gwen's talent as a physical therapist.

"We were good together." Gwen took her hand.

"It was a long time ago." Jac pushed her chair back and stood.

"We could try again."

Taking Max's harness she turned to go. "It should never have—" She bumped into someone. Citrusy, sweet perfume. Liz. No. Not this. Not tonight.

"Hello. I'm Gwen Gallagher."

"Liz Randall." Not a happy voice.

"Jac and I are old—"

"Excuse me." Jac hurried toward her cottage. She wasn't going to be part of this conversation.

Liz's mouth fell open as she stared at Jac's retreating figure.

"All that beauty and talent to boot. Good luck." Gwen shook her head and walked away.

What was that about? No, she'd heard enough of the conversation to know what that was about. She hurried after Jac and caught up to her as she was opening her door. "Not so fast." She followed her through the door and shut it. Hard.

Jac took off Max's harness and went to the kitchen.

"Are you a lesbian?" The silence gave her the answer. "That's a really big thing not to tell me." All the time they'd spent together and nothing had suggested Jac was a lesbian. "Why would you keep that a secret?"

"I don't discuss my personal life."

"But everything about my life is your business?" Resentment coiled in her gut.

"It's not the same thing." Jac ran her hands through her hair and pinched her temples between her palms.

"You were involved with Gwen."

"We dated briefly. So long ago it hardly counts."

"When long ago?"

Jac spread her hands flat on the counter. Her jaw worked and then she said, "Ten years. She was my physical therapist for my back problems."

"And?"

"I wasn't in a good place." Jac yanked a bottle of wine from the temperature-controlled cabinet and banged it down on the tile counter. She squeezed the foil cutter around the neck of the bottle and twisted. "Things went in a direction they shouldn't have."

"Seems like she still cares."

"I'm no more ready for a relationship now than I was then. I'm sorry you found out this way." Jac walked from the kitchen and held out a glass of red wine. "Peace offering?"

"I thought we were friends." She set the glass on the bar top.

"I'm not sure I'm ready for that either."

Liz's heart dropped. She considered Jac a friend. A good friend who knew her in ways no one else did. "I've held nothing back while you've shared very little. I don't even know how you afford expensive wine." God, had she just said that? Of course Jac's eyebrow went up. "Friends trust each other. Friends talk about their lives."

"I didn't ask for any of this."

That was it, wasn't it? "I don't want a one-sided friendship. I won't intrude in your life again." Liz knelt and hugged Max, then walked out. The band was playing another Goodman song, and she tried to let the snappy beat dispel the sadness. In reality, she'd had nothing with Jac but a business collaboration. The truth hurt. She stood at the edge of the cliff, gazing out at the dark ocean and the barest sliver of moon.

"I wondered where you'd gone off to," Peggy said, joining her.

"Why didn't you tell me?"

"What?"

"Jac. Lesbian. I just found out that they go together in the same sentence."

"It wasn't my place to tell you."

"Seems to be the theme tonight." She was being petty but didn't care.

"You have no idea what she's been through." The words were heavy, not at all a reproach. "Don't judge her too harshly."

"I've leveraged my future on her opinions. And I have no idea who she is."

"Yes, you do. In your heart you know."

They stood side by side. Music came from Jac's. Early Miles Davis. The melancholy sounds fit the mood perfectly and brought tears to Liz's eyes. The friendship that had become so important to her didn't exist. "I need to go. It was a lovely party." She headed up the walkway.

"Don't walk out on her. Please talk to her."

"This is the way she wants it." She should have gone to her dad's party. People who cared about her. People who were honest with her. Friends.

❖

Friendship. Why had Jac thought she could be friends with Liz? She'd never had friends. She'd never confided in people. Until Maria. She wasn't making that mistake again. Anger burst from the place deep inside that never stopped hurting and then fell away like fireworks collapsing in the sky. Liz was right. She had shared much and gotten little in return. *Friends trust each other. Friends talk about their lives.*

She put on Miles Davis to block out the obnoxiously peppy band, then returned to the kitchen, her thoughts in turmoil. She took a long sip of wine, then set the timer on the coffee machine and took two biscuits out of the container for Max. This day needed to end.

Peg knocked on her door and came in. "Are you all right?"

"How's Liz?"

"She wants to trust you. You don't give her much reason to."

"I've given her more than..." Jac swallowed around the lump in her throat.

"I know, honey." Peg's voice was gentle. Irritatingly gentle. "You two dance beautifully together."

Jac banged her knee on the corner of the cabinet as she walked out of the kitchen. "Damn it." She rubbed it. "If you're implying what I think you're implying, that's ridiculous."

"You can't hide your feelings from me."

"Liz doesn't want anything but friendship, and I can't even do that well."

"She's not Maria. I know it's not what you want to hear, but you should tell her the rest of it."

"No!" Jac kicked a barstool. It hit the floor with a crack. Max's nails clicked on the floor and he touched her leg. She dropped to one knee and stroked his sides, kissed his head. He'd never judge or betray her.

"You have to trust someone, sometime."

"No, I don't."

"She'll understand."

"You think I care what Liz Randall understands?" Jac pulled her shoulders back, stiff with anger.

"Yes. I do." Peg's footsteps crossed the living room, hard and fast. The door slammed.

Jac gripped the back of the recliner, dug her nails into the soft leather, then pressed her palm to her stomach. How had her carefully ordered life unraveled to the point where she was expected to explain herself to someone who was practically a stranger? She walked down the hall, Max by her side. Yes, Liz was a stranger. People she'd known a lot longer hadn't deserved her trust.

She undressed and went to the hot tub. To hell with anyone stupid enough to peek over the wall around her patio. Jets pounding her back, she tried to block out the band, tried not to remember how Liz felt in her arms. No. She would not be hurt again. Sweat gathered in her scalp, crawled down her face and neck. Parties. Gone. Dancing. Gone. Maria. Gone. Stephanie…Oh, God. Memories swarmed like mosquitos until she couldn't stand it. Tears joined the trickles of sweat. She wanted Liz's friendship. She wanted…

CHAPTER SIXTEEN

L iz hurried across the gravel driveway, resentment shifting to sadness and back again. Really, really big thing for Jac not to tell her. Why wouldn't she? Why all the secrecy? It hurt to realize she'd been imagining a friendship that didn't exist. She'd drive home tonight. Maybe her dad's party would still be going on.

At the end of the driveway, she stopped to empty pebbles from her sandals, bracing against the gatepost. She was in her car before she remembered the music she'd written out. Was it worth going back for? Yes. When she got back to the patio she didn't see Peggy anywhere. Office. Couldn't be hard to find. She'd retrieve the pages and be on her way.

The second door she opened along the hallway was an office. She flipped on the light. Desk in the corner, manila folder on top, a sticky note with her name. The wall behind her was covered in pictures not unlike the one at her dad's house. Family pictures. Very young Susanne and Jack with Mickey Mouse. Peggy and Jac as kids in front of a Christmas tree, two people behind them that she assumed were their parents. She stepped closer and studied another one.

Jac in a formal gown. Hair shorter. Young. Late teens? Next to a man in a tuxedo…No. She stared. Yes, it was. Leonard Bernstein. Frail looking, but unmistakably Leonard Bernstein. Jac held a trumpet at her side. A sound like a train roared through Liz's head.

Her gaze darted to other pictures. She brought her hand to her chest as understanding slowly dawned. These photos had one thing in common—a tall, slender, blond woman. Wearing an evening gown in most. A full orchestra behind her in some. Holding a trumpet in many. Shaking hands with known dignitaries in a few.

"Oh. My. God. Jacqueline Richards." Her mouth froze in an "oh" as she moved from one photo to the next, working her way along the wall, studying each one—running the gamut of the career of Jacqueline Richards, arguably the world's greatest classical trumpet player. When she reached the end of the wall, she clutched the doorframe and looked up. Right into Peggy's troubled eyes.

Peggy took the folder from her trembling fingers, led her back to the kitchen, and settled her on a barstool.

Liz was vaguely aware of the party going on around them. "Grandma took me to see her with the San Francisco Symphony when I was in high school. She told me to pay attention because we were witnessing genius. I was transfixed." Pieces slid into place. Jac's hearing music like a musician. A shudder whisked through her. She was a musician all right. "Why didn't she tell me?"

"It's complicated." Peggy's smile was that sad one Liz had seen before when she talked about Jac.

She made a noise somewhere between a squeak and a gasp. "The morning I surprised you with croissants and heard the sound of a trumpet coming from Jac's. That wasn't a demo CD you said someone had sent her, asking for her opinion. That was her." It had seemed odd at the time that someone would want Jac's opinion about a classical piece. Peggy looked apologetic, and she didn't know whether to be angry or laugh. She stared across the patio toward Jac's. Jacqueline's.

"A car accident...I remember reading about it." Liz frowned, trying to call up the memory. "Badly injured...speculation about whether she'd ever perform again. And then nothing."

"That sums up the last ten years," Peggy said, her tone flat.

"Why would she keep that from me?" Being a lesbian was the least of Jac's secrets. Jacqueline's.

"It's complicated."

"That's not good enough anymore." Liz bolted for the cottage, driven by outrage. Again, someone close to her, someone she trusted, had kept something crucial from her. *I was open and honest with her, and all she's done is lie to me.* She burst through the door, not giving a damn about Jac's precious privacy. "Jac!" Not in the kitchen or living room. Foolish. She must have had a good laugh helping the little jazz pianist. "Jac!" She marched down the hall. Bedroom door was open and she strode through. No Jac. French doors to the patio were open.

"Did you have a good laugh at my expense?"

"What the—Liz?" Jac. Hot tub. Naked.

Liz retreated, bumping into the door. It banged back against a dresser. She flinched, turned around, and froze. Peggy. In the doorway. Hands on her hips. Heat sprouted everywhere and deposited what Liz was sure was flaming red on her cheeks and ears.

Peggy took her elbow and led her back to the living room. "Sit."

Liz obediently dropped onto the couch and sat on the edge, hands tucked between her knees, trying to forget what she'd just seen. Peggy and Jac were talking, but their conversation was muffled behind the closed bedroom door. "Why didn't she tell me?" ran through her mind like a ticker tape. She'd been analyzing music with one of the most brilliant musicians alive. Known for strong opinions. Check. Known as a perfectionist. Check. Known for innovative interpretations. Check. But jazz? How did that fit? And why hadn't she gone back to performing? She looked up when she heard footsteps.

"Do I need to stay to make sure you two work this out?" Peggy acted like she was scolding children who should have known better.

Jac stood with her hands clasped, her light-blue sweat suit zipped up to her chin. Her face was flushed. Her mouth was a tight line. Max settled in his bed. Everything normal, but not.

Liz nodded, but she wasn't at all sure this could be worked out. She felt betrayed and very intimidated. All the celebrities she'd met today, and one of the biggest of them must have been laughing at her fan-girl excitement. She squeezed her hands between her knees to stop the trembling. The silence stretched. Not the usual comfortable silence between them. The bad, who's-going-to-talk-first kind.

Jac went to the kitchen and returned with two glasses of wine, setting one on the coffee table in front of Liz before sitting in her recliner. Silence swallowed them again.

"What do I call you?"

"What you've always called me." Jac's voice sounded hollow and distant. More silence. "I'm sorry."

"For what? Lying to me? Again? Playing me for a fool? Having fun at my expense?"

"You can't possibly think that."

"What should I think? A world-famous classical musician slums it to help me with my little jazz—"

"Don't ever say that again!" Jac looked angry and sad and broken all rolled into one. "I'm proud of that album." Jac had treated her music with respect and praise. She hadn't faked that.

All sorts of emotions lodged in Liz's throat—gratitude, awe, confusion, and back to resentment. "I thought we were friends."

"I'm terrible at friendship, but if I ever wanted to try, it would be with you." Jac's smile was heartbreaking.

"Will you tell me what happened?" Accident. Blind. Never performed again. It was going to be a sad story, but she needed to understand.

Jac's chest lifted with a deep breath, and then she nodded as she exhaled. Silence again, but the kind you couldn't do anything about. It was Jac's story to tell. Jac went to her sound system and put on Bill Evans.

Liz was relieved when Jac sat beside her on the couch. Max lay next to Jac, his paw protectively on her bare foot. The first song was over before Jac spoke. When she did, the words seemed to come from a deep, dark place, as if dragged unwillingly into the room. Liz closed her eyes and listened, carefully, the way she'd listen to a piece of music she wanted to understand.

Jac took a long sip of wine, gathering her thoughts. Was Liz worthy of her trust? She deserved the truth, but what if Peg was wrong and she didn't understand? She couldn't bear Liz's judgment. The rip current of guilt swirled through her, dangerous, but pointless to resist. It always took her back to that night. She gripped the cool, soft leather edge of the couch. "I was injured in a car accident on Valentine's Day, ten years ago." Factual. "It's not a pretty story." An understatement.

"That's why it's good we're friends."

She'd hurt Liz, badly, yet here she was, offering her usual kindness. Friendship she didn't deserve. "There was a woman. Maria.

My European agent's wife. I was doing a lot of engagements and she started traveling with me. You know how exhausting it is."

"I can't imagine doing it alone. Your husband didn't travel with you?"

"No." He rarely even attended her concerts, always too busy with the business of music.

"She seduced me. The first time. After that I was equally responsible." She waited. Liz wouldn't approve. Would she walk out? How far were the boundaries of friendship?

"She must have been special," Liz said, her voice gentle.

If only that were true. The rip current tightened its hold and Jac leaned forward on her elbows, trying to ease the pain building in her lower back. "For the first time in my life I knew what it was to be in love. Being with her changed everything." She drank more wine to steady herself as emotions churned in her stomach. Only Peggy and Roger knew about the affair. "We were in Chicago. Snow. It was beautiful. I performed Hummel. I was outside myself." They'd made love that afternoon, wild and passionate.

"I'd ordered a special dinner for us." Maria's favorite foods flown in from Italy. She drank from her wineglass, her hands trembling the way they had as she'd opened the champagne, anxious to toast their new future.

"I'd filed for divorce the day before. I told her I wanted her to leave her husband so we could be together." Maria's face frozen in surprise, the champagne flute to her lips. Surprise shifting to something else as she sipped. Something Jac hadn't expected. Disapproval. Rejection. Something she hadn't seen in those six months, the warmth of summer to the chill of that winter night. The best six months of her life.

"She said she wouldn't." *Not in the plan, darling.* A terrible shudder shot through her as it had that night. Shocked. Confused. Embarrassed. How had she misread things?

Memories and emotions surged through her, painful and demanding. "I left and went to a bar." It was a tiny precipice, omission on this side and truth on the other. She backed up and came at it again. "I went to a—bar. I don't know what I was thinking." New guilt slid next to the old guilt and squeezed her like a corset. Liz deserved the whole truth, and she couldn't give it to her.

"You were hurt."

Jac shook off the understanding in Liz's voice. There was no excuse for what she'd done that night. "On the way back to the hotel I was in an accident." That much was true. "Broken vertebrae and ribs. Head injury." She tossed the words out like a decoy, truths to cover the omissions. It was the best she could do.

"I'm so sorry." Liz wrapped her arms around her.

She felt like a thief, stealing comfort she hadn't earned, but Liz holding her felt so good. Friendship. Longing curled up from her center, and she let it have its way with her, used it to keep the guilt at bay. A word attached to the longing. Love. She was falling in love with Liz. When Liz finally let go, she could barely stay upright from the muscle spasms clamping down on her back. She went to her recliner and lowered herself carefully onto it.

"Do you have contact with Maria?"

"I haven't seen her since that night." For months she'd thought Maria would come to her. She'd both feared and longed for it. Now she'd traded one unrequited love for another. Max moved to his bed and she reached for him.

"If I were you I might not have said anything either. Like my not wanting to tell people about Teri. Thank you for trusting me. It doesn't change anything." A short laugh. "Well, maybe it does. You really like my music?"

Jac remembered that tone she'd once encouraged in everyone she met. Intimidation. Awe. Reverence. She hated the sound of it in Liz's voice. "I love your music."

"Thank you. Coming from—"

"Please don't." Another reason she hadn't told Liz. She already sensed a subtle imbalance of authority between them because of Liz's turning to her for help with the CD. She wanted a friend, not a fan.

"Is Winters your maiden name?"

"No. Richards is. I never took my husband's last name." He'd been angry, but she'd held her ground. "Winters is my mother's maiden name. I wanted to make it hard for the press to find me. I couldn't deal with all that after the accident." Or now.

Liz was quiet and then asked, "Why do you blog jazz instead of classical?"

"Don't quote me, but it's more interesting."

"Why didn't you go back to performing?"

"It took a year for me to go completely blind." A year of doctors assuring her she wouldn't lose her sight. A year of debilitating migraines on top of the excruciating back pain. More and more days of darkening vision until one day the shadowy grayness was gone, too. Damn experts. "Longer for me to recover from the back injury." They told her she'd never walk without a limp. "All my energy went into rehab and building a new life."

"But you play."

"Once in a while." Guilt jabbed her again. Not the whole truth, but she couldn't have that discussion tonight. She needed to take muscle relaxers and the heavy-duty pain medication, and go to bed before the back pain incapacitated her.

Liz was quiet again. Was she deciding if she wanted to be friends? Was Peg wrong that she'd understand?

"I need to be honest with you, too. I told my dad who you are."

"What?" Her pulse skyrocketed and her back seized as she jerked up straight.

"I told him you were the *Jazz Notes* blogger. I'm sorry. I was upset by something he said and it just came out. I should have told you sooner, but I was afraid you'd stop helping me with the CD."

Relief soothed the flood of adrenaline. Of course Liz couldn't have told him her real identity. "In the scope of things, that's a transgression worth excusing. Please don't tell him who I am."

"I promise. I also put your name on the album as co-producer." A pause and then, "Does that look mean you're amused or about to throw me out?"

Jac realized she'd raised her eyebrow, tilted her head, and crossed her arms. A look the press had labeled imperious. "Why?"

"I felt dishonest taking all the credit. I figured since no one knows you're behind the blog, it wouldn't do any harm. It still won't." She paused. "Except I broke a promise I made to you."

"Let's call it even." Should she tell Liz the rest while she had this opening? Her back muscles spasmed and she slumped back against her recliner, tilting it back to ease the pain. She wasn't up to it tonight.

"Can we be friends?"

"I'd like that." In a few minutes Liz would be gone and the darkness would be all she had.

"Can I stay here a bit longer?"

She really needed to go to bed.

"Sorry. You've probably had enough of me for one—"

"Stay." She'd have to wait to take the medications because they made her drowsy, but it was a small price to pay for more time with Liz. Two hours of talking music, some laughing, a bit of arguing as Liz's intimidation faded, and then Liz said good night with a long hug. No sooner had Liz left than Peg came to check on her.

"I'm exhausted and my back's bad."

"I told you she'd understand. I'm proud of you."

"Don't be. I didn't tell her all of it."

"It's a start," Peg said after Jac shared what she told Liz.

In the bathroom she swallowed a pain pill and a muscle relaxer. Sitting on the edge of the bed, she lifted the lid on the music box Liz had given her Saturday, a thank-you for helping with the CD. "Fond Memories," her favorite song from the album because of Liz's solo, filled her heart with a longing she hadn't felt since those months with Maria.

She nudged Max over with her knee and rubbed her palms over the cool sheets, then over her abdomen. Her body wanted…Her hand crept up, up, until it cupped her breast. She let out a ragged breath. Wanted…She slid her other hand lower, inside the silk pajamas. She was wet where she didn't want to be wet. She pinched her eyes shut, but tears squeezed through as she stroked her clit, poked her fingers inside, stroked some more. Not long. No soft kisses on her throat. No tongue circling her nipple. No murmured words of love. The orgasm rippled through her, unsatisfying, and then she had nothing but the dark, and the longing.

CHAPTER SEVENTEEN

Liz sat on Teri's stool in her dad's music room and stomped on the bass-drum pedal over and over, the vibration like a vigorous heartbeat. She needed Teri so much tonight. The CD-release party. The first show without her since college. She turned the gold band on her finger. The jeweler had polished it when she bought the new watchband last week. She tugged it over her knuckle and read the inscription that was almost worn off. *Yours Forever*. Teri was wearing hers when she was buried. Not forever.

"I worked hard on it, sweetie. Happy Anniversary." It had been two days ago. No one in her family had given any indication they remembered. Jac knew, but only because she'd asked so many times this week what was wrong. Blind, but more aware than anyone she'd ever met.

Her dad popped in wearing a long-sleeved black Polo shirt, his hair parted a little unevenly, as usual. "People want to talk to you before the show."

She rested her palms on the cool surface marked by Teri's drumsticks. "I want her to like it."

"You turned tragedy into triumph."

Is that what she'd done?

"I invited reviewers from the *Chron* and the *Merc*."

She wished he hadn't. What if her hand cramped? What if those bad pains shot up her arm? The ones that made her back off with her left hand.

"Momentum." He pumped his fist for emphasis.

Liz slapped the crash cymbal and the sound skittered around the space. Oscar lounged unfazed on the back of the couch, the tip of his tail swishing to some unheard rhythm.

"Come on, sunshine. Let's give them a taste of what Randalls can do." He held out his hand.

"I'll be right there. Really," she added when he frowned. She hit the bass drum one last time as the door closed. Taking four Advil from her pocket, she swallowed them with the half glass of wine she hoped would calm her nerves. She'd never been afraid before a performance. She hummed "Spring Time" for luck. Standing, she brushed wrinkles out of the gold silk pants, humming a different melody. "Carmel Sketches." She wished Jac were going to be here.

"Showtime, Oscar." He padded regally across the floor and rubbed against her leg, totally out of character for the aloof cat. He dashed over and jumped on top of the bass drum, then danced across the snares before scooting out the door. She covered her heart. "Thank you, sweetie."

Walking across the street to the club, Liz held the ends of the fiery-toned scarf Teri had given her the first night of their tour. "Let's set the jazz world on fire." Now their dreams were barely a puff of smoke. Could she fan them back to life? The parking lot next to the restaurant was full, as were both sides of the street. Her dad's promoting had paid off.

She wound her way through the packed club, shaking hands, accepting congratulations, answering questions. Doing what Teri had done so effortlessly. No condolences about Teri and she resented it. Had they forgotten her? Heading toward the green room behind the stage, she stopped at a table when she recognized her chiropractor. "Dr. Hammond. I'm so glad you could make it." Her wife, Carla, stood and hugged Liz.

"Hi, Liz, and it's Jamie, please. We wouldn't miss this. Our friends Penni and Lori," Jamie said, indicating the other women at the table.

After a few minutes of chatting, Liz said, "Hope you enjoy the show." She continued winding through the crowd toward Cassie, who stood to the side of the stage, talking with a woman. Flirting, knowing Cassie. If she had to let anyone take Teri's place, she was grateful it was Cassie. She was one of the best drummers in jazz and a longtime friend.

"You ready, girlfriend?" Cassie's tunic and trademark headband rivaled Liz's scarf for oranges and reds and looked rich against her mocha skin.

"I hope." She made fists with her left hand, praying it didn't fail her.

"I'll get you through it." Cassie put her arm across Liz's shoulders and squeezed. "Wow, haven't seen her around before. I'd remember."

Liz followed Cassie's gaze toward the entrance. Jac. She blinked. Yes. Sandwiched between Peggy and Roger. "That's my friend, Jac Winters," she said, hurrying toward her. God, she was happy to see her.

"Album co-producer Jac? You didn't tell me she was gorgeous."

Liz couldn't take her eyes off Jac. She looked like a mirage in silvery-blue crepe pants, white tuxedo-front shirt, and lacy white vest. Elegant. She was really here. Her chest loosened with each step closer. Peggy smiled broadly as they approached.

"Hi, I'm Cassie." She extended her hand toward Jac, then withdrew it, apparently realizing Jac was blind. She shot Liz a quizzical look.

"Cassie, these are my friends Peggy, Roger, and Jac."

"Cassie James of The Cassie James Band," Jac said. "Your last album was impressive."

Cassie's sunny personality rippled through her laugh. "Thank you."

"Carl Randall," her dad said, joining them. "You must be Peggy and Roger. I reserved a table up front for you." He appraised Jac before saying, "And this must be the famous record producer."

"I need to borrow Jac for a minute." Liz took Jac's arm and steered her around the edge of the crowd. "We're at the bar. Stool in front of you. Red or white?"

"Cab." Jac didn't sit.

Liz felt a hand on her shoulder and turned. Kevin. "Good luck, sis." He kissed her cheek.

"Kev, this is my friend Jac."

"I hear you're quite the wine expert. Let me see if I can impress you." He went behind the bar and poured two glasses.

"You have excellent taste," Jac said, after sipping it.

"I'll have it sent to your table," Kevin said, drinking most of his glass.

"How are you holding up?" Jac set the glass on the bar.

"Better. I'm so glad you changed your mind."

"Had to practice this friend thing. How am I doing?" Jac's face softened into an expectant smile.

"The best."

Jac took Liz's left hand and put something on her palm before sandwiching it between her hands. "I wore this for luck when I performed. You don't have to wear it. Just put it in your pocket."

Liz opened her hand. A gold musical note on a delicate chain. "Put it on for me?" She lifted her hair, and Jac hooked it inside her collar. "Thank you." She put her palm over where it lay against her chest as she stared at the blue eyes, wishing they could see what she couldn't say. She gripped Jac's hand, suddenly dizzy, as the past swarmed around her—a different club, a different audience. The last time she'd been onstage. Teri squeezing her hand before stepping away to the drums. Smiling at her before tapping her sticks together and setting them off. She'd be on her own for—

"It's all right, Liz."

She hadn't realized she'd made a sound. Her throat hurt like she'd swallowed a knife. Wrong. Everything was wrong.

"Liz." Quietly commanding.

Liz took the glass Jac put in her hand, forced wine down her throat. Fear ricocheted through her like lightning.

"You put my name on it. You're not alone."

Liz's heart did a roller-coaster loop, and when it landed she was able to take a deep breath. Not alone. Before she could stop herself she hugged Jac. To her surprise Jac hugged her back. She absorbed the strength and support she desperately needed. Not alone.

"Ready?" Cassie touched her back.

"Yes." She kissed Jac's cheek. "Thank you."

Liz made fists with her left hand as she stood to the side of the stage between Sammy and Regan. Sammy looked relaxed, as always, in his retro fifties-style shirt, fingering his sax. Regan, in tight black jeans and T-shirt, adjusted the strap on her bass and shifted her weight back and forth on her black Converse tennis shoes. She should offer them words of encouragement, but she had none. She felt like she was about to step out of a plane, and she had no idea if her parachute would open.

Her dad stepped to the center mic. "Ladies and gentlemen. Thank you for joining us. Jazz on the Side is proud to be the home of Up Beat. Tonight we're celebrating the release of their new album *Up Beat Live in New York*. I'm also proud to announce that they will be performing at the Monterey Jazz Festival in September."

Liz walked to the piano on unsteady legs. Sitting, she pulled the mic toward her. "We're thrilled to share this special night with you. We'd like to start with 'Fond Memories.'" She shifted on the seat and pumped the sustain pedal, trying to gather herself. She looked toward the audience. She couldn't see Jac, but she was out there. Not alone.

She nodded to Cassie, who counted them down. She and Jac had decided to put this song first because it was her longest solo and her hand would be fresh. It hurt, but she dropped into that place where nothing existed but the music—no past to mourn, no future to worry about, just the present moment and the sound springing from the piano. She sent notes flying through her fingers—playing and playing and playing before withdrawing and letting Sammy's wailing sax pick up the solo. She was vaguely aware of clapping and whistles, but she was too deeply inside the music to care. This was what she loved best in the world.

❖

Jac let out the breath she'd been holding and joined the wild clapping for Liz's solo. The power and beauty of it wound around her heart, blending with her own heartbeat. How had she thought she could miss this? She'd woken this morning knowing she had to come, knowing the need to share this night with Liz outweighed the threat of being recognized. Of course no one would give her a second look in a small jazz club in San Jose.

She noticed minor flaws in Liz's playing, but the band was on fire, clearly in the zone. She remembered how that felt, when time meant nothing and the music felt like a living thing inside and around her. She sat on the edge of her seat, heart pounding, consumed by the music. Consumed by Liz. Forty minutes later she stood to applaud the final song. She assumed everyone was standing, but she didn't care. It was a thrilling performance.

Finally, Liz spoke. "Thank you for helping us celebrate." She sounded relieved and happy. "We're going to take a break and then we'll be back. CDs are for sale by the door, and we'll be there shortly to sign them."

Back? Dad. Damn him. He should have waited to put Liz through this. Making her do another set was crazy.

"Well?" Liz asked from beside her.

"It was breathtaking. Truly." Jac gulped back everything she couldn't say. "I'm so happy for you."

"You're doing really well at the friend thing."

Chills went all the way to Jac's toes when Liz put her hand on her arm. "How's your wrist?"

"Tolerable."

"You don't need to do another set. You'll sell a million CDs and get rave reviews as it is."

"Dad wants a couple more songs. Any requests?"

"Whatever's easiest on your hand." Jac wanted to strangle that man. He and Malcolm were two of a kind. Business. "Are you coming back to Carmel tomorrow?"

"In time for our walk."

"Don't be late." Jac tried to look stern.

"What did you think?" Liz's dad asked.

"He means you." Peg touched her arm.

She knew that but didn't like the man's challenging tone. "Superb."

"Put that on your—"

"Dad!"

"I'd like to use the restroom," Jac said to Peg. Yes, strangle him.

"You should head to the signing table," her dad told Liz. "Half an hour and we'll do the encore."

We? Was it his wrist that was only six weeks out of a cast? She was still seething as she waited in the hallway for Peg to join her. Where were his priorities?

"Jacqueline Richards?"

Panic gripped her and she froze. No. Not this.

"I thought I recognized you sitting in the front row," the woman said. "You wouldn't remember me. I was a freshman at Juilliard when you were a senior. I always admired you." The woman laughed. "Not that everyone didn't idolize you."

Jac braced her palm against the wall, her head spinning. No. That was twenty years ago and a continent away.

"I was hoping I could buy you a drink and we could catch up."

She flinched when someone took her arm.

"Come this way." Peg. "I think there's a rear exit."

"Jacqueline?" the woman called after them.

"Get me out of here." She ducked her head.

"I'm trying." Peg's grip tightened.

"This can't be happening." Who was that woman? How could she possibly recognize her after all this time? She knew the answer. The fame she'd once cherished. A door banged open and she was outside in the hot night air.

"It's all right." Peg loosened her grip.

"No, it isn't." Jac tripped over something. "Were there people around?"

"I don't think anyone paid any attention."

"I shouldn't have come. I knew better."

"You didn't do anything wrong." Peg opened the car door. "I'll get Roger."

Jac slid into the backseat. The door closed and she gripped the edge of the seat, encased in silence except for her heart pounding against her ribs. Adrenaline flooded her, tensing her muscles, and fear coated her tongue with a metallic taste. Was the car under a streetlight? Would someone see her? She pressed the door lock. Calm down. She hadn't just left a concert hall. Autograph seekers and photographers weren't after her.

It seemed like forever before Peg and Roger returned, and then they were on their way back to Carmel. Would it still be safe there?

Would that woman tell others? The press? Would they figure out where she lived? Oh, God, she couldn't face that.

Liz collapsed onto her bed, too tired to take off her shoes. It was after two in the morning. The CD was out in the world. Now all that was left was waiting to see if it was well received.

Her body was vibrating, her ears were ringing, and her skin felt like it had been sandpapered from being around that many people. No sneaking off to a quiet corner while Teri mingled and talked with fans. Had she said the right things? Been enthusiastic enough? She'd have to post something on the website and Facebook. And get a video from the show up on You Tube. And check sales on CD Baby. And make sure Regan got the CDs packaged and mailed to purchasers. The million things.

Jac hadn't stayed for the second set, but that was okay. It must have been exhausting for her in all the commotion and without Max. They'd recap the show tomorrow. She fingered the pendant. Not alone.

CHAPTER EIGHTEEN

Eight, nine, ten...Jac headed back in the other direction, warm slate under her bare feet changing to coarse rug. Her living room felt like a cage instead of a sanctuary. That's exactly what her home would become if the press found her. Anxiety surged up her spine. *What about the accident, Ms. Richards?* The awful tugging in her gut started again, the rip current of guilt that always swept her back to that night. She swallowed more coffee to give her stomach something to churn on.

Had word spread already? Jacqueline Richards spotted in a jazz club? Was the press already looking for her? Damn it. She'd been Jac Winters, protected from having to answer questions about that night, for so long she'd become complacent. Now she'd put her carefully built life at risk the way she'd put her carefully built career at risk ten years ago. And for the same reason—a woman. Her reputation. All she had left of those years. It would be destroyed. She swallowed more of the lukewarm bitterness to chase away the anger and fear.

Liz. Everything was fine until Liz. Until feelings she shouldn't have made her reckless. Now there were consequences. There always were when you let your feelings exist outside of the music, let them rule your life. How many times before she learned that lesson?

She turned up the volume, filling her mind with sound to block out the endless loop of thoughts. Beethoven. Fitting. His turbulent emotions had given power and beauty to his compositions and caused disastrous consequences in his personal life. She'd run through his symphonies by dawn and was now working through his piano sonatas. She stiffened when she heard a knock. Three raps. Peg.

Unlocking the door she said, "I don't want lunch, either." She hadn't been able to eat breakfast.

"Well, I do. I'm starved. Sorry I'm late."

Liz. Late? Oh, damn, they were supposed to walk this morning.

Liz walked past her. "Are you all right? Hi, Max." Liz made smooching noises as she apparently petted him.

"Rough night." Was she still in last night's clothes? No. Sweats. Oh, hell, what difference did it make?

"I'm so glad you were there. It made all the difference. How about I take you to lunch today? I know this great little bistro on Dolores. We'll revive you with wine."

"I'm not walking today." Maybe never again. Carmel's protective stance toward celebrities had lulled her. She needed to be more vigilant.

"Okay. We'll drive. I'm pooped, too. I'll bet you have a ton of comments about the show you're dying to share."

"Go without me." Jac resumed pacing as the next sonata started. Which one was this? Oh, yeah, number eight, "Pathetique," one of her least favorite.

"I want to spend the day with you."

"And I want to be left alone."

"Are you upset with me because I did the second set? Is that why you left?"

She couldn't stand the hurt in Liz's voice. "Someone recognized me."

"At the club?"

"A woman. Said she was at Juilliard when I was. Did you hear anything after we left?"

"About you? No. That's why you left?"

She nodded, or at least she thought she nodded. Eight, nine, ten…turn. She stopped when Liz blocked her path and held her arms.

"Why are you so upset?"

"What if she told people and it got back to the press? I can't face them invading my privacy." *What about the accident, Ms. Richards?* Another shudder of anxiety shot up her spine.

"That seems like a big leap from someone you went to school with saying hello."

"You have no idea what they're like." Poking at her life. Examining it. Judging her.

"I have some idea."

"You're not Jacqueline—" She must sound crazy.

"Don't take this the wrong way, but after ten years, aren't you out of the spotlight?"

"The media is always looking for a sensational story."

"Retired trumpet player...okay, retired world-famous trumpet player living in Carmel is sensational?"

"I want to be left alone!" Tears coasted down her cheeks in the wake of exhaustion and the guilt that had owned her for the last decade.

"Hey, it's okay." Liz hugged her.

She shouldn't let Liz hold her. She should end the friendship. Now. Before her feelings made her any more reckless. The front door opened. Liz let go. Jac crossed her arms, trying to hold in the comforting feel of her.

"I'm glad you're here, Liz," Peg said. "Is everything all right, Jac?"

"No buzz after we left." Jac swallowed the last of the coffee and her stomach growled.

"It's going to be all right, honey." To Liz she said, "We loved the show. You must be elated and relieved."

"And starved. A picnic on the beach?"

"You two go celebrate," Jac said. She wouldn't see it coming. She'd have no way to escape from a reporter throwing questions at her. *What about the accident, Ms. Richards?*

"Not without you," Liz said.

"Take Liz to the beach where I painted her dad's painting. There's rarely anyone there. I'll throw together leftovers for you."

"Beach?" Liz asked, the question apparently directed at Max. His tail slapped the side of the recliner.

She shouldn't. She really shouldn't.

"Come on. I want to talk about the show. If we run into reporters I'll fight them off with forks and knives."

Should she risk it? One last afternoon with Liz and then she'd have to return to the life that kept her safe. "I'll hold you to that promise." Liz wouldn't defend her if she knew what she'd done.

❖

"Dad's going to love these pictures." Liz took another photo of the small cove that Peggy had captured beautifully in the painting. All that was missing were the clouds. It was a beautiful clear day with gentle surf.

"Keep me out of them." Jac tucked her hands into the pockets of her sweats rolled up to her knees.

"What, and miss a chance to make a fortune selling them?" She bumped Jac's shoulder and got the raised eyebrow she loved. She took several pictures of Max chasing the waves, his tail arcing water as it circled. She texted one of them to Peggy, adding, "All good. Having fun." Not quite true, but she didn't want Peggy to worry. Jac was quiet and tense, and she didn't know how to make it better for her. She didn't understand why Jac was so adamant about not having anything to do with the press. She'd been injured in an accident and retired. That didn't seem to warrant her panic about the press finding her. After discovering Jac's identity she'd Googled her and, from what she'd seen, the press had loved her. Some harsh reviews, but no one was immune to that. True, they seemed overly interested in her personal life, but then a female trumpet player of her virtuosity was rare.

Jac took Max's tennis ball from her pocket and teased him by waving it in the air. He crouched, then bounced around her, barking. She threw it and he charged into the surf after it.

"Dad loves the beach. I wish I could get him over to Carmel for a vacation, but he says not until after Monterey. He works too hard. Keeps adding shows to our fall tour. I can't imagine doing any of this without his help."

"It's admirable how supportive he is."

"I thought you didn't approve."

"It's a tough business. You can never have too much support. He reminds me of Malcolm, my ex-husband. He thought the music should accommodate the business." Max nosed Jac's leg. She took the tennis ball and heaved it down the beach.

"He managed your career?"

"Unfortunately. It took me too long to realize he was overbooking and over-recording me. It was always about money with him."

"Grandma had all your albums. I've been listening to them. It's a little intimidating if I think about it too much. Who you are, I mean."

Jac tossed her Max's tennis ball. "Don't think about it."

"Eww. It's soggy and sandy. Or is that dog drool?" Sand rained down on her as she threw it back into the water. She rolled up her jeans and waded in up to her ankles. Thirty seconds was all she could stand before she backed out of it. "Bad, bad dog," she said, as Max shook water and sand on them.

"She doesn't mean it," Jac said, kneeling to ruffle his ears.

"Your family was supportive, if Peggy's any indicator." Max raced toward a seagull that landed on the rocks at one end of the cove.

"Yes, but they weren't involved in the same way. I moved to Los Angeles to study with a teacher when I was ten, and then to New York when I was twelve."

"I can't imagine being away from my family so young."

"I was obsessed with the trumpet and determined to be the best."

"Peggy said your dad was in a jazz band. Why did you choose classical?"

"It wasn't something I decided. I'd been taking lessons from the trumpet player in his band. One day I heard Hummel's Trumpet Concerto in E-flat Major on a classical station in the car. I knew that was what I wanted. As soon as we got home I played a good part of the concerto from memory. They found me a classically trained teacher the next week."

"So the album covers are right that you were a child prodigy."

"I suppose, although I hate that term. I just knew the trumpet made me feel whole, as if it was part of me."

"Same for me with piano and composing. I've always heard melodies. Grandma helped me arrange them. I was lucky to have her. Did I tell you she performed at the Monterey Jazz Festival in sixty-four?"

"She'd be proud of you." A big wave washed up Jac's leg, soaking her sweats. She stopped and turned toward the ocean. "I love this feeling. The shock of cold. The tingle. The sting of salt. Feet sinking into the sand as the wave goes back out."

"Do you have a favorite beach?"

"One in Greece."

"I was thinking locally."

"Sand as soft as a blanket. Water so still it was like a lake." Jac seemed lost in memory. "White cliffs surrounding it. One of the best afternoons of my life."

Liz said nothing as they resumed their walk. How many times had a memory of Teri captured her in the same way? She had no doubt it was a romantic tryst Jac was remembering. With Maria? Jac had looked so heartbroken when she'd told Liz about her. What a terrible night that must have been—rejected by her lover, the accident. "I'd be happy with Hawaii."

"It's beautiful there."

"My dream vacation." All the music experiences they had in common and yet so many ways they were different. Maybe Jac's fame did justify her fears about being recognized. Maybe she was being naive because Teri had handled the press. "I'm hungry."

"Weren't you eating croissants all the way down here?"

"Now that the show's over I could eat and sleep for days."

"It's something, isn't it? The effect performing has on your body?" Jac swished her feet through the ankle-high surf. "I had a specific routine I followed the day of a show, trying to gather and focus my energy, gear it up so it peaked for that short time on stage. Then it would be over, and I'd be left with all this unused energy. It would take me all night to come down. I'd sleep a few hours, practice all day, interviews, rehearsals, and always planning the next recording."

"You make fame seem so glamorous." She laughed as Max lifted his butt and barked at an incoming wave before charging it. "I see a lot of people chasing it. Playing music is all that matters to me."

"That's why you'll be fine. How's your wrist?"

"Okay." She could barely tie her shoes this morning, and lifting anything was out of the question. She should have said no to the encore, but she didn't want to let her dad down. Most bands would kill to have a home club, and she wanted to do her part to make it successful. "Can I keep the necklace until after Monterey? Maybe it'll bring me luck there, too."

"I meant it as a gift." They walked for a while and then Jac said, "There's a tide pool at the end of the rocks up ahead. You should go explore."

"Like anemones and starfish?"

"So I've been told."

"Come with me."

"I'll pass."

"Something I'll bet you didn't do on that beach in Greece."

"You're right. Something I've always wanted to do. Not see starfish and anemones."

"Act blind and I'll treat you like you are." With a bit of "downslope the next ten feet" or "step up," they crossed the rocks and knelt by a shallow pool. Jac swished her hand in the water, and Max eyed the ocean on both sides of the peninsula like he didn't trust it.

"We went to the Monterey Aquarium a few years ago for my nephew's birthday. This is way better than the touch tank. Give me your hand." She put Jac's finger on one of the creatures attached to a rock.

Jac tilted her head, smiling, the tension from this morning gone, but not the fatigue. "Soft. A little sticky. Tentacles. Anemone?"

"Try this one." She moved Jac's finger to another creature.

Jac traced from the center out to each of the five legs. "Starfish. Like leather, only prickly."

"Keep your arm in the water, but pull up your sleeve." Keeping it submerged she set the starfish on Jac's hand.

A smile unlike any she'd seen made Jac's face radiant. Her cheeks were pink, and the wind blew her hair off her shoulders. Beautiful. Sitting back on her heels, she let Jac have the moment. Something soft settled in her belly. She'd made Jac happy. She took out her phone. Peggy would love a picture. She put it back in her pocket. Some moments were private.

"Tickles," Jac said as the starfish made its way up her forearm. Her expression was childlike, as if decades had been stripped away. "Is it safe for it to be out of the water?"

"For a few minutes." So much like Jac. So dependent on its environment. So fragile out of it. Jac's attachment to her home and Max and her daily routines was her world as much as this tide pool was the starfish's. She'd do whatever she could to protect Jac.

"This is better than waves on my feet," Jac said, holding her arm in the freezing water for several minutes while the starfish crawled off.

Max barked, a sharp, alarming bark, just before a wave crashed against the end of the rocks, lunging up toward them like a specter. She hugged Jac to shield her from the icy spray pelting them.

Jac threw her head back and laughed, her arms outstretched. "Do that again," she yelled as the water receded around their legs and Max licked Jac's cheek. "I dare you!"

"Do you want to leave?" Liz asked as they made their way back across the rocks, Max bringing up the rear as if guarding against another attack. They were both soaked and she was shivering.

"No. I want lunch and wine and a long nap."

"Okay, your majesty," she said, mimicking Roger. By the time they left, Jac seemed back to herself, as if the encounter with the wave had jolted her out of her obsession with the press.

Maybe she'd overreacted to being recognized. Maybe, like being ambushed by that wave, it would wash over her without sweeping her out to sea. Jac reached between the seats and petted Max. His fur was soft, almost fluffy, from the salt water. Relaxed and thinking clearly again, she realized the odds of that woman knowing anyone in the media were low. Peg said she looked embarrassed. She probably didn't think any more about it. She'd lay low for a few weeks, and she'd have to stay away from Liz's shows. She'd get her feelings under control before they caused any more damage. Friends. That's all.

Liz stopped the CD and replayed the song. "That's what I love about Ellington's compositions. I think I know what he's doing and then he surprises me."

"Your compositions, too." A few minutes later, tires on gravel indicated they were home. She stepped out and arched her back. Better. "Give me something to carry." She let Max out.

"Take these." Liz put a bundle of towels in her arms.

"Jacqueline Richards?"

Jac jerked her head toward the male voice and hugged the bundle as if it could protect her.

"I'm with the *San Francisco Chronicle*." His voice closer. "I'd like to ask you some questions."

"Go away!" Fear glued her feet to the gravel and her heart lodged in her throat. Ambushed.

"Hey, who are you?" Liz. Footsteps moving quickly on the gravel.

"*Chronicle*. I'm doing an article—"

"Leave her alone!"

"You're Liz Randall. Great. I want to talk to you about your collaboration with—"

"You can't be here," Liz said fiercely.

The house. Which way was the house? Jac took a step and bumped into the car. Damn it. She clutched the towels against her body, disoriented. Max hugged her leg, but he wasn't in harness. No way to escape.

"People loved your music, Ms. Richards, and want to know what happened to you."

"Go!" Liz. "You're trespassing on private property."

"What about the accident, Ms. Richards? You were at the peak of your career. Was that why you retired?"

"Leave me alone!" Jac swung her arm in front of her as footsteps approached.

"I've got you," Liz said, taking her arm.

Her legs quivered as Liz hurried her across the gravel, the reporter firing more questions at them. After what seemed like an eternity, Liz opened a door and she was in Peg's house. She was shaking from the adrenaline. Ambushed. Her worst nightmare.

"How was your afternoon?" Peg asked, when they made it to the dining room.

"There's a reporter out front," Liz said.

"Damn it. I'll get rid of him," Roger said.

"Sit." Liz took the towels and put Jac's hand on the back of the barstool.

Jac slid onto it and gripped the edge of the bar top. Liz held onto one shoulder and Peg the other. The press had found her. *What about the accident, Ms. Richards?* Scandal. Sensation. They'd milk it for all they could. There'd be no safe place.

"He's gone," Roger said.

"It'll be all right," Peg said.

"No." Jac's heart beat nearly out of her chest. Her reputation would be destroyed. All she had left. A strangled groan broke loose. After what she'd done she deserved to lose it. "I want to go home, Peg."

"I'll take you," Liz said.

Too exhausted to protest, she walked on legs that didn't feel like they'd support her. Max stayed by her side. She meant to say good night, good-bye, at the door, but the words wouldn't form as heartbreak stacked onto the fear and guilt. She'd lost her career. Wasn't that enough? Did she have to give up Liz, too?

"I left my car doors open. I'll be right back."

The silence was deafening, and she was cold, and her back pain was bad again. She fed Max and took Advil. After turning on Beethoven she paced, her mind tying itself in knots.

A knock and the door opened. "Roger sent this," Liz said. "If you get it right you get—"

"I'm going to bed."

"Don't shut me out."

"I'm not who you think I am. You don't want to be associated with me."

"Now you're telling me you're not Jacqueline Richards? Here." Liz put the bottle in her hand. "It's dusty and old and probably cost more than I make in a year. I'm afraid to open it."

"Liz—"

"I'm not leaving."

She took the bottle to the kitchen, opened it, and drank, searching for the courage to send Liz away.

"Hey, where's the swirling and sniffing? You can't just drink it."

She loved Liz for the teasing and for so much more. Friendship she hadn't known she wanted and now she had to give it back. "Petrus."

"What year?"

"Seventy-one." The year she was born. She poured a glass and handed it to Liz.

"Holy mother of God. That's like…"

"Enjoy it. Some things don't need to be described."

"Roger said dinner in an hour." The unspoken "I'm not leaving."

Did she have the courage to tell Liz the whole truth? *What about the accident, Ms. Richards?*

"I was thinking," Liz said when they were sitting in the living room. "I have a friend who's a freelance journalist. Give her an interview. Answer the questions about your retirement, but you'll be in control."

"I can't." Jac perched on the edge of the recliner, holding the glass to give her hands something to do. Max's food bowl slid on the floor as he licked it clean.

"Getting ambushed like that isn't right, but you were famous and then dropped out of sight. Millions of people loved your music. You can't blame them for wanting to know why you retired or if you'll perform again."

"There's more to it than my retiring."

"The blindness?"

"More."

"I can't help you if I don't know what it is." Always the kindness in Liz's voice.

"Working with you on the CD took me back. Close to what I had. Too close. I wanted to be part of your world. I used you. Like I used Stephanie." She hadn't spoken her name since that night.

"Who's Stephanie?"

"The woman I killed."

"That's not possible."

Oh, but it was. Jac took a shuddering breath, and emotions imprisoned for a decade broke loose like a torrent over a dam. A sob worked its way up from that cold, dark place. She couldn't hold it back, and then Liz was kneeling in front of her, holding her while hot tears of guilt and anger and loss ran down her cheeks. When the tears finally stopped, Liz let go.

"Here." Liz pressed Kleenex into her hand. "It's the accident. There's more, isn't there? Tell me."

Did she have the courage to tell Liz the parts she'd left out? She didn't want to. She had to. It would be the end of their friendship, but Liz deserved to know. "That night..." Rejected. Confused. Heartbroken. *No divorce. You're going to tell Malcolm it was all a ploy for attention. No, you're not going to start your own production company. If you want this*...Maria running her fingers down Jac's front...*everything stays as it is.* Her nipples tightening from the touch she craved. Maria smiling because she knew it. Grabbing her purse and fleeing.

"The bar I went to...it was a lesbian bar." She was Jacqueline Richards. Someone would want her. No change in the concierge's expression when he said there was one ten blocks away and would she like him to call a cab. The wait on the curb, in the snow, still in the slacks, silk blouse, and high heels she'd changed into before leaving the concert hall. Shivering and pacing, keyed up, glancing back to the lobby, expecting to see Maria running to embrace her, telling her it was a misunderstanding, and of course, they would be together.

"I can't imagine how hurt you must have felt."

She heard the sympathy in Liz's voice. Sympathy she didn't deserve. She should have gone to the hotel bar or gotten another room. So many choices she could have made that wouldn't have ended catastrophically. "I'd never been in a lesbian bar. It was Valentine's Day." Wall-to-wall women. Most dressed up, many wearing red. The unfamiliar music. Leaning against the bar, watching women dance and touch each other. Aching for Maria. So hurt and embarrassed. She trusted Maria. She loved her. How could she be so cruel?

A glass of champagne. Then wanting to dance, to be touched, to feel something other than emptiness. "A woman asked me to dance." Beautiful in a black cocktail dress. Short blond hair. Athletic looking. Nothing like Maria's full-figured dark beauty.

Liz touched her hand. Max scratched and then put his head back on her foot.

"She said she'd been at the concert, lavished me with praise, assured me she wouldn't tell anyone. Invited me to sit with her and her friends. We danced some more." At first the unfamiliar touches felt strange, but then she wanted more, anything to distract her from thinking about Maria. She should have left. She'd put her career in the hands of a stranger. So many bad choices that night.

"She kissed me." Pulling away at first, then kissing Stephanie hard, anything to chase away the ache for Maria. "I got the idea to go back to my hotel with her." Memories swam through her mind—

all those women, champagne relaxing her, someone wanting her. Reckless, but it had seemed right.

"To make Maria jealous," Liz said.

"I used her. I shouldn't have dragged her into my drama." So angry and hurt Maria hadn't come for her. The concierge knew where she'd gone. It wouldn't have been difficult to find her.

Filling her hands with Stephanie to drive away the pain. Making out in the back of the bar. She'd felt sexy and powerful at the time. Now she recoiled from the memory. Her emotions had been dangerously out of control.

"You did what we all do—ran from pain."

"She's dead and I'm not!" Jac clenched her jaw, blinked in vain to stop the tears, and forced herself not to rock with the anguish of it. She continued before she lost her nerve. Liz had to know the whole ugly truth, why she couldn't do the logical thing and give an interview. Why Liz needed to distance herself from any association with her.

"I insisted she come back to my hotel." How dare Maria toss her aside? She'd make her sorry. "She asked the bartender to call a cab, but it was going to be an hour. I was angry and told her she'd have to do better than that if she wanted to be with me. I was desperate to get back to the hotel."

"She said to wait. The next thing I knew, she was tossing car keys to me, but I said she knew the way to the hotel better than I did." All over each other as they hurried to the car. "It was snowing hard, and we were swerving and skidding. We should have pulled over." Cupping Stephanie's breast, kissing her. Desperate to feel something other than heartbreak. "Instead, I told her to hurry. I was scared but so upset I didn't care if we crashed. If I got hurt maybe Maria would care. I unbuckled my seat belt so I could touch her." Sliding her hand under the dress. No panties. Wet. Stephanie spreading her legs and rocking against her. Jac recklessly encouraging her.

"She was laughing and the music was really loud and we swerved some more, only this time we picked up speed. I grabbed for the safety handle and the car slid faster. Then there was screaming and the sound of crunching metal." It had happened so fast. Images flashed across her mind. Bad images. Bile rose in her throat and her pulse bounced erratically. She forced herself to continue.

"The next thing I remember, something hard and cold was under my cheek. I'd been thrown from the car. I couldn't feel my legs, couldn't stop shivering." Squeezing her eyes shut against the pain and the sight of the car crumpled into the corner of a building, steam rising from the hood. "I heard an explosion. Then nothing until I woke up in the hospital." She waited for tears, but all she felt was numb, as if the guilt and grief were all that had been holding her together and now she was splintering into pieces.

"I'm so sorry." Liz slid to the end of the couch and squeezed her hand.

"I can't talk to the press. They'll dredge up the accident. Find out what really happened. I was a married woman who went to a lesbian bar and left with a woman. That woman died because of me."

"I remember reading about the accident, but I don't remember any of this."

"Malcolm contained it to avoid publicity that could hurt my career. He didn't know about the divorce papers at first. He'd never tell me the details, but Stephanie's family didn't want her name in the papers. It was reported to the press as a one-car accident. It's my fault she's dead, and I have to live with that. If I hadn't lost control of my emotions…if I hadn't wanted to make Maria jealous…if I hadn't been touching Stephanie in the car…" Oh, God, she was responsible for a woman's death. She clutched the armrests as guilt and remorse shredded her.

"It was an accident. A tragic accident that changed your life. No one will blame you."

"They already have. Malcolm." Furious when he found out about the divorce. Furious about the bar. *How long have you been making a fool out of me?* Thank God he never found out about Maria.

"He's hardly impartial."

"And my teacher did." Jac cringed. Twenty years she'd studied with him. Twenty years his opinion had been the only one that mattered. She'd woken in a haze of pain in the dark hospital room. His face in the glow from the monitors, constricted with rage. His eyes pinpricks of contempt and judgment. He hadn't needed to say a word.

She covered her face. Max nudged her leg. He needed her reassurance and she had none to give him. "I knew better than to fall in love with Maria. I knew better than to let something be more important than the music. I didn't care. God help me, I didn't care. I let my emotions rule me. I lost the career he gave me. I killed someone. I deserve the blame." Tears were everywhere. Spilling out of her eyes. On her hands. On her chin. Sliding down her arms.

"It's all right." Liz was holding her again and it felt so good, like Liz could hold her together.

She wasn't strong enough. She wasn't. Her emotions were running away with her again and there would be consequences and she couldn't help it. She wrapped her arms around Liz and burrowed into that place she'd wanted to be since dancing with her. She pressed her face into the crook of Liz's neck and let it be all she felt. Warm skin. Her perfume mixed with the smell of the ocean. Pulse skipping against her cheek. Liz's hands rubbing her back. Soothing words. The world was alive with the sensation of Liz. When her tears stopped, Liz's hands stopped. Gradually, gently, she was deposited back to reality. She dried her eyes and blew her nose. She drank wine. She waited.

"Who's this teacher?"

"The one I moved to New York to study with when I was twelve." The flight to New York with her parents for the audition. All nerves as they walked up the steps to his apartment off Central Park. Her parents waiting while she was ushered into a windowless room. Putting her trumpet together with shaking hands as he stared at her from his wheelchair. Taking her hand and kissing it when she was done. *Excellent. Now we will make you divine.* "I wanted to be the greatest trumpet player in the world."

"You got your wish."

"It was an honor to be his protégé." How proud she'd been. "He said it would take total dedication, that I'd have to give myself to the music and only that. Distractions were for those in the orchestra, not those in front of it. He was right. I almost lost my career before it started." All he'd done for her, and in the end she'd failed him.

"What do you mean?"

"My first professional performance. The Boston Philharmonic Youth Orchestra." Did any of this matter? The press would dig out the details of the accident. The scandal of being in a lesbian bar. The scandal of being responsible for Stephanie's death.

"Jac?"

"At the private high school I went to for kids like me." She reached for Max. Loyal. Loving. He wouldn't blame her. "No one liked me much except one of the girls, an artist...we became friends. Instead of practicing, I'd sneak off with her. She was fun and it was exciting and I felt different when I was with her. It affected my concentration. The rehearsals were a disaster. The conductor yelled at me. My teacher was furious. I'd embarrassed him and he threatened to send me home. When he found out why...the girl wasn't at school the next day. I never saw her again."

"Oh, Jac. You didn't do anything wrong. You acted like a kid."

"I wasn't supposed to act like a kid. I was a professional musician." The scorching rebukes for weeks afterward. *Don't waste my time if you're not serious. How dare you let anything be more important than the music! Music! Your life is the music now!* Conductor's baton tapping against his perfectly creased black pants. His face so red she'd been afraid he'd have a stroke. The long, grueling practice sessions for months after.

"He sounds harsh."

"He made me what I am. What I was. Classical isn't like jazz. It's rigorous. He opened doors for me, created opportunities I wouldn't have been offered without him."

"He fed off your immaturity and made you conform to some ridiculous idea that music is somehow separate from life. We get emotion from life and feed it back into our music."

"When he played...there was so much emotion in it...like it was coming from inside me—joy, sadness, excitement, love. I would shake listening to him."

"That's how I feel when I listen to your albums."

"He taught me well. He taught me to find the emotion in the composer's notes and translate it through my trumpet so it was accessible to an audience. He taught me to become the music. He said that in order to do that I'd have to sacrifice my emotions and give myself completely to the music."

"Whether I play Brubeck or Bach, Ellington or Beethoven, I'm not trying to channel them. I'm trying to find what's personal in their music for me."

"He said emotions left to wander free outside the structure of the music were dangerous. He was right. When I fell in love with Maria, my feelings for her became more important than the music, and look what happened. I lost control. A woman died."

"I'd bet your love for Maria went into your music and gave it qualities it didn't have before. My love for Teri was always at the core of my music as well as my life. Love enhances our relationship to everything, including music."

Was that true? If anyone but Liz had said it, she could discount it. Those months she was with Maria, critics had raved about a new maturity in her playing. Her teacher was pleased. She'd never connected it with her love for Maria. She'd been terrified he'd find out about the affair. She was breaking the rules again. So many rules—how you held the trumpet, how you controlled your breath, how you practiced, how you dressed, how you ate, how you answered questions from the press. Devoting yourself to the music. Saving your emotions for the music. "An innocent woman died because I let my emotions take control."

"She died because of snow and slick roads and driving when she shouldn't have."

"She wouldn't have been in that car if I hadn't lost control. I used her." Liz didn't understand. "She's dead!"

"So are you!"

It hit her like a slap. She flattened her head against the recliner. Liz. Her face so close she felt her breath. Jac gripped the armrests so she wouldn't reach out for her. *Don't lose control. Don't do something foolish.*

"Locked up here with self-imposed guilt…" Liz's voice was gentle, soothing. "Hiding from your teacher's judgment…judgment you didn't—"

"It's the life I deserve." The guilt yanked harder.

"It wasn't your fault."

The whisper wormed its way inside her. Peg had told her that a thousand times. And now Liz. Was it true? The words burrowed deeper, sidled up to the edge of that whirlpool of regret and guilt. "That's not what the press will say. You don't want to be associated with me when it comes out."

"I already am associated with you because of the album. I'm not Maria. I'm not leaving you."

"You should."

"Haven't you paid a high-enough price?"

Coaxing, inviting words. A lifeline. Dare she reach for it? For the absolution Liz was offering? Liz, who'd been through tragedy and loss of her own?

"Hanging onto guilt gives you the security of thinking you could have changed the outcome. I want to believe that if I'd noticed Teri was tired..." Liz's voice broke. "If I was responsible, then I can do better next time. I can save someone I love. I can keep myself from hurting the same way. It's easier than believing it wasn't my fault, that it was beyond my control. The accident was just that. You loved and you got hurt and something terrible happened. It's not your fault."

Guilt pulled hard, handcuffing her to that night, to the darkness. Liz cupped her cheek. She wanted to grab her hand. Life. She wanted to let Liz unlock those handcuffs and pull her from the darkness.

"What are you afraid of?"

Longing washed through her. A new pain. This is what she was afraid of.

"I was afraid of playing again without Teri. I was afraid of making a CD and keeping the band together. I was afraid of going on without her. I'm not any more, because of you. I couldn't feel anything but sadness and loss. Now I have a future because of you. What are you afraid of, Jac?"

"You. I'm afraid of you. You made me feel again." Oh, God, had she said that out loud? "Music. You made me feel music again. I'm afraid I'll end up hurting you."

"I don't see how that's possible, but I'll take my chances. You helped me live again. I want the same for you."

Jac sucked in air and reached for Max as Liz backed away. She wanted to argue that her life was fine the way it was, but she knew that was no longer true. Liz had changed everything. Liz had brought music back into her life. Liz had brought love back into her life. The guilt was still there, but she resisted giving in to the current that was trying to whisk her back to that night. She'd been a part of what happened, but was she to blame for it? She was no longer certain, and that scared her. The guilt felt safer.

Liz opened the French doors and cool air trickled into the room. "Come on. It's a beautiful evening and I'm hungry again."

Jac didn't move. She had no more control over her feelings for Liz than she'd had over her feelings for Maria, and it terrified her.

"Don't let Malcolm or your teacher speak for everyone. Give the interview. Tell the truth. If I'm wrong, you keep yourself locked up here. If I'm right, and the accident is seen as just that, with two victims, you start living again. I dare you, Richards." Liz took her hand and tugged. Max nosed her other hand as if in agreement with Liz.

Part of her wanted to stay right here, in her safe and ordered world, away from the judgment that scared her more than isolation. But there was Liz's hand, strong and sure, and the offer of friendship she desperately wanted. Jac took a deep breath and stood, each step like heaving herself away from the binding weight of guilt. For this one night she didn't want to be alone.

CHAPTER NINETEEN

"Jac! Wake up!"

She was on her back. Why couldn't she see anything? A scream. She jerked. The car. Stephanie. She had to get to her. Where was the car? The dark was pierced by an orange blaze and a blast of sound and hot air. She tried to get up, but her legs wouldn't obey. She tried again, concentrated on pulling them up to her chest. Had to get up. Her legs moved, and searing pain in her back sent her tumbling back into the darkness and the scream that wouldn't stop.

"Jac!"

She had to get up. Her feet weren't on the ground. Where was the ground? She fought her way up. Stood. Arms wrapped around her as she fell forward. She hit the ground and pain sizzled through her back and down her legs. "Noooo!"

"It's all right."

Max licked her hand, then her face, and Jac knew where she was. And whom she was lying on. Last night. Dinner. Coming back here to talk some more. Sleepy. She must have fallen asleep. Liz must have slept on the couch. Her head was on Liz's chest. She tried to sit up and bit back a groan.

"What's wrong?"

"My back." No hot tub or exercises or muscle relaxer last night. Sleeping in the recliner. With her back already hurting, it had been a setup for disaster. She took deep breaths, trying to calm the panic and ease the pain. She hadn't had nightmares in years. "I can't do this." *I don't want to remember. I don't want to feel.*

"What do you need?"

"Leave. I need you to leave me alone." Jac rolled onto her back and bent her knees, trying to ease the pain.

"No."

"I'm entitled to my privacy."

"Okay. I'm officially assigning myself to see that you have it. Damn it."

"What?"

"My wrist." Liz sat up. "Some pair we are. Blind. Bum wrist. Bad back. Brokenhearted." Liz giggled. It grew to a laugh and she kept laughing.

Liz's laughter felt like a waterfall cascading over her, and Jac wanted to stand under it and let it wash away the fear and guilt and loneliness. She started to laugh. She didn't want to. None of this was funny. "Ow." Spasms seized her back, but she couldn't stop laughing as tears rolled out the corners of her eyes.

"Oh, gosh, I haven't laughed like that in so long I'd forgotten what it felt like. We have to be friends, Jac. Who else has been through what we've been through?"

"Go live your life. You don't need me anymore." She tucked her elbow against her side when Liz tickled her.

"Wrong answer." Liz tickled across her stomach.

"Don't." She grabbed for Liz's hand but missed.

Liz tickled the tops of her feet. "What? Did you say yes, I want to be friends with you?"

"Not fair." Jac flopped onto her side and curled into as much of a ball as her back would allow. The pain mixed with the tickling into a confusion of sensation. Max was dancing around them, and she figured by Liz's squeals that he was licking her face. "All right. You win." They were acting like children. She wanted to be angry, but it felt good.

"Say it."

"We can be friends." Jac struggled onto her back, resting her hands on her stomach, catching her breath.

"Close," Liz said, poking a finger into her ribs again. "I want to be friends with you. Say it."

She'd never wanted to see someone's face more than she did at this moment. She reached up, caught the ends of Liz's hair. Soft. Thick. She put her thumbs in the indent of Liz's chin and laid her fingers along her jaw. Her skin was warm and smooth. She moved her thumbs up to her lower lip. Warm breath puffed against her fingers as she went around her mouth. Twice. Liz was smiling and she ached to see her.

She put her fingertips on each side of Liz's nose and traced her cheek—the fleshy part and the bone, the dip under her eyes. She moved to her forehead, across and back, then her eyebrows. And lastly to her ears, slipping her fingers under the cape of hair hanging over them. She wanted to cup her cheeks but didn't. Her pounding heart reminded her she wanted to do more than that.

Setting her arms back on her stomach, Jac entwined her fingers to stop the trembling. "I want to be friends with you." Warmth flowed thick and slow through her body. She was happier than she'd been in a long time. The guilt over the accident was still there, but she was willing to let there be something else, too.

"It's been a long three days," Liz said, lying on her side with her head on Jac's shoulder. "You're not still planning on running away to your parents in Hawaii, are you?"

Last night's plan of escape. "No. I'll be lucky if I can get off the floor."

"I was serious about you staying with me."

"I may take you up on it, but I need to deal with the reality of my life. I was responsible for someone's death, and that's not going away."

"It was an accident."

"One I could have prevented."

"Has imprisoning yourself for the last decade brought Stephanie back?"

Jac tensed and pain shot up her back. "That's not the point."

"Isn't it? Famous trumpet player living as a recluse in seaside town? Will shutting yourself off from the world for the rest of your life bring her back?"

Jac's chest rose and fell in a staccato rhythm as breathing became hard and tears filled her eyes. "Got Kleenex?" she asked, trying to be funny, but the words caught in her throat.

"Settle for a T-shirt?" Liz turned Jac's head into the crook of her neck.

Jac's chin touched soft cotton, and her nose fit into a nook below Liz's ear. She pressed her hand against her stomach, willing the sob to stay put. Max lay next to her, his body stretched along hers.

"It's okay. You're human."

The sob gathered in her belly, climbed up through her chest, forced its way out her mouth. She grabbed for Liz as other sobs chased it—the new, fresh sobs about her lost career, then the heartbroken sobs about Maria, and finally, the old, angry, guilty sobs for Stephanie. "She was twenty-two," she choked out in broken syllables. "Only twenty-two. I would have traded places with her."

"I know. Me, too."

Jac touched Liz's cheek. She was crying, too. They held each other for a long time until no more tears remained. Friendship and love tangled together, so much more powerful than what she'd felt for Maria. She rolled to her back and wiggled her butt on the floor.

"How bad does it hurt?"

"Not as much as before." When it was this bad it never improved without weeks of chiropractic and massage, ice and anti-inflammatories.

"Shall we get you up?"

Liz moved away, and the loss made her heart fall in on itself. Of course Liz wasn't hers. She rolled onto her side. The pain was bearable.

"Give me your hand."

She did, and Liz helped her to her feet.

"How is it?"

"I can manage."

"Wrong answer. Friends don't get all 'I can do it myself' with each other. We're gonna have a lot of tickling before I get you trained."

"Now that's something my teacher never tried. You know what I want? A shower."

"Um, you're on your own for that."

"Could you make coffee? Unless you want to go home."

"I was invited for brunch, but I need to go home and shower, too. No coffee until I get back or you know what will happen."

Jac liked the teasing. Maria never—She cut off the thought. Halfway down the hall she stopped. "Liz?"

"Yeah?"

"Thank you." She started toward her bedroom, but Liz stopped her and wrapped her arms around her waist. A hug from a friend. So simple, but the wonder of it wasn't a small thing. Max nudged her leg and she put her hand on his head. Liz covered her hand. Friends.

"I'll be on time, Kev." Liz held the phone to her ear as she forked two more pancakes onto her plate. It was hard to hear him over the conversation. Roger opened another gift, and more laughter erupted when he held up the apron that said WHINE TIME.

"I'm going to strangle her. She didn't get the damn tickets."

Liz didn't have to ask who the "her" was. She rubbed butter on the pancakes and poured syrup over them. "Did you look for tickets?" Every year they got her dad concert tickets for Father's Day. This year was supposed to be Pat Metheny at the Mountain Winery.

"Sold out."

"I'll pick him up a shirt and tie in Carmel." Why couldn't Hannah ever be responsible?

"We always give him concert tickets."

"Sometimes always doesn't happen."

"They hold tickets back for VIPs. Can Jac score us some?"

"Jac? Why would you—"

"Dad told me she's that blogger."

Liz clenched her jaw. He'd promised he wouldn't tell anyone.

"I'll see what I can do." Jac was laughing at something Roger said. She looked younger. She looked happy. What a terrible burden she'd carried, believing she was responsible for someone's death.

Liz understood guilt. She'd always wonder if they would have beat the leukemia if they'd come home and started treatment sooner. She knew that wasn't any more logical than Jac blaming herself for the accident, but the guilt was there, sticky and hard to shake. She thought back to the tide pool and Jac's radiant smile. She wanted to give her more moments like that.

Liz walked around the table to where Jac was sitting. "Can I shamelessly impose on you?" She explained the problem.

"I'll make a call tomorrow."

"Thank you."

"It's what friends are for."

Liz kissed Jac's cheek. Friends who trusted each other and had shared much. Peggy caught her eye and lifted her cup. "Thank you," she mouthed, and then laughter erupted again as Roger opened another gift. She had friends. She had a life. She checked her watch. She could get used to the new band. And if she didn't hurry, she'd be late for her family's Father's Day party.

Chapter Twenty

Liz walked into her dad's backyard, just a bit late. It had been hard to drag herself away from brunch and from Jac. Peggy had assured her she'd keep Jac busy so she wouldn't go back to worrying about the press. Tomorrow she'd call her journalist friend about interviewing Jac.

"Sunshine," her dad called. His skinny legs stuck out below Bermuda shorts, and he wore the Diana Krall T-shirt from the concert they'd taken him to last year. He was pushing Kevin, Jr. in the swing.

"Not so high," Karen called, holding the back screen door open.

"It's all right," her dad called back, pushing him higher. Robbie kicked his legs up wildly in the adjacent swing.

"Kevin, I want to talk to you," Karen said.

Kevin shoved out of the chair, set the *Wine Spectator* magazine on the table, and drank the rest of his wine before walking to the house. His shorts and Polo shirt were rumpled like he'd slept in them.

Liz sat in the third swing. Her thighs squished together, and she wrapped her arms around the chains.

"I helped Regan get the CD orders mailed out yesterday," her dad said, giving her a push. "And posted three videos on YouTube."

"Thanks." She should have done those things, but all she'd wanted to do was celebrate with Jac.

"Okay, big guy, you ready? On three." Kevin, Jr. went sailing out of the swing. His squeal of delight turned to a scream of pain when he landed facedown on the ground.

Karen burst through the screen door and ran to him. "Let me see," she said, taking his face in her hands. "His chin's bleeding."

Liz hopped off the swing and knelt next to him. She fingered the scar under her chin. Same swing.

"He's a champ," her dad said, patting the boy's back.

"He's an eight-year-old." Karen gave Liz's dad a withering stare, holding her son as he cried.

"Let's go find a superhero Band-Aid," Kevin said. A look passed between Kevin and Karen before he carried his boy to the house.

"Robbie, come with me," Karen said, holding out her hand. "Mommy needs your help with something important." She let the screen door slam behind her.

"He's tougher than she thinks. He'll be fine," her dad said. "I have a surprise for you." His expression had an odd smugness. "Let's go to the study where we can talk." When they were inside his study, he turned on the desktop computer and angled it toward her. "*Chron* review."

"I don't read—"

"Read it."

She sat behind the desk and read. The first paragraph lavished praise on the album—one of the best of the year, a must-see band with a bright future. That was good. It singled her out for her composing, and the reviewer analyzed some of her songs. Okay. Then raved about her performance. That made her uncomfortable. It hadn't been her best.

The album was co-produced by—Liz's heart vaulted into her throat. *Jacqueline Richards, under the name Jac Winters.* No. How— She jerked her head up. Her dad was grinning. Liz put her hand to her throat. "Oh, no." The review continued about the influence Ms. Richards had on the album, said she was the voice behind the blog *Jazz Notes*, now lived in Carmel, and finished by speculating on whether this signaled she would be returning to the stage herself.

"I didn't recognize her either. Odd that she didn't tell you."

Liz ignored the ping of guilt for keeping that from him. She pressed her palms to her cheeks as she stared at the screen in disbelief, willing it not to be true. Oh, God, this was going to undo Jac.

"You got lucky, sunshine." He grinned again, a too-smug grin. "And you have me."

"What do you mean?"

"I overheard a woman telling her friend she couldn't believe she'd run into Jacqueline Richards. I recognized the name. Imagine someone that famous in my club."

Liz listened with growing dread.

"I asked if she was still here and she said no, but then told her friend she didn't know she was blind and went on about knowing her at Juilliard." Her dad looked like he'd just filled in the last word on a *Times* crossword puzzle. "You should have seen the *Chron* reviewer's expression when I told him Jacqueline Richards came to your show. When I told him she'd produced your album, I thought he'd fall off his stool."

The reporter yesterday was because of her dad? "I told you about Jac in confidence." Her voice rose.

"It's important to have a good relationship with the press. You won the publicity lottery, sunshine." That grin again.

"You sicced the press on someone you know nothing about?" Blood rushed to her face as she shoved out of the chair and faced him.

"She's a public figure." Irritation tinged his voice.

"She's my friend, Dad."

"Not if she didn't tell you who she was."

Liz braced her hand on the desk, dizzy as understanding dawned. Her words came out slowly, as if she had to invent each one. "You told him about Jac in hope of a favorable review."

"You were so close last year and lost your dream again because of Teri's illness," he said, as if consoling a child. "I don't want you to lose it again. She'd agree with what I did."

"No, she wouldn't."

His expression hardened. "Teri understood the game."

"We got gigs and great reviews because of our music."

"Grandma was as good as you, but how many people came to her living room to hear her perform?"

"That's not fair."

"I'm good enough to play professionally. Do you see me on my own stage? Talent isn't enough. Timing. Breaks. Publicity. Teri understood that."

"It's my band now."

"You keep doing what you do best and let me handle the rest." He put his arm over her shoulder and guided her to the door.

Liz scurried upstairs to her bedroom. She needed to think. She felt sick to her stomach. Oh, God, she'd have to tell her. Jac would never speak to her again. The look of panic on her face when the reporter confronted her. Her heart-wrenching story last night about the accident. She was in the hallway, headed downstairs for her phone, when she heard Kevin and Karen in his old bedroom.

Karen's voice was low but furious. "Do not let him put them on those swings again. He does what he wants without caring about consequences."

"He does a lot for us," Kevin said, sounding irritated.

"No. We do a lot for him," Karen shot back.

The door opened and Kevin barged into Liz, his mouth a hard line. She steadied herself with a hand to the wall below a picture of her at the piano as a child. He hurried down the stairs as Karen appeared in the doorway.

"Are you and Kevin okay?"

"We're seeing a marriage counselor." Tears pooled in Karen's eyes.

"I'm sorry." Their marriage had always seemed solid.

"What your dad did to your friend? It's not right." Karen gave her a quick hug before heading down the stairs.

Liz slunk into her bedroom and collapsed on the bed. No, it wasn't right. Would Teri have agreed with him? The thought shot her to her feet. Of course not. She needed to call Jac. How was she going to explain this? Two steps into the hall she stopped and looked at her dad's closed bedroom door at the end of the hall. Other voices. A memory she'd forgotten. High school. An English test the next day and she'd come up to get her notebook.

"It's an important gig," her dad said, his voice loud even through the closed door.

"She has a test tomorrow," her mom countered.

"I'll quiz her on the drive. We agreed we'd do whatever it took to help her get her dream."

"Her dream? Are you sure about that?"

"Do we have to force her to practice? She deserves her shot, Alice."

"Does that have to include taking her to bars?"

"I won't let anything happen to her. He's a big name. It was a lucky break his piano player got sick. I told him I'd give him a little something if he let Liz solo a bit. She'll get reviewed. It adds up. She'll get noticed by bands looking for pianists."

"She has a band."

"They're all right for another year."

"They're her friends."

"She can have friends or she can have the career she deserves. I wish I could talk her out of going to UOP. It's an unnecessary detour."

At dinner her mom acted like nothing had happened. She'd received great reviews for that show and it had led to other offers. Was she naive about the business?

When she went back downstairs, everything seemed the same. Rebecca was scrubbing potatoes in the sink. Kevin was in his chair on the patio, reading his magazine. Karen was kicking the soccer ball around on the lawn with the boys. Her dad was pulling weeds from between his prized tomatoes. And yet everything wasn't the same.

Car doors slammed, and a minute later Sammy and Regan walked into the backyard. "Hey, Pops," Sammy said, high-fiving him. "Awesome review," he said to Liz, bending his tall frame to hug her.

"Happy Father's Day," Regan said, her usual six-pack of Coke in her hand. She gave Liz's dad a one-armed hug that was more just leaning toward him. She ignored Liz and went to the kitchen.

Liz followed her. "Sorry I wasn't around yesterday to help with the CDs."

"Whatever." Regan put her Coke in the refrigerator.

This would go nowhere if she didn't ask the question. "What's wrong?"

"Nothing. Job got done."

"Regan—"

"I get it. We're so lucky to be in your band now you're hooked up with that famous woman."

"That famous woman likes her privacy. Like you. Now she has reporters hounding her."

"She gets credit. We get publicity. What's the big deal?"

"Grow up, Regan." Liz grabbed her cell from her purse. She was vibrating with anger as she stormed out the front door, slamming it behind her. She was long past caring about don't-slam-the-door rules. What were the rules? Anything was fair game for the sake of publicity? She was across the lawn and heading down the street when Regan caught up to her, hands buried in her pockets. "Don't you ever wear anything other than black?"

Regan stopped. "Fuck you. When you were given only one pair of new jeans and T-shirt a year and a mom who couldn't sober up long enough to do laundry or give you quarters to do your own, black didn't look as dirty."

Liz bent over and gripped her knees as laughter poured out of her. She was going to lose a friendship she didn't want to lose. She'd argued with her dad and she hated arguing. Now she was being mean to someone she loved. It had been a bad day and the sun wasn't even down yet. All she saw through eyes blurred by tears were the black Converse tennis shoes an inch from her sandals. "That's more words than I've heard from you in months," Liz said when she could breathe. She straightened, unsure what to expect. A smile barely broke the straight line of Regan's mouth. "Hug me, damn it."

Regan did. A real, full body hug, complete with a shuddering breath. "I'm sorry about your friend. Jac. That's not right she was outed like that."

"I need to make a call."

"Want me to wait for you?"

"No. I won't be long." Liz walked a block before making the call, wishing she didn't have to. No answer from Jac. She called Peggy. "I saw the review," she said when Peggy answered. "How is she?"

"Bad. She got a migraine. She's asleep finally."

She dropped to someone's lawn and cradled her head on her bent knees. "It's all my fault."

"You couldn't have known where this would lead. I want to strangle that woman who recognized her. I thought Jac was overreacting about her saying something to the media. Boy, they wasted no time. When she wakes up, I'll tell her you called. You earned the review, Liz."

"No, I didn't. I'm coming down in the morning. I need to talk to her."

"I can't guarantee she'll be up to it, but I'm always happy to see you. How's your party?"

"Not so good." She ended the call and continued around the block. She felt awful for not noticing what was going on with Kevin and Karen. Her dad's thoughtless behavior confused her. Come to think of it, Rebecca hadn't been her usual cheerful self lately, either. When had things started to unravel? Maybe it was for the best she wouldn't have a reason to be in Carmel. She needed to be here. When she got back to the house, Hannah was getting out of her car.

"I suppose you're not speaking to me, either."

"It's a big thing not getting the tickets."

"I forgot. I'm sorry. I've been busy with the restaurant and—Oh, never mind. God forbid if I'm not Hannah who always screws up."

Liz started to scold her but stopped. There were circles under her eyes and she'd seemed stressed lately. "Jac's going to get us tickets."

Hannah smiled. "See, I keep telling you, it's all about who you know. Good time in Carmel yesterday?"

"Not exactly." As they walked to the backyard, she filled Hannah in on what had happened.

"Why does Dad do stuff like that?" Hannah asked, disgust in her voice.

"He wants what's best for all of us," she said, but not with her usual certainty.

Hannah snorted. "You still believe that? He wants what's best for him."

She didn't defend him. They joined Rebecca in the kitchen. Yes, she was quieter than usual. Liz helped Hannah bake the chocolate cake they always had when the party was for her dad. This time Hannah didn't dress it up.

On the surface, dinner was the event it always was, but she noticed undercurrents of tension between Kevin and Karen, and Rebecca was definitely too quiet. Kevin, Jr. kept rubbing the neon-green Band-Aid on his chin. And in the middle of it all, her dad was his usual boisterous self, seemingly oblivious to the discord around him.

"Music time," her dad said, after he'd opened his presents.

"I'm taking the boys home," Karen said.

"Nooo," Robbie wailed, grabbing onto her dad's arm. "I wanna play with Grandpa."

"Whoa, big fella. Real musicians don't cry. Have you been practicing the chords I showed you?"

"Yes." Robbie beamed.

"Let's hear you." He took both boys by the hand and led them out of the living room. "Practice needs to be rewarded," he said as he passed Karen. "Why don't the boys spend the night?"

"Yay," they cried in unison.

Karen folded her arms, her face tight. "Does he ever not get his way?"

"You know how important music is to him," Liz said.

"Robbie plays that guitar your dad gave him because he wants the praise, but he loves baseball. Does your dad come to his games?"

"I don't know," Liz said, afraid there was a lot she didn't know. "I guess I haven't been paying attention since Teri's death."

"It's always been like this."

"Come on, Liz," her dad said from the back door.

"My hand's not up to it, Dad."

"You can do a few songs."

"I'm going home," Karen said, not looking at Kevin as she walked out of the room.

"I'm taking off," Hannah said. "Don't get upset, Lizzie. The condo's a little messy."

An hour later Liz joined Kevin on the patio. Her left hand hurt like hell. Why hadn't she just said no? "You should take a couple weeks off while the boys are out of school."

"Do you know what kind of mess I'd come back to?"

"Dad would—"

"He's terrible at running the restaurant. Mom ran it. He likes to talk to customers and come up with advertising schemes."

Liz rubbed her forehead and then drank some of Kevin's wine. "Why don't I know this?"

"You've always been kind of separate." He lifted one shoulder. "Promise me something?"

"What?"

"The band? Do it your way. With Teri gone, Dad's—"

"Did I hear my name?" Her dad walked toward them, the boys tagging along behind. "Why don't you boys run upstairs and put your pajamas on."

"They need a bath first," Kevin said.

"What do you think, boys? Bath or a story?"

"Story," they said. "Read us a story."

"Come on," Liz said to the boys. "Race me upstairs. Last one to the bathroom gets first bath."

"Liz—"

"It's fine, Kevin." She squeezed his arm.

"I'll be back in a bit," her dad said. "I want to check on the club."

"If I took them home would he even notice?" Kevin asked, after they'd tucked the boys into bed.

"Not until breakfast." A pattern Liz had never recognized before took shape. Her dad disappeared for the grunt work. Tomorrow morning he'd make a big deal out of cooking pancakes and bacon for the boys. Something he loved to do. A troublesome thought crossed her mind. Would they be as close if she hadn't become a musician?

"I've gotta go make up with Karen." Kevin gave her an unusually long hug.

Her dad was in the kitchen when she went downstairs for another piece of cake. "Is Rebecca all right?" She hadn't stayed to listen to them play. She was usually the last to leave.

"Fine. We need to start putting together your set list for Monterey. I've been thinking about it. We should open with—"

"I'll choose the set. And Dad? Don't do anything like what you did with that reviewer again." He looked hurt. She didn't care. "If the band makes it, I want to know we made it on our talent and hard work, not because you wheedled a review by violating someone's privacy." His face tightened. "Did you even think about the fact that the album will be seen as her creation? That all the years of work Teri and I put into the band are now irrelevant?"

He looked away, his jaw muscles working. "When you calm down, you'll realize I did the right thing."

Liz went to her bedroom and flopped onto the bed. She wasn't up to facing the messy condo. She'd started the day sure of her friendship with Jac and optimistic about the band's future. Her relationship with Jac would probably end tomorrow, and she was going to have to rethink her dad's role with the band. Messy. All of a sudden everything was messy.

CHAPTER TWENTY-ONE

L iz pulled up to the closed gate across Peg's driveway. It was like pulling up to a prison, and she was responsible. She shouldn't have told her dad about Jac helping her with the CD. She shouldn't have put Jac's name on it. She pressed the buzzer, her stomach churning. She'd give anything not to have to deliver the bad news. After a minute the gate swung open and she drove slowly over the gravel, probably for the last time.

"How is she?" Liz asked when Peggy opened the front door.

"I was about to take breakfast to her."

That was good, right? She followed Peggy to the kitchen.

"Coffee?"

"Please." Maybe they wouldn't throw her out before she drank it.

"Congratulations on the review in the *Merc*. I'm happy for you. Jac said your album got great reviews from other jazz bloggers."

"Thanks." It should matter, but at the moment it didn't. Liz carried the tray of food as they walked to Jac's. The fog was starting to burn off, and sunlight brightened patches of the blue-gray ocean. Peggy set breakfast on the dining table and poured Jac's coffee.

"Did you get hold of Mom?" Jac walked into the living room, brushing out her hair. She was wearing her fisherman-knit sweater over heavy pants. Max was by her side. He didn't come over to Liz like he usually did.

"I left a message."

"Don't go to Hawaii. I am so sorry." Liz gripped the back of the recliner, staring at Jac.

"Liz?"

"We want to give them a head's up about the article," Peggy said. "In case reporters—"

"It's my fault." Liz's breath caught in her chest. "My dad. He told the reviewer."

"Your dad?" Peggy asked, her voice accusing.

She watched Jac. All that mattered was Jac's reaction. Her heart felt ready to shatter. Every good thing that had happened this year was because of Jac. "He overheard the woman talking to her friend. He put the pieces together. He told—" She clenched her jaw. It wasn't her place to cry.

Jac's face softened into a sad smile. "He traded me for the guarantee of a great review."

Liz nodded and couldn't stop. If she kept her head moving she wouldn't fall apart. Peggy's mouth was open and her eyebrows rose, but all she cared about was the tender expression on Jac's face, not at all what she'd expected.

When that truth settled Jac said, "He didn't like that I helped you with the album." She walked toward Liz and stopped inches from her. "Do you like the album?"

"Yes." Tears filled Liz's eyes.

"You know you deserved a great review anyway, right?" After a minute Jac lifted her eyebrow. "Right?"

"I guess." Jac's eyebrow went higher. "Yes." She couldn't pull her gaze from Jac's blue eyes that seemed to take in every part of her. Liz's chest loosened and tension drained from her like water down a drain. They were still friends.

"Every review of the album so far has been great. It's the tribute you wanted it to be. Now keep me company while I eat?"

"Yes." She nodded and tried to swallow, and then she was hugging Jac and everything was all right in a way it hadn't been since Teri's death.

❖

"Fog's coming in." Jac lifted her face to the cool breeze after taking off Max's harness. Home. No one had approached them on their walk. She imagined her blog's email was flooded with requests for interviews. The door to her past had been opened and she'd have to face it, but not today. She'd always regret the choices she made that night, but maybe she didn't deserve all the blame. Liz's understanding and support now countered her teacher's accusing voice. This friendship had become the center of her life.

"Come to dinner?" Liz asked when they reached the patio. "I want to try a recipe from the new cookbook. You can bring the wine."

"Deal. What time—"

"There's my lovely Jackie."

Jac stiffened at the sound of her ex-husband's British-accented voice. "How dare you come here!"

"How dare you do an end around? 'No, Malcolm, I'm done with music. I'm just a blogger'. Now you produce an album, and rumor has it you're going to make a comeback." He snorted his contempt. "Did you think I wouldn't find out?"

"It's none of your business."

"Everything you do is still my business."

"Not that album."

"Perhaps. But that mediocre little jazz album will sell like hotcakes because your name's on it."

"What do you want?" She forced the question out as anger seared through her.

"Exactly what I've been saying for the last six months that you've been ignoring me." His voice was an angry singsong. "We need to capitalize on this being ten years since you retired. You agree to cooperate with the release of a best-of compilation celebrating your illustrious career. Thoughts on the pieces and composers, personal touches like what tea you drank before such and such a concert…you know the drill."

"And?" There was always something else. She was going to be free of him once and for all.

"Those four albums you owe me."

"Yes to the anniversary compilation on several conditions." Jac walked to the patio table and stopped in front of him, close enough that he couldn't stand up. She'd never liked his cologne. "I have complete artistic control over content and remastering. Fifty-fifty split. The

Carmel Bach Festival gets my share of the profits. You release me from my contract."

"You can't be serious. You forget I can ruin your reputation with a phone call to—"

"Someone beat you to it. I've scheduled an interview with a journalist. I'm coming clean about the accident. I should have done the honorable thing ten years ago. I'll take what judgment comes." She stepped back and held out her hand. "Deal?"

"Ten years you give me the runaround? And now—"

"You'll make a fortune. Take it or leave it. Be quick about it. I have a dinner engagement." Bluff. Pure bluff. She hoped he went for it. The silence stretched.

"Sixty-forty split," he said.

"Fifty-five, forty-five."

"You drive a hard bargain." He stood and shook her hand. "I taught you well."

"No, but I learned anyway."

"I'll have the papers drawn up. Aren't you going to introduce me to Ms. Randall?"

"No."

He laughed, and then what she assumed were his same ridiculous Italian loafers clipped across the patio.

"Wow," Liz said, nudging her shoulder. "That was a great impression of Jacqueline Richards. I assume that was your ex-husband?"

"Malcolm Phillips. Greedy bastard. Guess you'd better call your friend. Nap time." She headed toward her cottage, anxious about the outcome but feeling in control of her life for the first time in a decade. "What kind of wine should I bring?"

"Old cab."

Jac wiggled her fingers over her shoulder. Accidents. Some she ached to undo. Others were a precious gift.

CHAPTER TWENTY-TWO

*L*iz *kept her eyes shut, trying to hang onto the dream. Onstage, by herself, lights so bright she couldn't make out anything but the piano and a black curtain behind her. She was playing a new version of "Carmel Sketches"—bits of blues and swing, bits of what sounded like a fugue, some of the choppy Brubeck-like chords she loved. Music came from behind the curtain, faint at first and then louder. An orchestra. When she stopped, applause erupted from an audience she couldn't see.*

Opening her eyes she clamped down on the music running through her head. She wanted to laugh as she dashed for her grandma's piano. Jac was rubbing off on her. Fusion of jazz and classical wasn't new, but it was a new style for her. She'd been stalled on the arrangement of "Carmel Sketches." This was a welcome breakthrough. She couldn't wait to share it with Jac. She'd do her wrist exercises, take a shower, run to the bakery for the bear claws Jac liked, and be there early for their walk. Jac's eyebrow would go up, but this time in an amused way instead of a scolding "you're late again" way.

In the kitchen, she poured water into the coffeemaker. Enough for one. "What do you think of the new piece?" she asked Teri's picture on the bar top. She could still remember Teri's voice, but any answers were from the past, as was the smile that never changed. Kleenex was no longer part of her attire. Sadness captured her at moments, but she also had laughter and joy in her life. Being alone didn't scare her. She could start a fire. She was managing the band. She'd sold the Yukon and bought a used convertible, something she'd always wanted. She was composing again. Her life was moving forward. She was keeping her promise to Teri in spite of herself.

Blue sky and cool air greeted her on the patio. She settled in one of the cheerfully painted chairs by the new table. Well, a used table she'd bought last weekend at a garage sale with Peggy. She'd painted it yellow, and Peggy had added colorful flowers across the top. She sipped coffee and studied the garden, running through the Latin plant names Peggy was teaching her. "It's coming back to life, Grandma. Not exactly like you had it, but it's beautiful." Two juncos tossed water over their backs in the birdbath, and a jay pecked at a feeder hanging from the Japanese maple they'd pruned back into shape. It felt like home.

An hour later, bakery bag in hand, Liz hurried down the walkway to Jac's. She heard music coming from the cottage. She stopped and listened. That wasn't just music. That was a solo trumpet playing a sophisticated classical piece. Beautifully. By the time she reached the door her hands were clenched. Something else Jac had lied about. She couldn't sound like that without practicing regularly.

She knocked, then knocked louder, but the music continued. Finally, it stopped. As she brought her hand up to knock again, the piercing sound of a single high note, like the cry of a raptor, pinned her in place. The note went on and on and on. At last, it tailed off with such torment that Liz's breath caught in her chest. She understood that kind of pain. A long silence followed, and then she heard Jac cry out, "Max! Oh, God, no!"

She tried the door. Locked. She pounded. In seconds it was opened. The look of panic on Jac's face made her heart leap into her throat. "What happened?"

"Liz? Max. He's hurt. Hurry. Oh, God, I hurt him."

She rushed past Jac and found Max standing in the living room, blood on the floor by one of his front feet. Dozens of CDs and their shattered plastic cases littered the floor around him. She recognized the covers. Jac's albums. "Let's see what happened, big guy." She knelt and lifted his paw. He was as calm as Jac was frantic.

"How bad is it?" Jac knelt beside her, breathing fast, oblivious to the broken bits of plastic under her knees and bare feet.

"His paw's bleeding. Hold him so he doesn't step on anything while I get a towel." She hurried to the kitchen.

Jac held his collar and stroked his head, telling him over and over how sorry she was.

Liz brushed bits of plastic out of her way and knelt again, holding Max's paw and blotting the blood away. "There's a cut on the side of one of his pads."

"Where?" Jac worked her fingers down his leg and cradled his paw.

"Here." Liz put Jac's fingers on the cut.

"Noooo." Tears ran down Jac's cheeks. "We need to get him to the vet."

"I don't think it's that bad."

"I can't take the chance."

"Don't move until I sweep up. I don't want either of you cutting your feet. Broom?"

"Closet by the door." Jac held Max's collar again, rubbing his chest, her cheek on his, murmuring to him. The anguish on her face was heartbreaking.

What must it be like not to be able to see your beloved partner and make sure he was okay? Whatever had driven Jac to destroy her CDs had hurt her worse than it had Max. His wound was superficial. He'd be as good as new in a few days. What would it take to repair the damage to Jac? She pondered these questions during the ten-minute drive to the vet and the doctor's examination and assurance that nothing more than a compression bandage and topical ointment were needed. The trip home was equally silent.

"Thank you for taking care of him," Jac said when they'd walked to her cottage. She opened her door and stepped in, Max at her side.

"Wait a minute." Liz blocked the door from closing and followed Jac inside. "He's going to be fine, but I'm not sure you will."

Jac went to the kitchen and came back with a handful of dog biscuits. She walked Max to his bed and sat on the floor next to him, blood on her slacks. She fed him and stroked his back. Max rested his bandaged paw on her thigh. Partners.

"What happened?" She sat next to them on the warm slate, feeling like an interloper.

"It doesn't matter."

"Come on, we had a deal. Don't shut me out."

"I forgot I'm not Jacqueline Richards anymore." Jac's voice was sharp with bitterness.

"You miss being her." Liz scooted her back against the recliner, deliberately bringing their shoulders in contact. "I was going to surprise you with being early today. I heard you. I think you fudged the facts a bit about how much you play."

"I'm sorry. I wasn't ready to talk about it."

"I understand. It's your sanctuary. You've been playing all along, haven't you?"

"Not the first couple of years after the accident, but then...I couldn't live without it."

"What happened today?"

"I got caught up in the return of Jacqueline Richards—working on the anniversary CDs, the warm reception from the Bach Festival, your friend's enthusiasm for my music when she interviewed me. It's easy to say I'll never perform again, but..." Jac shook her head, still stroking Max.

"Hard not to want to." Weeks away from the piano and months without performing had left her feeling lost and edgy. She couldn't imagine how hard it had been for Jac the last ten years, deprived of the thing that had been at the center of her life. "Are you sure you can't?"

"My range is still what it was, but it would take years to restore my embouchure. I don't have the breath control, endurance, fingering technique..."

"Do you want to try?"

"I don't want people coming to see me out of sympathy or curiosity, comparing me to who I was. It's best I stay retired."

"Why haven't I heard you except for that one time a few months ago?"

"I usually practice in my soundproofed office and never when I know you'll be around. This morning I rebelled at the confinement."

Jac alone like that was more than Liz could stand. "Play with me."

Jac shook her head.

"I used to do a mean Bach." She nudged Jac's shoulder and got the raised eyebrow. "Let's borrow Peggy's piano." She waited. So much was at stake. Jac's heart and soul, and any chance she might perform again.

Jac frowned as if deep in thought, and her hand stilled on Max. Several minutes went by. Finally the hard lines of her face softened. "Are you sure you can keep up with me?"

Liz let out a sigh of relief as she pulled Jac up. "Let's find out."

Jac held her trumpet against her body as they walked to Peg's. It was a beautiful coastal summer day, sunny with a cool breeze. Max ambled along next to them.

"He's darn cute in the purple bandage."

"Is he limping?"

"Not a bit."

"I don't deserve his love," Jac muttered.

"You deserve love more than anyone I know. We'll work on the dating thing." Cassie had been asking Liz to set her up with Jac.

"No dating."

"We'll see."

"My sheet music is in Peg's office," Jac said when they were in the dining room. "Alphabetized by composer. Bach's Concerto in D Major."

The house seemed too quiet without Peggy in her kitchen, and Liz missed the yummy food smells that usually came from it. "You better be here when I get back." She headed toward the office, remembering the last time she'd been in it and the shock of discovering Jac's real identity. Now she was going to accompany her on Bach. She was as excited as she was nervous.

❖

Jac knelt beside Max, where he'd curled up on the bed in the corner. She rubbed his leg above the edge of the compression wrap. She'd lost control again and he'd been hurt. He licked her hand.

"He's all right." Liz squeezed her shoulder. "Give me a few minutes to warm up," Liz said, as she scooted the piano bench back and lifted the keyboard lid.

Did she want to do this? Peg had offered, but Peg wasn't Liz, and that's what it came down to. She wanted to know what it felt like to make music with Liz.

"That wall of pictures still freaks me out. Two presidents. A who's who of conductors. A queen?"

Jac wasn't that woman any more, and she didn't want Liz treating her as if she were. She fingered her trumpet, trying to gather the courage to do what she wanted to do. "Liz?"

"Mmhmm."

"Play a song from your album." Her stomach jittered.

"I want to play with you, not for you," Liz said.

"'Mad Dash.' Please?"

"All right, but then Bach."

Jac listened. Did she dare? Liz was almost to her favorite part. Heart pounding uncertainly against her ribs, she lifted the trumpet to her lips and joined in. Liz faltered but didn't stop. There would be questions, but right now all she wanted was the connection with Liz. She could have continued all day, but finally the song came to an end.

"You? Jazz?" Accusation mixed with confusion.

She sat next to Liz. "I dabble."

"You improvise pretty well for just 'dabbling.'"

"You liked it?" Her stomach went soft the way it did around Liz. "I've been working it out for weeks."

"I don't understand."

"I've been practicing to your CD through headphones hooked to my computer."

"You…my music. That takes some getting used to."

"Can we keep going?"

Liz started something that sounded like "Carmel Sketches." It wasn't a version she'd heard before.

"I can't improvise."

"You might not be able to do it on the spot, but what you did with 'Mad Dash' is original, sophisticated, and technically brilliant." Liz continued for several minutes. "This is why I came over early. I heard it in a dream. A new arrangement of 'Carmel Sketches.'"

"It's your sound. It's you, Liz."

"I'm scared. Where do I go from here?"

"Keep working with it. Let it evolve. I hear Ellington and Brubeck and Bach. How bad can that be?"

"How about we toss in some Richards?" Liz repeated the melody line, then again with chords. "Key, melody, and chords—that will give you the harmonic possibilities. Then stop thinking and let the music lead you."

Jac fingered the valves, both scared and excited. Could she do this?

"Play with me."

She lifted the trumpet, terrified she'd make a fool of herself but unable to refuse the invitation. When they stopped, Liz started again and Jac did better. The third time better still. By the fourth time, she was truly improvising. Music. Liz. Her heart beat with a new rhythm. Finally Liz stopped. Jac held her trumpet to her chest, breathing hard, sweat running down along her hairline. Happier than she'd been since before the accident.

"Jac? Oh, my God." Peg. Her voice shaky. A second later Peg wrapped her arms around Jac. She was crying. "I've dreamed of this. You have no idea..." Peg held her for a long time, laughing and crying. "Have you two been practicing when I'm not around?"

"First time," Jac said.

"What happened to Max, and why do you have blood on your pants?"

"Long story," Jac said, sitting beside Liz again. "I like the arrangement."

"Something's been missing in it. Now I know. It was you."

Jac didn't know what to say. That was a lot to digest. She'd imagined what it would be like to play with Liz but had never thought it a reality.

"It's a bit of a shock." Liz laughed nervously. "How did you learn jazz?"

"I haven't heard this story either," Peg said, pulling back a chair at the dining table.

"I went to a jazz club one night in New York." An act of pure rebellion after a vicious scolding from her teacher. "The sound did something to me, wound its way inside me. It was raw and powerful and mesmerizing." Dark, smoky, the quintessential club, so far from the concert halls she was used to. "Don't get me wrong, I listened to jazz, but I never felt it before, not in a way that made me have to explore it." In a way that made her ache all the way back on the subway, that made her wake up the next morning determined to master it.

"So, you studied formally?" Liz asked.

"I didn't dare. My teacher would have been furious." Jac shuddered. "I bought albums of the great jazz trumpeters and studied their techniques and styles. Experimented on my own. I kept going to clubs, the lesser-known, the better. I'd hang around after the last set and ask the musicians questions about jazz theory. 'You gotta feel it,' they kept telling me. 'Don't think. Feel. Don't get it right, just get it.'"

"Good advice. It's not easy to teach yourself jazz," Liz said, admiration in her voice.

"You never considered performing both?" Peg asked.

"I'd finally decided I was going to. That's part of what Maria was upset about. I wanted to start a production company and record with some of the musicians I'd heard in those clubs. Amazing musicians who deserved to be heard by a larger audience. I told her everything."

"Damn that woman."

"It's over, Peg." Jac knelt next to Max. He rolled onto his back for her to rub his stomach. Forgiven. Would Liz forgive her for keeping another secret?

"So you were letting yourself put your own feelings into the music through jazz," Liz said.

"I couldn't stop it any more than I could stop myself from falling in love with Maria. I'd become so arrogant. I thought I could have it all and, like Icarus, I was slapped down."

"Passion isn't wrong," Liz said.

"I can't forget that a woman died."

"Put those feelings into your playing. Transform them."

Was that possible? Were all emotions fuel for creativity? She loved the precision of classical and the challenge of searching inside the music for a connection with the composer, a way to bring their intentions to life for an audience. She loved the freedom of jazz where the personalities of the musicians, the place, even the culture at the time, came together in a sound that was always fresh, always new.

"This is for you," Peg said to Liz, setting something on the dining table.

Liz went to the table, and Jac heard the sound of paper tearing. Peg had told her she'd done a painting for Liz.

"Oh, Peggy, it's beautiful," Liz said.

"Your garden when it fills in."

"The future," Liz said quietly. "I have a painting of what the future looks like."

Jac startled when Peg sat beside her and hugged her again. So many things she'd kept secret from Peg and she now regretted it. She'd allowed guilt and fear to make her a prisoner, cut off from anyone and anything that could make her feel.

"This calls for a celebration," Peg said. "Stay for dinner, Liz?"

"On one condition," Liz said.

"Old cabs?" Jac asked.

"Oh, I'm in the mood for plenty of old cabs. I'm also in the mood for more music."

Jac smiled and tears stung her eyes. "Me, too." Practicing to Liz's album had patched something inside that had been broken for ten years. Collaborating with Liz might heal it. She'd thought long and hard since telling Liz about the accident. The guilt was still there, but not a rip current that made her powerless. She'd set events in motion that night but with no idea how things would end. She was human and she'd paid a high-enough price. She wanted music back in her life. She wanted Liz in her life.

She fingered her trumpet. Dare she let out the full spectrum of her emotions? Into the music? Into her life? The thought was thrilling and frightening and she had no idea where it would lead, but she'd go anywhere with Liz. "Let's do something else from your album. Then you can teach me more about how to improvise." That's what her life felt like lately—improvising around her friendship with Liz. It was a better life than she'd thought possible.

CHAPTER TWENTY-THREE

The leather booth in Regan's favorite diner creaked as Liz crossed her legs. She kept stirring the iced tea, although the sugar and lemon had dissolved. She was afraid to see Regan's reaction to what she'd just told her. Regan hated change, and she was pretty sure the band was headed for more change.

"Jac plays jazz?" Regan asked as she maneuvered an edge of the massive burger into her mouth. Her cheeks pushed out as she chewed.

Liz nodded. They'd been practicing every day for the last two weeks, hours on end. Some of the best music of her life. She dipped a thick-cut fry in ketchup and nibbled it. She had to admit it was yummy.

"Wrist is okay?"

"Great." It ached if she did too much, but it was getting stronger every day.

"She any good?"

"Yep." That was an understatement. Jac's talent was one thing to read about or hear on an album and another to witness in person. What she lacked in improvisational skills, and those were getting better by the day, she made up for with a tone that could melt butter and technique that allowed her endless creative possibilities. Liz felt a responsibility to nurture such enormous talent, and that scared her.

"That's cool she knows both jazz and classical."

"Cool? That's it? I thought you didn't like her."

"I never said that." Regan sucked on the straw in the stainless-steel blender cup.

"Since when do you drink chocolate shakes instead of Coke?"

"Since I like them. Is she going to join the band?" Regan salted her fries and then salted them some more. Where was the usual resentment of anything new?

"No. I don't know." The question that wouldn't go away. Jac seemed oblivious to the possibility. Peggy hadn't brought it up, but she could see the question in her eyes every time they played. "She's Jacqueline Richards."

"And you're Liz Randall. One of the top jazz pianists in the country, according to the article in the *Merc* after our show last week. Does she know our stuff?"

"Yeah." Jac worked out an improvisation to another song on an almost daily basis, as well as new variations on others. Peggy said she played late into the night. It was like she'd been let out of a cage and was making up for lost time. When they weren't practicing, they worked on arrangements. "I've been composing again." She'd been waking up and going to bed with new music swimming through her head.

"For the band, right? Not just you and her."

"For the band."

"When do we get to hear it?"

"It's not our sound. I've been fusing classical into it."

"That's been done. Modern Jazz Quartet, Mingus…" Regan shrugged one shoulder. "I know more than blues."

"I don't know where all of this is coming from. Honestly, I don't know where I'm going with it."

"Do you like it?"

"It's different."

Regan sucked down more of her shake. "It's not Teri."

Oh, God, she was going to cry. Liz nodded, a lump in her throat.

"I don't want to let go of Teri, either, but that doesn't mean we should stop new things from happening."

Why was Regan talking in sentences? Several at once? And embracing change? "Why aren't you wearing black?"

Regan gave a half smile and her eyes softened. "Dark green's pretty close. You want a different band?" Regan asked, looking away from Liz.

"I want this band, but I hear the new pieces as a quintet. Sometimes a full orchestra."

Regan slid fries around in the ketchup on her plate. "We wouldn't be having this conversation if you weren't considering her joining us."

"I don't know." She was barely used to Cassie on drums. Could she face another change? And Jac? It would alter their dynamics as well as their sound.

"What does she say?"

"I haven't talked to her about it. She doesn't want to perform again."

"She's gotta miss it. Do you want me to talk to her?" Regan smiled. "Just kidding."

"When did you get a sense of humor? Oh, gosh, I'm sorry."

"Nah, I deserved it. Life's better lately." Regan studied her plate, bangs obscuring her eyes. "I'm kinda with someone."

"That's great. When do I get to meet her?"

"You already have." The sheepish grin was adorable. "Vic."

"Vicky?" Of course. She should have realized. Regan was still part of her band, and Vicky had been to their Thursday-night gigs at the club. She'd thought they had their heads together talking music.

"Have a thing for redheads." Regan grinned for an instant.

Liz poked Regan's hand. "Smart, gorgeous, good heart, great musician…I'm happy for you."

"I want what you and Teri had. Sorry. That didn't come out right."

"It came out perfect."

"I'm different when she's around, like together we have a new sound." She smiled. A happy smile. "Bring Jac to a rehearsal."

"I'm not sure she would."

"Tell her to be there or I'll come get her on my bike."

She laughed. Jac on the back of Regan's beat-up motorcycle would be a sight.

"Can she jam?"

"Not at our level. I have her doing some of the same ear training I had you and Sammy do." Every day Jac had more questions about jazz theory. It was exhilarating, and a bit intimidating, to be teaching Jacqueline Richards.

"Bring her. I'll go easy on her." Regan winked. Actually winked.

"Dessert, ladies?" the waitress asked.

"Nah," Regan said, running her palms over the edge of the table, her heavy silver rings clunking over it. "Is your dad okay?"

"Yeah, why?"

"It's cool how much he cares," Regan said, looking serious. "But the new videos he's posted on the website? That's kind of weird."

"What do you mean?" The waitress cleared their plates, and Liz rested her forearms on the table.

"The ones of you as a kid."

"I didn't know." Liz shook her head. He wasn't himself lately—distracted and forgetful in a way she hadn't seen since her mom's death. "I'll talk to him tonight."

Regan nodded. "Gotta get back to work." She fished in her pocket and laid a twenty on the table. She was fanatical about paying her way. She knuckled the table next to Liz's hand. "It's your band, not his."

Liz nursed her iced tea, trying to gather her thoughts. Her dad was doing a lot of what Teri had done, especially booking shows and managing the website. She was grateful, but this new fascination with her past made her uneasy.

When the waitress asked again if she wanted dessert, she ordered a sundae. She wasn't sure which conversation she dreaded more—the one with her dad or the one with Jac about playing with them. Jac deserved to be back on a stage, and she couldn't deny that she was now a key part of Liz's new music. Whether Liz liked it or not, things were changing.

Chapter Twenty-four

Jac flew through notes on her trumpet, still not sure this was a good idea, but Liz had asked, and she'd do anything for her. That's why she was here in this stuffy room that smelled of sweat and old carpet, playing with people she barely knew, hoping she didn't embarrass herself. It was her fourth rehearsal with the band. Better than the last three, but still not good enough. She loved this song, and Liz's solo was coming up.

Sweat trickled down her neck, and she blew moisture from her trumpet as Liz took center stage. She tilted her head. There it was again. More evidence that something was wrong with Liz, besides the lack of her usual chattiness. Her playing had changed in the last week—less vibrant, less daring. Today it was lifeless and flat. Sad. You couldn't hide from your instrument. Was it the jazz festival? School starting in a few weeks?

Finally, she and Sammy joined in, and the song took off as Liz faded to the background. She let go of thought as she poured her emotions into the music, giving it everything she had. Life was risky and messy, and she could put all of that through her trumpet. Transform it. Liz had. She'd let grief and loss take her to a new place, but it hadn't destroyed her. Instead, new compositions were pouring out of her. A sound uniquely Liz. It was breathtaking, and she loved being part of what she was sure was the birth of Liz's future.

"Let's run through 'Carmel Sketches,'" Liz said. They worked on it several times each rehearsal and, although Jac wasn't privy to all of what happened with the band, she knew this was the test piece. If Sammy and Regan could shift into this jazz/blues/classical fusion that was evolving in Liz's music, she'd introduce more of her new compositions.

Jac had been waiting for this all evening. She'd worked out a new variation for her solo and wanted to surprise Liz with it.

"Rebecca has dinner ready," Liz's dad said. Like it mattered when the food was prepared in a restaurant kitchen. He didn't like "Carmel Sketches." She'd heard him complaining to Liz about wasting time on it. This band could bang out their signature songs in their sleep. Regan and Sammy seemed energized by the challenge, bringing more to the song with each rehearsal. Being part of the song's evolution was thrilling—so different from having a single run-through the day before a concert with an orchestra that was often less than welcoming to the star soloist invading their turf. Collaboration. A new way to experience music. She loved it.

"We'll be there in a bit," Liz said, sounding tired.

Jac blew a riff, hoping he'd leave. Out of respect for Liz, she hadn't confronted him about telling the reviewer. She didn't like him, or trust him, one bit.

"Hannah's waiting on us," he said.

Hannah probably wasn't in the neighborhood yet. She liked Liz's sister—feisty and outspoken, but under it all she clearly loved Liz. Lizzie. Jac had called her that a few times because it was fun to tease her.

Liz counted them off, and the song began with piano and soft cymbals. She waited her turn impatiently, her forearm muscles contracting as she fingered the valves. Primed. Finally, she put the trumpet to her lips and blew a single note, holding it like a seagull soaring, while under her the band played a rolling melody like the ocean. She and Sammy passed the melody back and forth, sax and trumpet trying to outdo each other, like two gulls high in the sky. He was giving her a run for her money today. Then it went into her favorite part—Liz's long, complex solo inspired by her enjoyment of Carmel's art galleries. It was subtle, with richly voiced chords and superb phrasing. Beautiful and emotional. Tears stung Jac's eyes every time she heard it. Then it was back to the ocean Liz loved and Jac's next solo. Five minutes later the song came to its gentle conclusion. She waited. Had Liz liked the new version? Silence. Then clapping.

"Those are some chops," Sammy said with his usual enthusiasm. He was like a puppy you just had to love. He'd endeared himself at the first rehearsal when he'd put Jac's palm to his face and said, "Hi, I'm Sammy." She didn't like being touched by strangers, but his move broke the tension, and Regan and Cassie jokingly followed suit.

"Better," Regan said, nudging her shoulder. This was a serious compliment in her no-frills style.

Last week, Regan had talked to her after rehearsal, a pep talk in a few short sentences about how she herself had sucked at jamming in the beginning. Their generosity was overwhelming and not at all what she was used to. The world of classical was harsh, or maybe she'd brought that out with the arrogance she now regretted.

"Sweet cakes," Cassie crooned. "Be still, my heart."

Jac smiled. She liked Cassie's warmth and humor, but not her interest in a date. She waited. Finally, she sensed Liz next to her.

"You could have given me a head's up." Tired, but pleased.

"And ruin the surprise?" She tightened her grip on her trumpet. She wanted to pull Liz to her and offer comfort for whatever was bothering her. All the long hours with Liz were glorious and the hours apart filled with an ache she'd never felt before. She was more in love with Liz each day and had no idea what to do about it. So she poured all that feeling into the music. "Did you like it?"

"It was beautiful. You're hearing more subtle things and responding to them."

"You're a great teacher."

Sammy started an old Coltrane standard. Regan picked up the rhythm and then Cassie. Jamming. They did it at the end of every rehearsal.

"You can do it," Liz said.

"No." She was getting better at improvising with Liz, but listening to several musicians and trying to fit in, that she wasn't up to. She walked to the too-soft couch and sat on the edge, reaching down to rub Max's head. He loved all the attention the band lavished on him.

"Take it easy on your hand," Liz's dad said from the doorway.

Did he know something she didn't? Was it hurting again? Maybe she'd pushed her too much. Damn it. She'd been soaking up Liz's time and attention with no thought for her. Finally the song ended, and then Liz sat beside her.

"We're going to do it again, and we want you to join us."

"No." She fingered the valves on her trumpet.

"Jazz isn't about being concert perfect. You're ready for this."

"Come on," her dad said, annoyance in his voice. "Dinner."

"We're not eating until you jam with us," Sammy called out. "And I'm hungry, so get your butt over here."

Cassie tapped her sticks together. Regan kept plunking the same annoying note. An invitation.

She did know the song. What if she came in on…she stood, her fingers trembling on the valves. She took her place between Sammy and Regan.

"We got your back," Regan whispered in her ear. "There are no wrong notes."

Jac put the trumpet to her lips, as nervous as the first time she'd stood in front of an orchestra, and shut out everything but listening and responding. She was breathing hard when they finished, but she couldn't stop smiling.

"Not bad for a stuck-up critic," Regan said, teasing in her voice. "You'll do."

"Whoo-hoo! Sign that girl up," Cassie said.

"Yeah, I can play with her," Sammy said.

A scary thought ran through her mind. Was that an audition? She walked to her trumpet case, took out her mouthpiece, and started wiping down her trumpet.

Sammy said, "Let's eat, Pops."

Regan said, "Missed you" to someone, probably Vicky. The door closed behind them.

"'Carmel Sketches' will be our encore at Monterey," Liz said, standing beside her. "I want you to perform with us."

Jac sank to the couch, emotions racing through her. Excitement. Panic. "It's not smart. What if reaction to my interview is harsh? I don't want it to taint your appearance."

"I don't care what public opinion is. I know you. What makes you think I'm not shamelessly using you for publicity?"

"I know you, too." She clasped her hands to keep from touching Liz and swallowed the words that were always in her heart. *I love you. I'd do anything for you. I want to be part of your life.*

"Then it's settled."

"What about your dad?"

"It's my band."

"I don't know—" Liz hugged her and words left her. Liz in her arms. Liz's cheek against hers. A shudder and tears. Liz's tears. "What's wrong?"

"Nothing." Liz stepped back and then the sound of her reaching into her pocket. She was back to needing Kleenex again.

"Is your wrist okay?"

"Almost a hundred percent. Let's get over there before Sammy eats everything."

The door banged open. "Hey, Jax," Hannah said. Apparently she took liberties with everyone's name. "I need to talk to you. Walk with me." The moment with Liz was gone.

"This conversation isn't over," Jac said, as she picked up Max's harness.

"Orange is Max's color," Hannah said as they walked toward the street. "He needs an orange harness."

"No, he doesn't."

"Okay, an orange bandana."

"Maybe." Hannah made everything seem like a good idea. "Topic?" she asked, or Hannah would be off on another tangent.

"Oh, yeah. Birthday. Liz's. The thirty-first of this month."

"That's what's bothering her." The first one without Teri. That was big.

"You're sharp. I like that about you. I also like how much better Lizzie's been since hanging out with you. So, we need to rescue her from this God-awful idea Dad has for her birthday. He wants to have a surprise party for her at the club and invite all her friends, who were also Teri's friends—a blast from the past."

"He wouldn't." Jac shuddered at how awful that would be for Liz.

"He would."

"Why don't I throw a party for her? An old-fashioned barbecue with hot dogs and hamburgers. A bonfire and roasting marshmallows on the beach. She loves the beach." Something she could do for Liz.

"Beach is exactly what I had in mind. Just a little farther west. I have an ex-girlfriend who's a manager at the Hyatt Regency on Maui. Your parents live on Maui. Voilà."

Jac stopped. "You want us, you and me, to take Liz to Hawaii? In…twenty days?"

"A couple less. Her birthday's on a Sunday, and I want to leave the Friday before. Come back on Monday. She starts classes on Tuesday. We'll make it an end-of-summer hurrah. Oh, yeah, I forgot to tell you that Teri's birthday was three days after Liz's."

No wonder Liz was sinking again.

"She'll need all kinds of distractions, and I have some ideas. We'll keep her so busy she won't have time to mope."

"Isn't your dad going to be upset?"

"That's the beauty of it. He can't be. You announce at dinner that your parents just called and want you to come over for Labor Day weekend, and you'd really, really love it if Liz would go with you since you're blind and haven't traveled and all that."

"What if she doesn't want to go?"

Hannah snorted. "Hawaii or weird party at the club?"

"Let me make a phone call. I'll be over in a minute."

"I'll wait. I don't need you getting crunched crossing the street and ruining our plans."

"Some of us use crosswalks."

"What fun is that? Stick with me and I'll show you how to live dangerously. Can I take your gorgeous dog for a walk while I wait?"

"Sure." She handed Max off to Hannah, amused by Hannah's constant chatter to him. She'd barely left Carmel in ten years. Hawaii. It was crazy. Could she? Her parents were back from Australia and would be thrilled if she visited. "I need you to listen to something totally impossible," she said when Peg answered, "and then help me figure out how to do it." She explained Hannah's plan.

"First thing tomorrow I'm taking you shopping," Peg said. "You are not wearing wool pants and sweaters to Hawaii. Shorts, sleeveless tops, swimsuit…"

Jac half listened as pictures of walking on the beach with Liz ran through her mind. Four days in paradise with her. Her life had become the biggest improvisation of all, and she loved every minute of it.

CHAPTER TWENTY-FIVE

Liz jerked awake and sucked in a breath. Hannah was nudging her elbow on the armrest between their seats. She rubbed her cheek. She remembered closing her eyes, but how had her head ended up on Jac's shoulder?

"Look." Hannah pointed out the window of the plane. The thin strap of her flowery sundress slid from her shoulder, and she pushed it back up.

"Which one is Maui?" Liz leaned across Hannah. The islands were tiny dots of green in the churning blue of the ocean.

"Second from the bottom," Jac said. "Good nap?"

"I've had softer pillows." Liz got the raised eyebrow she was hoping for.

"And the last time I was drooled on, it was Max."

"You're—not teasing." She thumbed the wet spot on Jac's blazer. "Don't tell Peggy I drooled on your new outfit." Pale-yellow blazer. Gold blouse. A brighter look, but then everything about Jac was brighter in the last few weeks. And her playing…a chill went up Liz's spine just thinking about it—elegant and sophisticated she was used to, but where had that sensuality and rawness come from? It was like Jac was reinventing herself through her playing.

"It's a great look on you, Jax," Hannah said. "You should have gone shopping with them." She plucked at Liz's jeans and lifted the hem of her limp T-shirt.

Liz swatted Hannah's hand. "They're comfortable." She wasn't about to tell Hannah she felt frumpy. Okay, so she'd let her wardrobe slip since Teri's death, but she wasn't dressing to impress a girlfriend. "Can we snorkel this afternoon?"

"You can." Hannah rubbed her palms together. "I plan to be—"

"Thank you for not sharing. Last weekend you were with…oh, I don't even remember her name. Your libido has the attention span of a mosquito."

"Bzzz." Hannah waved her hand, imitating a mosquito, and then pinched Liz's arm. "Yours could use a tune-up."

Her libido was fine. Frustratingly fine the last couple of months. Masturbating gave her relief, but it left out all the best parts—kissing, touching, being held. Sharing. How did you turn that off? Would it fade with time?

"How's yours, Jax?"

Liz scowled at Hannah. "Is everything about sex with you?"

"Shall I ask Kerri to fix you up?" Hannah asked Jac.

"Max makes those kinds of decisions for me, and since he's not here…" Jac shrugged.

"Don't encourage her." Jac seemed to find Hannah's antics amusing. Liz scowled at Hannah when she did the mosquito thing with her hand again.

"New song?" Jac asked. "You're humming again."

"I don't know I'm doing it. Teri said I hummed in my sleep." She was composing more than she had in years, and she loved the new sound.

"You hummed before you talked," Hannah said. "I'll bet Dad still has the first songs you wrote out with crayon. I'm surprised he hasn't posted them on your website along with all the other childhood memorabilia."

"I asked him to stop doing that." He was throwing himself into band business in an annoying way. Something was up with him, but he insisted he was fine whenever she asked. She nudged Jac's shoulder. "You're fingering on your pants."

"Touché. A new arrangement for the piece we worked on yesterday. It's funny how music owns us."

"Yeah, but who brings their trumpet on vacation?"

"Someone who in exactly three weeks will be back on a stage."

"Excited?"

"Terrified," Jac whispered, faking a shiver.

"I told you the reaction to the article would be favorable."

Jac pursed her lips. It was hard to get her to talk about it since it had come out two weeks ago.

Liz's friend had done a masterful job with the article. Yes, Jacqueline Richards had been in a lesbian bar and had left with a woman. Yes, she'd been married at the time. She'd detailed Jac's injuries and stated them as the reason she'd retired. She'd also done research on the accident, and they now knew that Stephanie's father was a powerful attorney who'd been running for judge at the time of the accident. Her friend's take on it was that he'd kept her name out of the media to avoid any scandal.

There'd been the expected gossip and rehashing of the accident, which had probably added to the spectacular sales of the anniversary CD collection. But the question most asked was whether Jac would perform again. She'd hired someone to handle relations with the press and managed to keep her life pretty much the way it had been. It was going to be blown wide open after her appearance at the jazz festival. Liz hoped she was doing the right thing by encouraging Jac's comeback.

"I hate this part," Liz said after the announcement about starting their descent. Jac offered her hand and she took it, telling herself she wouldn't squeeze as hard as she had on takeoff.

Frank and Susan, Jac's parents, were waiting for them. They sandwiched Jac in a long hug, tears in their eyes. Liz gave the moment the respect it deserved, then made them pose for pictures she texted to Peggy, as promised.

"Wow. I'm in Hawaii." She'd been dreading her birthday. Instead, she was on a tropical vacation. Life was surprising her lately in good ways.

Jac hooked her fingers on the inside of Liz's elbow as they walked through the small airport, Hannah chatting about local restaurants with Jac's parents. They'd practiced at home until she could guide Jac almost as well as Max. The last-minute plans hadn't left enough time to get Max certified to enter Hawaii because of the rabies laws. She veered them left and right around people and luggage. His job was harder than it looked.

❖

Jac held Liz's elbow as they walked beside her parents toward the entrance to the Hyatt Regency. They were meeting Hannah and Kerri for dinner. She missed Max terribly and hated being dependent on people to lead her, but she hated the white cane more. The trade-off for the dependency was the guarantee of being close to Liz. Her fingers were dangerously near Liz's breast, and her heart responded with too-rapid beats. Foolishness, but a delicious kind of foolishness she couldn't resist indulging. Nothing would come of her feelings. At least with Liz she knew that up front. She wouldn't be blindsided again.

"Wow," Liz said, her steps slowing. "The lobby is a huge atrium. Palm trees and plants everywhere, exotic birds in cages and on perches. Oh, my gosh, there are penguins over there."

"Would you rather stay here?" She tried to visualize the lobby from Liz's description. She'd been in hundreds of fancy hotels, but everything was new and exciting with Liz.

"Me and Hannah in one room? Disaster waiting to happen."

Good. Jac wanted to soak up every minute of this Labor Day weekend with Liz, the end of an idyllic six weeks since the day she'd first played with her. Long days of walking, sharing music, relaxed evenings with Peg and Roger. Friendship she'd never had. When they returned on Monday, Liz would stay in San Jose. Her classes started Tuesday. Jac would see her at band rehearsals until Monterey. Maybe on weekends after that. It wouldn't be the same, and she dreaded the impending change.

"Let's get a picture of the three of you for Peggy," Jac's dad said.

She smiled, but only because Liz's arm was around her waist. She didn't like having her picture taken, but she couldn't blame Peg for wanting to be part of this trip. Their relationship had shifted recently, like some barrier between them had come down. They'd talked a lot about the accident and the aftermath, cried a lot. Some strain that Peg always seemed to carry was gone.

"Lizzie!" Hannah joined them. "This is my friend Kerri. She's reserved a table for us in the bar, but I need to borrow Lizzie. We'll catch up with you."

MAKING A COMEBACK

Jac took her mom's elbow as they walked, wondering what Hannah was up to now. She'd planned all sorts of surprises to make the weekend special for Liz.

"I can't get over the fact that you're here," her mom said. "And hearing you play with Liz this afternoon...we can't wait for Monterey. Maybe it'll be the start of a new career."

"Not performing." It had been grueling when she had her sight. "I might produce albums." She was getting inquiries from some notable names in jazz. She still had moments when guilt settled heavily on her, but she was slowly accepting that Liz was right—it had been a tragic accident and she wasn't to blame. It was a better life than she'd thought possible.

❖

"Stop tugging on it, Lizzie," Hannah said as they walked down the sweeping staircase to the bar. "You look beautiful."

Who was she to argue with Hannah's fashion sense? "This hotel is kind of over the top." Postcard views everywhere she looked, and the tropical ambience was intoxicating.

"It's supposed to be. Fun and fantasy. That's what a tropical vacation is all about."

"I forget I'm the only one who hasn't had one." The bar was like something out of a movie with dark rattan furniture, lazily circling ceiling fans, and containers of tropical plants that gave it the sense of being a secluded hideaway. An aquarium took up the far wall. She recognized some of the fish she'd seen while snorkeling that afternoon. It was one of the best things she'd ever done.

"Doesn't Jax look yummy?"

"She's not a dessert." More like a cool drink—yellow pants and a pastel lime-green, sleeveless top. Yes, Peggy had outdone herself. Shorts and sleeveless fuchsia blouse this afternoon, and a midnight-blue swimsuit cut high on the hip that accentuated her shapely legs.

"Oh, come on. She might be a great trumpet player, but she's drop-dead gorgeous. And that outfit..." Hannah gave a long low whistle.

"I saw it." Geez, enough already. "Can we go shopping tomorrow? I want a new swimsuit." Maybe some new shorts and blouses.

"You're the birthday girl. Just not too early." Hannah sat next to Kerri, who greeted her with a tasteful kiss. They were a stunning couple—Hannah in an open-backed halter dress perfectly accessorized, looking every bit the sophisticated world-class chef; Kerri, suntanned and dark-haired, with an equally eye-catching dress.

Liz took the chair between Jac and her mom.

"You look lovely," Susan said. She was an older version of Jac and Peggy—slender, blond, blue-eyed.

"Tell Jax what you're wearing," Hannah said.

"Sundress. An early birthday present."

"Green that matches her eyes," Hannah said. "Fit-and-flare silhouette, cutout back, scoop neck, spaghetti straps. Knockout."

Liz felt a blush creep up her throat. Shorter and cut lower than she would have bought, but she had to admit she felt beautiful. Hannah taking time away from her reunion with Kerri to buy her a present was a sweet gesture.

"To beautiful women," Frank said, lifting a reddish-colored drink. Blond and blue-eyed, he looked every bit the laidback islander in the Tommy Bahama shirt under his linen sport coat.

Liz took a sip from the glass in front of her. Peachy, with a tang. Tropical. Was there alcohol in it? She couldn't taste it and took another long sip. Tropical vacation. Fun and fantasy.

"Here's to Sex on the Beach," Kerri said, lifting her glass.

Liz swallowed wrong and started coughing. Jac patted her on the back.

"The name of the drink," Hannah said. "Although…" She kissed Kerri, longer this time, then whispered something in her ear that made Kerri smile. Conversation shifted to best snorkeling beaches.

Jac leaned close. "I wish I could see how beautiful you look. Is that new perfume?"

"Birthday gift, too." Time for something new, Hannah had said, dabbing a bit of the delicately tropical fragrance on her throat. She squirmed on the seat. The new thong panties took some getting used to.

"I like it."

"Picture time," Frank said, pulling out his phone. They scooted their chairs together and the waitress took their group picture. After another round of drinks, they walked across to the restaurant.

"Wow. I think that's my word for the weekend. The restaurant…" Was a whole other kind of tropical. The super-romantic kind.

"Can you add some adjectives?" Jac squeezed her elbow.

"It's laid out like a pavilion. Dark except for candlelight. White tablecloths and place settings. Floor-to-ceiling wooden panels are folded back so the restaurant opens onto a large pond. View to the ocean beyond it. Palm trees, plants, a rock wall along the right that has a waterfall."

She pulled out Jac's chair and sat next to her. A waiter set another round of cocktails on the table, and Kerri ordered appetizers. "Two white swans are floating in the middle of the pond. Moonlight is reflecting off the water…" She let out a sigh, wrapped up in the beauty of the moment.

"Sounds romantic."

It was, and Liz's throat tightened. The swans nuzzled each other. Teri would say, "Like us, mated for life." But that wasn't true. The ache sucked the air from her lungs, and she put her hand over her chest. It hurt to be here without her.

Jac put her arm across the back of her chair and squeezed her shoulder. "I'm sorry Teri's not here with you."

"I don't know why we never made time for a trip like this." Jac's hand was hot on her sunburned skin.

"I have a whole list of things I would have done if I'd known I'd lose my sight. It's hard when the future isn't what you expected. I'm here for you if you want to talk about her."

"Thank you." Jac's friendship was the best kind—supportive without being intrusive, and she knew plenty about grief. "You know what. I'm on my dream vacation with my best friend and my sister. Teri would tell me to have fun, and that's exactly what I'm going to do." She held up her cocktail. "To Jac and Hannah for making my birthday special."

Cocktails and delicious food kept coming, and vibrant conversation kept her attention. For the most part. But then she'd notice the swans and the ache would capture her again. Finally, the meal came to an end. Liz took one last look at the swans as everyone got up to leave. She stood, then gripped the back of her chair as the room swayed. Or she swayed. Okay, there was alcohol in those drinks. When Jac took her elbow she said, "I'm a little unsteady. You should walk with one of your parents."

"Too much Sex on the Beach?" Jac's eyebrow was raised.

"Remember what happened the first night I had dinner with you?" She wasn't repeating the fiasco of tripping, maybe hurting herself again or, worse, Jac.

"I'll take better care of you this time." Jac put her arm around Liz's waist.

"Anyone up for dancing?" Frank asked when they were back in the lobby, spinning Susan around gracefully. "I know a great place."

"Definitely," Hannah said, pulling Kerri close.

"Definitely," Liz echoed. Her mind was a gentle fog, and she felt like she was floating. "I love it here." She sucked in a lungful of the warm, humid air that hung gently around her. She felt beautiful, not the sad mess she'd been for so long. She closed her eyes and then snapped them open as she tilted toward Jac, who steadied her with a hand to her stomach.

❖

The bar was in a strip mall, unassuming outside and in. Not tropical, and for a moment Liz wanted to protest.

"Not fancy," Frank said, "but great dance music." Several people called to Jac's parents as they commandeered a table next to the dance floor. A middle-aged couple in matching Hawaiian shirts swiveled their hips and flipped their arms to eighties rock.

"How about another round of Sex on the Beach?" Frank suggested, taking off his sport coat, giving the full view of the big yellow flowers on his olive-green shirt.

"Sure." The fuzzy edge of Liz's buzz was wearing off, and she didn't want it to. This wasn't great dance music.

When drinks had been delivered, Frank went to the jukebox, a sly smile on his face. A minute later Ellington's "Take the A Train" sprang from the speakers.

"We teach swing-dancing classes here," Susan said, sashaying out to the dance floor and into her husband's arms.

"Let's show them our stuff." Liz took Jac's hand. Swing dancing. Yes! She loved this vacation. She heard Kerri say, "I can't dance to this."

Oh, but I can. "Dance floor's fifteen-by-fifteen, your parents, and one other couple." They'd only danced at Peggy's Memorial Day and Fourth of July parties, but she'd never danced so easily with anyone. Jac spun her out, and there was just that swing beat, her feet moving to its sassy rhythm, and Jac's hands reeling her in, pushing her out, never letting go.

Another song began, and Jac swung her around to the new rhythm. She felt happy and beautiful, and this was the best vacation ever. They got a lot of looks and she couldn't stop smiling. Someone said, "Those two are terrific dancers." *Yes, we are.* Jac was smiling, too, her face flushed. They were good together.

The song ended and the next one started. Frank Sinatra. "Just in Time." One of her mom's favorites. Hannah held Kerri, and Susan moved into Frank's arms.

"I love this song," Jac said, pulling her close, cheek-to-cheek close.

"Me, too." Jac's thigh was a light pressure against Liz's crotch, her hand gentle on her bare back. In Jac's arms, dancing felt like soaring, and she melted into it. Jac hummed near her ear and she closed her eyes. Everything faded but the music and the delicious sensations of being in Jac's arms. Warmth and softness everywhere. Her lips found the corner of Jac's mouth—

The music stopped and Liz froze, trembling, too hot. Lipstick on Jac's skin. Hers. Oh, God. Her stomach tumbled. "I need some air." She stepped out of Jac's arms and hurried out of the bar, gulping in air, embarrassed, confused by the feeling in her chest. The wrong feeling. Oh, God. She'd almost…She paced and fanned her face, trying to cool down. Damn this tropical air.

"Why'd you run off like that?" Hannah fell into step beside her. "You and Jac make a stunning couple."

"I can't feel this. I can't." It came out as a choked sob, and Liz crossed her arms against the evidence puckering her dress. Damn the new lacy bra Hannah had given her.

Hannah stared at Liz's chest and her face softened. "Lizzie...it's okay to let yourself feel again."

"It's not!"

"So you're attracted to Jac. A little vacation romance. Can't you let it be okay?"

"Teri deserves better than me getting—" Tears filled her eyes and her nipples were still hard and she hated this vacation.

"It's going to happen sooner or later, Lizzie."

"Don't call me that." She turned her back to Hannah. "I don't feel well. I'll take a cab back to..." Hell, she had no idea how to get to Jac's parents' home. "She hasn't even been gone a year."

"Would it matter if it was next year? Ten years from now? When are you going to let yourself live again?"

Liz whirled on Hannah, rigid with anger. The anger faded when she saw the sadness on Hannah's face.

"I miss her, too, but not letting yourself live doesn't bring her back."

She'd said the same thing to Jac about Stephanie. No, it wasn't the same thing. How could she be in Hawaii and need Kleenex? She didn't resist when Hannah held her, trying so hard not to want it to be Jac's arms around her. But Jac wasn't safe anymore. "I am living. I'm playing and composing and—"

"Keeping busy. Just like Dad."

"So what? I'll be like those..." She sucked in a breath, desperate for composure. "Swans. They mate for life. They're loyal. If one dies—"

"Teri wanted you to keep living."

"Not this. She didn't mean this. Music. Monterey. She meant for me to go on with our dreams." Monday they'd be home. This would go away. "I can't talk about this." She'd be back in the condo. Back in her life where she belonged. Damn this vacation that had tricked her into feeling something she shouldn't. "Please make sure I don't dance with her again," she said as they walked into the bar.

"You can have Kerri. My toes are numb from being stepped on."

"I think she's hopeless," Liz said, grateful for the change in topic.

"Who cares if she can't dance? In bed she has great moves."

"Glad you're enjoying yourself."

"You could be, too. Don't let the past strangle the present."

Liz went to the bar and ordered an iced tea. She wanted to chase away the feeling of blurred edges.

"Are you all right?" Jac was next to her, her voice as tight as her face.

"Fine. Sorry. With the alcohol I got too hot." Did Jac know she'd been about to kiss her? Liz couldn't look at her. That funny feeling in her chest wouldn't go away.

"I'm tired. We're going home, but Kerri has another bar in mind. Why don't you go with them?"

"Okay." Liz was beat, but she needed some time away from Jac.

"Snorkeling again in the morning? Dad wants to take us to his favorite beach."

"Sure." She blocked out the memory of Jac in that suit as she sucked down the iced tea. The jukebox started up again. Bad eighties rock. Good. She ignored the stutter step her heart did when she remembered being in Jac's arms. Three days and they'd be home.

Jac sat at the table on her parents' deck. The middle of the night and it was quiet except for the faint sound of the ocean and the rustle of palm leaves. She turned her face into the warm, gentle breeze. Three more days of the tropical weather she'd always loved. Next week she'd be back to long pants and sweaters and water too cold to swim in. And Max. She missed his company and his steadiness.

That last dance. Carried away, she'd pulled Liz too close, lost in the feel and smell of her. Lovers, her body said. Thank God Liz left when she did. She'd been about to kiss her. Her sex contracted as arousal pulsed through her again. The cold shower, the self-administered orgasms, and she couldn't shake it. The pilot light of longing she'd felt the last few months was a furnace of desire threatening to undo common sense. Liz would never be over Teri. Not in that way. She squeezed the arms of the chair until her knuckles ached. After Monterey she'd come back here. Some time away from Liz. The slider opened. Please don't let it be Liz.

"Are you all right?"

"Fine, Mom. Couldn't sleep."

A chair scraped the deck beside her. "I'm glad you brought Liz over. I like her. She seems quite fond of you."

"It's nice to have a friend."

"Looked like more than that on the dance floor. You never looked happy with Malcolm. With Liz…you look like you belong together."

"There's nothing romantic between us." Jac hesitated and then said, "Except in my mind." It felt good to be honest with her mom. Before the interview with Liz's journalist friend, she'd told her parents everything. The affair with Maria. Her intent to divorce Malcolm. The events leading up to the accident. They'd been understanding and supportive…the best of parental love.

"You're in love with her."

Why had she thought she could hide it from her mom? She nodded and sadness swallowed the longing, putting it in its place.

"Have you told her?"

"She and her wife had the fairy-tale kind of love you and Dad have, Peg and Roger have. If she's ever ready for another relationship, and that's a big if, it won't be anytime soon." And it wouldn't be with her. Liz saw her as a friend and confidant and collaborator.

"Do you want a relationship with her?"

"I don't know." That was the other issue. The last time she'd been in love, it had ended disastrously. Liz wasn't Maria, but still… Did she have the courage to risk her heart again?

"Don't let what happened with Maria cloud the present." A long silence and then she said, "I'm so grateful you've let us back into your life." Her mom's voice cracked. "I'm so proud of you for doing the interview."

Without naming Maria, she'd been honest with Liz's friend about the circumstances of that night. All she'd put in the article was that Jac had left the hotel and gone to a lesbian bar. It made her wonder again where Maria was. She could probably find out, but she didn't want to know. She'd never forgive Maria for how she'd treated her that night or for not coming to see her after the accident.

She wasn't sure how she felt about the article. Relieved that she no longer had to hide. Uncomfortable about having to reveal personal details of her life. Surprised that the article had prompted more

discussion about whether she was a lesbian and about whether she'd
return to the stage than about the details of the accident. She'd always
wish she'd made different choices that night, but Liz was right—she
couldn't bring Stephanie back by hiding away.

"Promise me you'll come back often."

"I promise." Why had she cut herself off from everything and
everyone all those years? Yes, she'd come back here with Max after
Monterey and spend time with her parents.

CHAPTER TWENTY-SIX

Liz jerked the shower knob and cold water pelted her chest. Bad idea. Her nipples were overly sensitive. She covered them with her hands, sunburned skin tingling from the shock of the cold water. She'd woken up aroused and needed the unwanted feeling to go away. That damn dance Friday night. The memory of being in Jac's arms kept ambushing her.

She spun around and cold water beat against her back. She shivered, but the knot of arousal wouldn't go away. She put her hand between her legs and separated her labia. Wet. The thick, slippery kind of wet. Her clit tightened and a jolt of need flashed through her. No, no, no. Jac was gorgeous in her shorts and sleeveless blouses. She stroked. God, she needed to come. Jac in that swimsuit, rubbing in sunscreen with her long, elegant fingers. Her clit hardened under her fingers. Jac's thigh pressing against her sex with each step on the dance floor. The agonizing tease of it. The need to pull it against her, to satisfy the ache. Stroked harder. What would Jac's lips feel like on—

She plastered her palms to the tile wall. No, no, no. She was Teri's. She was not going to come to visions of another woman's touch. She ducked her head under the cold spray and waited for the torturous pulsing to subside. Damn Hannah and her tropical vacations. Tomorrow she'd be home in her condo where she belonged.

She dressed in the shorts and blouse she'd bought yesterday on the shopping trip with Hannah and Kerri. She stood at the window in the guest bedroom for a long time, watching the ocean take form out of the dawn—dark gray, then dark blue, and finally sparkling turquoise. Sunday. Her birthday. Thirty-three years old. She checked her watch. Almost the minute she was born. They'd always woken each other up at the moments they were born and made love. This time last year—No, it hurt too much to think about that.

She hurried to the kitchen for coffee. Everyone was on the deck. She joined them. Jac wore another colorful outfit, and her skin was a healthy pink from the sun. She should fasten another button on the blouse. "Wow, I've never seen a birthday candle in a…what is that?"

"Pineapple fritter," Susan said. "You'll want to ship a box home."

"Oh. My. Gosh," Liz said after the first bite.

"Picture," Frank said, catching her with powdered sugar all over her mouth.

"How many Tommy Bahama shirts do you have?" Today's was white with palm trees.

"He wore them all the time in Carmel. He was a local legend," Jac said, the first thing she'd uttered. She looked tired. Was her back okay? Damn, she hadn't bothered to ask. None of this was Jac's fault.

"We vacationed in Hawaii for the first time when the girls were teenagers," Susan said. "We had no idea we'd fall in love with the place or with scuba diving. You never know when something's going to jump out and grab your heart."

"Um, no, you don't," Liz said when Susan looked right at her.

"Ready for the best day of your life?" Frank asked.

No one would tell her what they were doing for her birthday. "Wasn't that yesterday?" Snorkeling in the morning at a pristine beach. She'd seen hundreds of colorful fish and a sea turtle in crystal-clear water. Jac and her parents had joined them after the shopping spree for the parasailing excursion that was Kevin and Karen's birthday gift. Jac was embracing her new life with gusto.

"Happy Birthday from us." Susan handed her a package.

"It's beautiful. Thank you." A scarf in ocean shades of blue and green. She put it around her neck and hugged Jac's parents. They'd made her feel so welcome.

Sliding a beautifully wrapped package across the table, Jac said, "Max wrapped it."

"Then he won't mind if I'm not dainty opening it. Oh, Jac, thank you." She held up the wind chimes and jiggled them. "What beautiful tones. I'll hang it in Grandma's garden."

Jac's smile looked forced. Something was bothering her. She'd been quiet yesterday, and her playing last night had been stiff and unenthusiastic. What if Jac knew she'd almost kissed her? Best to ignore it. Tomorrow they'd be home.

"Bus leaves in ten," Frank said, taking dishes to the house.

"Do you know where we're going?" Liz asked Jac.

"No clue." Jac gave a fake-innocent shrug.

"Liar. You'll pay for that." She started to tickle Jac, in keeping with their running joke about trust and honesty. She stopped. Not today.

"What did you say?" Jac realized her mom had asked her something.

"We're almost there. Are you excited?"

"Very." Something else she never thought she'd do. They talked about it for a bit, and then her thoughts went back to Liz. She seemed different since Friday night. Since they'd danced. At times Liz was herself, but then she'd drop out of a conversation, or her voice would sound strained or impatient. She seemed distracted when at the piano, and only wanted to play her older songs. When Jac had asked if she wanted to talk about Teri, she'd said "no" in a decisive way that made it clear the topic was off limits.

First birthday without Teri. A major performance in less than three weeks, just days before the anniversary of Teri's death. That was a lot to deal with. She wanted to help, but Liz was shutting her out. Did Liz know she'd been about to kiss her? Was she upset? She was afraid to say anything, and what was there to say? They'd be home tomorrow, and Liz would be back in San Jose. Seeing less of Liz would be painful, but it would allow her feelings time to settle again.

By design, Hannah was a few minutes behind them. A car pulled in next to them and doors opened. "Surprise!" They all yelled.

"Zip line?" Liz sounded more confused than excited.

"Dad's part of your birthday present," Hannah said. "Here, he's on the phone and wants to wish you Happy Birthday."

Jac waited by the car, listening to Hannah, who never tired of talking. She was also astute. Hannah had taken her aside last night and asked if she was all right. Then she'd said to be patient, an odd comment. Did she mean give Liz time to get over her birthday? Would everything be okay when they were back home?

"You're doing this, too?" Liz asked, beside her. She sounded worried.

"I've always wanted to." She'd never dared do things like this when she was performing because everyone was afraid she'd get hurt and ruin her career.

"Is it safe?"

"I'll make sure I'm strapped in."

"Funny. What about your back?"

"I'll know more after the first line."

"Peggy's going to want tons of pictures," Liz said finally.

"Not my job."

"You're probably more at risk from me tripping and taking you down with me."

"I'll take my chances." She held Liz's elbow as they walked over unleveled terrain, everyone chattering excitedly.

After signing releases, being fitted with harnesses and helmets, and listening to general instructions, they set out.

"Who's first?" their guide asked when they arrived at the first line.

"I am," Jac said.

"Way to go," Hannah said.

Her dad slapped her on the back and her mom said, "I'm so proud of you."

A few minutes later she was dangling in the harness with her feet off the ground. The harness squeezed her thighs, and she felt secure as she bounced in it. She tugged the straps around her chest. Tight. She felt up to where they were attached to a large clamp, like mountain climbers used, she imagined, which was fastened around a substantial steel cable. Her heart was pounding, but in a good way.

"Keep your hands and feet inside the ride at all times," the guide said, snugged up behind her.

In her next breath she was falling, an odd sensation of forward movement, bouncing on the cable, wind on her skin. She held tight to the strap at her chest.

In seconds he said, "Lift your feet."

She did and bounced against his chest as he ran across the landing platform to stop their momentum.

"Perfect," he said. "You're a natural."

When he released her from the cable, she turned in the direction of the cheers and bowed, which brought whistles and more cheers. The voice she searched for yelled, "Great performance, Richards!" Doing this was a thrill. Doing it with Liz was indescribable.

A few minutes later there was a scream as someone came across. Liz. Then feet running on the platform. "Oh my gosh, that's amazing! How was it?"

"Better than a standing ovation." Jac couldn't stop grinning.

"Your back?"

"Great. Don't worry about me."

Liz hugged her and something shifted, and Liz was like her old self. "Thank you for this weekend."

She couldn't speak as emotions choked her. So much she wanted to say. The next few minutes were a flurry of cheering and screams as Hannah, Kerri, and her parents took their turns. The rest of the morning was a nonstop sensory assault of zip-lining, hugging, laughing, and talking. Each line was longer. It was exhilarating. When they reached the last line, the guide pulled her aside.

"It's a double line—two people side by side. Do you want to do it without me?"

"Yes. With Liz." She could barely contain her excitement as he fitted her into the harness.

"You're all set," the guide said after getting Liz hooked on.

"Ready?" She held out her hand to Liz.

"Wait. He's not—"

"It's just you and me."

"But…oh, hell."

She squeezed Liz's hand as she lifted her feet. The wind blew hard against her as they fell through space. Liz screamed and Jac joined her. They laughed and squealed, and then, all too soon, they slowed and came to a stop

"Oooohhh!" Liz cried as they fell backward. This line didn't have a platform, and they would swing back and forth on the line until they ran out of momentum. "Don't let go!"

"Never." Tears stung Jac's eyes, but not from the wind. Today. Tomorrow. Three weeks of rehearsals and then? Monterey would launch Liz into the career she deserved. She'd do the fall tour and then there would be other tours and...Jac screamed, holding tightly, for these few precious moments, to the woman she loved.

Chapter Twenty-seven

"Best birthday ever?" Hannah stretched her arm around the car seat and tickled Liz's calf.

No, her best birthday was the year Teri gave her—"Yes, it is." No more sadness. Kerri was taking them to what she guaranteed was the best beach on the island. Secluded beach, Hannah had added, rubbing her palms together in that annoying way. Oh, heck, she was tired of being irritated at Hannah.

"It's certainly been my best birthday," Jac said, and everyone laughed. She was in high spirits after the zip line. "For my next adventure I'm skydiving."

"Awesome! I want to go with you," Hannah said.

"We're here." Kerri pulled off the highway onto a tiny dirt parking area.

"I don't see a beach," Liz said. More like a wall of jungle.

"That's why it's secluded." Hannah pulled Kerri into a kiss. "Last day in paradise," she said, popping out of the car.

It was, and Liz planned to make the most of it. Whatever that weirdness was with Jac, it was gone. She'd learned how changeable grief could be—a tornado one moment and vanished the next. Apparently attraction worked the same way. Hormones. A foolish moment.

Hannah and Kerri pulled beach bags and an ice chest from the car.

"I'll race you to the sand," Liz said, standing next to Jac.

"You don't know where it is."

"Neither do you."

Jac pointed to her right.

"I know better than to argue with your radar." Jac's fingers wrapped around her elbow, and they followed Kerri and Hannah along a trail so narrow they had to walk practically on top of each other. "Careful," she said, holding back branches so they didn't slap Jac's face.

Jac stopped. "Close your eyes."

She did, breathing deeply, opening her senses beyond the conversation between Hannah and Kerri that was fading as they moved ahead. She'd started this game, wanting to know what Jac's world was like. Well, as much as possible considering that she could open her eyes and see. Blindness was both disorienting and freeing. Sight was so dominant that it filtered out much of her sensory experience. She liked how its absence amplified other senses.

"I feel cocooned," Liz said. The warm, humid air was delicious against her skin, like a delicate piece of clothing. "I hear a bird trilling behind me. Branches moving overhead. A car driving by on the road. Something rattling the bushes. I hope it's not a snake." She peeked. "And the ocean, faint, and right where you said it would be."

"Smell?"

"Earthy soil smell. You. Me." The cocoon tightened around her. Jac smelled like ginger and musk, a new perfume.

"Good," Jac said, her hand tightening on Liz's arm, her pulse palpable in her fingertips.

Liz heard the in and out of Jac's breathing. The sweat-sticky skin of their arms touched. If she turned just a bit, their breasts— She popped her eyes open. Her heart accelerated like a sprinter off the blocks. The cocoon of heat was claustrophobic. "Come on." She hurried them along the path, their bodies as close as when they'd danced.

Jac stumbled and grabbed her waist. Their knees bumped and their breasts grazed for an instant as she righted herself.

"Sorry." Liz took forced, deep breaths as she slowed her pace.

When the trail finally widened, Jac stopped. "I don't know how to thank you for…everything." She seemed fragile in the midst of this jungle she couldn't see.

The poignancy of the moment touched Liz's heart, and the mood changed. She loved Jac's courage and strength, her willingness to trust and take risks, her thoughtfulness. She hugged her.

"This is the best vacation I've ever had," Jac said.

"You're teasing."

"I'm not. Liz, I…I…" She shook her head.

"What about when you were in Greece?" When Jac frowned, she said, "The day we went to the tide-pools, I asked what your favorite beach was. You were there with Maria, weren't you?"

Jac nodded, looking sad. What must it be like for her to live with memories of what her life had been—fame, excitement, exotic places?

"Come on, let's make our last afternoon special." She wanted Jac to be happy.

Jac smiled and everything was right again. Best friends.

"Wow." The trail ended abruptly at the most beautiful beach she'd ever seen. "Pristine. White—"

"Don't say any more." Jac tilted her head as if she was forming a picture of the gently sloping half circle of white sand. The forest that framed it extended down almost to the water on both sides. Secluded was right. The water was shades of turquoise and green, so clear it was like looking through glass.

"Does Kerri know how to throw a beach party or what?" Hannah asked as she and Kerri unrolled a large straw mat under a shade canopy. Hannah wriggled out of her shorts. "Last one in the water gets dunked." She picked up two sets of fins and a snorkel mask. "You're my date, Jax." Winking at Liz she took Jac's hand and led her to the water.

"Jac's beautiful," Kerri said, as they followed them.

"Um, yeah." Liz didn't realize she'd been staring at Jac's legs, specifically at where they disappeared into the swimsuit. She raced past Jac and plunged into the water. When it was up to her shoulders, she put the fins on, falling over only once as she worked her feet into them. After adjusting the snorkel straps, she swam over to join the others in a splash fight. Best birthday ever. Half an hour later she and Jac walked up the beach, jostling each other like kids.

"Water?" Jac asked when they were sitting on beach towels partially shaded by the canopy.

Liz pulled two from the cooler. Champagne and sushi for dinner, courtesy of Kerri.

Jac guzzled water, and chunks of ice slid off the bottle and onto her chest. They slid down between her—

Jerking her eyes away from the two peaks forming in Jac's suit, Liz was met with the sight of Hannah and Kerri waist deep in the water. Hannah's hand on Kerri's breast...Kerri's head thrown back. They wouldn't, would they? Right in front of her? She rolled onto her stomach and closed her eyes.

❖

"Lizzie's legs are in the sun," Hannah said. "Put sunscreen on so she doesn't burn?" Hannah pressed a tube against Jac's hand.

"You should do it."

"We're going for a walk." This wasn't the first time, and it was no mystery what they were doing. It irritated Liz, but Jac envied them.

Liz had been asleep for almost an hour, but she'd stayed awake, too keyed up to nap. On the walk from the car, in the quiet with Liz, their bodies touching, she'd almost blurted out...Thank God she hadn't. Telling Liz she was in love with her was foolish and pointless. Even though Liz hadn't talked about Teri since the first day, it was obvious that she was still so much a part of her life.

Hannah and Kerri's voices faded, and then it was quiet except for the wind moving through the palm trees and the irregular rhythm of the waves. Alone with Liz, she let her mind wander to all the places she wanted to touch her. She should wake her up...Squeezing sunscreen onto her palms, she rubbed them together, trying to get up the courage to touch her. Finally, she laid her palms on Liz's ankles and lightly, so as not to wake her, spread the sunscreen up her calves. Liz's skin was hot and the lotion seemed to melt into her. Bits of sand moved under her hands as they traveled up, up...smooth skin, firm muscles, knees, then more muscle and soft skin, soft skin, soft—

"What—that tickles," Liz said, turning over, slipping out from under Jac's hands.

"Hannah said your legs were in the sun." She dropped the container and jumped up. She pushed her feet hard into the sand as she hurried toward the water, hoping there wasn't a visible wet spot on her crotch. She waded out until her waist was underwater, and then deeper to cover her hard nipples. She dug her feet into the sand and swayed with the current. She wanted Liz so much it hurt.

"Do you want to swim again?" Liz asked.

Jac hadn't heard her approach. "Just enjoying the water." The end of the vacation was closing in, and her chest felt tight with impending loneliness.

Squeals and laughter came from the far side of the beach.

"Geez. I wish they'd be more discreet," Liz said.

"They're fine." She forced herself not to reach for Liz, not to pull their bodies together and kiss her.

"Will you think about going out with Cassie? I've known her a long time. I wouldn't trust you to just anyone."

"I don't want a relationship."

"Oh." Liz was quiet for a while. "Why not?"

Because of you. She held the words captive in her heart. "I like my life the way it is." *Stop asking me questions or I'm going to blurt out the truth and make a fool of myself over another woman I can't have.* She walked back to the beach through the pull of receding waves. Where was the mat? Liz caught up to her and led her to it. She dropped facedown on her towel. Her back would hurt tomorrow and it was rude to ignore Liz, but she needed time to collect herself.

CHAPTER TWENTY-EIGHT

Liz sat at the upright piano in Jac's parents' living room, waiting for Jac to get her trumpet. Her skin was hot from too much sun and sticky from the residue of sunscreen she'd had on all day. Her eyes stung from the salt water. Jac's parents wanted to hear "Carmel Sketches" one last time. Fine by her. It would relax her. She was exhausted physically from the long day, but keyed up and confused over feelings for Jac that wouldn't hold still. One minute everything was the way it had been between them. Friends. The next, her heart would skip a beat or she'd catch herself staring at Jac's body in a way she shouldn't.

Jac slid the mouthpiece onto her trumpet and walked toward the piano. Her skin was sunburned, and she was wearing the fuchsia blouse.

Liz started the song, wondering which improvisation Jac would practice tonight. Ah, that one. A newer one. She was watching her hands, thinking how amazing it was that her left hand felt normal, when Jac's playing changed. A subtle shift to more vibrato, then long notes as if she was pulling them from some place deep inside. Mournful. Beautiful. She quieted the piano to let Jac have her solo. She was making it up on the spot. Good.

It happened quickly, like a car accident you don't see coming. Rough, angry notes barked from the trumpet. Liz looked over her shoulder. Jac's expression was intense, almost a scowl, as if something dark was forcing its way up and out her horn. Liz fumbled a few bars. Jac had changed to a different key, a minor key. She was playing fast and powerful, like a train roaring down the tracks looking for something to run over. Something in her said this wasn't good, but she could only try to keep up. Jac had never improvised like this—raw and wild and risky, and she didn't want to embarrass her by stopping.

Jac was almost growling through the trumpet now, low notes that went right to Liz's clit. No, no, no. Her nerve endings felt scorched, and sweat broke out on her throat. She forgot what she was playing. Then thought ceased, and they were playing something that was "Carmel Sketches." And not "Carmel Sketches." It was intense and physical, and they were all tangled up with each other as if having sex. Cheeks hot, breathing fast, sweat dripping down her back, Liz pounded the keys. Her sex pulsed as if responding to Jac's trumpet. No, no, no. Minutes felt like days and like no time. Her mind collapsed into the music. This was exhilarating. This was dangerous.

And then as suddenly as it had begun, it stopped. As if she were waking from a fever, Jac's playing slowed and became moody. Liz looked over her shoulder again as she adjusted to the new tempo. Jac looked sad, almost broken, and her expression tore at Liz's heart. So much complexity. So much sensitivity. So much she didn't know about Jac.

Minutes later, Jac brought the song to a close with feather-light notes, and they were left with the remnant of what had happened, like confetti falling around them. Liz turned around on the bench. Jac's parents clapped, broad smiles on their faces. Sweat rolled down Jac's face, down her throat, inside her blouse. She really should fasten another button. She held the trumpet between her breasts as her chest rose and fell. She was smiling, a satisfied, relaxed smile, as if she'd—

Liz sat in the agony of skin too hot, and pressure pulsing in her center, and arousal draped over her like a thick sweater. She gripped the edge of the bench, bouncing her leg, fighting an overwhelming urge to put her hand between her legs. They were not playing that version at Monterey. They were never playing that version again. Never. "I need some water." She hurried to the kitchen and splashed water on her face, then gulped ice water.

When she returned to the living room, Jac was cleaning her trumpet, chatting with her parents like nothing had happened. Hadn't something happened?

"I'm going to turn in," she said after talking with them for a polite amount of time. She needed to be away from Jac with her wild playing and sleeveless blouses. She wanted her concealed in wool trousers and buttoned-down shirts. She wanted the old Jac. The Jac who played elegantly. The Jac who didn't make her feel things she didn't want to feel.

"Sleep well." Jac stepped toward her.

For an instant, Liz wanted to be swept into her arms. She walked past Jac. She couldn't hug her. Not tonight. She took a cold shower and then lay on the bed, arms and legs spread. A warm breeze teased over her skin. No, she was not going to touch herself. The urge would fade if she ignored it.

Long after the voices stopped and bedroom doors shut, she lay awake, her mind exhausted from trying to force reason onto a body that burned for what it wanted. Jac. Angry tears stinging her eyes, she thrust her hand inside the tight confines of her shorts. She needed release so bad. She wanted it in Jac's arms. She was attracted to Jac. Crazy bad attracted to her. No, no, no. She yanked her hand out and scrambled off the bed, wound tight by frustration and confusion. A walk would clear her head. Tomorrow she'd be home. This would fade.

She was out the front door and half a block away before she realized how dark it was. Houses were mere shadows and, without streetlights, she was afraid she'd get lost.

Back in the house, she went to the kitchen. She took a glass of ice water to the deck and closed the slider behind her. She felt fragile, like delicate glass that could shatter with the slightest touch, grasping at a past that time was turning into the brittleness of memories. The stream of days and years with Teri was fragmenting into disjointed images infiltrated with an overlay of new memories that didn't include Teri. Music that didn't include Teri. A dream vacation that didn't include Teri.

She loved Teri. She wanted Jac. It was that simple and that complicated, that achingly painful, and it squeezed the breath from her. How could her body betray her? She gripped the railing and stared out to the dark ocean as past and present squared off. Waves crashed to shore in the distance. The slider opened. Her heart leapt into her throat. For an agonizing moment, she didn't know if she wanted it to be Jac or not.

"I didn't know you were out here. I couldn't sleep." Jac's voice was like a soothing caress on Liz's overheated skin.

"There's the barest sliver of moon. It's a very black night." Sadness and longing engulfed her in equal measure. She swallowed the last of the water, holding the ice cubes in her mouth. Cold on her tongue, but they did nothing for the heat torching her. "What do you do when you want something you shouldn't want?"

"Of course you should want Teri to be here." Jac was inches from her, but her voice sounded distant.

"Not—" Jac was so beautiful, and longing spilled out of her, down her arms, into her hands. She clasped Jac's waist and pulled her close. Reason was chased away by the softness of Jac's lips, then the warmth of her mouth as she pushed past her lips. Jac's body stiffened, but her mouth softened. She kissed her until she needed air and then kissed across her cheek.

"I need you." Want. Desire. Tones long absent from Liz's voice rose from the place that ached for Jac's touch. She bit below Jac's ear and whispered, "I'm burning up." She returned to Jac's mouth and entered her, sucking her tongue, urging her to join in the dance.

"Liz." Jac pushed on her waist.

"Shh." She wrapped her arms tighter and pressed her sex against Jac's thigh, nuzzling her neck. "I need this. I've missed it so much. Touch me." Grasping Jac's hand, she brought it to her breast. She rubbed against Jac's palm, moaning with pleasure, her nipple a hypersensitive peak. "Please."

"Oh, God." Jac's voice was tight, almost frail. "Not this."

Need blocked out the words. She pulled Jac's hand to the place that throbbed, holding it against her sex as she rocked her pelvis…the seam of her shorts…Jac's fingers…she was seconds from coming, and it felt so good, so good…then Jac's hand was gone. She whimpered and rubbed her clit on Jac's leg. "I need to come so bad. Please."

"Not here. Not like this." Jac's voice was rough.

Liz hurried them to Jac's bedroom. Closing the door, she pinned Jac against it and kissed her deeply. She separated Jac's legs with her knee, rode Jac's thigh in a desperate search for release. "God…

please." Had she ever needed to come this bad? Her mind went blank to everything but the demanding throb in her clit. Days of wanting drove her beyond the barrier of the past and into a present sizzling with sensation. More. She needed so much more.

Jac gripped her arms and backed her to the bed.

Liz tumbled onto it, pulling Jac on top of her. She could barely see her in the dark. They were encased in hot and humid air tinged with the sweet smell of flowers. Jac had her undressed in seconds. She tried to unzip Jac's shorts, but Jac pinned her hands above her head and lay on top of her. Jac kissed her long and hard as she cupped Liz's breast and rubbed her thumb across the nipple, taking charge the way Liz needed her to.

Liz fought to free her legs, fought to open herself to the pressure she needed, but Jac restrained her. She groaned into Jac's mouth, twined her fingers in her hair, and rocked with increasing urgency against the constraint. With a final squeeze that made her clit contract, Jac released her breast and stroked up the outside of Liz's thigh, across her hip to her groin. Liz spread her legs. When Jac's fingers found her clit she arched into the touch, her breath coming in ragged gasps.

"Is this all right?"

"God, yes. Don't stop." A different hand, different fingers taking her toward the release she desperately needed, but they were familiar fingers, too, and she welcomed them. She bit her lip and wrapped her arms around Jac. Her ab and thigh muscles tightened as she was pushed toward climax. "Oh, God…it's so good…"

"Come for me," Jac whispered in her ear.

That was all the permission Liz needed. "I'm coming…so good…" The burn filled her belly and rushed down her thighs and up her torso and neck, combusting in a fireball in her head. Finding Jac's mouth, she feasted on her tongue as the orgasm rolled on and on in waves of pleasure and exquisite relief.

That first orgasm had primed her. She usually came more than once, but not right away. Tonight she needed more. Again. Now. She released Jac's mouth, panting from need and the heat. Sweat collected on their skin. Sweet fragrances encased them. She closed her eyes and dove into the sensations. "Take me. I need more." She pumped her pelvis in a frenzy of jerky movements, seeking the perfect contact with Jac's fingers. When she found it she sucked Jac's blouse between her lips to keep from screaming as her clit clenched and rocketed pleasure through the same scorched pathways. She clutched at Jac's back, frustrated by the clothes. Why was Jac still dressed? She tried to roll on top, but Jac resisted.

"Let me give you this." Jac's voice was rough and husky, but her lips were tender as she kissed Liz's throat, across her collarbone, down to her breast.

She might have protested if not for the heat of Jac's mouth surrounding her nipple, sucking hard, and her wet fingers mercilessly teasing her other nipple. "Your mouth. I want your mouth on me." She pushed on Jac's shoulders. "Please."

Groaning, Jac slid between her legs and licked the inside of her thighs, stopping short of where Liz needed her.

Liz's clit was full and aching for release, and she pushed in search of Jac's tongue. "Don't tease." The tip of Jac's tongue played against her and the pressure was too much, and too little, and she shivered. The pleasure of a lover's touch. When Jac flattened her tongue and lapped the length of her clit, a groan worked its way from deep inside her. The orgasm took her up and then crashed her back down like a slap. She held Jac's cheeks and lifted her mouth from her oversensitized flesh.

She floated as Jac kissed her softly on her inner thighs and labia. Her skin tingled. Her pulse beat a soothing rhythm through her body, spreading the aftereffects of the orgasms. Finally, she tugged on Jac's shoulders, ready to be wrapped in the arms that always made her feel safe. She sighed as tension drained from her.

Jac lay on her back and gathered Liz against her. "Sleep, Liz. Sleep." Her voice was like a lullaby.

She settled against Jac, drawing one thigh over her and draping an arm across her abdomen, her favorite way to sleep. Jac was still dressed, but Liz was too spent to do any more than scrunch the blouse into her fingers. Pretty blouse. "Thank you." She nuzzled into the hollow at the base of Jac's throat. "So good."

"Sleep," Jac said into her hair. "You're safe."

Liz woke into darkness as if from a fever. The smell of sex and Jac's perfume shrouded her. More. She needed to touch and taste.

She snaked her hand under Jac's blouse and rubbed circles on her abdomen. Muscles tightened. When she tugged the zipper, Jac clasped her wrist.

"No."

"I want to touch you."

"Go back to sleep."

She lifted her head, but Jac pulled it back to her shoulder. She touched Jac's face. Her jaw muscles were clenched. "Why can't I touch you?" Was there some physical reason?

"I just can't," Jac said, her voice tight and hard.

Tears came fast and hot. She'd asked for this, and Jac had given it to her. Her cheeks burned with embarrassment and she tried to sit up. Oh, God, what had she done? "I'm so sorry." She had to get out of here. Suddenly Jac's hands were everywhere—kneading, caressing, stroking. A scorching kiss catapulted her need into orbit again.

This night was not going to end yet. Not like this. Jac had what she wanted, had wanted, for months. If she hadn't been in love with Liz she might have refused. But she was, and her slim grasp on control had shattered like a limb in the face of the storm that was Liz's need. This was going to end badly. Liz would regret it no matter how much she'd pleaded for it. Anguish choked her. She could let Liz leave, but they had already crossed a line, and that truth would be there even if this went no further. With no good choice, she took what she couldn't resist.

Jac kissed Liz and kept kissing her, swallowing her protests, until Liz softened under her and kissed her back. This one night was all she'd have, and she opened herself to the feel and smell and taste of Liz. Her skin burned and her heart pounded as she pressed her fingers to Liz's opening and entered her, one finger, then another on the next stroke. Inside. Wet and slick and tight. As close as she could get. *Mine, but only for tonight.*

She memorized the tunnel that held her fingers—a soft, pulsing enclosure that responded to her intrusion by tightening and relaxing as she entered and withdrew. All too soon, the flesh encasing her fingers pulled tight around her, then threatened to expel her as Liz arched beneath her and came. Jac kissed her, cutting off Liz's words she didn't want to hear. Words lovers spoke. Words she feared were meant for another. Liz's fingers played against her scalp and then stilled. Her breathing settled and her body relaxed. She was asleep.

Jac rolled off Liz, breathing hard, her clit pulsing and burning. The night was thick with the scent of sex and sweat and tropical flowers, heavy with heat and humidity. Liz's wanton need had called to that deepest part of her she'd shut off a decade ago. She was dizzy with arousal, slick with sweat rolling down her sides and between her legs.

She unzipped her shorts and shoved them off. She lay on her back, against Liz's side, and pulled her knees up, spreading them wide. Liz stirred. *Please don't wake up.* She couldn't let Liz touch her. She'd never know if Liz was imagining Teri. Her panties were soaked with the evidence of her desire, and she needed release. Now. Right now.

She put her hand inside her panties. Wetness everywhere. She cupped her sex and rubbed her clit, hard, then lightly, teasing herself as muscles in her legs and abdomen tensed. She touched her breast, imagining Liz was fondling her. Her breathing was ragged, and her clit was hard and aching for release, and still, she kept teasing herself.

Finally she couldn't hold back any longer. She bit her lip as she came in her hand, flooding on her fingers, her clit twitching. Pleasure flowed through her like hot lava. Wetness dripped between her thighs, collecting in her crack. She was panting and the room was too hot. Fingers touched her groin. A shock. Her clit contracted and was Liz awake and damn this blindness and there was nothing she could do about anything as she came again. Liz's hand stayed on her groin, but her breathing remained the even rhythm of sleep.

She closed her legs and clasped Liz's hand. The ring. She'd never take it off. She'd never give Teri up. Jac lay awake in the never-ending dark, afraid to stay, unable to leave, trying to think of a single thing she could do to make this not end badly. Two hours later, she rolled onto her side and spent the next half hour memorizing Liz's body, delicate touch by delicate touch, before this night crashed to its tragic finale.

CHAPTER TWENTY-NINE

Jac had never touched a lover without benefit of sight. Her hands imprinted a landscape of planes and curves, soft skin, the slow rise and fall of Liz's abdomen, delicate curls above her sex, breasts that filled her palms. Liz's forearms were striped with muscles. Jac stayed away from her hands and the ring. She feathered her fingers through Liz's thick hair and held strands against her face, greedy to make a memory of every sensation. She put her palm to Liz's cheek to fix the shape of her face in her mind, then laid it on her chest, over the pendant she'd given her, absorbing the rhythm of her heartbeat.

She fought the urge to wrap her arms around Liz, as if she could squeeze time so it didn't move forward and take her from this moment. Her internal clock said it was near dawn, and she needed to leave before Liz woke. She couldn't bear to be here when the tears and the guilt and the remorse came. She wouldn't say things that weren't wanted. She wouldn't lose control. Not this time.

Carefully, she slid from the bed. She put on her shorts and straightened her blouse, then found Liz's clothes on the floor. She pressed the T-shirt against her face. A fusion of smells—sun and ocean and the new perfume. A reflection of this weekend. It took all her willpower to set it on the bed. Couldn't she take a memento for the years to come when the memory of this weekend was all she had of Liz? She would be the reminder that Liz had betrayed Teri. She'd lose Liz. She'd lose playing music with her. She'd lose everything.

She leaned back against the door for a long time, aching for Liz, forcing herself not to crawl back next to her. Finally she walked to her parents' bedroom and knocked. When the door opened she reached out and held tight. Her mom. "Take me for a drive? Please?"

Jac focused on the vibration of the car, the sound of the tires on the road, passing vehicles, the warm air coming through the open window, the rubber floor mat against her bare feet, the smooth leather of the seat under her thighs. Any sensation to replace Liz in her arms, under her hands, around her fingers. The night replayed itself in sensual detail as her mom drove, silent, except for the hand on Jac's thigh, a comforting touch that she was grateful for.

Traffic noise was steady with the morning commute by the time Jac felt composed enough to talk. "I couldn't stop it. I knew better, but I couldn't say no."

"You can't take the blame." Her mom's voice was kind, but stern, and she squeezed Jac's thigh.

"She was sad…her birthday, Teri's…she was reaching for the familiar, for what she lost, for comfort."

"She must have wanted to be with you."

The blatancy of Liz's need made her shudder. Her heart clenched itself into a hard fist. Had Liz been imagining Teri? "She'll leave me. Just like…" Jac let out a long, sad breath.

"She's your friend. She cares about you." Her mom was quiet and then said, "She's not Maria."

Jac was grateful the interview had forced her to tell her parents about Maria. They'd made her promise never to shut them out again. She was going to need their support to make it through this.

Her mom called her dad. "Is Liz up?…Yes, we're headed back." She started the car. "You need to talk to her. Please tell her how you feel, Jacqueline."

Could she? Was she that brave? "I don't deserve her even if she—"

"Don't ever say that again."

"The accident, Mom."

"Was an accident. No more blaming yourself. No more guilt. No more hiding. You forget how much beauty you've given the world through music. You deserve to be happy. You deserve love."

When they arrived home, her mom walked her to the deck. "We'll give you privacy, but know we're here for you."

Liz was packing. Jac waited on the deck, fighting the ache in her chest. Dare she hope last night had meant something to Liz?

Chapter Thirty

Liz came up from a deep sleep and rolled onto her back. She couldn't remember the last time she'd slept this well. She stretched. Her abs were sore. And her thighs. Oh, yeah, snorkeling three days in a row. Her eyes popped open and dread spread over her like cold rain, making her shiver. She was naked. This wasn't the guest bedroom. Jac. Last night.

No, no, no, no, no pounded through her like a bass-drum beat. She yanked the sheet up to her chin and clenched it to stop the trembling. The deck…kissing Jac…putting Jac's hand on…Oh, God. No, no, no. She squeezed her eyes shut, but that didn't prevent images from galloping across her mind. She jerked to a sit, hugging herself to fight back nausea. She'd forced herself on Jac. And Jac…her head spun. Passionate kisses. Jac touching her everywhere. Tender. Giving. Responding to her need. Giving her the relief she pleaded for. Her skin burned with the memories. Mind-blowing orgasms. Again and again.

They had made love. No. Jac had made love to her. Liz frowned. She'd tried to touch Jac…Heat burst on her cheeks. Jac hadn't wanted her to touch her. "I can't," she'd said, holding Liz's hands away from her. Oh, God, this wasn't happening. A strangled sob filled her throat.

Teri. She clasped her hands to her mouth. Yanked them away. They smelled like Jac. She felt like she was coming apart and couldn't breathe. She'd cheated on Teri. She'd taken advantage of Jac. She bolted from the bed as guilt and shame surrounded her. She needed to get out of here.

Her clothes were folded at the foot of the bed. More heat on her cheeks. When had Jac left? She dressed and hurried to the guest bedroom. She dialed Hannah's cell. It went to voice mail. Her hands trembled as she tried to find the number to the Hyatt. When she reached the registration desk, the clerk said no one by that name was registered. Panic gripped her. Had Hannah checked out? No. The room must be in Kerri's name. She started to call back, but she didn't know Kerri's last name and wasn't up to trying to explain it to the clerk.

Liz paced, twirling her wedding band and taking deep breaths until she was calm enough. She'd apologize to Jac and call a cab to take her to the Hyatt. She'd wait for Hannah. She'd get her seat on the flight changed. She stood in the hallway listening for voices. She heard Vivaldi's *Four Seasons* and then the sound of someone turning a newspaper page. That wouldn't be Jac. She straightened her blouse. Setting a smile on her face, she walked to the dining room.

"Good morning." Jac's dad was wearing a black Tommy Bahama shirt with white flowers. He set the newspaper aside and looked at her.

"Where's…" She cleared her throat. "Where's Jac?" she asked in a voice that came out too high.

"She and her mom went for a drive."

Liz gripped the back of the chair as her legs became jelly. Jac had left. What must she think of her? "Um, I need to call a cab. What's your address?"

"I assume you want to go to the Hyatt?"

"Yes," she said without looking at him, sure her face was many shades redder than the rest of her sunburned skin.

"I'll drive you when you're ready."

Oh, God, he knows. She hurried to the bedroom and bundled her things into the suitcase. Matching suitcases they'd bought for the band tour. Tears blurred her vision. Guilt slithered through her. "I'm so sorry, sweetie," she whispered.

The wind chimes were on the dresser. Taking them out of the box, she clutched them against her chest. Thoughtful. Jac was always thoughtful. She'd taken advantage of her in the worst way. God, the music last night. Jac's playing had ripped her open, changed her until she didn't know who she was. She wasn't someone who seduced her best friend. Or cheated on her wife.

Liz set her bags by the front door and went to the dining room. "I'm ready—" She gasped and put her hand to her chest. Her fingers closed around the pendant. Jac. Sitting alone on the deck. Her knees went weak and she collapsed onto the nearest chair.

Jac tilted her head and her shoulders stiffened.

She always knows where I am. Tears flooded Liz's eyes and she had no Kleenex. She wiped them away with the hem of her T-shirt as she walked slowly to the patio table and sat across from Jac. She had on the fuschia blouse she'd worn last night. Wrinkled.

"I'm so sorry." It was so true and such a ridiculous thing to say. Liz wanted it to be yesterday morning, with all of them eating pineapple fritters. She wanted to go back to last night and make a different choice. Stay in her room. She'd lost control in the worst way. The way that hurt people.

"It's been a hard time for you." Jac's voice was like the hug she craved, but her face was tight.

"I'm so sorry I used you." The sun was warm, and the ocean was blue, and palm trees swayed. Another perfect day in paradise. Except she'd ruined paradise. How did they go on from here?

Jac gripped the armrests, squeezing to keep herself together, squeezing to block the pain of her heart breaking. *Used her.* A stand-in for Teri. It was hard to breathe. She wasn't going to hear the voice she loved say the words she wanted to hear—"I love you." That's what last night had been for her, but for Liz it was reaching back for what she'd lost.

"There's no excuse." Sadness in Liz's voice. Then sniffling. Crying.

Why had she let it get out of control? She could have said something to stop it, something that would have let them sit here this morning with a little awkwardness, but not this chasm between them. She hadn't stopped it because she hadn't wanted to. It was too easy to fall into Liz's need, to let it give her the excuse to take what she wanted. To let it mean something it didn't. To pretend Liz was hers.

"I took advantage of your friendship in the worst way. I'm so ashamed."

No, she wasn't going to hear the words she longed to hear. Her throat tightened and she fought tears. She would not cry. "We're friends, Liz. We've weathered a lot together. We'll get through this." Friendship. If that was all she could have, she'd make it be enough.

"Okay. Yeah." Liz's voice softened. "We'll laugh about the vacation fling." Another sniffle.

Jac's heart caved in on itself. Is that what this would be? Like it didn't matter? "I love you," she wanted to sing out.

"It hurts so much. I'm not someone who...I don't..." A chair scraped on the deck. "I'm so sorry. So very sorry." Liz's footsteps across the deck, across the bamboo floor of the house, then the front door opening.

Jac focused on Vivaldi's *Four Seasons*. Clung to it. Concerto No. 4 in F Minor—"Winter." The door opened again. Liz? Was she coming back? They were friends. Of course she wouldn't leave it like this. A hand squeezed her shoulder and she grabbed it. The wrong ring. Her mom. She felt like she'd been punched as she let the tears flood down her cheeks.

Chapter Thirty-one

"Did Jacqueline tell you how she started with the trumpet?" Frank asked when they were on the highway headed to the Hyatt.

"No." Liz picked at the hem of her T-shirt, focusing on the ocean as her feelings shifted like the current—confusion, then regret, then guilt, then immense sadness, before cycling again.

"I was in a band, and we rehearsed in the studio Peggy uses for her painting. Jacqueline would sit in the doorway and listen to us. She was so serious." He paused and then cleared his throat. "One day we were up at the house getting snacks when I heard someone playing the trumpet. I made a joke about Wayne, our trumpet player, never leaving well enough alone. Well, Wayne was standing next to me. We went down to the studio. It was Jacqueline. She could barely hold it, but she had a look on her face like nothing I've ever seen. She was in love with that instrument. I bought her a trumpet the next day."

Liz had no idea what to say. Jac was special? She knew that. Jac deserved better than a friend who took advantage of her in a way she shouldn't have?

"We'll be at Monterey."

Her heart skipped. Monterey. Would Jac still want to perform with them? Could she play with Jac? "Thank you for having me," Liz said when Frank pulled up to the Hyatt. "Is Jac going to meet us at the airport?"

"I imagine so." Frank took Liz's bags into the hotel. "I like you, Liz. You've been good for Jacqueline. I hope you keep being good for her." He gave her a quick hug and walked out.

"I need to find my sister," Liz said to the clerk at the registration counter, hanging on to what little control she had. "I think her room's under...she's with an assistant manager named Kerri." She swiped away tears.

"Have a seat and I'll find her," the clerk said kindly.

Liz sat on the nearest chair and tucked her hands between her knees, looking toward the lobby with its tropical ambience. The vacation she'd always wanted.

"Lizzie?"

She launched herself into Hannah's arms. "Oh, God, I did something awful."

"Come up to the room," Hannah said.

"I don't want to see Kerri."

"She went to work." Hannah put her arm around Liz's waist and walked her to the elevator.

When they were in the room, Liz sank onto one of the chairs. The bed was a mess, and clothes were strewn everywhere, and she'd never been happier to be with her sister.

"Talk." Hannah sat across from her.

"I slept with Jac," she said in one long exhale.

"Good for you." Hannah's voice was too bright.

Liz clasped her hands. "I seduced her," she said in a voice as small as she felt. "What am I going to do?"

"Celebrate."

"No, not the good kind of seduced. I forced myself on her." She hugged herself and rocked. "I couldn't stop myself."

"Maybe she let you."

"What?"

"Maybe Jac let you seduce her."

"Trust me, she didn't." Jac pushing on her waist. Jac refusing to let her touch her. Jac saying, "Let me give you this." Why hadn't any of that mattered last night? She felt on the verge of collapse under the truth of what she'd done. "Can you please be understanding?"

"Yes, but I won't tell you what you want to hear." Hannah went to the bathroom and came back with Kleenex. "You let yourself feel. You acted on it. You didn't do anything wrong."

"Teri deserves better than a wife who seduces another woman."

"Teri's not here, Lizzie."

"I wanted Jac. I don't understand." She fingered the musical note on the end of the chain around her neck. "I still love Teri, but I wanted Jac." Love and desire had always had a single point of intersection—Teri. Now they were two forces pulling her apart. She let go of the pendant and pinched her wedding band. Love for Teri that would forever be trapped in the past. Desire for Jac that had demolished the boundaries of friendship.

"Your ability to feel love and passion doesn't stop because Teri's no longer the focus for those feelings. You don't betray her by letting yourself feel again. You do betray yourself if you don't."

"Not this. I can't feel this." She fell against Hannah as images of last night barraged her. "Not this."

Liz stood on the curb in front of the airport while Hannah said good-bye to Kerri with a few words and a very long kiss. She didn't see Jac. As they walked to the gate she kept thinking about the conversation with the groundskeeper at the Hyatt. She'd gone down to the lobby while Hannah packed. She'd wandered to the pond where he was feeding the swans.

"They're beautiful," Liz said, watching them gobble up the food. "I love that they mate for life."

"Yeah, most people believe that. The male's got a scar on his belly from a fight." He tossed out another handful of food. "That female left her mate for him, and there was quite a tussle over her."

She'd sat on a bench after the groundskeeper left, watching the swans float lazily, occasionally nuzzling each other. Everything she'd thought she knew about love now seemed suspect. She'd fallen in love so young, like her grandma, like her dad, like Kevin. She'd assumed it would last a lifetime. It hadn't. And then Jac…She tightened her grip on the luggage handle as they walked toward the gate. She still didn't see Jac.

"Best vacation ever?" Hannah asked when they'd taken seats in the waiting area.

"Yeah." She smiled when Hannah looked at her. The vacation had been a thoughtful gesture she'd always remember.

"I put a deposit on a place in the city last week."

Probably for the best since Liz wouldn't be going to Carmel anymore.

"It's time I got on with my life. My new job is the first step toward rebuilding my career."

"Just don't let your libido sink it." The airport looked the same as it had on Friday, but nothing was the same.

"That's not what happened."

"Your boss finds you in bed with his wife and—"

"I loved her." Hannah's voice was sharp.

"You said it was a fling."

"You all assumed that. Do you really think I'd be careless enough to blow up a career I spent fifteen years building?"

"So what happened?" Liz kept glancing toward the corridor but didn't see Jac. What would she say to her?

"She was practically a prisoner in the hotel while her womanizing, jerk-off husband came and went as he pleased. Arranged marriage." Hannah crossed her arms, looking off in the distance. "I started cooking her special meals to cheer her up. We talked, became friends. Then it became more. She was trying to divorce him. He caught wind of it, set us up to get caught, and trashed my career." She shrugged one shoulder.

"Why didn't you tell us?"

"What, and ruin another family myth—Hannah the party girl? Hannah with a different girlfriend every month? Hannah who doesn't understand love?"

"I haven't been fair to you."

"You had your own stuff to deal with, Lizzie. I don't even know if she's okay. How fucked up is that? Don't leave things in a bad place with Jax. You two have something special."

Had something special, until she ruined it. Jac still wasn't here. Liz checked her watch. She frowned and tapped the dial. The second hand wasn't moving. She covered it with her hand. No. She wasn't ready to let go of the past.

"We had some fun, didn't we?"

"I'm glad you're not moving back to some tropical island."

"Someone has to straighten out this family."

They announced the flight would begin boarding. Was Jac waiting until the last minute so she wouldn't have to talk to Liz? She stared out to the tarmac. The plane was waiting to take her home. Back to normal. Away from all this tropical nonsense. *Best vacation ever.*

CHAPTER THIRTY-TWO

L iz shoved through the music-room door and flung her satchel on the floor near the piano. Oscar flattened his ears as he watched her from his perch on the back of the couch, as if scolding her for being late. Again. Cassie, Regan, and Sammy continued to joke around, ignoring her, probably hoping she wasn't going to bite their heads off. Again.

"Hear from Jac today?" her dad asked, walking in behind her.

"No." Liz was exhausted from two weeks of classes and a full schedule of private lessons, on top of stress about the band and the festival on Friday. And always, every minute, worry about Jac. She hadn't seen or heard from Jac since Hawaii. She hadn't returned Liz's phone messages. Peggy didn't know when Jac would be coming home. Liz had stayed away from Carmel. Jac's message was clear.

"That's not professional." He looked tired and kept tugging his pants up. He'd lost weight. Probably stress over Kevin and Karen's separation.

Plopping down at the piano, Liz ran through a series of chords, hoping by some miracle it would be different this time. She winced. That same zinging pain shot up from her hand all the way to her elbow in spite of the extra Advil. Weeks of feeling normal and then bam. Ever since she'd returned from Hawaii, it hurt like hell. Different than after the cast came off. Worse. Tons worse. The kind of pain that made her nauseous.

"Short rehearsal tonight," Liz said. Regan and Sammy shared a look. Of course they should run through the whole set for Monterey.

They should be rehearsing every day leading up to the show. She hadn't told anyone about her wrist. She didn't need them any more worried than was normal before a big performance. She planned to rest it and load up on Advil, maybe Vicodin, and pray that in four days she could get through the most important set of her life. "I decided on the encore." Not "Carmel Sketches." If they got an encore. She was playing like crap, and they all knew it.

The door opened and everyone looked toward it. Liz plastered her palm to her chest. Air rushed out of her lungs, as if she'd been punched. Jac. Tanned. Sun-bleached hair. Wearing a Tommy Bahama blouse. Max at her side. Liz's heart galloped under her hand, and she swallowed hard as questions banged into each other.

"Missed a few rehearsals," her dad said, but no one paid attention to him. Sammy gave Regan a thumbs-up. Cassie caught Liz's eye and winked.

No one said anything as Jac released Max from his harness. He walked directly to Liz, tail wagging, and put his paws on the piano bench. She ruffled his ears and scrabbled her fingers down his back the way that made him wiggle his butt. God, she'd missed him. He settled on the floor on his spot by the couch, a respectful distance from Oscar. Her hands trembled as Jac took her trumpet from its case, ran through several arpeggios, and then blew a high C that went on forever. She couldn't get the last time they'd played out of her head.

Jac went to her usual position next to Sammy and nodded in Liz's direction.

Never taking her eyes from Jac, Liz started them off on "Carmel Sketches." Everything faded, and it was just Jac and the music they'd written together. Her wrist hurt like hell as she played with everything she had.

When the final note faded, all Liz heard was her heart beating against her ribs. Jac's improvising was daring, confident, and sensuous, a refined version of how she'd played the last night in Hawaii. Cassie clapped her sticks together. Regan slapped her guitar. Sammy whispered something to Jac, who nodded but didn't smile. Her dad folded his arms, looking smug.

"Let's do 'Spring Time,' 'Combustion,' and 'Soaring Hawk,'" Liz said. "Then we'll do another run-through of 'Carmel Sketches' and call it a night." Could she make it through four songs? She massaged her wrist. Her dad looked her way and she stopped. She was afraid to tell him it hurt.

Jac turned toward her and tilted her head, frowning, then went to the couch. Sitting with her trumpet in her lap, she petted Max through the three songs. When she joined them for "Carmel Sketches," she played even more beautifully.

"Great work," Liz said. She rubbed her wrist as everyone filed out, except Jac. Her heart was in her throat, and all she could think about was that night in Hawaii and how much she'd wanted Jac.

"Hello, Liz," Jac said, standing by the piano. "What's wrong with your wrist?"

"I don't know." Tears stung her eyes from the pain.

"Have you seen the doctor?"

"I will after the festival. I'm glad you came back."

"Monterey's important."

Liz's heart dropped. Jac came back for the show.

"Is this your last rehearsal?" Jac was all business. Not a speck of acknowledgement in her voice that they were friends.

"Yes."

"I'll meet you backstage Friday." Jac's distant, detached attitude sent chills through Liz. If she'd hoped for forgiveness, she saw no sign of it. Jac packed her trumpet and put Max's harness on.

"I'll walk out with you. Did Peggy drive you?"

"Mom did. No need to walk me out." Jac hesitated, and for an instant, something heavy hung in the air between them. Then she straightened her shoulders and left.

Liz followed a few steps behind, as if pulled by a magnetic force. It hurt so much to watch Jac walk away. She waved to Susan. The car pulled from the curb. A stab of longing made her want to chase it.

"You're looking like you lost your best friend," Cassie said, draping her arm over Liz's shoulders. "Don't take a genius to figure out something happened with Jac."

"A misunderstanding."

"If I was a betting woman, I'd say it was the romantic kind of misunderstanding."

"Save your nickels."

"Whatever you say." Cassie walked on ahead. "If losing her makes you play like you been lately, you better rethink what you're about, girlfriend."

"Cass, wait." No point denying it. "Things got out of hand and I made a mistake. I don't know how to fix it."

"For better or worse, T gave you this shot for the band. She can't give you happiness."

"I don't know what that is anymore."

"If you found it with Jac, you're a fool for letting her go."

"I'll always love Teri."

"What does that have to do with anything?" Cassie gave her a funny look. "You and Jac click. It's in your music. You can't hide or fake that."

"It's just music."

"It's just your heart singing. Why you being so stubborn? How many people are lucky enough to fall in love twice? Now go say good-bye to T and get on with your life." Cassie kissed her cheek. "I love you. Don't disappoint me."

"I want to talk to you after dinner about the fall tour," her dad said as Liz gathered up her stuff in the music room. "And I don't want to make you nervous, but an agent approached me about promoting you. He'll be at Monterey to hear a couple of groups, including you."

"Are we ready for that?" Something was seriously wrong with her wrist.

"You take the breaks when they come," he said. "Teri would be thrilled."

"Hey, Pops," Sammy said, poking his head in the door. "Gotta run."

"You're not having dinner?"

"Can't."

Regan walked in, her arm around Vicky. "I'll see you Friday," she said to Liz.

"We always have dinner together after practice," her dad said, frowning.

"Got plans." Regan had on blue jeans and a yellow T-shirt. Only her Converse shoes were black. Amazing.

"I guess it's you and me, sunshine," he said as they headed toward the restaurant. "I want your opinion on Louise's chicken potpie. She wants to put it on the menu."

"When's Rebecca coming back?" She'd been on vacation for the last two weeks, the longest she'd ever been gone. He said nothing. "What's going on, Dad?"

"Rebecca took a job in Sacramento."

"Why didn't you tell me?"

"You need to focus on the show."

"She's had job offers before."

"She wanted to date." So, Hannah was right.

"And?"

"Your mom was the love of my life. I can't replace her any more than you can replace Teri."

"You know what? I'm exhausted. I'm going home."

"I want to talk to you about—"

"Not tonight." Liz forced herself to drive home instead of to Carmel. What could she say to Jac in the face of her aloofness? Would they play Monterey and never see each other again? That's not what she wanted. After the festival, she'd find a way to restore their friendship.

Inside the condo, she heated leftover pizza and ate without tasting as she curled up on the couch with the TV on. At least the noise was company. She missed Hannah being here. So many things she needed to do and she had no energy for any of them.

The front door opened and Hannah bustled in with flattened moving boxes in her arms. "Why are you sitting in the dark?" She tossed the boxes on the floor and turned on a light. "Are you crying?"

Liz pressed Kleenex to the corners of her eyes. "I miss Jac so much."

"I know," Hannah said, sitting next to her.

The Kleenex wilted with the fresh rush of tears. "I'm in love with her. I can't help it." The instant she'd seen Jac walk through the door, she'd known.

"You two belong together." Hannah rubbed her back.

"I always thought I'd be like Grandma and Dad. One love. Mated for life."

Hannah snorted. "Life isn't a fairy tale, Lizzie. Love is precious whenever it comes, and you're a fool if you don't grab it."

"Jac came to rehearsal today."

"Did you tell her how you feel?"

"I'm afraid." A sob rose up and she gripped Hannah's hand. "She barely talked to me."

"You have to give her a reason to talk to you. Tell her. I dare you."

"I don't know how to say good-bye to Teri."

"Cancel your classes tomorrow. We'll go say good-bye together. Now scoot over." Hannah took a piece of pizza from her plate and turned the volume up too loud and everything felt right. New, but right.

CHAPTER THIRTY-THREE

Liz tightened her fingers around the bouquet of lilies on her lap, thinking back to the last time she was at this cemetery. Numb from grief, she'd walked between her dad and Teri's mom, pockets stuffed with Kleenex, hoping her legs didn't collapse under her. Monday it would be a year.

Hannah parked Liz's convertible beside the curb. Green lawn dotted with oak trees stretched to the boundaries of the cemetery. Vineyards went on from there. Pretty. Peaceful. They'd listened to the CD on the drive to Lodi, and they sat until the last song ended, the one with Teri's riveting solo.

They walked arm in arm, in the matching sandals they'd bought in Hawaii. The sun was warm on their backs, the sky a cloudless blue. Liz's heart beat slowly, reverently, as if recognizing where they were. They stood in front of the waist-high black marble headstone.

Teri Denise Carr
Beloved Daughter and Wife
September 3, 1981–September 22, 2013

Kneeling, Liz arranged the flowers in the vase they'd brought, adding water from a bottle.

Hannah kissed her fingers and touched them to the headstone, saying something under her breath. She gave Liz a quick hug. "I'll be by the car if you need me."

Liz pulled out the wad of Kleenex from her pocket. She put on Teri's favorite Giants baseball cap and sat on the grass with her legs tucked under her. A squirrel ran up the trunk of a nearby oak tree, an acorn in its mouth.

"I'm sorry I couldn't bring myself to come before. I've missed you so much. It's been so hard without you. I thought we'd be together forever." She picked a stalk of clover and twirled the stem in her fingers.

"The jazz festival is Friday. I got the CD out. It's getting great reviews. I'm composing again. It's not our sound, but I love it. You wanted me to go on with my life. I didn't think I could, but I have." She rubbed her palm over the prickly blades of grass. "I met a woman in Carmel. I need to tell you about her. Her name's Jac…" Liz talked and cried for a long time until she'd said it all. With each sentence, the strings that bound her heart to Teri's loosened. By the end she felt lighter than she had in a long time.

Finally she stood and ran her hand over Teri's name on the headstone. "I'm in love with Jac. I want a future with her, if she'll have me. I came to say good-bye, Teri." She waited for more tears that never came. She took off her ring, put it in her pocket, and walked to the car.

"Hear that?" Hannah asked. "That's Teri cheering."

One phase of her life was ending, and it was as it should be. Liz prayed another phase was about to start. She kept her eyes on the road ahead as they drove out of the cemetery, her thoughts on Jac.

"You're humming," Hannah said.

Liz pressed her hands to her chest. She was humming a new melody. Would there be a trumpet part in it? She pinched the pendant she never took off. She hoped there would be.

Chapter Thirty-four

Liz put her hand over her abdomen to calm the nerves dancing in her stomach. She'd pulled into this gravel driveway so many times in the last six months that it felt like home. She was worried about the reception she'd get today in light of Jac's aloofness on Monday. How did she apologize for taking advantage of her and then ask her to go steady? It was crazy. But…her heart did that wonderful flip-flop and then beat its new rhythm, the rhythm that had Jac in it. She owed her the truth.

She'd planned to tell her after the show Friday night but had woken up this morning with an aching need to see her. She barely made it through her morning classes before hanging an OFFICE HOURS CANCELED sign on her door and racing home. She'd packed and driven like a crazy woman down to Carmel. *I'm in love with her.* The thought made her insides go soft and her heart flutter, but it also made her tremble with fear. Was Hannah right that Jac had feelings for her, or would she make a fool of herself with an unwanted confession?

Liz let the engine idle, trapped in uncertainty. Finally, she turned it off and strode to the house. She couldn't stand the way things had been at the last rehearsal. If they were going to be onstage together, she had to do this. The awkwardness between them would show in the music, and that wasn't fair to Jac. There was too much at stake with her comeback. Taking a deep breath, she knocked on the front door.

"Liz." With the briefest look of surprise, Jac's mom greeted her with a warm smile. Or maybe she wanted to believe it was warm.

"Susan. I'm so glad you're here for the show. I'm sorry I didn't say good-bye in Hawaii." A funny little hitch added itself to her heartbeat. Maybe this wasn't a good idea.

"I hope you've come to see Jacqueline." Trumpet notes filled the house and a piano joined in. Show tune. Jac and Peggy. "Join us. We're having a late lunch."

Liz followed Susan, hands clasped in front of her to steady them. Frank was eating a salad at the dining table. He nodded at her. Peggy caught her eye. Surprise, and then she smiled.

She was afraid to look at Jac. Her heart was already galloping from just being near her. She closed her eyes and listened as Jac improvised to the well-known melody, twisting and turning it in a sophisticated riff. When they stopped, Liz was trembling, barely able to believe what she'd heard. Hawaii had changed Jac's playing. She was uninhibited, improvising with fearlessness and ease. She opened her eyes and looked at Jac, and her stomach did a slow roll. Oh, yeah, she was in love with her.

"One more," Peggy said.

"No more," Jac said. "I haven't had lunch yet." She was breathing hard, the trumpet against her chest. Wearing creased jeans and an orange linen shirt, sleeves rolled up to show those wonderfully muscled forearms, she was partly her old self and partly a new, more relaxed-looking self. So beautiful.

"One more or I'll hide the butterscotch pudding," Peggy said, motioning Liz over to the piano.

Heart pounding, Liz slid to the center of the bench and rubbed her hands on her jeans. Her wrist still hurt like hell with any movement. She didn't care if this was the last thing she ever played. It was her most important performance ever.

"Do I have to put up with that, Mom?"

"Yes." Susan poured iced tea from a pitcher and handed the glass to Peggy, who sat with them, her expression as welcoming as it had ever been.

"You always liked her best," Jac said with mock petulance, tucking hair behind her ear. She wore her diamond studs and diamond ring. She looked confident, not at all like the lonely mess Liz was. "What tune?" She lifted the trumpet to her lips.

Liz froze, her fingers above the keys. Longing swirled through her, like an ocean current, and she couldn't find her way out of it, trapped in forces about to pull her away from everything she'd known. It built like a crescendo until she couldn't keep it in. She let go…love and desire swept down her arms and into "Carmel Sketches."

Jac lowered the trumpet, a look of shock on her flushed face. She started to walk away.

Liz's heart plummeted, but she didn't stop. She needed to have this conversation with Jac, and if the only way to have it was through the piano, then that's what she'd do. Those zinging pains in her wrist made her wince. The melody she'd heard in her mind leaving the cemetery filled her, and she let it come through, raw and fresh, the sound of the future she wanted. She played her part hoping, against the evidence of Jac's back, that she'd play hers.

Susan went to Jac, took her arm, and whispered something. Jac stiffened. Susan spoke again, and Jac's shoulders lifted as she took a deep breath, then dropped as she let it out.

Peggy, Susan, and Frank went to the patio, closing the French doors. Max moved to Jac's side and sat, as if blocking her from leaving.

Liz kept going—apology for what she'd done in Hawaii. Telling Jac how much she'd missed her. Then confessing how much she'd wanted her in Hawaii.

Jac turned toward the piano and tilted her head, her mouth in that sad half smile.

Liz repeated that passage. *Yes, I wanted you so much it drove me to do something I shouldn't have. I took advantage of someone I love. Yes, someone I love.*

Finally, Jac lifted the trumpet and joined her.

She didn't know how long they played, or even what they played—jazz, classical—it blended and separated, climaxed and softened, surged and ebbed, fusing into something new. She couldn't take her eyes off Jac, blurred into soft edges by tears. When she'd said all she had to say, she dropped her hands to her lap. Only then did she realize her wrist was free of pain.

Jac didn't stop. Her sound went sad, deeply sad, then angry sad.

She wanted to run to Jac, to hold and comfort her. She sat and listened, waiting for her future to be determined.

Jac's sound shifted, becoming less sad, then ended in a flurry of dissonant confusion. She held the trumpet between her breasts, her chest rising and falling, her expression unreadable. "Why are you here?"

"I miss you." She gripped the edge of the bench to keep from throwing herself into Jac's arms. She wouldn't force herself on her again. "I miss us."

"Is there an us?" Jac's voice was gentle but sad.

"There was. I want that again." *Please tell me you forgive me.*

"Your wrist. It's better."

"Not until just now." She rubbed it, made fists. No pain. She wanted to laugh with relief, but the pain in her chest was still there. No sign of forgiveness. "I'm so sorry about Hawaii."

Jac set her trumpet on the table and was out the door, long strides taking her across the patio before Liz was barely off the bench.

Liz caught up to her and tried to keep pace as Jac headed toward her cottage. "Please let me explain."

Jac kept walking. Max trotted beside her.

She grabbed Jac's arm, holding tight when Jac tried to yank free. "I want to be with you." Damn it. That's not the way she wanted to say this.

Jac pried Liz's hand off and froze, frowning. She sandwiched Liz's left hand between hers, then traced each finger. "Where's your ring?"

Liz entwined their fingers. "I'm not wearing it. I—"

Jac's face constricted into a dark, angry storm. "Don't play with me. I've been some pathetic stand-in for Teri. Sounding board on your CD. Composing muse. Bedmate. I'm not here for you to take advantage of!"

Liz clamped her hand to her mouth as Jac fled. She flinched when the door to her cottage slammed shut.

"I'm so sorry, Peggy." Liz ended the call, edged forward in the chair, and rested her chin on her hands. Fog saturated everything into a dull, damp, flat white. The wind chimes Jac had given her sounded in the breeze, making her want to cry.

"Jac won't talk to Peggy. I'm so messed up. I hurt her again, Hannah. I've never seen her so upset."

Hannah sat next to her and laughed at something on her phone.

"What do I do now? I love her, and all I do is hurt her."

"She hasn't been with anyone in a long time. You can't expect her to know how to do it any better than you."

"Thanks."

"For cancelling my date and coming down here? You're welcome." Hannah texted something, probably to the date she wasn't with. "This garden's kind of cool. When you said you were restoring it, I had visions of the plants in perfectly straight rows and Grandma saying, 'Don't touch.' Everything with her was 'don't touch' and 'don't make a mess.'"

"It was?"

"Oh, please. Don't tell me you don't remember her yelling if we got within ten feet of her precious cranberry glass in the window. And who doesn't have a lawn or sandbox for their grandkids?"

"She baked cookies for us."

"Did she ever let us help?"

"I guess not." Liz made a fist. Yeah, it hurt again. Maybe Peggy's piano had some magical healing power.

"She was kind of a tyrant, Lizzie."

"She was not."

Hannah held up her hands in an appeasing gesture. "You were her favorite. You had a different relationship with her than Kevin or I did. You had the talent she could mentor. You found your 'one true love,'" Hannah emphasized the words with her fingers, "at a young age. You fit the Randall family myth. Kevin found a way to belong by marrying young and staying with the restaurant. I was always on the outside."

"You're blaming Grandma for—"

Hannah shot to her feet. "I'm not blaming anyone for the choices I made." She dipped her head to smell one of the new roses Liz had planted. "I'm saying all of us had a lot of expectations on us and not a lot of room to be ourselves."

Liz sat back against the chair, surprised by Hannah's comments. She'd been close to her grandma. She searched her memory for anything they'd done that didn't involve music. "So, you left to..."

"Be my own person. You can't have a real life until you have that."

"But..." Liz lifted her gaze to Hannah, understanding for the first time what the rules had been. Approval, belonging, support had come at a price. She'd fit in. She'd worked hard to please her grandma and her dad. She'd become what they wanted, but not her own person.

"Come on." Hannah tugged her to her feet and danced them across the patio and into the house. "Since I gave up my date, you get to take me to dinner."

Liz pulled into a parking space on Ocean Street half a block from the restaurant. The convertible was so much easier to park than the Yukon. They were shown to an elegantly set table on the atrium patio warmed by heaters and dimly lit with candles. The host held her chair while she sat. She shot back up, bumping the table.

"What?" Hannah turned and looked toward the table in the corner. "We'll go somewhere else." Hannah took her arm and led her out. "Don't melt down on me, Lizzie." On the sidewalk she said, "It might not be what it looks like."

Liz sucked in the cold air as her heart crumbled into little pieces. "No, it's exactly what it looks like." Jac and Gwen, her former physical therapist. Clinking wineglasses.

CHAPTER THIRTY-FIVE

"Time to go," Hannah said, ending the call.

"I'm not going anywhere." Still in the sweats she'd slept in, Liz downed the last of the cold coffee and banged the mug back on the table. Hannah had forced her to sit on the patio, but that was as much as she could manage. Her chest ached. Her wrist ached. How was she going to get through tomorrow night?

"Come on. I'll help you pick something to wear."

"Hannah." The damn wind chimes sounded again. It was a cheery blue-sky day and she felt awful. She'd handled things badly with Jac yesterday and she couldn't get the image of Jac and Gwen out of her mind.

"That was Peggy." Hannah sat next to her. "Jac's heading out for her walk. You better hurry if you're going to catch her."

"I'm the last person she wants to be with, and ditto for me. Why is Peggy calling you?"

"Grow up, Lizzie. You had a fairy-tale life with Teri. You had a love where there was never a wrong note or missed step. Sometimes love is messy and off-key. Sometimes it makes you do foolish things, the exact opposite of what you want to do. Sometimes people push away because pulling close is too scary. You and Jac belong together."

"Wait. You—Peggy? You—"

"Meddled. Good thing we did. You two are clueless."

"Are you telling me…Hawaii? You and Peggy set that up?"

"Best vacation ever?" Hannah's smile and gleeful eyes were like sunshine on a cloudy day and sprinkles on a cupcake.

"You're…" Liz couldn't finish as emotions choked her. She'd been so wrong about Hannah.

"Best sister ever? I know. Now go talk to that gorgeous trumpet player. As soon as I get you sorted out, I need to focus on Kevin. I'll bring him and Karen back together. Dad and Rebecca? Not so sure."

"Dad's pretty stubborn."

"He's pretty scared of change and pretty locked into this 'one-love' nonsense Grandma started. Life's short, and it's time we all started grabbing what makes us happy."

"How did you get so smart?"

"It's what makes me a great chef. Paying attention to how things fit together. Now come on." Hannah tugged Liz up. "You've got a date."

❖

Liz caught up with Jac several blocks from Peggy's and fell into step beside her. "Hi."

"What are you doing here?" Jac looked sexy in jeans and a crisp white shirt open at the collar, sleeves rolled up. Her military-straight posture and lengthening strides screamed, "Go away." Max gave Liz a quick glance and then ignored her, focusing on his job.

"We need to talk." Half a block of stony silence made Liz think this might be a bad idea. "We're not performing tomorrow night with things like this between us. Either we work this out, or you can play solo."

"You wouldn't dare."

"Try me."

"Leave me alone."

"I'll be on your walks every day until we're friends again."

"Stalking me?" Anger was practically sparking off Jac.

"If that's what it takes." Two blocks later, Jac hadn't said a single word, and Liz was almost running to keep up with her. Hannah's words came back to her. "Sometimes people push away because pulling close is too scary." Who could blame her? She hadn't given Jac much reason to trust her. Okay, and Jac was stubborn, too. She tickled her ribs.

"Don't." Jac clamped her arm to her side.

A few steps later, Liz tickled her again. "Say you want to be my friend."

Jac stopped. "I don't want to be your friend! I want to be your lover!"

"And I want to be yours!"

"I'm not a stand-in for Teri!"

"I'm not Maria!" Great. Now they were in a childish shouting match. Liz turned to go, afraid she'd say something she'd regret. Oh, the hell with manners. She had nothing to lose. "And another thing—" She turned around and ran into Jac, who'd stepped toward her. She grabbed Jac's waist to steady her.

"Are you going to forever be knocking me over?" Jac lifted her eyebrow, a hint of a smile at the corners of her mouth.

"Yes. Are you going to forever be sneaking up on me?"

"I haven't decided yet."

"I love this smile." Liz traced Jac's lips. "Can I kiss you?"

"No. I don't know. No."

"Chicken." Liz tightened her grip on Jac's waist.

Tears poured down Jac's cheeks as if a faucet had been turned on. "I'm terrified," she said in a whisper. "I love you so much, and if you break my heart, I won't survive. I won't, Liz. I can only be friends. Just friends."

"Shh." Liz held Jac as tenderly as she could. It couldn't have been easy for her to say that. Her heart swelled with love for the woman who was strong and yet so fragile. "It's all right, honey. I want there to be an us. Friends is an us. A beautiful us." Max pressed against their legs, as if reminding them he was part of this.

"Do you have Kleenex?"

"No, but I have thumbs." Liz brushed the tears from Jac's cheeks and kissed the corners of her mouth.

"I don't think friends kiss each other."

"Your rules, not mine. Now are you taking me to lunch, or not?" Liz craved so much more, but she wasn't going to force herself on Jac. She would be whatever Jac needed her to be.

Lunch at the Bistro was an extravaganza. "Where have you been?" Tony asked, coming out to the patio to greet them. He pampered them with delicious food, including a decadent dessert. Jac pretended not to recognize the wine, to Tony's immense delight.

Jac was quiet on the walk home until they'd left the busy downtown streets behind. "In Hawaii…" Her stride became shorter with each step. "That night. For me. It was making love."

"I know." Liz adjusted her stride to match Jac's. "My body knew it. My mind hadn't caught up yet. When you tried to push me away on the deck, then wouldn't let me touch you, I didn't understand it was your way of protecting yourself."

"I couldn't say no to you. I wanted to be with you so much. I was afraid I was a substitute for Teri. I couldn't let you touch me. It would have broken me."

"I wanted *you* that night. You. Not Teri. I was in a bad state after watching you parade around in shorts and sleeveless blouses with too many open buttons and that swimsuit. Oh, my. You can't look that gorgeous around me and expect me not to want you."

Jac undid another button on her shirt.

"Don't." Liz clamped her hand over Jac's as she moved to undo the next button.

"And if I want you to touch me?" Jac sounded shy.

"I'll touch you with all the love in my heart." They continued in silence along residential streets. A comfortable silence. Liz studied the gardens she knew almost as well as her own from months of walking this same route with Jac. Their relationship had changed with the seasons as surely as the gardens—the flush of new growth in spring had phased into the flowers of summer, and now a hint of fall foliage tinged some of the Japanese maples.

Finally, Jac spoke again. "I fell in love with you the first time I danced with you."

"Memorial Day?"

"I'm a sucker for a beautiful woman dancing in my arms." Definitely a smile.

Liz nudged Jac's shoulder. "You know how to make a girl feel special."

Jac took her arm, elegant fingers curling around her elbow. "You're the most special. I wanted to tell you in Hawaii so many times."

Liz shuddered as sensations rolled through her. Warm sensations. Jac's fingers felt like they'd always been there. Like they belonged there. "You did with every thoughtful gesture. I fell in love with you dancing, too. The first night in Hawaii."

"I almost kissed you. I thought you knew and that's why you left the dance floor so abruptly. You were different after that. I felt guilty."

"God, we're a pair. I left because I almost kissed you. I wanted to so badly. I was worried you knew, and that's why you kept your distance."

"I was afraid I couldn't keep my hands off you or I'd blurt out I love you or burst into song or something equally inappropriate. That last afternoon at the beach undid me."

"What was with your playing that night? I almost came on the piano bench."

Jac's smile grew huge. "Yeah?"

"Don't do that tomorrow night."

"And if I do?"

Liz tickled Jac's ribs. "Are you going to kiss me? Like in the next few seconds?"

Jac stopped. She looked scared again.

Liz stepped so their bodies touched and closed her eyes. "I hear water being sprayed against something, a woman laughing, cars a few blocks away. I smell you and me. I feel your shoes against mine, your legs against mine, your breasts against mine. I feel you and only you. I feel us."

"You're getting better." Jac's voice was soft.

"I'm hoping I have a lifetime tutor." Liz held Jac's waist and kissed her, and kissed her, and kissed her on a peaceful Carmel street on a beautiful day. "We should walk faster. If I don't touch you soon, I'm going to burst."

Us. Jac entwined their fingers as they walked to her cottage. Lovers. She felt gloriously alive. And terrified. She made it as far as the bench along the walkway before fear bullied her onto it. Wind blew across her shoulder, a cooling contrast to the sun's warmth. Liz sat beside her. Max leaned against her leg. Sandwiched between the woman she loved and the dog she adored, she felt paralyzed. "I don't know if I can do this. Maybe we should give things more time, in case you're not sure."

Liz took her hand, lacing their fingers back together. "I won't force myself on you, but I won't pretend I'm not sure of what I want. I didn't expect to fall in love with Teri, but I knew it was right. I didn't expect to fall in love with you, but I know it's just as right."

Jac rested her hand on Max's back. Just sitting here like this with Liz was more than she'd thought she would ever have. Friends. And now Liz was telling her what she'd longed to hear. Offering her everything she wanted.

"What about you? Are you sure? I saw you with Gwen last night. I wasn't stalking you." Liz squeezed her hand. "If you want to date—"

"You. I only want you. Gwen called after I returned from Hawaii. In a moment of anger that I'd again fallen for someone I couldn't have, I agreed to dinner. There will never be anyone for me but you."

"Then can we move on to the having-each-other part?"

"We need to talk about my blindness." Not the conversation she'd choose to have right now, but a necessary one. A deep sadness welled up. It hadn't mattered, or she'd pretended it hadn't mattered all these years, and now it mattered a great deal. "My life has complications."

"I haven't noticed any complications, except that you get stubborn sometimes and your stride is too long."

Another reason she loved Liz. She had no doubt Liz honestly believed it didn't matter. "Having a blind friend is one thing. Having a blind lover…there's so much we won't be able to share, so much I won't be able to do for you." Jac wanted to see this moment so badly she trembled. Just this one moment, damn it. When Liz gathered her into a hug she wrapped her arms around her. Was there no end to the sadness clouding this perfect offering of the future she wanted?

"I could tell you we shared zip lines and snorkeling and beautiful sunsets and I never once felt a lack of sharing with you. That's not what this is really about. It's about sharing our bodies. It's about taking your clothes off this time. It's about my seeing you and your not being able to see me."

Jac nodded into the crook of Liz's neck, embarrassed and relieved that Liz understood. She hadn't seen her body in ten years. She had scars from the back surgery. Liz was ten years younger.

"This is new territory for both of us. I'm as nervous as you are, honey. Please take this step with me." Liz cupped Jac's cheeks and planted feather-light kisses at the corners of her mouth. "Let go. I've got you."

She kissed Liz with all the passion swirling through her, every part of her aroused and wanting. Lovers. She wanted to be lovers with Liz. Before her mind could throw up any more excuses, she stood and took Liz's hand.

In her bedroom, doubt returned. Jac clasped her hands, listening to the sound of Liz lowering the zipper on her jeans, of shoes discarded, of clothes tossed on the chair behind them. Undressing. Her belly quivered with anticipation and knotted with fear. Then Liz was in her arms, warm, soft skin against her hands as they kissed, their tongues caressing with abandon.

Liz lifted Jac's hands to her cheeks. "Touch me."

A delicious slow burn built deep in her abdomen as she slid her fingers down Liz's throat, over the bounding pulse, and down the delicate chain to the pendant she'd given her. She slid her fingers along Liz's collarbones to her shoulders, taking her time. She remembered everything about Liz's body from Hawaii, but those had been stolen touches. This was permission to explore. Down the straps of her bra, along the edges of the lacy material to the V, then around her ribs to the clasp. Jac's breathing quickened. That moment when a woman's breasts were freed always aroused her. She undid the clasp and slid the straps down.

"You're teasing me." Liz's voice was breathy. Desire. For her.

"I am, and I'm teasing myself." When she stroked the outsides of Liz's breasts with the backs of her fingers, Liz let out a long sigh. She cupped them and rubbed the nipples with her thumbs. Soft became hard, and Liz leaned into her touch. She found Liz's mouth and sank deep into the sweetness and warmth.

"Can I undress you?" Liz kissed along her jaw.

Her breath caught. Was she ready for this? Lovers. Easy to say. Easy to want. Was it safe to give herself to Liz? She had no way of knowing any more than she could see the zip-line landings. She wanted the exhilaration and freedom of jumping into the unknown. She wanted it with Liz. She undid the buttons on her shirt, slowly, parting the material as she went.

"Teasing again," Liz whispered. "You're so beautiful." Liz slid the shirt off her shoulders, then laid her hands over her lower back and fingered the raised flesh of the scars. "All of you. I'm dying to touch you. Please."

Desire scooped her up, and Jac was falling into the intimate quiet of a lover's voice, the passion-laced touches that left hot trails on her skin, the scent of bodies wanting. She held Liz's palms against her breasts, then rubbed them across her nipples until they felt huge and hard. She let go, and Liz kept fondling them as she licked along the edge of Jac's bra. When Liz bit her nipple, Jac's clit contracted. She needed Liz. Wanted Liz. "Lovers," she whispered into Liz's mouth before another passionate kiss. When Liz lowered the zipper on her jeans and unhooked her bra, she let her. Naked except for panties, she rocked against Liz's thigh as a demanding kiss shredded her reserve.

"Nice rhythm." Liz matched her rocking, her sex wet on Jac's thigh. "I want to make love to you."

Jac groaned and pulled herself from Liz's thigh as fear dominated her. "I haven't made love with anyone in a long time."

"Afraid some parts might be rusty?" Liz kissed the base of her throat. Her touch soothed. "We have the rest of our lives to get to know each other. Lie down with me?"

Jac settled on the soft flannel sheets with Liz tucked against her. She reached over the side of the bed to pet Max. "Sorry, buddy."

"We'll let you up later," Liz said. "The tip of his tail is wagging, and he's looking at us like he approves. I'll never interfere with the bond you have with him."

"He hasn't been himself. I think he missed you as much as I did."

"Can I lie on top of you? Will your back be okay?"

Jac nodded and spread her legs. Liz covered her, and everywhere their bodies touched, long-dulled nerve endings burst to life. She wrapped her arms around Liz as they lay cheek to cheek, hearts beating against each other.

"Feel that? It's our rhythm." Liz circled her nipple with a delicate touch.

"Now who's teasing?" Jac squirmed.

"Do you like your breasts touched?"

"I used to. And sucked. Bit." Arousal took her to that place where everything softened and became just about her lover. Liz.

"Thank God. You might have to have me surgically removed. I go crazy for breasts, and yours make me think I landed in paradise." Liz closed her mouth around Jac's nipple, biting gently, then sucking hard.

"Mmm." She'd forgotten the exquisite ache that came from a lover's touch. She was so lost in Liz's touch she could barely think. Liz's mouth was sending her to places she'd never been. "So good, love." She flooded from arousal, embarrassed before she remembered she didn't need to be. Liz's hand crossed her abdomen and dipped inside the waist of her panties. She wasn't ready for this and clasped the probing fingers.

Liz rolled onto her back. "This is what you do to me." She put Jac's hand against her sex.

Wetness coated Jac's fingers. She sucked in a breath as heat rushed through her. The heel of her hand brushed soft hair as she explored the folds of Liz's labia and circled her opening. So invitingly slick.

"Make love to me." Liz pulled one knee up, opening herself.

Desire sparked through her at the invitation. She kissed Liz as she touched her clit, cataloguing Liz's responses—hitch in her breathing, an involuntary tensing of her abdominal or thigh muscles. Learning her lover's body. Liz groaned in her mouth and she kissed her harder. "I'm so in love with you." She bit Liz's nipple, and Liz twisted under her.

"Make me come." Liz's voice was thick with need.

She entered Liz, withdrew to stroke her clit, entered again, keeping a slow rhythm.

"Don't tease." Liz gripped Jac's shoulders as she rocked her pelvis, moaning, breathing fast.

Jac added a second finger and pushed in as far as she could, paused in that hot encapsulation, then withdrew to the tight ring of Liz's entrance. She stroked Liz's clit with her thumb, matching the rhythm of her fingers. She kept her mouth fastened to Liz's breast. She needed as much sensation as she could get. Everywhere she touched Liz was hot. "Come for me, love." Liz tightened around her fingers in a surge and release, like the ocean.

Liz's hips stalled in their rocking and her arms tightened around Jac's neck. "I feel you everywhere. Ahh...so good...coming for you, my lover."

Jac lightened her touch on Liz's clit and kept moving inside her. "Come again. I want more of you." She took Liz to the edge, backed off, took her again, feeding on the desire surging through every moan, through Liz's hands rubbing erratically on her back, through Liz's passionate kisses.

Liz thrust hard onto her fingers, arched herself into Jac's hand, and broke the kiss. Her breath came in short exhalations against Jac's face. "I love you so much."

Jac floated with Liz's orgasm, the movements of her body, the smell of her delicately tropical perfume from Hawaii. She wasn't prepared when Liz guided her onto her back, separated her legs, and settled on top of her. Before she could protest, Liz took her breast, and all words faded as Liz made love to her with her mouth. She tensed when Liz slid her panties off, but let her. And again when Liz stroked up her inner thigh and into her center, against her clit. She wanted to give herself to Liz, but when Liz's finger touched her opening, she clasped her wrist. "Tell me again that you love me."

"With all my heart." Liz's tender kiss mirrored her words. "Tell me what my being inside you means." Liz pressed her fingers gently against her opening.

Jac ached to swallow Liz's fingers, but she couldn't. Not yet. "It's the most intimate thing I can let someone do to me," she said against Liz's cheek. "Letting your fingers inside me is letting myself be owned by you, letting myself be played by you. Please don't go inside me unless you're sure of how you feel." She wrapped her arms around Liz's back and held tight, afraid to let go and afraid not to.

"I'm sure I'm in love with you. I'm sure I want us to be connected in the deepest way."

"You're in my heart. If I let you inside my body, I'll be lost. I won't be the same again, and I'm scared."

"We're already deep inside each other. Let me love you."

Trusting the love in Liz's touch and in her words, Jac guided Liz back to her opening and pressed onto her fingers, arching her neck at the exquisite feeling of being filled. She surrendered to the gentle intrusion, the warm mouth sucking on the sensitive skin at the base of her throat. "More. I need more fullness. Add another..." She moaned when Liz slipped in a third finger.

"Tell me what you want." Liz kept her movements slow, going deeper with each thrust. "You're so beautiful, so wet."

"Curl your fingers. Ahh...perfect." When Liz started to slide down her body, she stopped her. "Stay. I need to feel all of you against me." She tangled her fingers in Liz's hair and pulled her into a hard kiss. She was close, spiraling to a new beginning in the arms of the woman she loved. "Fortissimo, love. Make me come." The orgasm gathered in her belly like a storm and swept through her in waves of pleasure she didn't know existed. New. Everything was new with Liz. "Don't stop," she said when Liz withdrew her fingers. When they entered her again, fast and hard, she came in a rush of hot fury that shoved away doubt as fire speared through her body, blasting through long-dormant channels. It burned away everything before Liz. She wrapped her arms around Liz and rocked shamelessly on her fingers, losing control in the safety of her arms. "I'll never get enough of this. Enough of you."

Jac flipped Liz onto her back and had her mouth on Liz's clit before her own orgasm ebbed. More. Liz. Everything became Liz— smell and touch and taste and the beautiful sound of Liz crying out her name when she came.

Time and time again they took each other, skin against skin, fingers and hands coaxing and caressing, mouths searching and reassuring. Finally they lay spent in each other's arms.

"How's your back?" Liz asked.

Jac scooted her butt around. She'd been in some awkward positions over the last few hours, but it didn't hurt at all. "Great." She pulled Liz's thigh across her abdomen.

"You know what? My wrist doesn't hurt. Oh, my gosh, I completely forgot about it." Liz peppered Jac's cheek with kisses. "We're good for each other in so many ways."

"We have a show tomorrow." Jac rubbed up and down Liz's thigh, lost in the wonder of holding her.

"Nervous?" Liz asked.

"Not at the moment. You. Us. That's all I want."

"Me, too." Liz punctuated her words with a kiss that started tender and ended with passion that left them breathing hard. "Cassie, Regan, and Sammy are coming to my house tomorrow around noon. You should be there. They need to know about us."

"They don't already?"

"They need to know things are good between us. They're stressed enough without the kind of tension there was at Monday's rehearsal."

"Agreed. Stay with me tonight. We'll have to make an appearance up at Peg's, but I can't bear to be away from you. Roger and my dad have been grilling every night and I'm sure we can rustle up some old cabs."

"I want to invite Hannah to join us. We'll have to endure a healthy dose of gloating from her and Peggy. I found out this morning they were in cahoots on Hawaii and Peggy called her when you left this morning."

"Do you think we would have figured it out on our own?"

"Absolutely. But think how much of this we would have missed." Liz stroked Jac's clit. "Let's see how long you can stand this."

Turning onto her side to face Liz, Jac slid her fingers into Liz's sex. She was so very wet. "And you, this."

"Come with me, honey." Liz took Jac's breast in her mouth.

"I'll go anywhere with you." They touched each other and kissed until they cried out and held tight to each other. "I love you," she said into Liz's mouth, feeling the words said back to her as their tongues met and danced.

When they were lying contentedly in each other's arms again, Liz said, "Max's head is on his paws and he's looking pathetic. Can he come up?"

Jac patted the bed and Max jumped up, did three circles, and settled by their feet. "He thinks it's nap time."

"So do I," Liz said. "I didn't get much sleep last night."

"And you won't get much tonight." Jac pulled Liz against her and laid her hand on Max. Long after Liz and Max were asleep, Jac lay awake, her heart fully alive, pumping joy and hope through channels hungry again for life.

CHAPTER THIRTY-SIX

Backstage. Jac remembered the last time as if it were yesterday. It was hard not to think about the last time she'd performed. The night that changed her life. The night that sent her down a long, dark tunnel. Liz had brought her partway out of that tunnel with friendship and, now, love. Would tonight give her back the rest of what she'd lost? She was vaguely aware of people moving about the room, laughing, bantering the way musicians did. Her awareness was on the nervousness that made it hard to stay in the metal chair off in a corner. She wanted to preserve her anonymity as long as possible.

"You're thinking." Liz sat next to her in the too-hot room somewhere behind the Jimmy Lyons Stage, the main stage at the festival.

"I still feel you everywhere." They'd made love so many times throughout the night and early morning that her skin tingled as if they were still touching. Their consummation had been everything she could have wished for—like a symphony that had quietly introspective passages, passionate outbursts, and beautiful harmonies.

"Me, too." Liz put her hand on Jac's lower back, her voice a husky whisper.

"How are Regan, Sammie, and Cassie?" She shifted her focus to Liz's hand and let the warmth of it ground her.

"Regan's in rapture talking to Derrick Hodge. He about has her convinced to learn double bass."

"She'll like the sensibility of it, and it will give you composing options."

"Cassie's mingling with just about everyone because she knows just about everyone. I'm lucky to have her, both for her talent and for her festival experience. Sammy's tagging along with her, and his eyes get wider every time she introduces him to someone else."

"Regan and Sammy can hold their own with anyone here."

"So I've told them, but it wouldn't hurt coming from you, too. How are you doing?"

"Scared to death."

"Remember the zip line we went across together? I'm right here with you."

"Liz," a male voice said from in front of them. "Welcome to the 58th annual Monterey Jazz Festival. It's an honor to have you opening the event. Is everything all right?"

"It's great, Tim," Liz said. "May I introduce—"

"She needs no introduction."

Jac stood and shook his hand. "It's an honor to be here." Tim Jackson was the artistic director of the Monterey Jazz Festival. He'd heartily agreed to her appearance and to keeping it under wraps.

"I have an escort ready to stand with you while Liz is onstage. Let me know if you need anything else. Sound check in half an hour."

"You'll make sure my mic's set up right?" she asked Liz, sitting back down.

"Just the way we talked about. I'll take very good care of you."

Half an hour later, Jac waited in a room backstage during the sound check, listening, getting a feel for the sound system. Missing Liz. When the band piled back in, they were quiet, and she felt the tension. "You're some of the best musicians I've ever played with. I'm honored to be onstage with you."

"Likewise," Cassie said, kissing her cheek.

"You look like the picture of calm." Liz took Jac's hand. "Everyone thinks I'm giving you a pep talk so smile and nod, but what I really want to say is I love you, and I want to rip your clothes off and make love to you again."

Jac put her hand to her chest, hoping her reaction wasn't painted on her cheeks. "I love you, too." Everything was contained in those few words. Liz was everything.

"You look beautiful. Midnight blue's a great color on you. Reminds me of that swimsuit. Mmm." Liz straightened the stand-up collar on Jac's jacket.

"Don't get me worked up or I'll play like I did at my parents'." She'd been carried away by her feelings and hadn't imagined the effect it would have on Liz.

"You won't get cold feet and skip out on me, will you?"

"Never, love. Go make beautiful music."

Liz squeezed her fingers and was gone in a commotion of voices. Backstage was always hectic, but more so because she didn't have sight to orient her. How different would it be performing blind? Would she trip on a cord or run into a mic or speaker? No, Liz would be with her. She fingered her trumpet, warming it while it soothed her nervousness.

"It's a pleasure to have Liz Randall back on our stage with her band, Up Beat," Tim Jackson said through the mic. "Her new release, *Up Beat Live in New York*, has been heating up the jazz charts all summer. For the oldsters in the crowd, Liz's grandmother, Mildred Randall, performed here in 1964 with the Woody Herman Orchestra. Two generations of great jazz pianists. Without further ado...Liz Randall and Up Beat."

Jac's heart beat fast and strong, immensely happy to be part of this monumental evening. Part of Liz's future. The forty-minute set seemed to last forever, and she lost herself in every graceful note, every cascading melody and surging harmony. Liz's playing was brilliant, and the band was clearly in the groove. Applause built with each song, as did her excitement. Liz would get the recognition she deserved.

"I'll take you to the stage entrance," her escort said.

She held her trumpet close to her body as he led her through a tunnel of voices. Applause erupted after the final song. Whistles, calls for more, and then Liz was by her side, and her heart settled.

"Miss me?" Liz's hand was warm in hers.

"Terribly. It sounds like your hand is fine."

"Of course. I have you. Ready to make your comeback?"

Nervousness skittered through her. "I don't ever want to be alone again."

"Never." Liz kissed her cheek.

She held tightly to Liz's elbow, heart pounding, as they walked onto the stage. Sammy, Regan, and Cassie followed, congratulating each other. Back on a stage. It was a wondrous feeling. A new beginning she desperately wanted.

"Center stage," Liz said. "Usual arrangement. Mic's a foot in front of you. You're ready for this." Then Liz was gone and fear engulfed her. She couldn't see. She'd play badly. She'd make a fool of herself and—Someone touched her shoulder.

"Hi, I'm Sammy."

Jac let out a long breath, the tension broken by his humor.

"Ladies and gentlemen," Liz said through her mic. "It's my great honor to announce our special guest performer, Ms. Jacqueline Richards."

She fingered her trumpet, dropping into herself and shutting out everything but the music running through her head. There was a pause, then applause that went on and on and on.

"They're standing," Regan said into her ear. "Take a bow."

She did, and then, mercifully, Liz started "Carmel Sketches." She let go into the music that told the story of how they fell in love. The song took life and they all played like they never had before, as if they were of one mind. She held her final high C for as long as she could, and the song finished on a resounding chord series from Liz. The audience erupted into applause, and whistles, and cries of "bravo."

Jac held out her hand and Liz was there, linking her arm, keeping her promise not to leave her alone. Regan linked her other arm and they took several bows amid calls for more.

"Better get me offstage. You have a second encore."

"Do 'Mad Dash' with us," Liz said.

"You're not going anywhere," Regan said, pressing against her. Hands held her shoulders—Cassie and Sammy.

Jac's heart lunged into her throat. The first song she'd played with Liz. She hadn't practiced it with the band. She remembered the zip line, how it felt to stand at the edge of the unknown—freedom just a step beyond fear.

"It's all about letting go and trusting those around you," Liz said before stepping away.

She listened to Liz's piano leadership, and to Cassie and Regan's solid rhythm, and to Sammy's sax as they started the song. Desire surged through her—desire to be part of this band. Putting the horn to her lips she joined in. Collaborating. Belonging. She poured herself into the piece. Letting go. Making it up in the moment. Trusting. It was glorious and then, all too soon, it ended. She'd improvised onstage. She couldn't stop smiling.

Thunderous applause covered them. A wall of sound. Electric. Alive. Coating them with its energy. The vibration of it swept through her, lighting up her cells. Bringing her back to life as a musician. She'd forgotten what an audience's appreciation felt like—a huge burst of joy. Liz and Regan put their arms around her waist, and she was encased by people who cared about her. She was loved and alive. She'd never forget this night.

"That was quite a comeback, Ms. Richards," Liz said as they made their way backstage.

Gripping her trumpet, Jac fought back panic as people bumped her. Hands grabbed her. Voices everywhere. People called her by name. "Don't leave me." She clung to Liz's elbow. She had no sense of where she was in the commotion, no way to protect herself.

"Never." Liz stopped, put her hands on Jac's waist, and pressed against her, orienting her. "We can sneak out if you want, but this is your moment, honey."

"It's our moment." She was breathing fast and sweating. She hadn't thought through to what would happen after the show. The press. Fans. She felt very blind and wanted to be home, in her recliner, in her—No. She wanted to be with Liz. She wanted to perform again. "Don't let go."

"Great set," a man said, as he passed them. "Nice horn playing."

"Jason Moran," Liz said, humor in her voice. "A pretty nice welcome to jazz for you."

Welcome to jazz. Exactly where she'd been heading a decade ago. A long detour, but she finally felt back on track. High on post-performance adrenaline, she was barely aware they were descending steps.

As they walked across the uneven ground in the warm evening air, cameras clicked and people called out to Ms. Richards or Ms.

Randall. They stopped. Bodies were too close. Liz stood in front of her shoulder, shielding her. Jac kept her arm linked through Liz's as questions were asked. Voices without faces. Hesitant questions at first, as if they didn't know what to make of Jac's performance. Then questions about the accident. Questions about whether she'd be returning to the classical stage. And finally, a male voice asked if they were romantically involved with each other.

"That's enough for now," Liz said, and then they were walking again. "I need to be somewhere I can kiss you."

Jac raised her eyebrow. "That's your department."

❖

Liz pulled over to the curb two blocks from Peggy's. She needed a few more minutes alone with Jac before the celebration party. This day she'd been dreading for six months had become one of the best days of her life. Making love with Jac had been breathtakingly sensual and deeply renewing. The show had been the best performance of her life.

"Happy?" Jac asked.

"I'm so high I may never come down." She cupped Jac's neck and pulled her into a kiss, swirling her tongue in her mouth, breathing hard, her body vibrating with energy. "I want you to play with us full-time." She rested her forehead against Jac's and rubbed her thumb over the spot where it had been cut the day they met.

"I'm not at your level, love."

"After tonight, that's not a valid argument." She kissed Jac again, soft and slow. Love surged through her veins, and her body hummed with euphoria and relief.

"I'd be lying if I said I didn't want to. Being onstage…I had no idea how much I missed it. Traveling and performing with a blind person isn't as easy as—"

"There are a lot of ways you're not easy." Liz got the raised eyebrow she was hoping for. God, she loved this woman. "Blind isn't one of them."

"You really don't mind, do you?"

"I mind that you were deprived of your sight. I mind that you lost your career. I mind that you've been in pain and alone." Her throat closed around all the tragedy she wished Jac hadn't been forced to endure. "I want us to be together in all ways."

"Fused." Jac took Liz's hand and entwined their fingers. "Blended. Inseparable. Different styles that merge, becoming something entirely new. Like the music we make together."

"Yes. We each have our own voice and we have a collaborative sound." She squeezed Jac's hand. "Then it's settled." Jac was quiet, the kind of quiet that meant something was wrong. "What?"

"If I play with you…" Jac's jaw tightened and her face became hard.

"Yes, your name will get attention for a while."

"You heard the questions tonight. Your set was brilliant. You've been playing brilliant jazz for years. They should have directed all their questions to those facts."

"I've never cared about anything but the music. I want to play with you and to hell with what the press does with it. Now do you want to collaborate with me, Ms. Richards, or not?"

Jac tried not to smile. "Demanding band leader, aren't you?"

"Yes. Don't forget it." A shiver ran through Liz. A déjà-vu feeling. They were going to do great things together musically.

"What about that last question?"

Liz took Jac's mouth in a possessive kiss. "Yes, we're romantically involved. End of quote."

"You've talked it over with everyone?"

Liz snorted. "If I don't convince you to join us, they'll fire me." "Your dad?"

"He'll have to come to terms with quite a few things." She wasn't looking forward to the conversation she needed to have with him about Jac. "Do you want to perform classical again?"

"I don't think so, but when I'm with you, anything seems possible."

"For me, too." She kissed Jac again, startled when headlights flooded the interior. Hannah got out of her car and hurried toward them.

"Enough necking," Hannah said. "Party can't start without you."

"You taking good care of my dog?" Jac asked.

"Front seat and we're holding paws." Hannah had insisted Max ride home with her, since he'd sat with her during the show. "I think

I'm in love. He's the perfect date. And I told you orange was his color." She'd tied an orange bandana around his neck.

"We'll be right there." Liz took Jac's hand in both of hers. "You're in my heart. You're in my music. I love you. I want to be with you for the rest of my life."

"I love you with all my heart, Liz. I want you in my life always."

She kissed Jac every way from tender to bruising, until finally she was afraid Hannah would come after them. "Let's celebrate."

She pulled through the stone gateposts and parked next to Roger's SUV. When they reached the patio, she led them around tables to a cacophony of clapping and congratulatory shouts from family and friends. She stopped next to Hannah, and Jac knelt to pet Max. The band had not only survived, but it had a shining future. She had not only survived, but she had a future with the woman she loved. She wanted to celebrate all of it.

"I'm so happy for you both," Jac's dad said, handing them glasses of champagne, probably expensive champagne, knowing Roger. "It looks like you're very good for Jacqueline," he whispered to Liz.

Jac's mom wrapped her arms around both of them. "I'm so proud of you."

Peggy's gaze was glued to them, a huge smile on her face while she brushed tears from her eyes, the perfect mirror to the emotions swelling and surging through Liz.

She missed Teri, but it was a missing filled with peace and the sense of completion. Teri was here in spirit, and she had no doubt she was cheering Liz's new life.

"To Up Beat," Roger shouted, lifting his glass. When the group quieted, he said, "I've never heard a performance like you gave tonight. Knowing what you've all been through, your achievement is even more memorable. Here's to your very, very bright future."

When the cheers died down, Roger held up his glass again. "To my sister-in-law. Jac, your talent needs no mention, but your courage does. Here's to your stunning return to the stage. May tonight be the first of many."

Liz kissed Jac on her tear-dampened cheek as everyone cheered. A shiver shot through her. Not just Jac. Jacqueline Richards. She was going to make sure this was the first of many performances for her lover.

"My turn," Liz hollered. "We've been asked to play a special show tomorrow evening on one of the other stages." She'd been surprised and thrilled when Tim approached her after the set to request an encore performance.

Wild applause erupted. Regan, Sammy, and Cassie crowded around them, whooping and hugging and high-fiving. A band in all the best ways.

"I'd like to say a few words," Liz's dad said, stepping forward.

Liz glanced over her shoulder when Hannah squeezed it.

"Will he ever leave well enough alone?" Hannah asked, rolling her eyes.

"He deserves his moment." He might be overly enthusiastic, but she owed this night as much to his years of support as she did to Teri's foresight.

"I've never been more proud of my daughter than I am tonight. She's fought her way back from tragedy and has earned this night of triumph."

"Makes you sound like a gladiator," Hannah said.

Jac blew out a snicker.

"I'm honored to announce that one of the top agents in the business, Malcolm Phillips, has offered to represent Up Beat. This time next year…"

Liz didn't hear the rest of what her dad said as she dissolved into laughter. Jac's face went from shock to anger, and then she joined in laughing. Her dad scowled at them. Peggy's expression was priceless incredulity, and Roger just shook his head.

"How do you think that happened?" Liz asked Jac after another round of cheers died down and people dispersed to help themselves to the catered sandwiches and salads.

"Revenge for the interview I gave your friend, and a reminder he's still around. I don't care. Nothing could ruin this night." Jac looked radiant. She'd come offstage with a mantle of confidence, like she'd reclaimed an essential part of herself.

"I need to talk to Dad. He needs to know about us."

"If you'd rather wait—"

"No. I plan to be glued to your side all night." So much love filled Liz's heart it squeezed the air from her lungs.

"Don't be long." Jac kissed her hand. "I love you so much."

"I love this smile." She traced the precious half smile she'd never get tired of. Interrupting her dad's ear-bending speech to Regan and Sammy, she led him toward the bench along the walkway to Jac's.

"We did it, sunshine! Grandma would be so proud of you. Malcolm will have the contract to me in a couple of days and—"

"Malcolm Phillips is Jac's ex-husband."

He looked puzzled. "I didn't know." And then delighted. "Which confirms that he's one of the best agents in the business."

She put her hand on his arm. "He's an unscrupulous scoundrel who's caused Jac no end of trouble."

After a minute, he said, "I'll make other inquiries. After tonight's show, we'll have agents lining up to represent you."

"Slow down, Dad." There was no easy way to do this, and she hated throwing ice water on his enthusiasm. "I'm in love with Jac. We're romantically involved," she added, in case there was any doubt in his mind.

"You're just infatuated with her fame and—"

"No, Dad. I love her."

The confusion on his face was heartbreaking. "I don't understand how you can love someone else."

"I started listening to my heart. It's capable of loving again. Yours can, too."

"No." He shook his head. "I'll always love your mom."

"We can't keep Mom or Teri alive by refusing to let love capture us again," she said, as gently as she could.

He leaned forward, elbows on knees, shaking his head. "I had my one true love. Like Grandma." The usual pride in his voice had a hint of a crack. Kevin and Karen's separation had hit him hard. "I'd be afraid I'd forget all the good times with her."

"You don't stop remembering. You make new memories to blend with the old." She wasn't giving up, but it wasn't tonight's battle. "I want you to be happy, Dad."

"Watching you get your dream makes me happy. We need to add gigs to your tour."

"I've asked Jac to join the band full-time."

He was quiet for a moment, and then nodded. "That's good for the band."

"And for me."

He studied her, as if searching for something, and then looked away. "I only want what's best for you." He fiddled with the buttons on his sport coat. It seemed too big on him, like the last year had worn him away. "You know that, don't you?"

"Of course."

"Is there going to be a place for me? With the band?"

The uncertainty in his voice tugged at Liz's heart. Yes, he'd made mistakes, but hadn't they all? "You've always been part of the band and always will." She hugged him for a long time, certain of his love.

Sammy met them on their way back to the patio. "Hey, Pops. Let's get you some food. You're at my table."

"Thank you," Liz mouthed to him.

Jac stood and pulled back the chair next to her as Liz approached the table where she sat with her family, Max lying beside her.

She always knows where I am. Jac's attentiveness was one of so many reasons she loved her.

"Drink up, love." Jac slid a glass of red wine toward her. "It's—"

She clamped her hand over Jac's mouth. "I don't want to know how expensive it is. I just want to enjoy it." She put her arm around Jac and kissed her. She tasted of wine and love, and she couldn't get enough.

"Welcome to our family," Jac's mom said, a huge smile on her face. "Will you come for another visit soon?"

"We'll be on tour the next few months," Jac said, her voice full of pride as she explained she'd be joining the band.

Peggy leaned close. "I'll stop saying this someday, but you two make a beautiful couple. You were my first choice for sister-in-law."

"I love you and Roger almost as much as I love Jac. You gave me reasons to laugh again. You let me come back to life."

"You brought Jac back to life, and I'll always be grateful."

Jac stood and held her hand out to Liz. "May I have this dance?"

"Did you sneak this into the mix?" A medley of jazz standards had been playing.

"Of course." Jac's eyebrow went up.

"Are you always going to be so romantic?" She melted into Jac, into her confident lead, as Frank Sinatra's voice crooned out "Just In Time," the song they'd danced to in Hawaii.

"Yes." Cheek to cheek, they moved in a lazy circle that covered no distance and all the distance in the world, from alone to coupled. "I miss that dress you were wearing the night we danced in Hawaii. All that bare skin. Mmm."

"I miss your hands on my skin." The flame of arousal that had been simmering all night became a hot burn.

"Soon, love. Soon. Anticipation makes it sweeter." Jac's breath warmed her cheek as she hummed the melody and Sinatra sang the prophetic lyrics about being rescued by love just in time.

Liz shifted so Jac's thigh was between hers and felt Jac smile against her face. She sucked in a breath, and her heart skipped beats when Jac pressed into her sex. The thin silk pants they both wore made it feel like skin on skin. She scraped her mouth across Jac's cheek, and the rest of the short dance was one long, heated kiss.

"My turn with Jax," Hannah said, stepping next to them when a new song began. "Go rescue Dad."

Liz could barely force herself to let go. Everything felt right in Jac's arms. When she opened her eyes, her dad was watching her. He looked away, but not before she saw the confusion on his face. She went to him, tugged him from his chair, and danced with him. She wanted to tell him it could be Rebecca in his arms. She hoped one day it would be.

Everyone wanted to dance with her and everyone wanted to dance with Jac. It was well after midnight before the party wound down. As she made her way back to Jac, Regan and Sammy intercepted her. "We're taking off," Regan said, her arm around Vicky's waist. She looked happier than Liz had ever seen her.

"You played like…" Liz shook her head as her throat tightened. She hugged Regan for a long time, and even better, Regan hugged her back. "Meet us here at noon tomorrow. Peggy's fixing lunch for us."

"I wasn't sure about…" Regan shifted her weight and put a hand in her pocket, but kept Liz's gaze. "What Teri did. Setting us up for the festival. But we're going to be okay, yeah?"

"We're all going to be okay." Monday was the one-year anniversary of Teri's death. It wouldn't be an easy day to get through, but Teri's death wasn't the lighthouse in her emotional life any more. She had someone she loved, who loved her in return.

"Is Jac part of the band now?" Regan sounded hopeful.

"Yes."

"Good. I'm glad you're with her." Regan grinned and pulled Vicky closer. "Love changes everything."

"We want to stay with you after the fall tour," Sammy said. "We like the new style."

"Good." She reached up to hug him. "I want us all to have the future we choose."

Cassie approached as they left. "Damn, that gorgeous trumpet player of yours can dance. I should have tried harder." She bumped Liz's shoulder. "Just kidding. Happy?"

"Indescribably."

"You deserve all of this, girlfriend—the band, the woman, the fame you're gonna get. I'm proud of you."

"Thank you doesn't seem to cover all you've done for me this year, Cass."

"You can add one more thing. I'll play your fall tour."

Liz cupped Cassie's cheeks and kissed them several times. Not having to find another drummer right away took a big worry off her mind.

"On one condition. You get yourself a trumpet player full-time. It's a good sound."

"Already done." Liz returned to the table, to the woman she loved. "I want to kiss you in the worst way."

"Yeah?" An easy smile spread over Jac's cheeks.

"Yeah." And she did.

"Not again," Hannah teased them as she squeezed their shoulders.

"I'm happy for you, sis," Kevin said. He bent to kiss Liz's cheek. "Congratulations, Jac." He extended his hand.

Jac stood and hugged him and then Hannah, who laughed at something Jac said to her.

"Kev's going back with me. You get to tell Dad," Hannah said. That was going to be an interesting drive. Knowing Hannah, she'd get Kevin and Karen back together.

"You're pretty amazing," Liz said, hugging Hannah for a long time. Now that Hannah was back in her life, she'd never lose her again.

"So are you. Be happy, Lizzie."

Her dad was one of the last to leave, and she walked him to his car. "I'll see you tomorrow."

"You bet, sunshine." He unlocked his car and then turned back to her. "I was wrong to tell the reviewer about Jac. I didn't want you to lose out again. I'm sorry."

Liz hugged him. "Thanks, Dad."

"It's a great album. Momentum!" He pumped his fist in the air.

Liz waved to him as he drove away. It had been a year of loss and challenges and shifting roles for everyone in her family. As she walked across the gravel driveway, she thought back to the day she'd met Jac and Peggy. Now they were family. Her steps felt light and sure. She'd found her way to new music and new love. A future she was committed to. She wanted the same for Hannah, for her dad and Rebecca, for Kevin and Karen.

Jac was waiting for her on the bench along the walkway to her cottage. "Can Max and I interest you in a stroll on the beach?"

"Sounds like the perfect ending to the day."

The beach was deserted, the moon barely a crescent in the star-filled sky. They walked barefoot in the soft sand above the water line, the rhythmic cascade of waves a comforting accompaniment, the breeze just cool enough. Liz threw Max's tennis ball into the surf. "I'm going to move to Carmel."

"That's a long commute."

"I don't want to be away from you for a minute."

"What if I rent a place in San Jose? We can stay there part of the week while you teach. I'd like to live in my cottage when we're here. I can add on a room for your grandmother's piano." They walked for a while, taking turns throwing the ball for Max, and then Jac said, "I was wrong."

"About?"

"Teri applying to the festival was an act of unimaginable love. I didn't understand. I couldn't understand until I fell in love with you. I want to love you as well as she did."

"You do." She took Jac's hand. "I learned how to love with Teri, and I'm learning it all over again with you."

"I don't expect you to avoid talking about her. You must be feeling a lot of different things about tonight and about the one-year anniversary of her death coming up Monday."

"I am, and I promise I'll talk about it. Right now, I want to bask in our love and the connection that makes me sure we belong to each other. I wouldn't have wished loss and grief on either of us. It's like we were tossed in the ocean and carried away by currents that stranded us far from where we thought our lives were headed. We made our way back. Together. I wouldn't want to be anywhere but here with you. I'm crazy about you, Ms. Richards." Liz draped her arms over Jac's shoulders and kissed her. "Dance with me?"

Jac took her in her arms, and everything faded except where their bodies touched and their tongues explored each other's mouths. Heat built quickly with Jac's thigh between her legs.

Liz didn't realize she was humming until Jac said, "Thank you for describing it. I feel stars dancing on my skin, a sliver of moon fighting the darkness, white feathers of waves rolling onto the sand. And inside it all, I feel the heartbeat of your love."

"Our love. Fused."

"Can I interest you in a little sex on the beach?" Jac's voice was deep and raw and so sexy Liz shivered.

"Getting kind of risqué, aren't you?"

"Improvising and collaborating, love. Isn't that what you're teaching me?" They were at the rock wall at the end of the beach. Jac sat against the rocks and motioned Liz to settle between her bent legs. Max sprawled beside them. She tunneled her hands inside Liz's blouse.

Liz rested her head against Jac's shoulder, sheltered in her arms, soft sand beneath her, waves playing a rhythmic serenade. A perfect night.

"What's that you're humming?" Jac nuzzled her cheek.

"Our future, honey." She lifted her head and kissed Jac, humming the new melody that would become their greatest hit—"Making a Comeback."

About the Author

Julie Blair has always believed that fiction is one of life's great pleasures. From the time she was old enough to hold a book, escaping into worlds where anything is possible and endings are usually happy has been a favorite pastime. Growing up a tomboy before it was fashionable, Julie attached herself to sports, especially softball, which culminated in her pitching in the Women's College World Series. Finally forced to grow up and get a real job, she landed in restaurant management for a decade before entering the rigors of chiropractic school. She has been a chiropractor for over two decades.

Julie has sat atop the ruins of Machu Picchu and stood five feet from mountain gorillas in Uganda, but her favorite place is curled up on her couch with her Labradors, Magic and Mandy, reading or writing. Living in the quiet of California's Santa Cruz Mountains, she enjoys gardening, hiking, red wine, strong coffee, smooth jazz, and warm fall afternoons.

Books Available from Bold Strokes Books

Making a Comeback by Julie Blair. Music and love take center stage when jazz pianist Liz Randall tries to make a comeback with the help of her reclusive, blind neighbor, Jac Winters. (978-1-62639-357-8)

Soul Unique by Gun Brooke. Self-proclaimed cynic Greer Landon falls for Hayden Rowe's paintings and the young woman shortly after, but will Hayden, who lives with Asperger syndrome, trust her and reciprocate her feelings? (978-1-62639-358-5)

The Price of Honor by Radclyffe. Honor and duty are not always black and white—and when self-styled patriots take up arms against the government, the price of honor may be a life. (978-1-62639-359-2)

Mounting Evidence by Karis Walsh. Lieutenant Abigail Hargrove and her mounted police unit need to solve a murder and protect wetland biologist Kira Lovell during the Washington State Fair. (978-1-62639-343-1)

Threads of the Heart by Jeannie Levig. Maggie and Addison Rae-McInnis share a love and a life, but are the threads that bind them together strong enough to withstand Addison's restlessness and the seductive Victoria Fontaine? (978-1-62639-410-0)

Sheltered Love by MJ Williamz. Boone Fairway and Grey Dawson—two women touched by abuse—overcome their pasts to find happiness in each other. (978-1-62639-362-2)

Asher's Out by Elizabeth Wheeler. Asher Price's candid photographs capture the truth, but when his success requires exposing an enemy, Asher discovers his only shot at happiness involves revealing secrets of his own. (978-1-62639-411-7)

The Ground Beneath by Missouri Vaun. An improbable barter deal involving a hope chest and dinners for a month places lovely Jessica Walker distractingly in the way of Sam Casey's bachelor lifestyle. (978-1-62639-606-7)

Hardwired by C.P. Rowlands. Award-winning teacher Clary Stone, and Leefe Ellis, manager of the homeless shelter for small children, stand together in a part of Clary's hometown that she never knew existed. (978-1-62639-351-6)

No Good Reason by Cari Hunter. A violent kidnapping in a Peak District village pushes Detective Sanne Jensen and lifelong friend Dr. Meg Fielding closer, just as it threatens to tear everything apart. (978-1-62639-352-3)

Romance by the Book by Jo Victor. If Cam didn't keep disrupting her life, maybe Alex could uncover the secret of a century-old love story, and solve the greatest mystery of all—her own heart. (978-1-62639-353-0)

Death's Doorway by Crin Claxton. Helping the dead can be deadly: Tony may be listening to the dead, but she needs to learn to listen to the living. (978-1-62639-354-7)

Searching for Celia by Elizabeth Ridley. As American spy novelist Dayle Salvesen investigates the mysterious disappearance of her ex-lover, Celia, in London, she begins questioning how well she knew Celia—and how well she knows herself. (978-1-62639-356-1)

The 45th Parallel by Lisa Girolami. Burying her mother isn't the worst thing that can happen to Val Montague when she returns to the woodsy but peculiar town of Hemlock, Oregon. (978-1-62639-342-4)

A Royal Romance by Jenny Frame. In a country where class still divides, can love topple the last social taboo and allow Queen Georgina and Beatrice Elliot, a working class girl, their happy ever after? (978-1-62639-360-8)

Bouncing by Jaime Maddox. Basketball Coach Alex Dalton has been bouncing from woman to woman, because no one ever held her interest, until she meets her new assistant, Britain Dodge. (978-1-62639-344-8)

Same Time Next Week by Emily Smith. A chance encounter between Alex Harris and the beautiful Michelle Masters leads to a whirlwind friendship, and causes Alex to question everything she's ever known—including her own marriage. (978-1-62639-345-5)

All Things Rise by Missouri Vaun. Cole rescues a striking pilot who crash-lands near her family's farm, setting in motion a chain of events that will forever alter the course of her life. (978-1-62639-346-2)

Riding Passion by D. Jackson Leigh. Mount up for the ride through a sizzling anthology of chance encounters, buried desires, romantic surprises, and blazing passion. (978-1-62639-349-3)

Love's Bounty by Yolanda Wallace. Lobster boat captain Jake Myers stopped living the day she cheated death, but meeting greenhorn Shy Silva stirs her back to life. (978-1-62639-334-9)

Just Three Words by Melissa Brayden. Sometimes the one you want is the one you least suspect. Accountant Samantha Ennis has her ordered life disrupted when heartbreaker Hunter Blair moves into her trendy Soho loft. (978-1-62639-335-6)

Lay Down the Law by Carsen Taite. Attorney Peyton Davis returns to her Texas roots to take on big oil and the Mexican Mafia, but will her investigation thwart her chance at true love? (978-1-62639-336-3)

Playing in Shadow by Lesley Davis. Survivor's guilt threatens to keep Bryce trapped in her nightmare world unless Scarlet's love can pull her out of the darkness back into the light. (978-1-62639-337-0)

Soul Selecta by Gill McKnight. Soul mates are hell to work with. (978-1-62639-338-7)

The Revelation of Beatrice Darby by Jean Copeland. Adolescence is complicated, but Beatrice Darby is about to discover how impossible it can seem to a lesbian coming of age in conservative 1950s New England. (978-1-62639-339-4)

Twice Lucky by Mardi Alexander. For firefighter Mackenzie James and Dr. Sarah Macarthur, there's suddenly a whole lot more in life to understand, to consider, to risk…someone will need to fight for her life. (978-1-62639-325-7)

Shadow Hunt by L.L. Raand. With young to raise and her Pack under attack, Sylvan, Alpha of the wolf Weres, takes on her greatest challenge when she determines to uncover the faceless enemies known as the Shadow Lords. A Midnight Hunters novel. (978-1-62639-326-4)

Heart of the Game by Rachel Spangler. A baseball writer falls for a single mom, but can she ever love anything as much as she loves the game? (978-1-62639-327-1)

Getting Lost by Michelle Grubb. Twenty-eight days, thirteen European countries, a tour manager fighting attraction, and an accused murderer: Stella and Phoebe's journey of a lifetime begins here. (978-1-62639-328-8)

Prayer of the Handmaiden by Merry Shannon. Celibate priestess Kadrian must defend the kingdom of Ithyria from a dangerous enemy and ultimately choose between her duty to the Goddess and the love of her childhood sweetheart, Erinda. (978-1-62639-329-5)

The Witch of Stalingrad by Justine Saracen. A Soviet "night witch" pilot and American journalist meet on the Eastern Front in WW II and struggle through carnage, conflicting politics, and the deadly Russian winter. (978-1-62639-330-1)

Pedal to the Metal by Jesse J. Thoma. When unreformed thief Dubs Williams is released from prison to help Max Winters bust a car theft ring, Max learns that to catch a thief, get in bed with one. (978-1-62639-239-7)

Dragon Horse War by D. Jackson Leigh. A priestess of peace and a fiery warrior must defeat a vicious uprising that entwines their destinies and ultimately their hearts. (978-1-62639-240-3)

For the Love of Cake by Erin Dutton. When everything is on the line, and one taste can break a heart, will pastry chefs Maya and Shannon take a chance on reality? (978-1-62639-241-0)

Betting on Love by Alyssa Linn Palmer. A quiet country-girl-at-heart and a live-life-to-the-fullest biker take a risk at offering each other their hearts. (978-1-62639-242-7)

The Deadening by Yvonne Heidt. The lines between good and evil, right and wrong, have always been blurry for Shade. When Raven's actions force her to choose, which side will she come out on? (978-1-62639-243-4)

Ordinary Mayhem by Victoria A. Brownworth. Faye Blakemore has been taking photographs since she was ten, but those same photographs threaten to destroy everything she knows and everything she loves. (978-1-62639-315-8)

One Last Thing by Kim Baldwin & Xenia Alexiou. Blood is thicker than pride. The final book in the Elite Operative Series brings together foes, family, and friends to start a new order. (978-1-62639-230-4)

Songs Unfinished by Holly Stratimore. Two aspiring rock stars learn that falling in love while pursuing their dreams can be harmonious— if they can only keep their pasts from throwing them out of tune. (978-1-62639-231-1)

Beyond the Ridge by L.T. Marie. Will a contractor and a horse rancher overcome their family differences and find common ground to build a life together? (978-1-62639-232-8)

Swordfish by Andrea Bramhall. Four women battle the demons from their pasts. Will they learn to let go, or will happiness be forever beyond their grasp? (978-1-62639-233-5)

The Fiend Queen by Barbara Ann Wright. Princess Katya and her consort Starbride must turn evil against evil in order to banish Fiendish power from their kingdom, and only love will pull them back from the brink. (978-1-62639-234-2)

Up the Ante by PJ Trebelhorn. When Jordan Stryker and Ashley Noble meet again fifteen years after a short-lived affair, are either of them prepared to gamble on a chance at love? (978-1-62639-237-3)

Speakeasy by MJ Williamz. When mob leader Helen Byrne sets her sights on the girlfriend of Al Capone's right-hand man, passion and tempers flare on the streets of Chicago. (978-1-62639-238-0)

Venus in Love by Tina Michele. Morgan Blake can't afford any distractions and Ainsley Dencourt can't afford to lose control—but the beauty of life and art usually lies in the unpredictable strokes of the artist's brush. (978-1-62639-220-5)

Rules of Revenge by AJ Quinn. When a lethal operative on a collision course with her past agrees to help a CIA analyst on a critical assignment, the encounter proves explosive in ways neither woman anticipated. (978-1-62639-221-2)

The Romance Vote by Ali Vali. Chili Alexander is a sought-after campaign consultant who isn't prepared when her boss's daughter, Samantha Pellegrin, comes to work at the firm and shakes up Chili's life from the first day. (978-1-62639-222-9)

Advance: Exodus Book One by Gun Brooke. Admiral Dael Caydoc's mission to find a new homeworld for the Oconodian people is hazardous, but working with the infuriating Commander Aniwyn "Spinner" Seclan endangers her heart and soul. (978-1-62639-224-3)

UnCatholic Conduct by Stevie Mikayne. Jil Kidd goes undercover to investigate fraud at St. Marguerite's Catholic School, but life gets complicated when her student is killed—and she begins to fall for her prime target. (978-1-62639-304-2)

Season's Meetings by Amy Dunne. Catherine Birch reluctantly ventures on the festive road trip from hell with beautiful stranger Holly Daniels only to discover the road to true love has its own obstacles to maneuver. (978-1-62639-227-4)